James von Leyden first visited Morocco in 1985, leading to a life-long love affair with the country. He divides his time between Lewes, East Sussex and Oualidia, Morocco.

You can follow James on Instagram at
www.instagram.com/jamesvonleyden.

Also by James von Leyden

A Death in the Medina

Last Boat from Tangier

JAMES VON LEYDEN

CONSTABLE

CONSTABLE

First published in Great Britain in 2020 by Constable

A CIP catalogue record for this book
is available from the British Library.

ISBN: 978-1-47213-064-8

Typeset in Adobe Garamond by Hewer Text UK Ltd, Edinburgh
Printed and bound in Great Britain by Clays Ltd, Elcograf S.p.A.

Papers used by Constable are from well-managed forests and other responsible sources.

Constable
An imprint of
Little, Brown Book Group
Carmelite House
50 Victoria Embankment
London EC4Y 0DZ

An Hachette UK Company
www.hachette.co.uk

www.littlebrown.co.uk

For Czarina

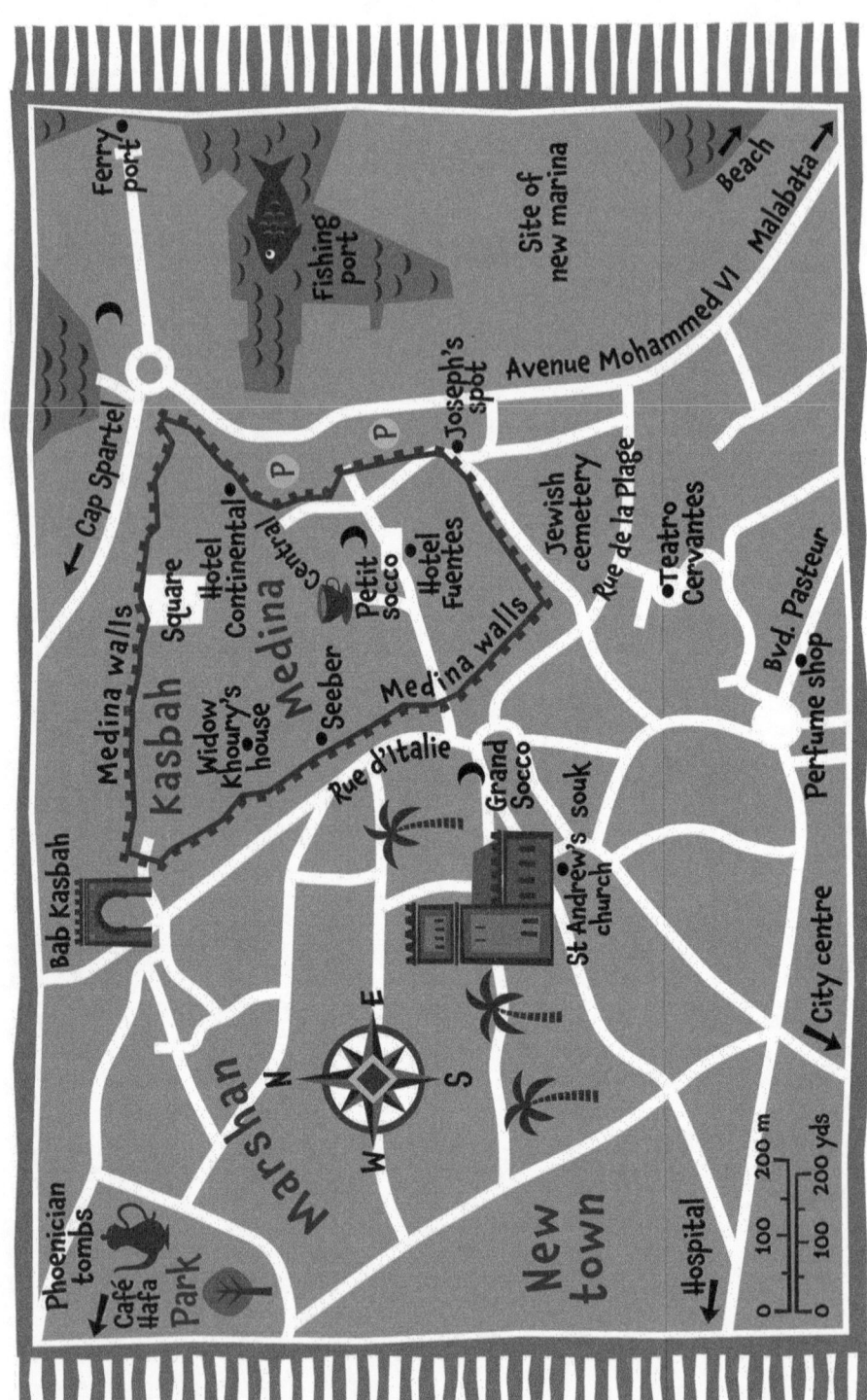

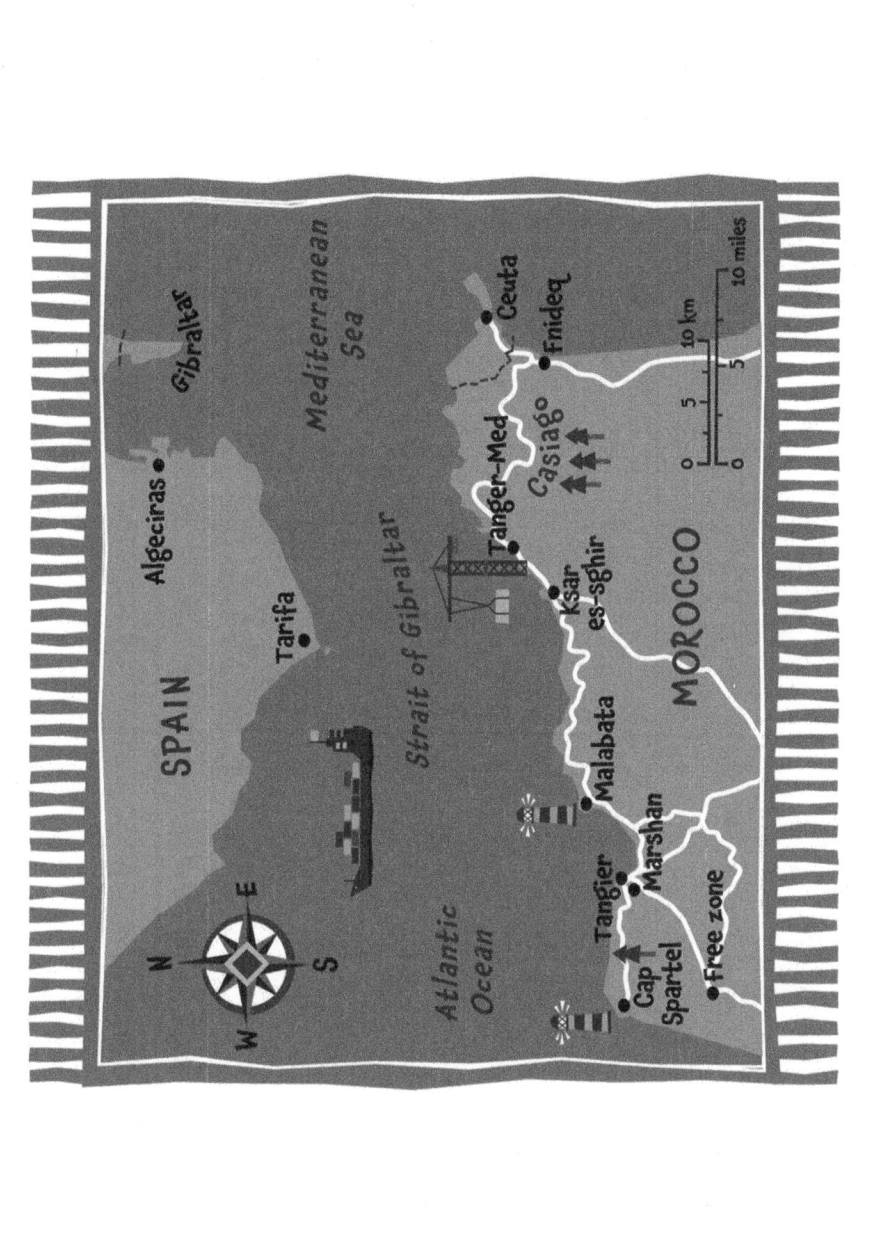

Prologue

It was a forty-foot container. From where Abdou was standing it looked no different from the thousands of containers that passed through Morocco's ports every day. However, a shipping container was like a corpse before an autopsy: you could scrutinise it on the outside, perform tests and x-rays, but until you opened it up there was no way of knowing what secrets it contained.

Two weeks ago, when he first arrived in Tangier, the assignment seemed routine. He had helped ports with their inspection procedures before. But this was different. This was a crime so shocking that it would reach the ears of the King, cause an international outcry and lead to changes in government policy. It was galling, therefore, that he had to let the container go. What choice did he have? The container was travelling without documentation. There was no bill of lading, no handling agent, no consignee, not even a seal on the doors. The container could be shrugged off by the port and the shipping company as an aberration, a container-in-a-million that had slipped through the net. It filled him with anguish, but if he wanted to catch the perpetrators he would have to let it go.

He hadn't mentioned any of this to Karim. Partly for security reasons: both his mobile phone and his email had been hacked. But there was another reason. Once Karim and his superiors found out what was going on the investigation would be taken out of his hands. He was only a junior lieutenant, after all. It was Karim who had launched the nationwide contraband operation two years earlier; Karim who conducted the liaison work and the press conferences. But Karim had given the case to him and Abdou was determined to prove he could handle it on his own.

A cold wind whipped off the harbour, causing the lamp masts to rattle and ruffling the tarpaulins in the storage yard. Abdou blew on his hands and flexed his fingers. He checked the time: 17.37. He had arranged to meet the chief of police at 19.30.

Just then, he glimpsed something out of the corner of his eye – a flash, or a shadow. Looking down the line of containers all he could see was an empty expanse of concrete stretching to the perimeter fence. He cocked an ear: the only sounds were the rumble of low-loader lorries and the distant *clank* of containers from the quay. It was probably a seagull. There were dozens of them flapping around, although God knew what they found to eat in a container terminal.

It all happened so quickly. A heavy arm shoving him against the steel doors. Sharp words in a language he didn't understand. Lying on his back, staring up at faces, two of which he recognised. A wonderful feeling of contentment, like a wave washing over him. Then nothing.

Chapter One

Three days later

On the sports ground of the police college cadets were running around the track. It was Friday morning and the four hundred-metre race was their last activity before lunch. Among the male runners were two girls wearing the red tracksuits of the commissioner corps. One of them, short and slight of build, was neck and neck with the leader. As they came down the last straight she edged in front. Her legs were tired and oxygen fought to get to her lungs, but she had beaten boys before, racing down obstacle-strewn alleyways where the gaps were narrower and the bends were sharper and the ground was studded with metal drain handles and loose cobblestones . . . As she flew past the finish line the instructor jabbed his stopwatch.

'Four-twelve, Talal! Four-thirteen, Hakimi!'

The man, his hair shaved close to his scalp like the other male cadets, stopped and stood with his hands on his knees, recovering his breath.

The girl went up to him. She had dark, intelligent eyes and a scar over her left ear.

'Good race,' she panted.

Instead of replying, the man spat on the ground then stalked off.

'Take no notice, Ayesha,' said the other girl as she came off the track. She took a breath then shouted at the man's retreating figure: 'Some people still haven't come to terms with the fact that the college admits women!'

Ayesha Talal and Salma Mernissi were both twenty-two years old and room-mates at the Institut Royal de Police in Kenitra. Salma wiped her face with a towel while Ayesha took a drink from her water bottle. The instructor came over. He was a well-toned young man whose otherwise handsome features were disfigured by a broken nose. He picked up Ayesha's tracksuit top and handed it to her with a smile.

'Well done.'

As they walked off, Salma made mischievous eyes at Ayesha. Ayesha laughed. 'What?!' She flicked Salma with her tracksuit top.

Laughing and joshing, the girls made their way across the parade ground, past cadets marching in formation. They discussed arrangements for the weekend.

'Are you going to stay for lunch?' asked Salma.

'No. A quick shower and I'll be off. I told my mother I would be home by seven. The neighbour is making couscous.'

'Don't forget we have a class on Critical Incident Management on Monday.'

'I'm taking my notes.' Whether I look at them is another matter.

'I'll test you when you get back!' Salma wagged a finger. 'No excuses!'

Their voices echoed across the foyer of the accommodation block. It was a modern, three-storey building with female quarters at one end. The girls walked down the corridor and Salma unlocked the door of their bedroom. The room was compact: two single beds with wardrobes at their foot and a desk between them. Salma untied her ponytail and threw herself on her bed while Ayesha went off to shower and change. A few minutes later she reappeared in a black trouser suit and took her overnight bag from the wardrobe.

'There's still time to get a weekend pass if you're quick.'

'I have to finish my essay. Another time, *inshallah*.'

Ayesha looked at her room-mate with admiration. She didn't have Salma's aptitude for study. But the fact that her grades were almost as good as Salma's was proof that the Royal Institute measured success by ability on the assault course and shooting range as well as in the classroom and laboratory.

As the call to prayer rang out, Ayesha joined a stream of cadets heading to the gates – dressed, like her, in the off-duty uniform of dark suit, white shirt and black tie. One by one they collected their mobile phones at the gatehouse. The rules about mobile phones were strict. As the principal told them on their first day, the cadets were there to become officers, not to check their Facebook status. Under no circumstances were phones to be brought into the college. They had to be handed in at the gate-house on arrival and signed out on departure. With every aspect of their lives regimented from six in the morning until ten at night it was little wonder that the cadets laughed and joked and called their loved ones as they streamed out of the gates.

Ayesha stood at the roadside and put her hand out. A *petit taxi* pulled up.

'The station,' she said, getting in.

Ayesha's heart always skipped a beat when she took a taxi. But the driver, a young man in a green *jellaba*, seemed pleasant enough, and the Quranic chanting on his radio was reassuring.

In common with other Moroccans who worked or studied, Karim Belkacem and his sister Khadija returned home for their midday meal. In Karim's case it meant a fifteen-minute scooter ride from the police commissariat near Marrakech's Jemaa el Fna to the family riad at the northern end of the medina. Today was a warm spring day and the swifts were soaring and screaming as Karim parked his *moto*. He walked into the courtyard and looked up at the railings on the second storey of the house, as if searching for something. Then he draped his jacket over the disused fountain, removed his shoes and entered the *salon*.

The room was long and narrow with a high ceiling and a shelf unit on which stood a forty-six-inch television. Karim greeted his mother and sister, sat down at the low table, dipped his fingers in couscous and turned his attention to the television. His mother, Lalla Fatima, had bought the television shortly after Karim's father died, and it was always switched on during mealtimes – an intrusion, Karim thought wryly, that his father would never have allowed. Khadija liked to catch the morning chat shows before she went to work and never missed the soaps at lunch and dinner.

Like Karim, Khadija had a slender nose and the green, almond-shaped eyes of an Amazigh, or Berber, from the Chleuh tribe of southern Morocco. But good looks were all they shared. Khadija was not ambitious, content to earn a meagre salary as secretary for a law firm. She had put all her efforts into attracting a rich husband. Since the engagement fell through, two years ago, she had lost interest in her appearance. Her cheekbones had lost their definition and she wore baggy track bottoms to hide the fact that she had put on weight.

'Khadija!' Lalla Fatima said sharply. 'Your brother is home.'

With a sigh, Khadija flicked to the news channel. The news shows were the only programmes that Karim watched. He followed Al Jazeera as intently as Khadija followed her soaps. A police officer – so Karim believed – should know what was going on in the world. How else was one to make sense of a new edict from the government or understand the joblessness that drove a man to steal?

On that Friday lunchtime the news channel carried a report about a mass assault on the Ceuta border which had taken place the previous night. The footage made uncomfortable viewing. Migrants from sub-Saharan Africa were trying to scale a six-metre-high fence topped with razor wire while commandos from the Moroccan police attempted to pull them down. On the Spanish side the Guardia Civil were trying to repel the invaders with high-pressure hoses. One young African in a sodden khaki jacket and woollen hat had managed to make it over the wall. He was running around making victory signs at the cameras while the Guardia Civil chased him.

'Why's he so cheerful?' asked Lalla Fatima. 'They're going to catch him, for sure!'

'Ceuta is part of Europe,' Karim answered between mouthfuls of couscous. 'Once a migrant makes it into Ceuta they can claim asylum. They can go anywhere in Europe, get a job, bring their families.'

'Ha! Did you see that?' Khadija pointed. 'That guy who fell? The police are giving him a kicking!'

Lalla Fatima was appalled. 'There's blood coming from his head! I can't bear to watch!' She reached for the remote control.

'*Bletee!* Wait!' Karim stayed her with his hand. He was both fascinated and repelled by what he saw. The operation was a free-for-all, the police pouncing on any Africans who fell to the ground and beating them with batons. Such aggressive behaviour reflected badly on the Sûreté. It certainly compared unfavourably to the more disciplined approach of the Spanish Guardia Civil.

Lalla Fatima put aside the remote. 'Where do they come from, Karim, all these migrants?'

Karim had seen reports of King Mohammed VI making official visits to other African capitals, but beyond Niger the countries seemed to merge into one another. He shrugged his shoulders. 'I don't know.'

'The *Afaraqa* are not like the Syrians,' Khadija declared. 'The Syrians have got a reason to flee. There's a war going on in their country. The *Afaraqa* just want fancy cars and houses – stuff they've seen on television. They should stay at home and get a job!'

'Shh! I'm trying to listen.'

Khadija persisted. 'Have you seen the blacks begging at the traffic lights? The women with babies on their backs? I never give them anything. We have our own beggars to look after!'

'When did you last give money to a beggar?'

With an exasperated sigh, Karim turned up the volume. It nearly drowned out the sound of the telephone that was ringing from the courtyard. But the phone kept ringing and Khadija went out to take the call. She returned a few minutes later.

'That was Ayesha. She's coming to Marrakech this weekend.'

Lalla Fatima's face lit up. 'God be praised!'

'She'll visit us on Sunday morning, *inshallah*.'

'With Lalla Hanane?'

Khadija shook her head. 'You know how frail Hanane is.'

Lalla Hanane was Ayesha's birth mother. She had given birth to Ayesha in a remote mountain village during a cholera epidemic. With her husband out of work, and two other children to feed, Hanane had been forced to give up the infant for adoption. The Belkacems took Ayesha in and brought her up alongside their own children. At the age of twenty, Ayesha was reunited with her mother, now living on her own not far from the Belkacems. Ayesha took her duties as a daughter seriously. She returned from police college to do the housework and keep her mother company. But what she enjoyed most was visiting the Belkacems, where she could relax and gossip like in the old days. *I have two mothers*, she told Salma. *With Lalla Hanane I can be a daughter. With Lalla Fatima I can be myself.*

Karim was too absorbed in the television to pay attention. It was only when he was getting ready to return to work, and Khadija was grumbling about having missed her favourite

Turkish soap opera, that he registered that Ayesha was coming
to see them.

Riding back to the commissariat, Karim was in two minds
about Ayesha's visit. He wanted to see her but he also dreaded
the prospect. This conflict was not new.

As a boy of four, Karim had been entranced by Ayesha's
arrival in the Belkacem household. He dangled toys and sang
songs to her while ignoring his sister of the same age. He
wondered at her fierce determination to walk, her precocious-
ness in mastering the stairs. When he started running around
with the other boys from the neighbourhood he brought
Ayesha with him. At first the other boys were grudging. In
time, however, Ayesha's fearlessness and penchant for mischief
won approval. She was always the one who took the greatest
risks and ended up in the most serious scrapes. When the boys
took turns to steal mandarins on market day she vanished into
the crowd, returning a few minutes later staggering under a
watermelon. She didn't do it to impress the other boys. She
did it for Karim.

When Karim was sixteen and Ayesha thirteen their relationship took a different turn. They met after school to share
gossip, jokes, dreams, observations, feelings, secrets. Sometimes
these trysts took place at the nearby flea market of Bab
el-Khemis. Or they chatted on the roof of the riad, which they
had made their private domain. Karim would gossip to Ayesha
as she hung out the washing. He would help her with her
homework or they would lie together on the old mattress,

Ayesha's head on Karim's chest, and talk about spending their lives together.

Ayesha and Karim regarded each other like cousins. But they were brother and sister in the eyes of Islam. Any intimacy, any closeness, was forbidden. This caused Karim endless torment. He moved away to police college and embarked on relationships with other women. Ayesha, too, moved out to her mother's house and then to police college. But they couldn't avoid meeting occasionally and when they did there was a pull, an attraction, that made it hard for Karim to concentrate on anyone or anything else. The day would come when Ayesha married another man but until then, Karim decided, any encounter with her was best avoided.

The first thing he saw when he arrived at the police station was Bouchaïb, the parking attendant, leaning on his crutch and grinning.

'Only three hours until the match, Mr Karim!'

'What match is that?'

'Raja are playing Wydad. It's going to be close but I think Raja will win! They won against Tunis last week!'

Karim had no interest in football and he didn't pretend otherwise. He walked up a flight of outside steps to his office. He shared the room with two other officers. One was his deputy, Abdou. For the past eighteen months they had been collaborating on an investigation into fake medicines: poor quality copies of life-saving drugs bought by patients who couldn't afford the real thing. The other officer was Noureddine, a senior commander who presided over the two young lieutenants like a stern uncle. As Karim entered he was surprised to see Noureddine talking to the station superintendent.

'*Salaam ou-alikum!*'

The superintendent's voice was grave. 'The Tangier police just called me.'

Karim nodded warily. As part of their investigation he had sent Abdou to help at the port of Tanger-Med.

'Abdou's gone missing.'

Alarm bells rang in Karim's brain. The Chinese cartels who manufactured fake drugs were known to be vicious. Many had switched from narcotics trafficking to fake drugs because the risks were lower and the profits greater.

'How long?'

'Three days.'

'His mobile . . .?'

'Not responding.'

It was Noureddine's turn to speak. 'Tomorrow is Saturday. If Abdou hasn't surfaced in the next twenty-four hours you're to leave for Tangier on the night train.'

On Saturday morning a young black man arrived outside the north-eastern corner of Tangier medina. Called Bab Dar Dbagh, The Gate of the Tannery House, the corner was perfect for a selling his wares. The position was elevated with a view over the harbour. No one harassed him, there was a ledge to sit on and an attendant let him use the nearby lavatory free of charge. After checking that there were no police around, Joseph opened his Adidas bag and took out twenty pairs of sunglasses. He arranged them on the ground in two neat rows with the wings of the glasses extended. Next, he took out five telescopic umbrellas and placed them next to the sunglasses. Rain or shine, he would make money.

Unfortunately, today was neither sunny nor rainy. It was one of those cold spring days in Tangier when the sun struggles to penetrate thick banks of cloud. For the first two hours few people came past. After disembarking from the ferry most tourists went up to the medina by one of two routes: Port Gate or Tannery House Gate. Today they all seemed to be using Port Gate. Joseph didn't mind. He was happy gazing at the harbour. He watched a gendarme wander out of his hut on the quayside, light a cigarette and check his mobile phone. On the boulevard, a couple strolled arm in arm then stopped to look at the hoardings for the new marina. Between the marina and Tannery House Gate was a large car park where two men washed cars. With hundreds of motorists using the car park the men had more work than they could handle. A few weeks ago an impatient motorist asked Joseph to wash his Peugeot 305 using a standpipe and an old sponge. Joseph cleaned the car from top to bottom but all he got for his efforts was a parting jeer. *Bslemma, azzi! So long, nigger!*

The advantage of selling sunglasses and umbrellas was that no one could cheat him. He decided which items to sell and how much to charge. He favoured cheap goods that everybody wanted and that he could scoop up in five seconds if the police arrived.

As the sun came out the air became warmer and the road grew busier. Joseph laid out another five rows of sunglasses: Ray-Ban, Giorgio Armani, Gucci, Cartier. At three o'clock, the ferry arrived from Tarifa. Shortly afterwards groups of day trippers came walking past. A Spanish girl stopped to buy a pair of Ray-Bans for two euros.

Out at sea, he could see a white line of breakers. Joseph knew all the moods of the sea: the glassy surface on a calm evening, the metallic glint that presaged a change in weather. He wondered what had happened to his neighbour who left the camp a week ago. He had promised to send Joseph a text. Perhaps he'd got his phone wet. Salt water was bad for mobiles, everyone knew that. You could wrap your phone in three layers of plastic but once it came into contact with the sea, all bets were off. Joseph reached in his pocket and felt the reassuring outline of his Samsung. He'd taken it to the shopping centre that morning and managed ten minutes' charge in a floor socket before he was chased away by a security guard.

There was the ferry, going back to Tarifa. Tarifa sounded like a nice place. Sandy beaches and fancy restaurants. Maybe his neighbour from the camp was sitting at one of them right now with a big grin on his face.

Catching the Saturday night train to Tangier had one benefit: it gave Karim an excuse to avoid seeing Ayesha. The train was busy, and there was a crying infant to contend with, but at least he had a seat and the overhead lights weren't too bright. As the night wore on the warmth drained from the carriage and he put on his jacket. The old woman sitting opposite was snoring, a drool of saliva on her lower lip.

Unable to sleep, Karim played games on his phone. Abdou always used to pass the time with puzzle books and Karim was annoyed with himself for forgetting to buy a sudoku book at the station. When his eyes started hurting he gazed through the window. They were crossing the Doukkala plains: mile after mile of moonlit wheat fields interspersed with sleeping hamlets.

Karim cast his mind back to eighteen months ago, when he and Abdou had first uncovered the counterfeit drug trade. They found that antibiotics, painkillers, heart drugs and cancer medications – drugs whose high price put them beyond the reach of everyone but the well-off – were being copied by Chinese factories and shipped into the Maghreb by the container-load. In many cases, the fake drugs contained nothing more than glucose. Sometimes they were cut with harmful substances like rat poison.

Under normal circumstances Karim would have handled the Tangier assignment himself. But because he had sidelined Abdou from a previous operation in Agadir, and felt he owed Abdou a favour, he gave the job to him. Going north would be an adventure, he told him. Tanger-Med was the biggest and most modern port in Morocco. Abdou could check out the latest scanning and logistics technology. He could impart his knowledge to the Tangier authorities and earn their gratitude in return.

It was only on Friday afternoon, when he learned of Abdou's disappearance, that Karim looked more closely into events at Tanger-Med. Since 2011, seizures of fake drugs had risen steadily. Then, about six months ago, the seizures tailed off. In December – the last month for which statistics were available – there hadn't been a single confiscation. The authorities were still seizing heroin, guns and other contraband. Just not fake medicines.

Karim hoped that there was a simple explanation for Abdou's disappearance. Perhaps he had gone undercover to monitor security procedures. God willing, Abdou would be waiting for him at headquarters on Monday morning, smiling broadly and asking for the latest gossip from the precinct.

'*Qahwa?*' The old woman opposite was holding out a thermos flask and a cup of coffee.

'Thank you,' said Karim. The coffee was sweet and milky.

'*Dar Bida?* Are you going to Casablanca?' The woman's skin was as wrinkled as a walnut. A strand of grey hair straggled out from her headscarf.

'Tangier.'

'*Tanja?*' The woman flinched slightly.

'Yes.'

'Your first time?'

Karim nodded.

The old woman leaned forward and wagged a bony finger. 'A beautiful city. But a dangerous one.'

Karim laughed.

The woman sipped her coffee and gazed at him silently.

'Don't worry, *a lalla*. I'm a police officer. I've been all over the Maghreb.'

'Tangier is not like the Maghreb.'

'How so?'

The woman stared at him for a few more minutes. 'People get lost there.'

Karim laughed again but his laughter died on his lips as he realised that this was precisely the reason why he was going to Tangier. The woman's eyelids closed and she fell asleep, the flask still in her hand.

It was Sunday morning and Ayesha was at the Belkacems playing with Safee, the pet monkey. Safee had lived an eventful life. As an infant he earned a profitable income for his owner by climbing on the shoulders of tourists in Jemaa el Fna. When he proved more interested in yanking earrings than posing for photographs, Safee was sold to a Frenchman who gave him as a gift to his girlfriend. The monkey escaped from the girlfriend just as she was about to get rid of him and turned up one night on the Belkacems' roof, where he was adopted by Ayesha. The family dubbed him Safee – 'enough' – because he was always causing mischief. *Safee, come down here; Safee, give back the remote control; Safee, leave the bird food alone.* Karim had a wooden cage made for him, but Safee preferred to clamber up the railings and observe proceedings from on high. When Ayesha moved out to live with Lalla Hanane the responsibility for looking after Safee fell to Khadija, a duty which she resented.

'I brought some cooked chicken as a treat,' said Ayesha, taking out a food storage box.

'You needn't have bothered,' Khadija snapped. 'He gets leftovers every night.'

'He opens the bin and eats the vegetable peelings,' sighed Lalla Fatima. 'It won't be long before he can open the fridge.'

Ayesha gave a laugh, swinging Safee from her shoulder and placing him on her lap. 'You're a clever little rascal, aren't you?' She nuzzled his forehead. 'When I've finished college you can come and live with me, God willing. Until then, you have to be a good boy and not annoy Khadija!' She looked around the courtyard. 'Where's Karim?'

'In Tangier.'

'What's he doing there?'

'Looking for Abdou. The poor boy has disappeared.'

Ayesha knew Abdou well. He had been a frequent dinner guest at the riad in the old days. Once, on the way back from a summer outing to Ourika, where Abdou's family lived, Lalla Fatima declared that Abdou would make a fine match for Ayesha; a comment that caused Ayesha to laugh and Karim to bite his lip and change the subject.

'Was he on an Operation MEDIHA assignment?'

'Operation what?'

'You know – the fake drugs investigation that Karim set up with the *gendarmerie* and the customs authorities.'

'Yes, he was, poor boy. But Karim is sure he will track him down, *inshallah*.'

Despite Lalla Fatima's words Ayesha was sure that Karim would be worried. Any missing officer case was cause for concern. And Abdou wasn't just any officer: apart from herself and Lalla Fatima, he was the person that Karim felt closest to. On every level the disappearance was disturbing. How annoying, therefore, that Karim had already left for Tangier! They could have taken the train together as far as Kenitra and discussed the case.

'Come, tell us, Ayesha,' said Lalla Fatima, 'what marvellous things are they teaching you at college?'

'Meema, really! Anyone would think that Karim hadn't been to the same college!'

'Yes, but you're a *woman*! Remind us how many female cadets there are.'

'Five.'

'And how many men?'

Ayesha laughed. 'Nine hundred.'

'Five women and nine hundred men! Imagine that!'

'Stop, Meema. You'll make her blush.' Khadija envied the fuss that her mother made of Ayesha. It should have been *her* returning to the riad to show off her newborn baby. The last thing she imagined two years ago was that she would still be living at home, looking after a *monkey*!

'And Salma?' asked Lalla Fatima. 'How is she?'

'Studying hard for exams.'

'I hope *you're* studying hard.'

'I scored top marks in Self-defence. And I won a race on Friday – against eighteen men!'

'Lalla Hanane must be so proud of you!'

'She *is* proud, but she misses me when I'm at college. She can't bear for me to be away.' Ayesha checked the time. 'I mustn't stay too long.'

'The poor woman! She's suffered so much. It's not surprising that she clings to you.'

'Speaking of which – she had a letter from Abderrahim. She waited for me to arrive so I could read it to her.'

One of the things that Ayesha learned on being reunited with her birth family was that she had an older brother, Abderrahim. He was serving a three-year sentence in the country's maximum-security prison for belonging to a banned Islamist organisation.

'He says he's working in the kitchen, doing menial tasks. He doesn't mix much with the other prisoners.'

'What sort of men are they?'

'Godless men, according to Abderrahim. But he's eating well and says that his health is good.'

'*Al-hamdulillah!*'

'He's learning a new skill: plastering.'

'I can't imagine Abderrahim as a plasterer!' said Khadija. She had known Abderrahim before he was incarcerated and remembered him as a rather formal young man with Islamic robes and a long beard.

'Does he have a date for release?'

'*Ma arfch*, I don't know,' said Ayesha, pushing Safee off her lap.

'You should take him food, Ayesha. Make him a tagine, or some nice *kofta briouats*.'

'Meema, I'm in class all day! I can't just go to the kitchen and start cooking!'

Khadija pursed her lips. 'From what I've heard, the food in prison is terrible.'

'At the very least, take some fresh fruit.'

Although she nodded and *inshallah*'ed Ayesha had no intention of visiting Abderrahim. Having a criminal for a brother was shameful for anyone, let alone a trainee police officer. Ayesha never mentioned Abderrahim at college, not even to Salma, and that was the way she wanted it to stay.

They heard the sound of breaking china and Khadija jumped up with a cry. 'Safee! Get out of the kitchen!'

Karim could smell the tang of the sea even before the train pulled into Tangier.

He located the prayer room at the back of the station and attended dawn prayers with a scattering of railway employees and construction workers. Afterwards he ate in a snack bar surrounded by scaffolding. The sun had risen when he finally stood outside the station, blinking. It was his first time in Tangier and it took him several minutes to get his bearings. A new terminus was being built, many times the size of the old one. On the far side of the road a crane loomed over a half-built tower block. Like Marrakech, Tangier seemed to be in a frenzy of construction.

The medina, where Abdou's hotel was located, lay three miles away, but the weather was fine and Karim had spent ten hours on the train so he decided to walk. He followed the road down to the sea. *There it was*, the Mediterranean: a strip of blue-grey above a vast, curving expanse of sand. He crossed a boulevard lined with modern hotels and apartment blocks then took off his shoes and walked barefoot across the sand, past boys playing football and middle-aged joggers in tracksuits. When he reached the sea the water was so cold it made him gasp.

He sat on his holdall and took out his binoculars. Across the choppy waters of the Strait, so close that he could almost reach out and touch them, were green hills, wind turbines, houses, a church, a marina and a ferry terminal: *Europe*. Apart from the church, the view was disappointingly ordinary – more like the view across the river from Salé to Rabat than the prospect of a different continent. A cargo ship moved slowly across his field of vision, its long deck piled with containers.

It was peaceful sitting by the gently lapping waves, his feet buried in sand and the sun warming his back, watching the boats and wondering where they were heading. After an hour he got up and walked back towards the road. At the traffic lights he saw his first migrant – an African woman with an infant strapped in a shawl, moving between the lines of cars.

He gave her the change in his pocket then climbed uphill in the direction of the medina. The tourist shops sold the usual tat: carpets, leather bags and brightly coloured pottery. As a Moroccan, Karim was of no interest to the owners and they looked straight past him. Near the brow of the hill he peeked inside the entrance to a fish market. A vast hall echoed to shouts and the slap of fish on slabs.

Crossing the road, he took a right turn past a pair of gates marked *Cimetière Juif* then followed the walls of the medina down towards the sea. When he reached the bottom of the hill he realised that he was back where he started. He saw an African man – Joseph – standing on the corner of the road selling sunglasses and considered asking him for directions but instead he enquired at a grocery store.

'Hotel Fuentes?' The shopkeeper replied. 'I know a better hotel.'

He sang its praises so enthusiastically that Karim thought he must be on commission, but Karim insisted on the Fuentes and the man pointed.

'Take the steps, follow the alley and you'll see it on the corner.'

In a few minutes Karim came out in a little square, so narrow it looked like someone had pushed the buildings together. According to a street sign this was the *Souk al Dakhel*, the *Petit Socco*. Moroccans and Westerners sat at café tables watching a steady procession of passers-by: hunched figures in *jellabas*, workers in hi-vis vests, children selling paper tissues, tourists with rucksacks on their chests, porters in blue work-coats, smart women in raincoats. Karim's nostrils picked up mint and the sweet smell of kif. To his left, on the side of the building, was painted: *Hotel Fuentes.*

The interior of the hotel was dark and cavernous, its corniced ceilings and peeling archways suggesting a once-luxurious establishment that had fallen on hard times. He climbed two flights of steps to a first-floor café. Just outside the door to the café stood a desk, overlooked by a faded tourist poster. A clerk sat at the desk with a sleepy-eyed man in a grubby *jellaba*. Guessing that this was the reception desk for the hotel, Karim asked if they had a bed for the night.

'Yes, sir!' The clerk sprang to life. 'With a washbasin!'

'How much?'

'Forty dirhams.'

'For a single room?'

'A single room?' The clerk tutted indulgently as if Karim was a country bumpkin who didn't know how the big city operated. 'No, *sidi.* For a shared room. You won't find a single room in Tangier for forty dirhams.'

Karim peered into the café. It was a large room with square columns, a balcony and a mirror at one end. Men were watching television or chatting over cigarettes and mint tea.

'*Shahal d-leelat?*' The clerk asked. 'How many nights?'

'Four, maybe more.'

'I'll tell you what – the hotel isn't busy right now so I'll give you a room to yourself. How does that sound?'

Karim turned around. 'Forty dirhams is still a lot of money.'

Recognising Karim's accent, the sleepy-eyed man joined the conversation. '*Wesh nta Marrakchi?* Are you from Marrakech?'

'Yes.'

'There's another Marrakchi staying here.'

Karim's ears pricked up. 'He's a friend of mine.'

'Your friend hasn't been here for five days,' exclaimed the clerk. 'He left on Tuesday and since then – *walou*, nothing!'

Karim improvised. 'His mother is sick.'

'Your friend owes me two hundred and ninety dirhams!'

'Don't worry. When he comes back he'll pay you. In the meantime, I'll stay in his room.'

The bedroom, on the second floor, had a high ceiling and faded yellow floor tiles. Three single beds lined the walls. There was a sink with a tap, a flimsy wardrobe and a set of French windows. On one bed Karim recognised a neat pile of Abdou's clothes. He walked over to the sink and ran his finger along a crack in the bowl.

'How much did you say the room was?'

'Forty,' the clerk replied in a weary voice.

'I'll give you thirty. Here's two nights in advance. And if my friend doesn't come back I'll pay his bill as well, OK? *Wakha?*'

When the clerk had gone Karim kneeled down and pulled Abdou's holdall from under the bed. It was a similar size and colour to his own. Inside were more clothes, a washbag, a woollen hat, a tin of cough sweets and a phone charging cable. There was no sign of Abdou's notebook, nor his gun.

Karim stepped out onto the balcony, which trembled under his weight. He could see the tops of the heads of passers-by. Hearing the loudspeaker from a nearby mosque, he washed his face and arms in the basin, dried them on his towel and laid his prayer mat neatly in the space between the beds.

It was late when Ayesha arrived back in Kenitra. She checked in her mobile phone in at the gatehouse and signed the register. She found Salma in the reference library, working at a computer.

'Just give me a minute,' said Salma.

Ayesha browsed the bookshelves while she waited. The shelves fanned out from a central area which contained eight desks, a coin-operated photocopier, two armchairs and a magazine rack with back issues of *Police* magazine. As most cadets preferred to work on study assignments in their bedrooms, the library was little used. Ayesha was surprised to see a section titled *Shorthand and Typing* – subjects long gone from the syllabus.

The two friends walked across the dark parade ground to the dormitory block.

'How was Marrakech?'

'Tiring. But I spent an hour at the *hammam*.'

'With your mother?'

Ayesha gave a sigh. 'Alas, she's too weak. She refuses to go out. She just sits all day holding my hand.'

'May God preserve her!'

'Do you remember that lecture we attended on post-traumatic stress disorder? I think my mother has it.'

'You should take her to the *tbiba*.'

'The doctor? What can the doctor do? They can't bring my father or sister back from the dead.'

Lalla Hanane had never recovered from the double tragedy that engulfed the family shortly before Ayesha's return. The Talals had not been much liked in the neighbourhood – under the patriarchal control of Omar Talal they kept largely to themselves – but even the most sharp-tongued of their neigh-bours agreed that no woman should have to endure the horrific death of their daughter and the consequent decline and death of their husband, both within the space of a month.

'On a positive note, there was a letter from my brother.'

'Karim?'

'No, my *birth* brother.'

Salma stopped in the corridor. 'You never told me you had a birth brother!'

'It's . . . embarrassing.' Two male cadets walked past and Ayesha lowered her voice. 'I'll tell you later.'

'You've made me curious!'

'We've got an hour to talk before lights out.'

'Tell me now! Is he an eligible bachelor with great career prospects in search of a beautiful and academically gifted wife?'

'Er . . . not exactly,' laughed Ayesha.

When Joseph returned to the camp he noticed a four-wheel drive vehicle parked under the trees. Then he spotted two strangers – Moroccans – among the tents. The taller of the men was wearing a Lacoste tracksuit and talking to Marie-Louise, a young woman from Kinshasa. She was making enthusiastic gestures but her baby suddenly started wailing from the tent. Babies were a no-no, a dead giveaway; on a calm night you could hear a crying baby a mile off. Sure enough, with a sign to his colleague, Lacoste Man moved on to the next tent.

He would find it hard to get customers. Half of the camp had already left, including Joseph's neighbour. Joseph now occupied his lean-to under the eucalyptus tree. It was a good site, sheltered and close to the fire, but not much use in a downpour: Joseph could feel the first fat drops of rain. Anxious to get his laundry inside, Joseph plucked the clothes from the branches above his head. As the sleeve of his puffa jacket rode up it revealed the name *Joseph*, inked in large letters on the inside of his forearm.

With a flick he unrolled the plastic sheeting over his lean-to then wandered over to the fire. Jean-François, his friend from Ivory Coast, was heating rice and milk in a battered saucepan. The tall Moroccan arrived at the fire at the same time as Joseph. He squatted down on his haunches.

'Speak English? French?'

'*Français,*' Joseph replied.

'*Mauvais temps.* Bad weather.' Lacoste Man spoke French with a heavy accent. 'Better on the other side.'

'*Oui.*'

'They need fruit pickers. Strong men.' He gave Joseph's biceps a squeeze. 'Sixty euros a day.'

He held out a photograph. It showed a fishing vessel with twin outboard motors. Joseph narrowed his eyes. Sometimes the people smugglers tempted you with a picture of a powerful boat, rather like pimps enticing you with photographs of a beautiful girl, when what awaited you was a skeletal wreck.

'Only eight thousand dirhams – with life jackets.'

Joseph and Jean-François shook their heads. Rain drops spat in the fire.

'*C'est un très bon prix.*'

Joseph shook his head again. He didn't have eight thousand dirhams, nowhere near.

Lacoste Man got to his feet. 'Another time, *inshallah*.'

Joseph watched the two men walk back to their Cherokee Jeep. Judging by their car, these guys made good money. Perhaps they were telling the truth about the boat after all.

'Hey!' Joseph realised they had forgotten the photo. He got to his feet, waving the photo in the air. '*Vous l'avez oublié!*'

But the men were already in the car and Lacoste Man was turning the ignition. A split-second later the trees flashed white and there was an explosion like a thousand guns going off. Joseph was flung to the ground and a shower of metal fell around him, mixed with raindrops. When he raised his head, flames were roaring from the windows of the jeep. The driver was a blackened corpse, his Lacoste tracksuit melted into his flesh.

Chapter 2

Karim awoke to the sound of rain. To his intense annoyance, he had slept through his alarm. He sat under a leaky awning in the Petit Socco, watching the raindrops plop into a *nuss-nuss* – his favourite coffee, half-and-half espresso and hot milk – wondering what excuse he could give the commissioner for being late. He hurried down the hill to the boulevard, shoes sloshing on wet cobblestones, and waited for a taxi. Downtown Tangier was grim: bleak modern buildings and tawdry shops, their windows plastered with *Sale* banners.

The taxi dropped him a block away from a Catholic church, in a large car park of vans with riot shields. He walked past a commando with a machine gun and signed in at the front desk. The downtown prefecture was more imposing than his commissariat in Marrakech, with an aura of brisk efficiency. Climbing the stairs to the sixth floor, past plain clothes officers talking in twos and threes, Karim felt like a child on his first day at school. He ran his hand through his wet hair and adjusted his tie.

'Ah, Lieutenant Belkacem. *Merhaba*, welcome! The local smugglers will be quaking in their boots, ha ha!' The police chief was a well-built man of forty, dark hair greying at the temples.

His suit was elegantly tailored, unlike the cheap suits most detectives wore, and he wore a white shirt open at the collar. 'My name is Sidi Mohammed Layachi, but everyone calls me Simo.'

Karim followed him across an open-plan office, observing how the men looked up as the chief strode past. He spoke over his shoulder. 'You're famous here, you know. You started the whole thing. Our narcotics team was getting worked up about heroin and cocaine while containers full of fake Tramadol were being smuggled under our noses!'

'I – er –'

'How was your journey? Tiring, I expect! A few years from now high-speed trains will get you from Casablanca to Tangier in two hours, so they tell me!'

Simo showed Karim into a large glass-panelled office where a man was waiting. Karim's hopes rose, then fell: it wasn't Abdou, but a small, older man. He sat to one side, eyes fixed on the floor. The commissioner went to a desk twice the size of any that Karim had seen and pointed to a chair. Karim draped his wet jacket over the back and sat down. A large framed photograph of the King looked down from the wall.

'Coffee?' Simo lifted his phone and muttered a single word, then leaned back in his chair.

'Dear Abdou! A charming man. So unfortunate that he's gone missing. But let's not jump to conclusions. Perhaps he got trapped in one of the containers – people can survive in those things for weeks. And he's only been gone for five days.'

'Six.' It was the first word Karim had spoken.

'Oh, that's nothing.' Simo batted the thought away with the back of his hand.

'So you haven't discovered what happened to him?'

'What can I say? We've searched the port from top to bottom. We've examined the CCTV footage. Mind you, we've been busy with other things – student demonstrations, a gas plant explosion, a visit by the King . . .'

'When was he last seen?'

'The King?' Simo laughed. 'Or Abdou?'

'Abdou,' Karim replied testily.

'He was caught on camera at around 17.40 on Tuesday in Terminal 1. There are two terminals at Tanger-Med. He was inspecting the storage yard in Terminal 1. One minute he's there, then *plaf* – he's gone.' The police chief passed a paper across the desk. 'This is a list of all the ships that called at the terminal while Abdou was in Tangier, up to and including the night he disappeared.'

Karim studied the list, trying to find a shipping name he recognised.

'Hicham here was Abdou's driver.' Simo addressed the other man. 'Tell the lieutenant what happened.'

'Yes, sir.' The man spoke in stops and starts, avoiding Karim's gaze. 'I didn't take Mr Abdou home that day. I dropped him as usual at the Tanger–Med prefecture at nine o'clock, on, er, Tuesday morning – the fifth of March – and told him that I was very sorry but I, er, couldn't pick him up that evening. He said no problem, he would get a taxi outside the Gare Maritime.'

The door opened and a secretary entered with a tray of coffee. Karim noticed that there were only two cups.

'Why couldn't you pick up Mr Abdou – I mean, Lieutenant el-Mokhfi?'

'I had a meeting at my son's school, sir; he got himself into trouble . . . I told Mr Abdou about the meeting – we always chatted on the journey – and he said, "Don't worry, I'll make my own way back." '

'Did he give you any idea what time that would be?'

'No, sir.'

Simo interrupted. 'We think he was looking at empty containers.'

'Tell me about the ships berthed in Terminal 1 while he was in the yard.'

'There were two vessels,' replied the commissioner. 'The MSC *Santa Cruz* was being loaded with Renault cars, bound for Rotterdam. There was also a medium-sized ship, the COSCO *Oceania*, registered in Panama and heading for Abidjan. We checked them out. Nothing suspicious.'

'Could Abdou have got onto one of the ships?'

Simo shook his head. 'No one can board a ship without permission from the captain.'

'Was anyone with Abdou?'

Simo held his palms out. 'Someone from the port authority or terminal operator should have been accompanying him. That was an oversight. But Abdou wanted to be on his own. He was very clear about that.'

'Witnesses?'

'There were people at the terminal – drivers, crane operators, security men – but no one saw him in the hour before he disappeared.'

Karim turned to the driver. 'Hicham – you picked up Lieutenant el-Mokhfi from his hotel every morning?'

'Yes, sir. That is – I waited in the car park below the hotel. Cars are forbidden in the Petit Socco.'

'You said he chatted to you. Did he tell you what he was working on?'

'No, sir. He was discreet – a proper police officer.'

Simo got to his feet. 'Let's ask Larbi. He's head of police at Tanger-Med. Finish your coffee – it's a forty-five-minute drive.'

They ran to the car to avoid getting soaked. The few pedestrians in the street were carrying umbrellas or sheltering in doorways. As they headed out of town, along a highway lined with apartment blocks, Simo asked Karim where he was staying.

'The Fuentes? It's a fleapit! Five years ago we closed it down for prostitution! It's no place for a police officer. I told Abdou the same thing, but he wouldn't listen! What is it with you Marrakchis? Stay at my house. I have a nice place in Casabarata. As long as you're in Tangier you're my guest. So that's decided – I shall phone my wife and tell her to expect you for dinner.'

'Thank you, but I prefer to stay at the hotel.'

'Now you're offending me! What possible reason could you have for staying at a hotel . . . unless you want to have fun with the girls! Beware! Tangier girls are pretty, but they'll steal your money!'

'I don't want to chase girls. I'm here to find my colleague.'

'As you wish. *Keema bgheetee!* But don't say I didn't warn you!'

For the rest of the journey the two men chatted about families and work. Eventually the motorway crossed a mile-long viaduct, curving towards the sea, culminating with an overhead sign: *Tanger-Med.* Karim sat up to get a better look. Before him stretched industrial parks, harbours, construction sites, container depots, a vast road network, landscaped gardens, modern office blocks, a long breakwater and twelve of the biggest gantry cranes Karim had ever seen.

This wasn't a port – *it was a city!*

The lecture room consisted of two long tables with a white-board. Twenty cadets sat facing each other in belted fatigues and black turtleneck sweaters. As the instructor walked in they stood to attention.

The instructor was a man in his forties with a dark uniform and a name band above his breast pocket: *CHOUKRI*. After motioning his audience to sit, he took a marker pen and wrote *Critical Incident Management* on the board.

'Who can tell me the difference between an ordinary incident and a critical incident?'

One man put up his hand. 'It's more serious?'

The instructor gave him an icy stare.

'Give me an example of a critical incident. Anybody?'

Another cadet piped up. 'A hostage situation, sir, a terrorist incident or a suspected homicide.'

'Correct. And what is common to those three situations?'

'The degree of risk?'

'*Besahh*, exactly.' Choukri wrote the word *Risk*. 'A critical incident is one in which there are serious risks involved. How should an officer respond if they're first on the scene of a critical incident?' He turned to Khalid Hakimi, the cadet who Ayesha had beaten in the four-hundred-metre race.

'You – Hakimi – what would you do?'

Hakimi stood up, flustered. 'Call for backup, sir?'

'That's not the first thing.' Choukri looked at the others. 'Anyone else? How should an officer behave in a critical situation?'

Salma got to her feet. 'Assess the risk, sir, and weigh up the appropriate response, involving other officers as necessary.'

'Excellent.' He wrote the word, *Assessment.* 'And what is the overriding aim?'

'To ensure the safety of civilians and minimise the loss of life, sir.'

Choukri nodded approvingly. 'You may sit. Risk assessment means weighing up the benefits against the possible harms. You may only have one second to reflect, but you never – repeat, *never* – act before assessing the risk. If you do not follow this procedure, people may die. Hakimi!'

'Yes sir?'

'Remind us what the primary function of a police officer is.'

'To assess risk, sir?'

'Wrong.'

'To enforce the law, sir.'

'Wrong.' He looked around. 'Anybody? How about you, Talal?'

Ayesha got to her feet. 'To protect the citizen, sir.'

'Correct. We are at the service of the people. In a critical incident you always take action to protect civilians. Remember that before you embark on a high-speed car chase or use your gun in a shopping centre. The only thing that separates a first-rate police officer from a second-rate one is that he or she thinks before they act. Talal!'

'Yes, sir?'

'Would you say that you are good at assessing risks?'

Ayesha's face reddened. 'I do my best, sir.' A titter went around the room.

'Imagine that you're negotiating with a terrorist. The suspect is armed. Would you wait for backup?'

'Not initially, sir.'

'Why not?'

'By the time backup arrived people might be dead. I would try to manage the situation myself.'

Choukri addressed Hakimi. 'Do you hear that, Hakimi? Talal would not call for backup. It looks like you're on your own.' The other cadets all laughed, except for Hakimi, who looked like he wished he could sink through the floor.

Opened in 2007, the port of Tanger-Med is the biggest port in Africa. It is the result of the strategic vision of His Majesty King Mohammed VI to create an industrial and commercial hub of international dimension. With the opening of Tanger-Med 2, scheduled for 2016, the two deepwater ports will handle three million containers a year—

'And to think that sheep were grazing here a few years ago!'

Simo chuckled as he strode into the reception area where Karim was watching a promotional video. Accompanying Simo was another officer of commissioner rank, Larbi, a short, weary-looking man in his early fifties. His brown nylon suit and black shirt made Karim think he must be unmarried, for no woman would let her husband leave the house in such ill-matching clothes. His thinning hair was combed over his head and a cigarette was jabbed between the fingers of one hand.

Larbi gave Karim a damp handshake and led the way into a ground-floor office.

'This was where your colleague worked.'

'*Works*,' Simo corrected. 'Let's not jump to conclusions.'

One wall of the room was covered in monitors showing CCTV footage from various locations in the port. A man in plain clothes and headphones sat at an end desk, toggling between the screens. Karim reached down to the mouse on Abdou's desk and a screensaver appeared of waterfalls in the Ourika Valley, Abdou's birthplace.

'I have his password if you need it,' said Larbi.

'Have you been through his documents and emails?'

Larbi nodded. 'There's nothing that might indicate what happened to him.'

Simo spoke. 'We think he was following a hunch of his own when he went missing.'

'Where was he last seen on camera?'

Larbi went over and spoke to the man at the end desk. A moment later the footage on one of the wall monitors changed to archive. The assistant fast-forwarded until Larbi told him to stop.

'This is Terminal 1 last Tuesday afternoon at 15.50.'

Karim approached the screen to get a better view. He could see the backs of two figures in hi-vis vests and hard hats, dwarfed by a stack of containers.

'The man on the right is Abdou,' said Simo.

Karim could make out Abdou's profile. The man next to him was wearing a striped scarf but it was impossible to see his face.

'Who is he?' asked Karim.

'One of our men,' said Larbi. 'He accompanied Abdou to the terminal but left soon after. He says that all they talked about was the cold.'

'Can I interview him?'

Larbi lit another cigarette. 'He's on annual leave. He'll be back in two weeks.'

'And the ship in the background?'

'The *Santos*, Panamanian flag,' said Larbi. 'We have all the details.'

The footage switched to another camera which was trained on two rows of containers, five units high, at the end of the storage yard. The ticker now read 17.37:27. 'An hour and a half later we picked him up here.' Abdou's youthful face passed underneath the camera.

'Is that a torch in his hand?'

'Yes,' said Larbi. 'He's between stacks J2 and K2. The letter refers to the block number and the number to the row. Each row is divided into sub-rows.'

'Is the entire terminal covered by security cameras?'

'Yes.'

'No,' corrected Simo. He exchanged glances with Larbi. 'There are a few blind spots, between the rows and at the end of K2.' He addressed the man with the headphones. 'Show the lieutenant the footage from camera nine.'

The screen changed to a different view with the ticker on 17.37:28. The footage ran for several seconds without any human presence.

'He should appear now,' said Larbi. 'But he goes into the blind spot and after that we don't see him on camera again.'

'Let me get this straight,' said Karim. 'You're saying that my colleague never left the port?'

'No, I'm saying that we have no record of him doing so.'

Karim took a few moments to absorb this information. He turned to Larbi. 'What was Abdou helping you with, exactly? Improving security? The scanning of inbound containers?'

Larbi regarded Karim stiffly. 'What do you know of our problems here at Tanger-Med?'

'Come now, Larbi!' said Simo. 'The lieutenant here has visited every port on the Atlantic coast!'

'Tanger-Med is different.'

Karim returned Larbi's stare. 'I know that Tanger-Med is the main entry point for Chinese goods – including fake drugs.'

'You're talking about logistics.'

'No, I'm talking about trafficking,' said Karim.

'This is to do with economics.'

Simo tried to mediate. 'The government wants to bring business to Tanger-Med. That means luring traffic away from rival ports like Algeciras. Now, it takes sixty seconds to scan a container. Some of the ships that stop here have ten thousand containers to unload. There are often four ships in port and another six waiting outside. If we scanned even ten per cent of inbound containers the delays to turnaround time would make the port uncommercial – it would put off potential customers. So, yes, trafficking is taking place. But we're under pressure to reduce the number of inspections.'

'To how many?'

'One in every hundred.'

Karim was shocked. 'At Casablanca they scan six containers out of every hundred!'

Larbi shrugged. 'We're thirty times bigger than Casablanca.'

'Did Lieutenant el-Mokhfi suggest a solution?'

'No,' said Larbi.

'That's not strictly true,' said Simo. 'Abdou suggested checking all containers from China, but Chinese containers account for almost fifty per cent of traffic. After we told him we could only carry out spot checks Abdou seemed to lose interest. He went off to do his own thing.'

That did not sound like Abdou, thought Karim. The last time they spoke, ten days before he disappeared, Abdou had grumbled about the obstructiveness of the port authorities, but their reaction wasn't unusual as far as Operation MEDIHA was concerned; nobody liked outsiders telling them what to do.

'How many containers did he check?'

'Six or seven. The last one was on a Chinese vessel, the *Pacific Star*, on the second of March. Three days before he disappeared.'

'Did he find anything suspicious?'

'Nothing at all.'

'Can we visit the terminal?'

'Of course,' said Simo. 'I haven't got security clearance so we'll go in Larbi's car.'

Larbi gave Karim an orange jacket to wear. It kept the rain off but it did nothing to soften his dislike of the man.

It was a fact: if you stood in the same place for weeks on end you saw things others missed. From his little patch at Tannery

House Gate, Joseph observed that one of the attendants in the car park made more money than the other attendants by claiming never to have change. If a customer handed him a five-dirham coin he would point to his empty pockets and the customer would drive off in exasperation. Then there was the shopkeeper across the road. He sold hash pipes and fishing tackle – an unlikely combination until you considered the shop's patrons: dead-eyed men whose sole means of earning a livelihood was to cast their lines on the rocks above Merkala Beach. The young chap who ran the store next to his was always laughing and joking with his customers but when alone his mouth drooped and he stared morosely at his mobile phone. Every so often a tall man with a harelip would stop by and engage him in conversation, then leave without buying anything.

Joseph thought about the explosion in the camp. Jean-François said that there was a war going on between rival people smugglers. Franco, the chef from Conakry, thought the bomber was a migrant; a man whom the two Moroccans had cheated. Others worried that the police would use the explosion as an excuse to evict them. To everyone's surprise, at seven o'clock that morning a tow-truck arrived, loaded the burned-out vehicle and drove off – with the corpses still inside!

Joseph hadn't eaten anything all day. Seeing the boiled eggs and flatbreads piled on the counter of the grocery store made him feel hungry. *The hungry people of Africa all end up in Tangier, like scum rising to the top.* A nasty Moroccan said that to him once.

At mid-afternoon a man in a robe stopped and bought one of his umbrellas. A short while later, a middle-class Moroccan couple came out of the Hotel Nahda, looked around, then went off in opposite directions. When his hunger pangs became unendurable Joseph walked across the road and bought a boiled egg and a flatbread. He put the egg in the bread, sprinkled it with salt and pepper then took it back to his spot and ate it under his umbrella. He checked the time on his phone: 16.15. His sister Gloria would be delivering her laundry. She collected clothes in the evening, washed them at night, ironed them in the morning then dropped them off again. It took her two hours to get around the village. One day he would buy her a little scooter with a box on the back. One day.

The terminal entrance lay half a mile from the waterfront. From that distance the gantry cranes looked like vultures picking at a carcass. Karim noticed that the guard at the gate was wearing an unfamiliar blue uniform.

'Who handles security here?'

'A private company called EDS.'

The three police officers got out of the car and a smart-looking man hurried over with a golf umbrella. Raindrops glistened on his nylon suit.

'*Salaam ou-alikum*. Driss El Hajjem, director of port security.' He shook Karim's hand. 'Let's wait in the hut until the rain stops.'

Larbi muttered something about a meeting and drove off. The others sheltered in the guardhouse. Karim asked the security director if he thought that Abdou was still somewhere in the terminal.

'If you want my opinion, I think your colleague strayed

into a container by accident and the container is now some-where on the high seas. He could be alive or dead.'

'You don't think he was eliminated?'

'Killed, you mean?' The security director shook his head. 'We would have found his body by now.'

'You work for EDS, is that right?'

'Correct.'

'Is security tight in the terminal?'

'Yes.'

'Do you trust your men?'

El Hajjem laughed. 'They can't pick their nose without me knowing about it.'

'But do you *trust* them?'

'Yes.'

'Simo mentioned blind spots.'

'There are a few blind spots,' the other man conceded.

'Suppose my colleague got trapped in a container which is still somewhere in the terminal. How would you know?'

'Your colleague would call for help on his phone. Or else he would bang on the side.'

'Would anyone hear him? The truck drivers look like they're wearing ear-protectors.'

'*Someone* would hear,' said Simo.

'Have you scanned the containers in the yard?'

'There are seventy thousand containers here!' laughed the security director. 'We could never scan them all!'

Karim's green eyes flashed. 'If you *did* scan them you could tell if there was someone inside!'

Simo interrupted. 'Scanning them would be pointless, Karim. The containers change all the time. This is a trans-shipment hub. Containers come off one vessel then remain in the storage yard for a few days – sometimes only a few hours – before being loaded onto a second vessel for shipping to their final destination.'

'I know how trans-shipment works,' Karim said testily.

'Then I'm sure you also know that containers are sealed at their point of origin,' said El Hajjem. 'They're locked tight. If there's a seal on the doors there's no point scanning them to see if someone got inside.'

The rain had given way to a mist, grey and watery. The three men donned hard hats and walked towards the storage yard. The security chief offered Karim two rubber nozzles.

'Ear plugs.'

Karim shook his head. If there were unusual noises in the storage yard he wanted to hear them.

Up close, the container stacks were like canyons, multicoloured ravines that rose on both sides. Low-loader trucks with flashing lights came back and forth to the stacks, pausing to be relieved of their loads by straddle carriers. Karim listened for shouts or tapping sounds but the nearer they got to the waterfront, the louder the clanking and whirring became.

The security chief raised his voice. 'We'll take a look at the quayside then go to the block where your colleague disappeared.'

They approached the first of two docked ships, a colossal vessel that spanned the length of the quay. Cranes were simultaneously loading and unloading containers while vehicles and forklifts buzzed about them.

'In the old days it took a hundred men to unload a ship,' shouted Simo. 'Now two men can do everything.'

Karim tilted his head back at the crane operators in their cabins high on the pale blue gantries, wondering how the world looked from their viewpoint. A young man came over carrying a clipboard.

'Faisal Berrada,' he shouted. 'Operations manager for APM, the terminal operator.' He motioned them towards a hut so they could speak more easily.

'What do you know about the missing police officer?' Karim asked when the noise had subsided.

'We spoke a couple of hours before he disappeared.'

'What about?'

'Our men intercepted a shipment of fake sleeping pills last year. He wanted the details.'

'Which were?'

'Oh, the usual. False compartments. A third of the container was filled with the goods listed on the manifest. The other two thirds was hidden behind a false wall.'

'Where did the lieutenant go after that?'

'The storage yard.'

'Shouldn't you have accompanied him?'

Faisal rubbed the toe of his boot on the floor, prodding some loose chips from the wood. 'Not my responsibility.'

Faisal's nonchalant manner made Karim bristle. 'Whose responsibility was it, then?'

'The port director.'

'And where is the port director?'

'In Rabat.'

Karim lost his temper. 'By Allah! A police officer is missing. He could be suffocating in a container, he could be held hostage, he could be floating out at sea!'

Simo put his hand on Karim's arm. 'Karim, this is the first time anything like this has happened. There's no established procedure.'

A truck drove up to the hut and the driver came through the door, taking off a pair of earmuffs. He looked startled, as if he hadn't expected to find men in suits gathered there.

'Who are you?' spluttered Karim.

'One of the drivers.'

'Did you see my colleague before he disappeared?'

'No.'

Karim's heart sank. This was going to be harder than he feared. He was being pushed from pillar to post like a customer complaining to a government ministry. He turned to Simo in desperation.

'Is there somewhere I can pray?'

When Karim returned from the prayer room he spotted Simo waving from the storage yard. A large number *2* was stencilled on the ground beneath his feet.

'Ah, there you are,' said Simo. 'This is where Abdou was last seen on camera.'

Behind Simo was a tower of five containers. Karim tried to picture his friend in the same spot six days ago and he was hit by a stab of grief, deep in his stomach. Standing with his back to the ground-level container he took a few moments to collect himself. He looked around. It was thirty feet to the wire perimeter fence. He moved to the right and a security camera came into view. He moved back two paces: now he could no longer see the camera. While he was taking photos, Faisal Berrada, the terminal manager, came over. Karim addressed his next question to him.

'What do you know about the container that was here last week?'

'We're still trying to trace the serial number.'

'I thought everything was computerised.'

'We only track the rows the containers are in. The containers move around constantly. But we'll find out where it's gone, don't worry.'

Karim gave a sweep of his arm. 'Out of all these containers, how many are empty?'

'Very few. There's one in E7. Shall we take a look?'

A few minutes later the three men halted in front of a blue container. Faisal lifted the locking bolts and opened the doors. Karim peered inside then stepped back.

'*Zid nta.* You get in.'

Faisal looked at Simo, who gave the briefest of nods. Faisal entered the container and Simo closed the doors.

'Can you hear us?' Karim said. There was no response. 'Can you hear us?' he shouted. His words were followed by a muffled thump. 'Tell him to keep thumping,' Karim said, walking away. At a distance of only ten feet the sound was inaudible above the background noise. He walked back to Simo.

'If Abdou didn't have a hard object to bang against the wall no one would have heard him.'

'I think we should let Faisal out now, don't you think?'

The terminal manager came out, a nerve in his cheek twitching with irritation.

'Your turn.'

Karim stepped inside the cavernous interior and walked halfway down the wooden floor. 'Close the doors,' he called to Simo. 'But don't lock them.'

The doors reverberated and the darkness swallowed him up. It would have felt claustrophobic were it not for shafts of light coming from two ventilation grilles towards the rear. Reaching up on tiptoe, Karim tugged at one of the grilles. Try as he might, it wouldn't budge. He walked back to the door and pushed it open.

'Were you afraid we were going to lock you in?' grinned Faisal.

'Not at all. I wanted to prove that if the door closes when you're inside you can push it open. The doors cannot lock by themselves.' Karim grasped the handle on the outside of the door and twisted it shut. 'The handles must be lifted, twisted and pushed down. Getting locked in a container is virtually impossible. Unless, of course, another person does it from the outside.'

'The lieutenant might have tripped and knocked himself out,' Faisal said hastily. 'If a security man was passing and saw the door open he would have locked it.'

'Without checking if there was someone inside? Isn't one of your primary duties to check for stowaways?'

Faisal seemed at a loss for words.

'How many containers have ventilation grilles?' asked Karim.

'Four out of every ten.'

'Would a man suffocate in a container without ventilation?'

'Hard to say. If the container was empty he could probably survive on the air inside. If the container was full, on the other hand, or if the ventilation grilles were blocked by boxes, then he might suffocate.'

'Shall we get a coffee?' Simo said brightly.

Instead of taking the motorway Simo and Karim drove back along the winding coast road. The clouds were low and the far side of the Strait was wreathed in fog. Karim aired his thoughts.

'If Abdou somehow ended up inside a container he's dying or already dead. If he fell into the harbour his body would have turned up by now. No one has mentioned a third, and more likely, scenario.'

'Which is . . .?'

'He was murdered. We know the Chinese traffickers are dangerous. If they thought that Abdou was going to disrupt their business they would take steps to eliminate him.'

Simo tutted. 'Come on, Karim! The last inspection – the one on the *Pacific Star* on the second of March – was carried out by EDS. Abdou was just a bystander. If the Chinese were going to take revenge they would have done so against Driss El Hajjem.'

'Abdou was the one who ordered the inspection.'

'Faisal and Larbi inspect containers all the time! It would be different if Abdou had found something, but he found nothing – nothing at all.'

'That scarf on the CCTV footage – the one worn by the police officer who was talking to Abdou on the night of his disappearance – did you recognise it?'

'No. Why do you ask?'

'Just curious.'

Simo stopped near some electricity pylons and got out of the car to relieve himself.

Karim gazed up at the mountainside. It was dotted with gnarled trees, gorse bushes and what looked like dark boulders, half-hidden by the mist. He got a sudden shock: the boulders were black faces staring down at him.

Simo followed his gaze. '*Afaraqa*. Africans.'

'What are they doing?'

'Waiting.'

'To cross?'

'Yes.'

'Where do they live?'

'In the forest.'

Karim watched the men, who made no attempt to hide themselves. As the detectives got back in the car, one of the Africans lifted an invisible cup to his mouth, as if he was thirsty and asking Karim for water.

Hastening up from the car park, Karim noticed Joseph standing by the roadside with an umbrella. Joseph gave Karim a smile and held the umbrella towards him, his bare arm protruding from his jacket.

'*Combien?*' asked Karim.

'*Cinquante.*'

'*Trente.*'

'OK.'

Karim noticed the tattoo on the inside of Joseph's arm.

'Is that your name?'

Joseph gave a nod.

'Where are you from, Joseph?'

'République Démocratique du Congo.'

'My name's Karim. I'm from Marrakech. We only use umbrellas in Marrakech to keep the sun off our heads!'

'It's the same in Congo.'

Karim opened his wallet but it was empty.

Joseph smiled. 'Pay another time. I'm always here.'

With a wave, Karim hurried on up the steps to the alley and the doorway of the hotel.

'Good evening, Mister Marrakchi.'

The clerk was sitting at the reception desk with his sleepy-eyed friend.

'*Salaam*,' replied Karim.

'I bet you wish you were in Marrakech now, eh, mister?'

'Not really. I have things to do here.'

To Karim's surprise, the man in the *jellaba* started singing.

> Marrakchi girls have the loveliest eyes
> Casaoui girls are full of surprise,
> Tanjaoui girls have expensive tastes,
> Rabati girls have the slimmest waists.

It was a popular song from a few years back and the man sang it surprisingly well. As Karim went upstairs with the key, the man's voice followed him.

> Fassi girls cook the tastiest dishes,
> Nadori girls succumb to your wishes.

As Karim reached the door of his room he paused, then went back down to the desk.

'Did anyone go in my friend's bedroom before I arrived?'

'No, *sidi*,' said the clerk. 'No one at all.'

The other man started singing again.

> The only girl I long to see
> Is the girl who waits at home for me.

Chapter 3

Karim slept fitfully. In the early hours he was awoken by the French windows crashing open with the wind. Outside, the square looked mournful, the cobbles glistening in the rain. Karim closed the windows then took the blanket from Abdou's bed and added it to his own. He lay on his side and stared at the empty bed. Abdou was the nearest thing he had to a brother. Apart from Noureddine, he was the only officer in the Fourth Precinct that he liked, and who liked him in return. They went out most mornings for coffee. They worshipped in each other's mosques and spent time together in the *hammam*.

Would Abdou ever see his beloved Ourika Valley again? Would he know the joys of marriage, of fatherhood? Of watching an infant take its first steps or seeing a daughter's face light up when he came home with a treat from the souks?

Karim's melancholy ponderings were interrupted by the call of the muezzin. *Prayer is better than sleep.* He washed, unrolled his mat and said his prayers. Then he lay down, this time wearing his tracksuit for extra warmth. At last he slept.

Rising early, he grabbed his towel and marched down the corridor to the shower. To his dismay, when he turned the tap, there was a clanking in the pipes followed by a freezing trickle.

He shivered under it for ten seconds. As he towelled himself dry he decided he would spend the morning going through the files on Abdou's computer then return to the terminal. Perhaps the port director would be back from Rabat.

Coming out of the bathroom he spotted a maid cleaning the floor. She was bending from the hips, the cloth in both hands, and swaying from side to side.

'You need a mop!' He laughed.

After the usual courtesies he asked her about Abdou. She smiled.

'A nice man, *dreef bezzaf,* very polite.'

'When did you last clean his room?'

The maid rested her hands on her ample hips. 'I clean it every day!'

'Does he normally leave the room tidy?'

'Yes, *sidi.* Very tidy. Except one day, when was it – Wednesday. His clothes were on the floor.'

'And his bed? Had it been slept in?'

'Now that you mention it – no, it hadn't. Is the gentleman all right?'

'Fatiha!' The desk clerk was glowering at the end of the corridor. 'Come down and clean the café.'

Karim thanked the maid, then returned to his room and dressed. He put on Abdou's grey hoodie, which was thicker than his own, and grabbed the umbrella. Outside he hastened to a cashpoint machine to pay Joseph.

But when he arrived at Tannery House Gate, Joseph was nowhere to be seen.

Simo Layachi preferred to conduct morning business from the congenial surroundings of Café Amine, a block from the prefecture. The commissioner had a sweet tooth and the proprietor of the café received daily deliveries from a French-run patisserie. As Karim scurried past in the rain he heard a tap on the window.

'Come inside and shelter, my brother!'

Simo introduced another man sitting at his table – a uniformed officer with a beak-like nose. Karim shook hands.

'How did you sleep?' asked Simo.

'Not well.'

'Ah-ha!' Simo winked at the other man. 'I told Karim he should stay at my house. Clean sheets, comfy bed and the best food in Tangier. There's still time to change your mind, my brother!'

Karim laughed but declined the invitation. When he and Abdou were on assignments for MEDIHA they always put up in a cheap hotel. If they accepted hospitality or stayed in an official billet they were vulnerable to pressure from the local police.

'My wife insists you come for dinner on Wednesday,' Simo continued. 'I hope you like seafood.'

'*Barak Allahu fik*, thank you.'

'Now, what will you have to drink?'

'*Nuss-nuss*.'

Simo relayed the request to the waiter.

'Karim is the man who launched Operation MEDIHA,' Simo said to the other officer, whose name was Jibrane. 'He's Marrakech's number one detective.'

Karim grimaced at the unwarranted praise.

'Is that right?' asked Jibrane, with the hint of a sneer. 'How are you liking Tangier?'

'I like it a great deal. Although I still haven't found my way around the medina.'

'The medina is really very simple,' Simo smiled. 'If you're going uphill then you're heading towards the Grand Socco or the kasbah. If you're going downhill then you're heading towards the sea.'

'And if you're on the level?'

'Nothing is on the level in this city.'

They all laughed.

'Are you planning to return to the port today?' asked Simo.

'Yes.'

'I cannot come with you, unfortunately. The lieutenant and I have a pressing matter to deal with in Boukhalef.'

Karim was secretly relieved. He wanted to have the run of the port without Simo at his shoulder. He had seen the way men snapped to attention when the chief was around. Witnesses might be more willing to open up if he spoke to them in private.

'*Makayn mushkeel.* No problem. But how shall I get there?'

'I've organised transport.'

'You're lending me Abdou's driver?' Karim said hopefully. This was a bonus. He had questions to put to the driver.

'Ah, no, he is on another job.'

'So how—?'

Simo dangled a set of car keys. 'On the right of the car park. A blue Dacia.'

Joseph waited patiently in line at the butcher's stall, staring at the immaculate suede slippers of the woman in front of him. He wondered how Arab women managed to keep their shoes clean with so much mud around. The butcher hacked a kilo of prime lamb and put it in the grinder. Joseph's handful of change wouldn't cover such a delicacy. All he could afford was scrag end of lamb, which Marie-Louise would use to prepare dinner for him and his friends. They all contributed to the cost apart from Marie-Louise, who had no means of earning money. A year ago, the police had evicted her and her husband from their apartment and thrown the husband in jail. After his release he tried to cross to Spain in a kayak but drowned. Now Marie-Louise was on her own with three young mouths to feed.

'I was next!'

A large woman in a blue dressing gown barged in front of him. Joseph didn't mind. He was happy to plan his day. He would return to the camp and drop off the food with Marie-Louise. From there it was a one-hour walk to Tannery House Gate. He looked up at the sky, full of dark clouds: perhaps he would sell more umbrellas. And if he walked home via the petrol station he could charge his phone out back.

The butcher served him with his usual cheerful smile and Joseph wondered why all Moroccans couldn't be as friendly. The camp was a twenty-minute walk away and he set off down the middle of the street, avoiding the potholes filled with rainwater. Boukhalef was the oddest neighbourhood he had ever set eyes on. The government had built tower blocks for a business project that never happened and the blocks had been left to rot, without plumbing or electrics. Many of the apartments were now squatted or owned by gangs who occasionally sublet them to migrants like Marie-Louise and her family, charging double the going rate.

'*Comment ça va?*' He greeted a little girl playing in the road but her mother came out of a doorway and shooed her inside. He reached the end of the tower blocks and set off across a rubbish-strewn wasteland made up of eucalyptus, patches of palmetto scrub and a bog filled with metal drums. Even Kisangani wasn't so full of rubbish!

He was already thinking of the stew that Marie-Louise would prepare, the meat slow-cooked until juicy and the vegetables caramelised so that they melted in the mouth, when a police van overtook him, siren blaring. Smoke was rising above the trees. His pulse quickened. Had there been another explosion? He started running.

When he arrived at the camp, police in riot gear were smashing everything in sight. Where Jean-François's tent once stood was a blazing pyre of wooden planks, clothes, sleeping bags and life jackets. Joseph heard shouts and the crackle of walkie-talkies. Three migrants were being bundled into the back of a van; all the other men seemed to have fled. Marie-Louise was standing in the middle of the site, cradling her baby and pleading with a hawk-nosed police officer who was scattering gasoline from a jerry can.

Joseph turned and ran all the way back to Boukhalef. Once at the tower blocks he hid on a staircase, his heart hammering. After ten minutes a convoy of riot vans drove past. When Joseph was sure the coast was clear he stole back to the camp-site. A few migrants were picking through the wreckage but there was no sign of Marie-Louise or any of his friends. Under the eucalyptus tree he found his Adidas sports bag, checked that the contents were safe, then swung the bag over his shoulder and headed across the fields towards the Perdicaris forest. After wandering for several hours he found a deserted building site, crawled inside a concrete pipe and fell asleep.

Larbi scowled.

'A desk and a computer? Did Simo sanction this?'

Grudgingly, he summoned his subordinate – the man who'd played the CCTV footage the day before – and told him to do what was necessary.

'Is that everything?' Larbi snapped.

'For now, yes,' Karim replied calmly. 'But I will need you to take me back to the terminal.'

'Look, I have other matters to attend to—'

'In one hour.'

The officer whistled when Larbi had left the room.

'That was telling him!'

The man, Ali, was in his twenties with a pleasant, open face. He was a lieutenant studying in his spare time for a master's degree in Maritime Studies.

Karim was curious. 'Is it true that the Strait of Gibraltar is the busiest stretch of water in the world?'

'*Besahh!* Absolutely! A hundred thousand ships a year, bringing us books, light bulbs, toys, that phone in your hand and all the equipment in this room!'

'*The ships that course upon the sea laden with the things which profit mankind,*' said Karim, quoting the Quran.

'Indeed, my brother. The world would grind to a halt without container traffic.'

'Tanger-Med seems to be doing very well from it.'

'That's because it sits on the Line of Zero Deviation.'

Karim looked blank.

Ali explained. 'Ships travelling from Asia to New York or Rotterdam can call at Tanger-Med without deviating from their course. They don't lose any time, and as we know, *al-waqt ghalee*, time is money!'

'Is Algeciras on the Line of Zero Deviation as well?'

'Of course.'

'So there is competition between the two ports?'

'Yes.'

'What about the ships that don't continue through the Strait? There must be many Chinese ships that finish their journey at Tangier?'

'To trans-ship, you mean? Indeed. The ULCVs – the Ultra Large Container Vessels –and the small, local ships . . . Tanger-Med is where they connect. The local carriers take the containers on the last leg of their journey.'

Karim thanked Ali for his help. 'May God reward you for your efforts.'

When he had gone, Karim opened the browser and started looking through Abdou's files. There was an inventory of cargo on the *Pacific Star*, details of counterfeit drug seizures in Tanger-Med, a list of Chinese exports to Morocco. Abdou's browsing history was humdrum – local weather and tide conditions, mainly. Karim rubbed his eyes, then opened a new document on his screen and created a table with two columns. At the top of the left column he typed: *Dead.*

Accidental death outside container (e.g. drowning)
Accidentally trapped inside container (followed by suffocation or dehydration)
Murdered outside container
Deliberately trapped inside container

He typed above the second column: *Alive.*

Trapped in container at sea (with access to drinking water?) but unconscious or mobile out of range
Trapped in container in port but unconscious or mobile out of charge
Hostage/kidnapped
Spain?

Larbi appeared in the doorway in his police jacket. 'Let's go.'

Karim didn't move. He asked the question that had been on his mind since first learning of Abdou's disappearance.

'Why have seizures of counterfeit drugs gone down? In the first six months of 2011 the port confiscated, let me see, a hundred and fifty tons.' He consulted Abdou's screen. 'Yet in the last six months they only stopped twelve tons.'

Larbi didn't seem fazed by the question. 'The traffickers have switched to easier ports, like Nouakchott or Abidjan.'

'So the threat to the Maghreb is over?'

'That's not what I meant.' Larbi ran a hand through his thinning hair. 'The traffickers have found other ways – overland, for example, or via a port like Casablanca. Now, I'm very busy. Can we get the visit to the terminal over with?'

'I've changed my mind. I want you to phone the terminal and tell them that I'm coming on my own.'

'You haven't got clearance.'

'You're the chief of police. Get me clearance.' In a milder tone Karim added, 'After all, you said you were busy.'

The security guard peered at Karim through the driver's window then waved him through. Karim took a hi-vis jacket and a hard hat from the boot of the Dacia and crossed the storage yard between two bays of refrigerated containers. God help Abdou if he was trapped in one of those!

In the wharf he noticed that the ship was different to yesterday's. The terminal manager, Faisal Berrada, was talking to an official under one of the giant gantries. The wheels of the gantry were so large they came up to the men's shoulders. While he waited for Berrada to finish, Karim timed the crane operation. It took ninety seconds for the spreader on one boom to descend into the vessel, grip a container, travel along the boom, lower the container onto an empty truck, then travel back. It took a few seconds longer for the second boom to do the operation in reverse, taking outbound containers from another line of trucks and placing them in the ship's hold.

A truck braked to a halt near him.

'*Salaam ou-alikum.* Back again?' It was the driver who had turned up in the hut the previous morning.

The driver shook hands. 'You're a colleague of the missing officer, aren't you? My name is Saïd. Have you learned anything yet?'

'Very little.'

'It's really very unfortunate.'

They stood and watched the crane operation for a few minutes.

'Tell me, Saïd,' said Karim, 'how long does a container remain in the yard before it gets taken away?'

'The average is three days. A container that stands still is losing money!'

'So the containers that were here last week have all gone elsewhere?'

'The majority, yes.'

'You met my colleague?'

'Yes. He was here most days.'

'Do you think he was trapped in a container?'

Saïd sighed. 'I feel bad about it – I really do. He should have been accompanied. Container yards are dangerous places. There's a lot of heavy machinery.'

'So what do you think happened to him?'

The driver looked around to check that Faisal Berrada still had his back to them.

'He was at the waterside a few times. He could have fallen in.'

'Where?'

'*Nshoufou.* Let's take a look.'

Karim climbed into the cab of the truck and they drove off, zigzagging to avoid crossing the paths of other trucks. When they reached the eastern end of the terminal they stopped at a barrier which separated Terminals 1 and 2. They were in a sort of no-man's land, equidistant from the vessels berthed in the two terminals. Karim noticed that Terminal 2 was operated by a different company, called Eurogate. Their gantries and vehicles were colour-coded white, in contrast to the blue of Terminal 1. Standing next to a capstan, Saïd and Karim peered down at the water sixty feet below.

'You think he could have fallen in here?'

To Karim's surprise, Saïd's answer was breathless, fearful.

'Can I be frank?'

'Of course.'

'I'd say it was almost impossible. Nor do men get trapped in containers. It simply doesn't happen.'

'Go on.'

'I think your colleague was silenced.'

Karim felt a jolt. This was the first time that anyone in Tangier had voiced the possibility of foul play.

'That is a serious allegation.'

'It's just a hunch.'

'What's it based on?'

Saïd pretended to point to the water. 'Listen – I'm just a driver. But I've seen containers leave and enter the port without paperwork. They get waved through the barrier. I wasn't here the night your colleague disappeared but another driver saw a Sûreté van in the stacks. I spoke to Commissioner Larbi about it.'

'What did he say?'

'He said that he had the situation under control.'

Just then Saïd's walkie-talkie crackled. After answering the call his voice returned to normal, as if his conversation with Karim had never happened.

'It's my lunch break. Shall I drive you to the gate?'

'No, thank you, I'll walk.'

Saïd put his hand on Karim's arm. 'Stick between the markings on the walkways. *Redd baalek.* Be careful!'

The offices of the Tanger-Med Port Authority were situated on a landscaped hillock overlooking the port. Inside, it was like a glorified public relations agency, with bright-eyed employees, marble floors and display boards decked with plans and photographs. The CEO, Ben Jelloun, was an unsmiling man of thirty – young, Karim thought, to hold such an important position. He showed Karim into a canteen. Karim chose a dish from the self-service buffet and the two men sat by the window.

'I had to go to Rabat yesterday,' said Ben Jelloun, picking at a salad. 'Did you find out what you needed to?'

'I'm still looking. Tell me, Mr Ben Jelloun, you're in charge of the biggest port in the country. Yet both terminals, along with security, are run by private operators.'

The director shrugged. 'That's the way things are done now in the Maghreb.'

'But presumably it means you have less oversight – less idea of what is going on?'

'As I said, that's the way things are done now in the Maghreb.'

'Do EDS do a good job?'

'They're very efficient,' Ben Jelloun replied guardedly.

'Commissioner Larbi told me that only one per cent of containers get checked.'

'Opening containers is time-consuming. The handling agent has to be present. We have to photograph everything.

We have to produce paperwork and inform the owners. That takes time and time is—'

'Money. I know. So do you subscribe to the theory that my colleague got trapped in a container?'

'The container at K2 had a seal on it. It was loaded next day and transhipped to Le Havre. The authorities inspected it for us. The seal was still intact and it contained nothing but agricultural implements.'

This was news to Karim. Faisal Berrada, the terminal manager, had told him that he hadn't been able to trace the container at K2. When he put this to Ben Jelloun he shrugged.

'We only found out this morning.'

'So where is Lieutenant el-Mokhfi? Or his corpse?'

'Ah. That's for you and Commissioner Larbi to establish.'

'But it's not in Terminal 1?'

Ben Jelloun shrugged again.

Karim continued. 'Do you think that Lieutenant el-Mokhfi visited Terminal 2?'

'No. He would have been seen. We have floodlights and cameras all over the terminals.'

'But there are blind spots and areas of darkness.'

'Yes.'

'Such as between the rows of containers.'

'Yes.'

'Let's say, for the sake of argument, that I was planning to assault a man in Terminal 1. If I knew that he was standing in a spot *not* covered by cameras, that would make my task easier, wouldn't it? I could creep up on him from behind through the dark alley between the rows of containers. Correct?'

'An assailant would still have to do something with the body.'

'Unless they took it back the way they came.'

'True.'

'So we have established that an attack was feasible.'

Ben Jelloun demurred. 'It's very unlikely.'

'Unlikely, but *feasible*?'

'Yes.'

'How do you check outbound containers – the ones that come into the port by road then leave by ship?'

'We're building a new nineteen-hectare Export Access Zone, capable of processing up to two thousand lorries a day—'

'But now? How many lorries do you process now?'

'Around eight hundred,' the director admitted. 'Container traffic has grown very fast at Tanger-Med. Sometimes we only have time for spot checks.'

'I heard that running a port is a cut-throat business.'

'I would prefer to use the word *competitive*. But Tanger-Med is holding its own.'

'Are you at all concerned that seizures of counterfeit drugs have fallen dramatically?'

'It has come to my attention.'

'You're not worried?'

'I have every confidence in our security procedures.'

'But tightening security procedures is what my colleague came to help you with?'

Ben Jelloun gave a nod. 'Yes.'

'If the port developed a reputation for weak security that would be bad for business, presumably?'

'Very bad.'

'Worse than a delay in turnaround times?'

'From the Port Authority's point of view, yes.'

Karim took a few moments to digest this information. It conflicted with what Larbi and Simo had said about the economics of running a port.

'I believe my colleague carried out a check on a container from a Chinese vessel, the *Pacific Star*.'

'Correct. The contents corresponded to the manifest. Nothing but t-shirts, sweat tops, track bottoms and trainers. We forwarded the container to the customer.'

Karim took out his notebook. 'What was the name of the company?'

'Best Century Clothing.'

'Where are they located?'

'In the Free Zone.'

'Here at the port?'

'No, the Free Zone in the city.'

When Joseph woke it was late afternoon and his shoulder ached from lying on concrete. He was afraid to go back to the camp. Even if he could rebuild his shelter, the place was now jinxed. He had heard of another camp at Casiago, but it was over thirty miles away.

To compound his worries, his phone was out of charge. He couldn't call Jean-François to find out where his friends had gone. Morocco was a scary place for a solitary migrant. The sooner he crossed the Strait, the better. He checked his body belt: seven two-hundred-dirham notes, three hundred-dirham notes, a fifty and a creased twenty.

He replayed Sunday night's explosion in his head. The police must think the migrants were responsible and they had carried out the raid as a punishment. Or the police had planted the bomb in the Moroccans' Jeep deliberately, to eliminate the traffickers and use it as a pretext for eviction of the migrants. Things had got worse, no question. When he arrived a year ago he hadn't even been fingerprinted. Now the police beat you up, threw you out of your apartment and destroyed your camp. It wasn't as if you wanted to stay in their shitty country!

He poked his head out of the pipe. There was mud everywhere. A hectare of land criss-crossed with caterpillar tracks, as if the woodland had been cleared and levelled. Apart from the pipes there was no sign of any construction work. He sat back down inside the pipe and chewed at the hunk of meat he'd bought. He'd eaten raw meat before. When he was crossing the Sahel he ate a dead falcon lying by the side of the road. Since he couldn't think of anything else to do, he went back to sleep.

Sometime later he was woken by headlamps and the sound of a car engine. Night had fallen. From his hidey-hole he saw three men get out of a car. The darkness was broken by the flicker of a cigarette lighter, laughter and the clink of bottles. The men were probably harmless, drinking alcohol in secret, but Joseph wasn't taking chances. Who knew what three Moroccans might do if they found a migrant in their drinking den? He crawled to the other end of the pipe then made a wide detour around the men's car before walking to the main road.

Hicham, the police driver, looked in the rear-view mirror and nearly had a heart attack.

'Leaving early?' Karim's face loomed from the back seat.

'Yes,' Hicham stammered. 'It's – I cleared it with police dispatch. My wife called me. My son hasn't come home. He – he sometimes goes to Malabata to smoke kif with a friend.'

'I'll go with you.'

Hicham was aghast. 'But—'

'We can talk on the way.'

Hicham reversed out of the prefecture and along the streets of downtown. The place looked better by night, Karim decided. The shops were bright, the pavements bustling with well-dressed Tanjaouis returning from work or heading out for the evening.

'Tell me about the trips you made with Lieutenant el-Mokhfi.'

'I – I told you everything. I usually waited for him in the morning in the car park under the Hotel Continental. Then we drove to Tanger-Med. I collected him from the port around six, either from the prefecture or from Terminal 1. Some nights I collected him much later, around midnight.'

'What was he doing on those nights?'

'I don't know, sir. He didn't discuss his work.'

'On Tuesday – the night he disappeared – did anyone else know that you weren't going to pick him up – that he had to make his own way home?'

'*Momken*, perhaps.' Hicham thought for a moment. 'The details were on the system.'

'At the port?'

'And downtown. The police dispatcher knows my schedule a day in advance so that if an officer needs a car they can check who's around. I swear – if I could have the time again I would go back to the terminal and wait by the gate – I swear on the Holy Quran! I would demand that the guard go and look for him, I would look for him myself!' Hicham's eyes welled. 'He was a good man, Mr Abdou. The other officers – they sit in the back of the car and use their mobiles but he . . . he always sat up front and chatted to me.'

That sounded typical of Abdou and, for a moment, Karim's eyes pricked as well.

'What did you chat about?'

'The news from Syria, the Africa Cup of Nations – everything.'

'But not work?'

'No. He was very professional.'

They were driving along the curve of the marine boulevard, the lights glittering like a pearl necklace.

'He never said anything unusual?'

'There was one occasion. I didn't attach much importance to it at the time, but now you mention it . . .'

Karim leaned forward. 'Go on.'

'It was last Monday, the day before he disappeared. We were talking about my son. I said that he was irritable and rude all the time. I was worried that he was smoking kif after school. Mr Abdou told me that his work had taught him an important lesson – not to look for dates in the olive tree.'

'What did he mean by that?'

'That there might be another explanation for my son's behaviour.'

'Outward signs can be deceptive?'

'Yes.'

They passed a succession of glitzy nightclubs, most of which were shut at that early hour.

'We're almost at Malabata. Shall I take you home, sir?' Hicham asked hopefully.

'No, let's look for your son. Where does he usually go?'

'To the lighthouse.'

A few minutes later they turned off the highway. At the end of the track was an old lighthouse with a faded five-pointed Moroccan star on the tower. Nearby, among the pine trees, was a small café with outside tables and chairs that a waiter was stacking up for the night. Hicham questioned the waiter and showed him a photo, but the waiter shook his head. Hicham's mobile rang and Karim strolled to a balcony over-looking the Mediterranean. It seemed like a popular beauty spot, with views across to the lights of Algeciras.

After a short while, Hicham came up to him with a grin. 'That was my wife. My son is at home. He went to the mall to buy a joystick for his PlayStation.'

'*Al-hamdulillah*, thank God. It seems that Mr Abdou was right, after all.'

When they arrived back at the police station rain was falling.

'You're a good man, Hicham,' said Karim. 'May God protect you and your family.'

By the time Karim parked the Dacia at the foot of the medina raindrops were hammering on the roof. He spoke through the window with a parking attendant in a plastic poncho and agreed a weekly price, then stepped out of the car, unfurled his umbrella and hurried up the hill. Once again, there was no sign of Joseph. He hadn't been there in the morning and now he wasn't there in the evening! Then again, who would stand outside on an evening such as this? The grocery store owner was huddled in his shop with the hood of his heavy woollen *burnous* over his head.

The steps leading up from Bab Dar Dbagh were a series of tiny waterfalls. Traipsing up the lonely alley to the Fuentes, his feet slopping in his shoes, put Karim in mind of a melancholy song by Fairouz. It was about the days of cold and winter, when the streets are under water, and a girl comes from her house to meet her lover only to find that he has forgotten her. Just thinking of the song brought tears to Karim's eyes.

When he reached the hotel he took his key wordlessly from the clerk, went to the room and lay down with the blanket over his head. Alone in Tangier, worn out with worry for his missing friend, his thoughts went to Ayesha. He wondered if she was studying or laughing with her room-mate. When she laughed, his spirits soared. When she was tight-lipped, everything seemed cold and drab. If she was near, people and events passed by without making an impression. A man could rob a bank ten feet away and Karim wouldn't have noticed.

No one knew how he felt, apart from Ayesha. It was unthinkable to tell others of his feelings for her. Ayesha was as much his sister as Khadija, their siblingship defined by centuries of religion and taboo. But love was stronger than taboo. And so Karim's mind, when he was feeling sad after a frustrating day like today, would turn to Ayesha.

Karim was so absorbed in his gloom that he didn't hear the first gunshot. But there was no mistaking the second. A violent crack, just below his window. He jumped up and rushed to the balcony. A figure was lying face down on the cobbles. Two bystanders were gawping from the other side of the square. Karim was down the stairs and in the square in seconds. The victim was a male, mid-thirties, wearing a hoodie, black jeans and trainers. There were two entry wounds in his chest. Judging by the size of the holes, they came from a powerful handgun. As he felt for a pulse Karim scanned the square, but all he saw was a widening circle of blank faces. A waiter stood in the doorway of the Café Central.

'What happened?' Karim barked. 'Did you see it?'

The waiter shrank back. 'No, mister, I was inside.'

'Call the police and an ambulance.'

'Is he dead?' someone asked.

Karim nodded.

'I saw it,' said a grizzle-haired man pushing a cart filled with gas bottles. 'He was arguing with another man and the man shot him.'

'Did you get a good look at the other man?'

'No. He was wearing a *jellaba* with his hood up.'

'It was an *azzi*, a black,' came a voice from outside the Café Tingis.

'How do you know he was black?' asked Karim.

'He, er, sounded like he was black . . .'

'What did he say?'

'I didn't hear . . .' The man's voice trailed off and he sat down again.

'It was a young man,' said a woman wearing a green caftan.

'No, he was an old man, at least fifty!'

Karim appealed for calm. 'Listen, everybody. If you saw anything please stay until the police arrive.'

Instantly, half the crowd dispersed. A few minutes later an ambulance came into the Petit Socco, its siren echoing and its lights flashing off the buildings.

Karim gave his details to a harassed-looking police officer. Once the officer had established that Karim hadn't seen the shooting he moved on to the gas-bottle vendor and the waiter – the only two witnesses who had stayed in the square.

It was Karim's first experience of a killing that involved fire-arms. Apart from their use for hunting, or by the police and army, guns were almost unknown in Morocco. To Karim's surprise, the incident left him feeling energised, as if the frustrations of the day had finally found an outlet. The shooting was shocking, but it was a neutral event, a police matter that he could consider and evaluate on a purely professional level. There was something, however, that he had to do first.

The mosque was an old building with a green doorway and stucco frame. A worshipper directed Karim to a fountain in the courtyard where he washed his hands, rinsed his mouth and face, put his feet under the tap and dried himself with a towel. Kneeling with his hands on his thighs, Karim placed his palms on the ground and rocked forward, touching his forehead to the ground. *Glory to Thee, O Allah, and Thine is the praise, and blessed is Thy name, and exalted is Thy majesty, and there is none to be served besides Thee.* It was half-past eight when he came out of the mosque, feeling fully restored.

He walked the short distance back up to the Petit Socco to find the police had disappeared, along with any forensics. Maybe they'd been and gone while he was at the mosque. Nonetheless, it was surprising that there were no traces of the shooting, not even a police line. The rain had stopped and customers were sitting outside at the Central, smoking and drinking tea, their collars and hoods raised against the cold. The atmosphere was subdued and he saw people staring at him and whispering. Then he heard a loud voice.

'*Labas, kulchee bekhir?*' The sleepy-eyed man was sitting at one of the tables, smoking kif in a long-handled *sebsi* pipe. 'Everything OK? If you need anything while you're in Tangier, just ask. Mokhtar is my name!'

Karim regarded him warily. He could have been fifty or seventy – it was impossible to tell. His brow was wrinkled under the hood of his jellaba and his wide mouth was curled in a grin.

'Do you know about the shooting?'

'No, mister! I wasn't here.'

Karim brushed past him into the café to ask the waiter about his statement to the police, but the waiter was busy and told him to come back later. To Karim's annoyance, when he walked away, Mokhtar got up and trailed after him. Halfway up Rue Siaghine Karim stopped at a stall selling CDs and DVDs. He leafed through the racks and picked out a CD of Fairouz songs. Mokhtar peered over his shoulder.

'Ah, Fairouz! The Lebanese Nightingale!' He started humming a popular Fairouz tune. Karim gave Mokhtar a venomous stare and stalked out. He crossed the road into an indoor market and wandered along aisles of brightly lit stalls selling preserved lemons, dates and spices in red, yellow and orange pyramids. Karim paused at a fruit stall to sample a strawberry.

'Strawberries from Agadir!' chirruped Mokhtar.

He's worse than a puppy, Karim thought. To shake him off he trotted up some steps into the Grand Socco. The square was larger and more open than the Petit Socco, with a patch of greenery in the middle. People were milling around, eating in restaurants, strolling through the park or looking at the notices outside a cinema. Karim stepped into a chemist, Mokhtar on his heels.

'You want contraceptives?' Mokhtar whispered.

Karim asked the girl behind the counter for antibiotics. She took three different types of amoxicillin from the shelves and he examined them one by one.

'You have an infection?' Mokhtar hissed.

After verifying that the medicines were genuine, Karim thanked the girl and walked out.

'You're not buying anything?' asked Mokhtar, hurrying to keep up. 'Where to now, mister? The kasbah? Something to eat?'

Karim stopped to look around. He noticed a man wearing a scarf similar to the one he'd seen in the CCTV footage at the port.

'What's that scarf?'

'Which scarf, mister? The green and white one? It's a Raja supporter's scarf, mister. I know where you can get one for forty dirhams – maybe thirty-five!'

Karim paused for a moment, wondering if Mokhtar might be useful, after all. He ran his fingers over his chin.

'I need a shave.'

Mokhtar gave a broad grin, revealing teeth like cracked tombstones.

'Come!'

ي

The barber was a slight man, his spine misshapen by scoliosis. He made up for any physical disability with firm fingers that pinched Karim's cheeks as he applied the lather. The two other swivel chairs were empty. Next to the mirror was a tier of glass shelves with a dusty bottle of aftershave and a curling postcard of a seaside resort.

'Leave the upper lip,' Karim told the barber. 'I'm growing a moustache.'

He could see Mokhtar in the mirror, grinning inanely from the seats at the back of the shop and making thumbs-up signs. Every so often Mokhtar passed a comment to the barber or the slack-jawed young man staring at his phone nearby.

Karim spoke suddenly. 'That guy who died in the square this evening. Who was he?'

The barber's eyes flickered but he said nothing.

'Riff-raff,' muttered Mokhtar. 'Probably a drug dealer.'

The boy on the chair took out his earphones. 'That's not what I heard. I heard he was a people smuggler.'

Karim stared at the boy's face in the mirror. 'You mean he smuggled migrants?'

'That's just talk,' said the barber, his hand turning Karim's head back to centre. 'What would a people smuggler be doing in the medina?'

'Maybe he'd just come from that African place,' said the boy. 'What's it called, Chez something.'

'Chez Kebe,' said the barber. He scraped the last bit of foam from Karim's face then lathered it for a second pass.

'What's Chez Kebe?' asked Karim.

Mokhtar dismissed the remark. 'Oh, it's just some restaurant where the Africans hang out.'

The barber rubbed Karim's face dry with a towel. 'Eyebrows?' Karim nodded and the barber put a comb to his eyebrows and snipped along the line.

Outside in the alleyway Mokhtar hissed at Karim. 'You can't say things like that, mister.'

'Like what?'

'People smuggling! It's dangerous. You don't know who's listening!'

'Do *you* think he was a people smuggler?'

'*Shh!* I don't know!' Mokhtar looked around. It was late and the alley was deserted, most of the shops closed. 'If you want my opinion, he was some lousy drug dealer who got into a fight. Where to now, mister? You want a girl?'

'Take me to the African restaurant, Chez Kebe.'

'It's closed, mister! A waste of time!'

'Show me anyway.'

With a lot of sighs and mutterings, Mokhtar led him down a series of dark alleyways.

'There! You see? Closed!'

They were standing in front of metal shutters, above which were painted the words *Chez Kebe*.

'Take me back to the square.'

Within two minutes they were back in the Petit Socco.

'Mokhtar. That's your name, right?'

'Yes, Mokhtar. At your service! And you are Karim. *The generous one,*' he said pointedly, referring to the Arabic meaning of *karim*. When Karim blithely walked off, he coughed.

Karim walked back to him. 'You want me to be generous? I can be generous. Did anyone search my friend's room last week?'

'I don't know, mister.'

'Then you're no use to me.' Karim prodded Mokhtar in the chest. 'Find out what happened to my friend and you'll discover that I can be very *karim* indeed.'

Chapter 4

The instructor was late for the morning lesson and the cadets were chatting in the lecture room.

'I don't know why we have to have a lecture about crowd control,' Ayesha grumbled. 'It would be better demonstrated on the parade ground.'

'You know how keen Choukri is on learning from past mistakes,' said Salma. 'He probably wants to give us a history lesson – tell us about the bad old days of the riot police.'

'What do you mean?'

'You know – the special unit set up after the Casablanca bombings. They were an elite squad – they got to wear smart uniforms and drive around in shiny SUVs. Unfortunately they got too big for their boots and killed a demonstrator in Laayoune. Then again . . . Choukri's prepared a projection screen. Maybe he wants to show us footage from Ceuta.'

'The assault on the border wall? That was so shocking! It was a lesson in how *not* to control a crowd.'

'Perhaps that's why he wants us to see the footage.'

Ayesha was so engrossed in the conversation that she didn't notice that Khalid Hakimi was staring at her.

'Hey, Talal!'

A smile was playing about Hakimi's lips. Ayesha exchanged nervous glances with Salma.

'Did you come to Kenitra because of your brother?'

Hakimi spoke so loudly that everyone stopped to listen. Ayesha could feel the blood rise to her cheeks. Was Hakimi trying to insult her – implying that she had only been awarded a place at Kenitra because of Karim's success at the college four years earlier? If so, it was a lie!

'What are you talking about?'

'I hear he's a dirty cocksucker.'

The effect on the room was electric. All eyes turned to Ayesha.

'My brother is a police officer!'

'That's not what I've heard.'

Ayesha tensed. Salma put a hand on her sleeve.

'I've heard he's in prison.' Hakimi looked around triumphantly. 'Right here in Kenitra.'

Ayesha's mouth opened but no words came.

'He's one of the bearded ones. Do you hear that, comrades? A terrorist. He must be proud of his little sister, making it to police college. Or does he want to blow us all up?'

Everyone held their breath. Ayesha picked up a pen and pretended to write something.

'Do you have anything to say, Talal? What's it like being the sister of a jihadi? *Allahu akbar!*'

Ayesha jumped to her feet. Clutching the pen, she vaulted her table in a single bound, grabbed Hakimi's arm and tried to jab the pen into his hand. Hakimi rose from his seat in surprise, trying to push her off. At that moment Colonel Choukri came into the room. The other cadets sprang to attention. Choukri's eyes fell on Ayesha and Hakimi. There was absolute silence.

'What do you think you're doing?' Each word fell like a hammer blow. 'Were you – *fighting*?' He lingered on the word as if it referred to an activity beyond human comprehension.

'Stay behind after class, both of you. Talal, go back to your seat.'

Ayesha walked around the table, her face burning with shame. For the rest of that hour she hardly took in a word. Every so often Salma looked at her with concern. When the lesson was over the others filed out, leaving Hakimi and Ayesha standing. Colonel Choukri closed the door.

'Do you have anything to say?'

Hakimi examined the beret in his hand as if he'd found an interesting pattern.

'Talal?'

Ayesha bit her lip. The worst punishment – the one she feared most – was a black mark on her record. It would prejudice her chances of a good position after graduation.

'It was a misunderstanding, sir.'

'A misunderstanding?' The instructor walked between the tables. 'A misunderstanding is when you go to the wrong classroom. A misunderstanding is when you take notes incorrectly. Two cadets fighting like hooligans is not a misunderstanding. Perhaps you've forgotten where you are. This is the Institut Royal de Police, an elite institution under the personal jurisdiction of His Majesty King Mohammed VI. To be given a place here is an honour and a privilege. Do you understand?'

The two cadets nodded meekly.

'I said: do you UNDERSTAND?'

'Yes, sir,' they chorused.

'There are many things you are expected to learn here. Leadership ... marksmanship ... but the most important thing is discipline.' Colonel Choukri rubbed down the white-board then folded the cloth and placed it neatly in a tray. 'Last week migrants attacked the Ceuta wall. You saw what happened. The police response was a disaster. A shambles. Why? Poor discipline. Officers losing their heads. We must have discipline in the modern police force.'

He put on his cap. As he was heading to the door he turned around.

'I am giving you both an official warning. Two warnings and you're out. No appeal, no redress. Is that clear?'

'Yes, sir,' they replied.

The Free Zone of Tangier lay south of the airport. An industrial park of soulless factories, empty roads and mani-cured lawns, the place resembled a film set after the actors and crew had gone home. Karim had difficulty finding the premises of Best Century Clothing company, so discreet was the nameplate by the door. After showing his police ID to the receptionist he was received by a courteous Chinese manager.

'*Ki dayr? Labas?* How do you do?'

Wang-Wei Zhang had an eager smile and an impressive command of Moroccan Arabic. 'I learned the local dialect,' he told Karim as he led him upstairs, 'because I wanted to be able to talk to our employees, none of whom speak French or English.'

His office on the second floor was small and functional, with the customary portrait of the King.

'This is just a routine enquiry,' Karim began. 'I learned that there was an inspection of one of your containers on the second of March?'

Zhang consulted his computer screen. 'Yes. A container from Guangdong. There was a problem with the goods or the documents?'

'No. But the police officer who carried out the inspection has disappeared. We do not know what happened to him.'

'That is terrible! *Llaherhamou.* May God have pity on him!'

Karim found it impossible to tell if the manager's surprise was genuine. He also found it disconcerting holding the conversation in Arabic.

'I'm trying to establish the course of events leading up to his disappearance. Can you explain what was in your shipment?'

'*Lehweyj.* Clothes. We have a shipping agent at Tanger-Med who can show you the documents.'

'What do you do with the clothes once you receive them from China?'

'We add crocodiles! Stripes! Swooshes! Polo players! We turn ordinary clothes into designer clothes.'

'That's all you do? Sew on logos?'

'The stitching has to be done by hand. We are very high quality!'

'Could you show me around?'

Zhang smiled. '*Tbiat al-hal,* naturally.' He led the way onto a high-level walkway. They were in a hangar-like space with a high roof criss-crossed by fluorescent lights. Below, two conveyor belts with items of clothing moved, carousel-like, around a cluster of female employees bent over sewing machines. Along each wall stood storage racks filled with cardboard packing cases.

'Do you sell your clothes in the Maghreb?'

'Thirty per cent, the rest go to Europe. We have a warehouse near Cadiz.'

There was something about the operation that mystified Karim. 'Why don't you add the logos to your clothes in China?'

Zhang gave a conspiratorial wink. 'Because of your country's free trade agreement with the European Union. If we put the logos on here we can sell the goods in Europe without paying import duty.'

They descended the far end of the walkway and emerged in an outside area where men were stacking a lorry.

Karim picked up a cutting knife. 'Do you mind?' Without waiting for a reply he sliced open a box and took out a Lacoste shirt wrapped in polythene. It was as good an example of fake merchandise as he'd seen. He replaced the shirt and thanked the manager for his help.

'*Mahrba!* You are welcome. And please – keep the shirt!'

The Carrefour supermarket was busy. Joseph plugged his mobile phone into a wall socket and pretended to read the back of a packet of washing powder. After five minutes an officious employee spotted the phone and asked him to leave. Joseph slung his Adidas bag over his shoulder, walked across the car park, crossed the highway and traipsed up the steep hillside to Marshan. He paused to catch his breath and call Jean-François but, despite several attempts, he got no answer.

Skirting the royal palace he headed down through a jumble of streets and municipal gardens until he came to the Anglican church of St Andrew.

At one time St Andrew's boasted a full congregation. The English community went there to worship, christen, marry and, when they died, to be buried underneath the palm trees in the churchyard. Their numbers, however, were dwindling. The church only kept going thanks to a constantly changing population of sub-Saharan migrants.

Joseph was on good terms with the caretaker and he tapped on his window for the key. Unlocking the heavy wooden door of the church he looked around to make sure he was alone. The interior was simply decorated, with white walls, a wooden ceiling and a Moorish chancel arch, over which ran a stucco frieze inscribed with the Lord's Prayer in Arabic. Joseph plugged his phone into a socket then sat in a pew and said a prayer for forgiveness.

At midday an elderly Englishwoman called Agnes arrived with a basket of flowers. She smiled at Joseph then disappeared into the vestry, coming out a short while later with vases and secateurs. Joseph watched her cutting and arranging the flowers. She was trying to make the modest number stretch to two vases. Joseph walked over and picked up the secateurs.

'*Je peux* . . .?'

Agnes nodded uncertainly. Joseph went out into the churchyard and cut sprigs of bougainvillea and hibiscus, along with a few fronds from a palm tree. It was hard work, and the palm fronds left him with cuts on his hands, but Agnes was delighted and Joseph's conscience about stealing the church's electricity was salved.

He reseated himself in the pew and turned his mind to the question of where to sleep that night. He had seen beggars and drug addicts lurking among the bushes in the Mendoubia Gardens, a short distance from the church, but he was worried that they might attack him. A hostel was beyond his means and the beach was patrolled by police.

'Will you lock up, dear?'

Agnes left with her empty flower basket. Joseph stared at the vases on either side of the chancel. Then he unplugged his phone and returned the key to the caretaker's cottage.

'It's not as bad as a black mark.'

The girls were in the canteen, Ayesha sitting forlornly over a cup of coffee from the vending machine while Salma did her best to reassure her.

'Once you graduate nobody will be any the wiser. But you have to be on your best behaviour from now on. You should have told me that your brother was in prison here in Kenitra!'

'How do you think Hakimi found out?'

'That's not important. What's important is that you are a sweet, obedient cadet who sticks by the rules.'

'What do you know about Hakimi?'

'I know he's the second-fastest runner in our class,' Salma chuckled. 'Why?'

'Because I've given him another reason to hate me. He might try to get revenge.'

'I doubt it. He's on a warning, just like you. Your destinies are linked until you graduate.'

'I can't believe how stupid I was.'

Salma nodded. 'Shame is an expensive business.'

'How do you mean?'

'He attacked you because he was ashamed that you beat him in the race. And you retaliated because you were ashamed of your brother. This country runs on shame.'

'Have you nothing you're ashamed of?'

Salma shrugged. 'I ate two chocolate bars on Sunday.'

Ayesha laughed. At that moment, Hakimi walked into the canteen with two of his friends.

'Remember,' hissed Salma, 'best behaviour!'

Tourists strolled through the Petit Socco, their noses in guidebooks, while schoolchildren in white tabards laughed and chatted on their way home for lunch. Karim stood outside the hotel wondering what to do with the rest of his day. The idea of returning to the port and having to deal with Larbi and the others was depressing. He decided to take a walk to clear his head. Perhaps he could find out more details of last night's murder.

He headed in what he thought was the direction of Chez Kebe but the alleys looked different by day and he had trouble retracing the route he had taken with Mokhtar. He was as bad as a tourist, lost in the medina! One alley, empty apart from cats basking in the sun, turned out to be a cul-de-sac. Recalling what Simo had said about the slope, he turned uphill towards the kasbah and, to his surprise, quickly found himself outside Chez Kebe.

The restaurant was tiny, no more than a handful of tables, most of which were occupied by sub-Saharan Africans. The only seat that Karim could find was on a table with three German backpackers. A smiling Senegalese woman brought him a dish of chicken marinated with mustard and lemon and Karim tucked in, enjoying the good-natured banter at the tables around him. The idea that any of these amiable individuals would own a gun, let alone use it to kill a man, seemed preposterous, and he wondered who else might have fired the shots in the Petit Socco.

The German backpackers spoke good English. They told him they had just come off the ferry from Spain and were heading to Chefchaouen. Mention of the ferry brought a spark of hope; perhaps Abdou had gone to investigate a lead in Tarifa. As Karim left, he asked the smiling waitress if she'd heard about the killing in the square and her mood changed abruptly.

'The police have already been to ask questions. I told them to look elsewhere. Why would one of these poor unfortunates' – she gave a sweep around the restaurant – 'risk everything by killing someone? They want to go to Europe, not some *degolas* Moroccan prison!'

Continuing uphill Karim came to a blue-and-white alley filled with brightly painted plant pots. It turned out to be another dead end but as he was turning back he noticed that one of the houses had a sign advertising a room to let. Out of curiosity, he knocked. The woman who answered was in her fifties, slim, with a grey caftan and headscarf. Her name was Khoury. With an apologetic smile she told Karim that she was a widow and rented the room to *naas maaqoulin*, sensible people. He asked to see it and she led the way across a tiled floor dotted with ficus and sanseveria. Karim enquired if the plants outside were hers and she nodded, adding that she looked after nineteen cats as well. The bedroom was plain, with a single bed and a window that gave on to a flower-filled courtyard.

'*Alf ryal*, fifty dirhams.'

Karim pointed to a door in the courtyard. 'Does that lead to the kasbah?'

'Yes. But it's quicker to return the way you came.'

Karim thanked the widow and filed the address away in his mind as a backstop. As he rejoined the main street he heard a familiar voice.

'Hey, mister!' Mokhtar sidled up to him. He was wearing a striped robe and a pillbox cap. 'Shall I walk with you?'

'No, I want to be alone,' snapped Karim.

Mokhtar kept up his cheerful patter. 'I asked about your friend but nobody has seen him!'

'What about the man who was killed? What do you know about him?'

'He was a people smuggler, like I told you.'

'You told me he was a drug dealer.'

'*Tsk*. Same difference.'

'Who killed him?'

'I don't know.'

'What's this street called?'

'Ah. That I do know. Jnane el-Captane. Did you like the room?'

Karim spun round. 'Were you spying on me?'

'No, mister. Calm down. Why are you getting so agitated?'

Karim chose not to answer. After a few minutes they came out in a large cobbled square where two boys were kicking a football. There was an old building that looked like a museum and Karim could hear strains of music drifting from a doorway. He would have liked to sit and call Noureddine, but Mokhtar was busy with a running commentary.

'Over there is Dar Zero! Odd address, don't you think? Over here is the old palace of Sultan Moulay Ismaïl! I can get you in free! Want to take a look?'

'No.'

Karim continued to an archway at the northern end of the square which had a view of the Strait.

'The sea!' Mokhtar declared triumphantly. 'Give me your phone and I'll take a picture of you.'

'No.'

Karim walked down some steep steps to the main boulevard, Mokhtar in tow. He was humming a tune and didn't seem in the least put out that Karim wasn't paying him attention. As they approached the entrance to the fishing port Karim noticed a guard checking cars.

'What's he looking for?' he said, addressing his comment to the air.

Mokhtar walked up to his side. '*Afaraqa.* They hide in the boots of cars then stow away on the fishing boats. Why do you want to go in there, mister? Your friend went to a lot of places but he didn't go there!'

Karim pressed on past the barrier. Mokhtar hung back for a few minutes, then started following again, quickening his step until he had caught up with Karim.

'Your friend ate dinner in Chez Hassan on Rue d'Italie, he had breakfast at the Manara Café, which is not the best café if you want my opinion, he prayed at the city mosque, same as you. Every morning he got into a car across the road, same as you. Are you a policeman as well?'

Karim stopped. 'How do you know he was a policeman?'

Mokhtar shrugged. 'I know things. Are you a policeman as well?'

'Maybe.'

Karim suspected that Mokhtar was holding back information and, sooner or later, with the help of a bank note or two, he would cough it up. They walked along a silent row of warehouses and cold stores, past two men in oilskins carrying a swordfish, then turned onto the bustling quayside. The fishing boats were in harbour, their bright blue and red hulls bobbing in the afternoon sunshine. On the quay, heaps of mackerel, skate, turbot and halibut were being bartered over by wholesalers and housewives while fishermen sat mending their nets, baiting hooks or simply smoking and chatting. Karim stopped to enjoy the scene. He liked fishing harbours. The raucous sounds and the smell of fish guts were a sharp contrast to the anonymity of Tanger-Med.

'Are you hungry, mister? I know a good place!'

Karim remembered his invitation for dinner at Simo's.

'Another time.'

'What about a nice mint tea?' Mokhtar said hopefully.

Before Karim could reply, a man who had been mending nets caught sight of Mokhtar and stormed over, his face twisted with rage.

'Son of a prostitute! Where's my money?'

He shouted abuse at Mokhtar, who cowered with his hands in front of his face. The fisherman kicked him on the shin then cuffed him on the head. Caught off-guard, Mokhtar fell spreadeagled on the slippery quayside. With a triumphant sneer, the other man wiped the sole of his shoe on Mokhtar's front, leaving a trail of slime on his *jellaba*. This was too much for Karim. He slammed the man against the wall.

'What do you think you're doing?'

'Don't interfere!'

The other man lunged at Karim but Karim parried the blow, holding the man's hand in a vice-like grip.

'Calm down, my brother, there's no need to get aggressive.'

He showed the man his police badge.

'Sûreté de Marrakech?' The man scoffed. 'This is Tangier, in case you hadn't noticed! You have no authority here!'

'Is that so? I'm on my way to see the police commissioner. Simo Layachi, he's a friend of mine. Do you want him to come down here and sort this matter out?'

'If you're a police officer what are you doing with this filth?' the man said, jabbing his chin at Mokhtar. 'Oh, of course – he's an *informant*.'

'Get lost! Or you'll spend the night in prison!'

The man stared at Karim, then spat on the ground and returned to his nets. Karim helped Mokhtar to his feet.

'Thanks, mister,' said Mokhtar, wiping himself down. 'That bastard says I owe him money. But he's the one who owes *me* money!' He limped away, looking over his shoulder and pouring forth a stream of insults, each more florid than the last.

'May God put him in a huge cauldron and burn him in the fires of hell! May God slice him open with a fish hook and make him pick up his entrails with his own hands!' Mokhtar continued in this vein until they arrived back in the Petit Socco.

ي

The only place Joseph knew that was safe and where he could get a cheap meal was Chez Kebe. The place was already busy at six-thirty in the evening. Kebe's smiling wife served him a delicious *poulet yassa*. Having eaten nothing apart from raw meat for two days Joseph fell on the food with gusto. All the talk in the restaurant was of the killing of the people smuggler in the Petit Socco. Some thought the police were behind it. Joseph described the eviction of the camp at Boukhalef and the others listened sympathetically. A man he knew, a Ghanaian, gave him the address of a squat near the bus station.

As he was crossing the Petit Socco on his way to the new town he heard a shout. Reluctantly, he walked up to a café table where Karim was treating Mokhtar to a mint tea. Mokhtar ran his eyes over Joseph. He spotted the Adidas bag and the tattoo on his arm.

'Don't talk to him, mister,' he hissed. 'People are watching!'

'Nonsense!' Karim pulled up a chair. 'Sit down, Joseph. Where have you been?'

Joseph remained standing. 'I've been . . . *à l'église.*'

'You mean the Catholic church – near the police station?'

Joseph shifted awkwardly. 'No, St Andrew's.'

'It's next to the Bou Abid market,' Mokhtar muttered.

'Do you go there often?'

'I – I go every Sunday at eleven o'clock. Sometimes I go at

other times.' He didn't like the look of the Moroccan man in the *jellaba*.

Karim pointed at the injury on Joseph's hand. 'You've cut yourself. Do you want me to get you a plaster?'

Joseph put his hand in his pocket. 'It's nothing.'

The waiter came up and murmured in Karim's ear. 'What are you doing? You'll scare away my customers!'

Karim turned around angrily. 'Leave the poor fellow alone! What harm has he done you? Yesterday you claimed you didn't see the gunman, even though he fired the gun right in front of your nose! Now you start attacking an innocent man. I suppose you think he was responsible? Bring a Coca-Cola!'

'Who for?'

'Him, of course!'

But when Karim turned back Joseph had disappeared.

The altercation in the square had spooked Joseph. Instead of continuing to the bus station he turned uphill to the kasbah, then worked his way through the back streets to Marshan. He liked Marshan. He liked the wisteria-covered villas, the parkland where youths sat playing games of *parchay* under fairy lights. He rested on a bench and called Jean-François. This time his friend answered. The news wasn't good. Marie-Louise's whereabouts were unknown. Jean-François and some of the others were hiding in the hills above Sidi Kancouch and hoped to reach Casiago tomorrow. He urged Joseph to join them but Joseph was reluctant.

'If I leave Tangier I can't earn money!'

'Those days are gone, my friend. Tangier is no longer safe.

Viens! There's a road block at Malabata but the police will be too busy checking cars to pay you any attention.'

Eventually Joseph agreed to set off at dawn. It was now ten at night. He stole across the park to Marshan cemetery. A few months earlier he had earned money in the cemetery by filling bottles with water from a standpipe and selling them to mourners who came to water the graves of their loved ones. He climbed a wall at the back and found a tomb to hide behind. After an hour it grew cold and he got up to stamp his feet, looking over the wall at the dark sea far below.

Propping his head on his Adidas bag he lay down again, hoping the rain would hold off until morning. It gave him the creeps to sleep among the dead but, for the time being, it was safer than sleeping among the living.

Casabarata was a mixed neighbourhood of low-rent apartments and modest villas. Simo's residence was one of the latter, a two-storey house half-hidden by palm trees. If it had been located in an exclusive suburb like Marshan or the Old Mountain the villa would have been worth millions. As it was, it looked like the home of a middle-ranking public servant who had done well for himself.

The *salon* was modern, open plan, with a grey rug and a polished European-style dining table. Karim gazed at the abstract paintings on the wall and decided that he didn't care for the indecipherable shapes. In one corner of the room were two divans in blue-and-yellow brocade, arranged around a low table. Simo's daughter, a diminutive twelve-year-old in a head-scarf and tracksuit, came in with a basket of oven-warm bread, smiled shyly at Karim and retreated. Apart from a brief *salaam*, Simo's wife stayed hidden in the kitchen.

Simo filled Karim's glass with lemonade. '*Kul*, eat.'

Karim ogled the feast in front of him: tagine of squid with tomato and *harissa*; tagine of sea bream with *chermoula* and preserved lemons; salads of aubergine, cauliflower and French beans, a plate of hand-cut chips and little bowls of green and black olives. He helped himself to some fish and told Simo about the killing in the Petit Socco.

'I heard he was a people smuggler.'

Simo gave a snort.

'You don't think so?' asked Karim.

'On the contrary. We know he was a people smuggler.'

Karim noticed that Simo didn't seem as good-humoured as usual; he was tetchy, on edge.

'Smuggling is what that this city does best. Eighty years ago it was currency. After that, guns. Then came hashish. Now it's people.'

And fake drugs, Karim reflected, but he kept the thought to himself.

'Right now, the city is at the centre of a war between rival gangs.'

'The gangs are killing each other?'

'Yes.'

'So the man in the Petit Socco was killed by a rival?'

'Almost certainly.'

Karim thought of the bullet holes in the man's jacket. 'Do you think Abdou got mixed up in this?'

'No. Abdou disappeared at the port.'

'How can you be sure?'

'I know what goes on in this city.'

'Yet you don't know what happened to Abdou!'

Simo stopped eating. 'You are a guest in my house, Karim. Please do not insult me. I am taking Abdou's disappearance very seriously and soon we will establish exactly what happened.'

Karim let the matter drop and conversation turned to Operation MEDIHA.

'It started with an investigation into the sale of fake designer goods. No one else wanted the case until I picked it up.'

'Did it originate from the Interior Ministry?'

'No. The Europeans provided funds.'

'If the Europeans ask us to do something, we leap into action,' Simo said tartly.

'I suppose they were concerned about all the pirated goods in the Maghreb. One month into the investigation Abdou and I realised there was a much more serious trade going on in pharmaceuticals. Many are made by European companies like Sanofi or Hoffmann-La Roche so of course the Europeans wanted us to take action.'

'Like I said: if the Europeans ask us to do something, we jump.'

'You make it sound like we're their servants.'

'We may not be their servants but they're sure as hell our paymasters. We make their clothes, we operate their call centres, we grow their fruit and vegetables, we provide their holidays . . .'

'But Simo – we reap the benefits! Take fake drugs, for example. Our citizens benefit from having drugs that are properly licensed – medicines that do what they're supposed to do. Don't you agree? A year ago I had to visit two mothers in Amizmiz who had given their babies antibiotics for whooping cough. Do you know what was in the tablets? Strychnine! The babies died.'

'You're right, it's a bad business. Did you make any arrests?'

'Yes. The importer is now serving a ten-year jail term.'

'Tell me – what was Abdou like as a detective?'

'First-class. He always knew if a customs officer or pharmacist was corrupt. He could take one glance at a packet of Avastin and tell if it was fake from the typeface, the glue or some other detail that I didn't even notice.'

'Did he ever take bribes?'

The question caught Karim by surprise. 'Of course not!'

'Forgive me for asking,' said Simo. 'But we have to keep all lines of enquiry open. One possibility is that Abdou colluded with the traffickers.'

Karim was incandescent. 'You should consider the much more likely possibility that he has been silenced! Eliminated by the very criminals you're supposed to be hunting!'

'And your evidence for this is – what? I understand your frustration. Perhaps you feel a little guilty, too, for sending a junior officer to handle such an important assignment. But at the moment we have no corpse, no suspect, no motive. Abdou found nothing and made no arrests. We've interviewed all the people who were in the terminal around the time of his disappearance. It could be weeks or even months before we find him. Have some more tagine – my wife will be disappointed if we don't finish it.'

'He could still be in the terminal,' Karim said through clenched teeth.

'Karim – as we have explained to you, there are seventy thousand containers in the terminal and they come and go twenty-four hours a day.'

'If one of your men disappeared while he was on assignment in Marrakech my colleagues would move heaven and earth to find him. What about that factory in the Free Zone? The one whose containers Abdou intercepted? Have you carried out a search?'

'I can assure you that they make nothing but clothes.'

'They may be a front for the cartel.'

'*Cartel?*' Simo laughed. 'You've been watching too many American thrillers! Life isn't that exciting here in Tangier. We have a few problems with migrants and people smugglers, but we're more concerned about our pensions. As I keep saying, we'll probably find that Abdou's disappearance is very ordinary, nothing glamorous at all.'

Simo clapped his hands and his daughter returned, clearing the table and setting down a bowl of fruit. Karim was still simmering with anger.

'Everyone I talk to in this city acts like they have something to hide.'

'That's because we don't like outsiders,' Simo laughed. 'Everyone says the Fassis are arrogant sons of bitches but we Tanjaouis are ten times worse. We sit up here with our feet in the Mediterranean and our noses in the air. You know what we call other Maghrebis? *Nass dyel dakhel.* People of the interior. Idiots, in other words. Have a strawberry – they're delicious.'

Karim heard high-pitched yelling and two seven-year old boys came charging into the *salon* with plastic lightsabers. They took one look at Karim then chased each other around the room. Simo grabbed a youngster and wrestled him onto his lap.

'Children!' Simo laughed. 'They're a *baraka*, a blessing, are they not?'

It was after eleven o'clock when Karim left Simo's house. It was a clear night, with a sliver of moon. He was tired after the events of the day but something – a nagging guilt, a sense that he'd wasted the afternoon and that time was running out to find Abdou alive – made him drive back to the Free Zone. He flashed his police badge at the entrance gate.

The place seemed busier by night. The avenues and lawns were bathed in an eerie glow and almost every factory and warehouse showed signs of activity. The Free Zone, it seemed, was as heedless of the normal working day as Tanger-Med.

When he arrived at Best Century Clothing, Karim crept along the side of the building. Light shone from a row of high windows, underneath which were the metal casings of air-conditioning units. Karim felt the smooth, slatted steel wall. There were no bumps or crevices where he could get a hand or foothold. He saw two wooden pallets near a side door and carried them, one under each arm, to an area of wall directly below a window. He leaned the first pallet at a thirty-degree angle, then propped the second on top so that it was flush with the building. Putting his toes between the struts he climbed up until his feet were on the top of the upper pallet and his head was level with the air-conditioning units. With one hand on the AC unit for support he peered over the windowsill. Inside, everything looked similar to morning except that, instead of Moroccan women, the workers all seemed to be black-skinned men. What were they doing? Karim stood on tiptoe to get a better view. Suddenly the pallet disappeared from under him. He was dangling with his hands on the bracket of the AC unit. At first he thought the pallets had collapsed, then a torch beam lit up his head.

'I'm a police officer,' Karim gasped. 'Help me down!'

'A police officer? That's a good joke!'

A security guard was staring up at him, a torch in one hand and the lead of a vicious-looking Alsatian in the other.

'As God is my witness!'

The guard stood back on the grass. 'I think I'll just wait until you fall.'

Karim's arms were beginning to tire. It was twenty feet to the ground and he could easily break an ankle. Using every ounce of strength he pulled himself up then grabbed the top of the metal box. He hoisted himself onto the unit and crouched for a moment, hoping that the bracket would support his weight. Then he looked at the roof. Disheartened to find that the gentle slope was as smooth as the wall below him, he spotted a metal stud, no bigger than his thumb, halfway to the ridge. Kicking off from the AC unit, he managed to get his right foot onto the roof. Thank God he was wearing trainers!

From below he heard the sound of a walkie-talkie and a menacing snarl from the Alsatian. Holding onto the stud with the fingertips of his left hand he slowly manoeuvred up the incline. It took him several minutes and his clothes were smeared with filth but he managed to reach the ridge. He straddled it with one foot on either side and stood up unsteadily, then walked towards the rear of the building, the torchlight trained on him like a performer on a high wire, the guard keeping pace with his progress.

At the gable end he halted, teetering above the loading bay. Several factory workers had joined the security guard, whom he could now see clearly, staring up at him with a mixture of curiosity and hatred. There was something about the guard . . . At that moment a truck slid out from below. Karim caught a brief glimpse of an *X* spray-painted on the trailer and, without pausing to think, he leaped towards it. He landed with a thud and toppled over, only just managing to stop himself from falling off the side. The lorry gathered speed as it turned into the central avenue with the unleashed Alsatian charging after it at full pelt. Crouching on his hands and knees, Karim could see the entry gate looming. He climbed down the locking rods on the back of the container, nervously eyeing the slavering beast closing in on him. As the truck slowed to go through the barrier Karim jumped onto the road, rolling as he fell. He picked himself up, raced to the car, fumbled with the keys, got in and drove off as the dog slammed against the door.

On the drive back into Tangier, drenched with sweat and laughing hysterically, he remembered why the guard looked familiar: he was wearing the same blue uniform as the security men at Tanger-Med.

Chapter 5

Karim woke with a sore throat and dry blood on his hands. As he stepped out of his bedroom for a shower it occurred to him that he hadn't seen the maid, Fatiha, for two days. Nor did there seem to be any other guests staying at the hotel: the place was empty, silent.

A short stroll down Rue de la Marine took him to the mosque where he had prayed the day before. He removed his shoes and washed his feet in the fountain.

Glory to Thee, O Allah, and Thine is the praise, and blessed is Thy name, and exalted is Thy majesty, and there is none to be served besides Thee.

When he emerged half an hour later he decided that he needed a different perspective. He started by having breakfast in the Tingis. The café was smaller than the Central but it occupied a better position, looking down the slope of the Petit Socco. The breakfast was tastier as well: wheat-and-semolina pancakes with honey, a saucer of green and black olives, freshly squeezed orange juice and the best café *nuss-nuss* he'd had since arriving in the city. Mokhtar was nowhere to be seen.

He decided he'd better check in with Noureddine. His superior answered on the first ring.

'*Salaam ou-alikum*. From the fact that you haven't called until now I assume that you haven't found Abdou.'

'God alone knows where the poor fellow is. Everyone thinks he is trapped in a container.'

'And you? *Ash baan lik?*'

'For Abdou to be inside a container the door would have to have been shut and locked by someone else.'

Karim told Noureddine everything, from his experiences at the port to the search of his hotel room and the inexplicable presence of migrants at the clothing factory.

'With each day that passes the more I am convinced that Abdou was eliminated, probably by an organised crime group. It pains me to say it, but that's my guess.'

'What does the CCTV footage show?'

'Abdou was in the storage yard of Terminal 1 on the day he vanished. But there's a blind spot in the yard so we have no record of the moment of Abdou's disappearance.'

'What was he doing in the yard?'

'Checking containers.'

'What was he carrying?'

'A torch.'

'Was it switched on?'

'No.'

'Had night fallen?'

'No.'

'So how do you know it was a torch?'

'He was examining containers!'

'How do you know he was examining containers?'

Karim bristled. 'Because he was in the middle of the container stack, far from the quayside! What else would he be doing?'

Noureddine replied in his usual, measured fashion.

'Before Abdou left for Tangier he asked my advice on what to take. I suggested he take a small telescope – a *monocular*. In my opinion, a monocular is better than binoculars because you can see just as far while keeping one eye on what's going on around you. And since a monocular is designed to be held in one hand it allows you to keep the other hand free – for your gun, for example. On CCTV footage a monocular might look like a torch. Check the footage again.'

From the stairs of the lecture block the cadets were observing a search-and-arrest procedure. The instructor led four men in black uniforms and balaclavas to a hide-out – in reality, one of the lecture rooms. Ayesha and Salma were on the stairs peering over the heads of their male colleagues.

The instructor pointed at the door and one of the commandos used a two-handed ram to pretend to batter the door down. With a sweep of his arm the instructor ordered his men inside.

'Remember to use hand signals,' the instructor told his students. 'Restrain the suspect or suspects. Minimise harm and loss of life. Above all, make sure that your team does not disturb any evidence.'

While the other cadets listened attentively, Ayesha was pondering Salma's words in the canteen the day before. Why was she so ashamed of the fact that her brother was in prison? He had been locked up on the flimsiest of pretexts, according to what Karim had told her. Apart from membership of an

Islamist association Abderrahim had done nothing wrong.
And if he had done nothing wrong shouldn't she support him,
find a lawyer, at the very least pay him a visit?

At the back of Ayesha's mind was the fear that her brother
would turn out to be like her father, a religious maniac who
ruled his family with fear. He made his eldest daughter, Amina
– Ayesha's sister – cover her hair at all times and refused to let
her leave the house at night. All this Ayesha had pieced
together since Amina's death. But what if Abderrahim, like
Amina, had suffered at the hands of their father? Shouldn't she
show him some compassion?

By now the commandos had brought out the 'suspect' and
were pinning him to the floor.

'Pay attention,' Salma murmured out of the corner of her
mouth. 'I don't want you getting expelled.'

'It wouldn't be so bad,' whispered Ayesha. 'If I wasn't around
you could study all night.' They both giggled.

'Hey! You two!' The instructor was staring at them. 'What
was the last thing I said?'

'Restrain the suspect,' Salma answered immediately. 'Search
the premises without disturbing any evidence – *sir*!'

'You – Talal!'

'Yes, sir?'

Ayesha felt a plunge in the pit of her stomach. Fortunately
this instructor was kindlier than Colonel Choukri.

'Please pay attention. Next time you could be the officer
leading the raid.'

'Yes, sir!'

'I've decided to help you, mister.'

Mokhtar arrived when Karim was on his second *nuss-nuss*. He arranged his robe on the chair opposite and opened a leather pouch. Karim waited impatiently while he filled his pipe with pinches of kif.

'Someone *did* search your friend's room.'

'Who?'

'God alone knows.'

'*Who?*' Karim repeated angrily.

'Two men. Wearing jeans and blousons.'

'Off-duty cops?'

Mokhtar shrugged. '*Momken.* Maybe.'

'Did they take anything?'

Mokhtar lit his pipe with a match and exhaled a cloud of smoke. 'Ah. That is the question.'

With a sigh, Karim put a purple twenty-dirham note on the table. Mokhtar carefully folded the note and placed it in his pouch.

'They took a notebook.'

'How do you know?'

'I was sitting at the desk with my friend. I heard one of the men say to the other, *ateelih al-ktiyyeb*, give the notebook to him.'

'Give it to whom? The chief of police?'

'Not the chief of police.'

Mokhtar drew on his pipe and grinned. With a sigh, Karim placed another twenty-dirham note on the table.

'A purple note!' Mokhtar let out a vaporous cloud of smoke. 'I like the green ones better. And the brown ones best of all.'

'Is that so?' Karim opened his wallet and took out a two-hundred-dirham note, more than he earned in a day, and held it between two hands. 'How about a *blue* note?'

Mokhtar's eyes widened but Karim snatched the note away.

'You get it when you find my friend.'

Reluctantly, Mokhtar picked the twenty-dirham note off the table. 'Mohammed Mansouri.'

'Who?'

Mokhtar started coughing. 'Can you buy me a mint tea, mister, *ma shiba*? With wormwood?'

Seeing this as another delaying tactic, Karim grabbed Mokhtar's wrist. 'Who is Mohammed Mansouri?'

Mokhtar coughed some more. 'May God spare you, please, *a Si Karim, shwiya atay*, some tea for old Mokhtar?'

Exasperated, Karim hailed the waiter and gave the order.

Mokhtar settled happily back in his seat, lit his pipe and inhaled until the kif was red hot. 'He runs a security company. Out on the Tetouan road.'

The premises of EDS Security were on Route de L'Abattoir, near the N2 highway leading out of Tangier. The area was a ragbag of vacant lots, sleazy cafés and car repair workshops. As Karim turned into the depot, the rolling doors and forecourt reminded him of a fire station. Several vans and lorries carried the EDS logo. In a prefabricated office he found a woman stapling receipts and he asked to see the director.

'Do you mean the manager? Or the boss of the company?'

'The boss.'

The woman directed him to an anonymous building two blocks away. Karim took the lift to the seventh floor and found himself on a gloomy landing. Like many Moroccan offices the headquarters of EDS Security were in a converted apartment.

'I'm here to see Mohammed Mansouri,' he told the woman in the headscarf who answered the door.

Without a word she led him down a corridor. Karim noticed a *salon* to the left, the divans covered with piles of paperwork. On the right he caught a glimpse of a room with a fax machine, then a windowless kitchen with pink wall tiles. The last room was dark, the window shuttered, and at first Karim couldn't see the shaved head and bull-like neck behind the desk.

The room was plain: a few rugs, a filing cabinet and a wall-mounted display with muskets and rifles. The two men exchanged the usual pleasantries.

'Simo told me about you,' Mansouri said guardedly.

As he took Karim's hand in a vice-like grip, the detective decided that Mohammed Mansouri could have been a night-club bouncer in a different life. He was powerfully built, with a barrel-shaped chest and tattoos on the back of his hand. Tattoos on a Moroccan man were rare, regarded by strict Muslims as a desecration of God's handiwork. Mansouri caught Karim's stare.

'They're Berber symbols. See here – the ear of wheat, that stands for life and death. This one is an axe, representing anger and destruction. And the concentric diamonds are to ward off evil spirits.'

'You are Berber?'

'I was born in a remote region of the Rif mountains sixty-three summers ago. You are Berber as well?'

'Yes. My father came from Talatast, in the High Atlas.'

Mansouri switched to dialect but Karim interrupted him.

'I don't speak Amazigh dialect. I was raised in Marrakech.'

'I see,' said Mansouri, clicking his teeth. 'So you have spent your whole life in Marrakech?' He made it sound like something to be ashamed of.

'Yes. Apart from eighteen months at police college.'

'My mother gave birth in the morning and went back to the fields in the afternoon. Soon afterwards she and my father died and I moved in with my grandfather. The first thing he did was take me out of school and teach me how to shoot.'

'I'm not here to discuss education, or the lack of it, Mr Mansouri. You are the owner of EDS Security?'

'Are you good with a gun?'

'What?'

'I asked if you could shoot. They must have taught you how to shoot in college?'

'I was the best marksman in my year.'

'The best marksmen come from the Rif.'

Karim pointedly got out his notebook. Unlike Abdou, he rarely took notes but he found that interviewees paid more attention when he did.

'Can we get back to EDS? How long has the company been in existence?'

'Do you like rifles?' Mansouri opened the cabinet and took out a musket. 'Here, take it.'

The musket was almost six feet in length, the barrel decorated with panels of chased silver and the stock inlaid with silver and coral.

'Most people think these old muskets are just good for *fantasias*,' said Mansouri. 'But for twenty years this gun ruled Ketama. Chieftains quaked before it.'

Despite wishing to get the interview under way, Karim was fascinated by firearms and he didn't need much persuading to examine the gun. He noted the number *1279 AH* engraved beneath the cock, corresponding to the year 1862.

'Take a look at this one,' said Mansouri, selecting another rifle. 'A Chassepot, made in France around 1874.' Karim exchanged the musket for the Chassepot and looked through the sight. 'It's a bolt-action breechloading rifle,' continued Mansouri. 'Accurate to a thousand feet. I bought it from a man who said it belonged to the great warlord Abd el-Krim himself, who used the gun to defeat the Spanish at the Battle of Annual.'

Karim replaced the gun in the case. 'Do you wish firearms were still legal in Morocco?'

'It would make my job easier.'

'Tell me about your job. Do you only work for the Tanger-Med Port Authority?'

Mansouri sat down with the musket across his lap. 'No. I supply security for companies in Tangier, Tetouan and Al-Hoceima.'

'You've done well to get the contract for Tanger-Med.'

Mansouri regarded him carefully. 'I'm good at what I do.'

'I spoke to your security director – Mr El Hajjem. That's a Riffian name, isn't it?'

'Riffians follow orders.' Mansouri cracked his knuckles, as if to emphasise the point.

'What duties do EDS carry out for the Port Authority?'

'We guard every wharf, building, entrance and sector. At the ferry port, for example, we check for drugs, explosives and firearms.'

'Do you open containers?'

'All the time.'

'Have you found many counterfeit pharmaceuticals?'

'Not recently. The traffic has switched elsewhere.'

'Why do you think that is?'

Mansouri shrugged. 'Tanger-Med has the best scanners and the best security.'

'Do you check for stowaways?'

'*Maalum*, of course.'

'Single men or groups of people?'

'Both. We've found them curled around engines or hiding in the wheel arches of lorries. Last week, we caught two men who crawled along a culvert to get into the terminal.'

'Apart from opening containers, what else do you do in the terminal?'

'We check documents, stop pilfering, keep an eye out for terrorists . . .' Mansouri gave an impatient sigh. 'Let's cut to the chase. You're here about your missing colleague. Do you want my opinion? He shouldn't have been prowling around on his own. He only has himself to blame if he fell or hurt himself.'

Karim put his notebook down. 'Let me tell you something, Mr Mansouri. My colleague and I have been investigating ports for the last two years. And in every case we have found collusion between traffickers and port officials. So the reason my colleague was *prowling around on his own*, as you put it, is that we have learned not to trust anyone who works in the port area – including the police and customs.'

'The police, the customs . . . they're idiots. That's why we were brought in. We're professionals.'

'Is it professional to conduct a search of a policeman's bedroom?' Mansouri's eyes flickered, but he said nothing. 'You ordered a search of my colleague's room at the Hotel Fuentes.'

'We were looking for clues – something that might explain his disappearance. We didn't find anything.'

'But you took his notebook.'

'Notebook?'

'You took my colleague's notebook.'

'No, we took a book of sudoku. There was nothing in it. I threw it away.'

'That's convenient,' Karim said drily.

Mansouri cocked the gun, still lying across his knees.

'We're only contracted to guard the port. We're not responsible for looking after visitors. Your colleague could be in the Bering Strait for all I know.' He let the cock fall on the nipple with a *click*, then replaced the musket in the display case.

'Go back to Marrakech. Let us handle things. If your colleague hasn't turned up by now he won't ever be found. He's *amtt*.' Mansouri snapped the case shut. 'That means "dead" in Amazigh dialect.'

It took Joseph twelve hours to reach Casiago. He walked the coast road, hiding whenever he saw an official-looking vehicle. His trainers were shoddy and his feet were soon covered in blisters. In addition, he was struggling with the Adidas bag: thirty umbrellas made it very heavy to carry. When he reached the electricity pylons he decided to jettison the whole lot. He laid them in a neat line on the side of the road, as he would have done at Tannery House Gate, as a free gift for passing motorists. Maybe a passing goatherd would take one. Half a mile on, he stopped. What was he thinking of? The umbrellas were his livelihood! He ran back, stuffed the umbrellas back in his bag and carried on walking.

It was a cloudless sky, the air filled with wild oregano and the sweet smell of mimosa. Once or twice he saw black-faced figures on the hillside. He gave a comradely wave but didn't stop to talk. What was the point? If they had a plan for getting across they wouldn't tell a stranger like him. His thoughts turned to Marie-Louise and he hoped that she was somewhere safe. Sleeping in the wild was no life for a single mother with small children, far from shops, doctors and running water.

At noon he bought a tin of tuna and a flatbread and sat on the beach at Ksar es-Sghir. Coming from a landlocked country he hadn't seen the sea until he arrived in Tangier. The first thing he did after his year-long journey was take a selfie on Tangier beach and send it to his sister Gloria. Even now he could stare at the waves for hours.

On the other side he saw cars driving over the hills and along the shore. *Andalusia!* Even the word sounded magical. The people inside the cars were the luckiest people in the world and they didn't even know it. They could go anywhere, do anything.

All he had on his side was hope. Louis, one of his friends from the camp, told him about a time he tried to cross the Strait. He set out with a dozen others on a misty night without a moon. They reached an uninhabited island off the Moroccan coast and, thinking they'd arrived in Spain, they jumped in the water, eventually swimming back to where they started. Joseph couldn't swim. When God was gracious enough to guide him across he decided that he would only step in the water when he could see the bottom. He would prod it with an umbrella!

On his right he observed a row of cranes and a ferry boat setting out cross the blue expanse. That must be Tanger-Med. He had heard about the port, which had many more boats than the port of Tangier. Some migrants he knew had tried to stow away on the ferry boats but they had all been found by sniffer dogs. As he drew near to the port he saw police cars and high fences with security cameras. To avoid them he turned off the highway into the mountains. According to Jean-François, Tanger-Med was three hours' walk from the camp. With luck he would get there before nightfall.

Mokhtar was probably the least reliable informant in the world. His brain was addled by kif, for one thing. And his loyalty was questionable. According to Noureddine, who was strongly against their use, informants were desperate people who would say anything for money. Could Mokhtar have been mistaken about the book that the room-searchers took? In Mokhtar's words, one of the men said 'give him the notebook'. It was a fact that Abdou used a notebook – one which would contain evidence that might point to his abductors and put them behind bars. But *ktiyyeb* could mean 'little book' as well as 'notebook'. A sudoku book, which Abdou was also in the habit of using, could legitimately be described as a little book. So Mokhtar might be wrong and Mansouri might be right when he claimed that the men found a book of sudoku puzzles. But why would the men be so keen to give Mansouri the book . . . unless they had been told to search for Abdou's notebook? Perhaps they took the book as proof that they had searched the room thoroughly.

Karim called Simo from the medina carpark and asked if he had authorised the search.

'Yes.'

'Why didn't you send police officers?'

'I didn't have any to spare. We were busy with demonstrations and a hundred other things!'

'Mansouri's men could have disturbed evidence. They're not trained to do a search.'

Simo harrumphed. 'They search buildings all the time. Besides, I wanted to eliminate that possibility that Abdou was in his room. Time was pressing. Abdou might have had a heart attack, for all I knew.'

'You could have found that out with a phone call!'

'You've seen how the hotel is run. I'd prefer to have a security man check the room than some clerk and his kif-addicted friend.'

'How do you know the clerk has a kif-addicted friend?'

After the briefest hesitation Simo replied.

'Abdou told me. Why do you think I tried to persuade him – and you, for that matter – to come and stay at my house?

Anyway, the only thing that the EDS men found in Abdou's room was a sudoku puzzle book.'

'You never mentioned the search to me.'

'Apologies, my brother. I didn't think it was important. We've done everything we can. So have you. You've interviewed everybody you need to. You should return to Marrakech and await news.'

'No. I'm going back to the port.'

'I wouldn't do that.'

'Why not?'

'What's the point? You've interviewed Larbi, Ben Jelloun, el Hajjem and Berrada . . . you've seen the footage at the prefecture. All the containers have gone, bar a handful. When every container has arrived at its destination and been accounted for, perhaps then we will be able to establish what happened to Abdou.'

'I want to go back to the port.'

'No!' Simo said with a vehemence that took Karim by surprise. 'Forgive me, Karim, I didn't mean to lose my temper. Look – I have a suggestion. You said that the clothing factory may be a front of some sort.'

'Yes.'

'Let me see if I can get authorisation for a night raid. We'll search the place from top to bottom. If we find so much as a packet of Valium I'll arrest the lot of them. OK?'

'*Wakha*, OK.'

Feeling considerably better, Karim got out of his car and walked up through Bab Dar Dbagh to look for Joseph.

'He's not there, my brother! He hasn't been there for days!' The storekeeper beckoned Karim over. 'Do you need another umbrella?'

'No, I haven't paid him for this one!'

'Maybe he's gone to Spain. Or he's been rounded up and put on a bus to the Algerian border. I wouldn't mind going there myself. They have more sunshine than we do in this godforsaken city.'

Karim cracked a boiled egg on the counter and sprinkled it with salt. 'As a Tanjaoui I would have thought you'd be used to the rain.'

'I'm not a Tanjaoui. I'm from the Souss. My name's Samir, pleased to meet you.'

'I'm Karim,' he said, munching. 'The pleasure's all mine.'

'My father owned a farm near Taroudant. Almonds, barley and a little maize. But there was a drought and my father fell into debt. We came to Tangier when I was twelve.'

As Samir chatted he took butter from the fridge, weighed out small amounts of flour and issued phonecards with breezy efficiency. He bantered with his customers, often carrying on several conversations at once. Karim couldn't help comparing him with Ayesha's father, Omar, who had also run a *hanout*.

Omar Talal dispensed his goods in stony silence. He had never given credit, refused to stock sanitary towels and shooed away children who came in with a few ryals for a sweet. He closed his *hanout* four times a day to go to the mosque instead of performing his prayers in the back like other shopkeepers. Despite this, his shop would have prospered in the busy neighbourhood of Sidi bel Abbès were it not for one unfortunate fact. Omar Talal couldn't read or write. Customers would point to non-existent offers on the sides of packets and cheat him out of money, which made him even more bad-tempered and resentful.

Karim paid Samir and said farewell. He wandered past Port Gate, along walls cascading with nasturtiums or draped with long skeins of silk for weaving. He halted at the door to a communal bakery and peered into the dark interior filled with the fragrance of fresh bread and wood smoke. Maintaining an uphill direction, he crossed a tiny courtyard where boys were spinning tops and climbed a flight of blue-and-white steps until he emerged, hot and sweaty, at Bab Kasbah.

Keen to explore further, he pressed on to Marshan. Coming out in the green parkland, he noticed an area of patchy earth and rock that looked over the Strait. He walked towards the edge and sat on the edge of a hollowed-out slab filled with rainwater and crisp packets. Above him a jet was emitting a white contrail. Down below, container ships made furrows in the sea.

He hailed two girls in headscarves sitting nearby. 'What's the name of this place?'

'The Phoenician Tombs,' said one. She was pretty, with an olive complexion and dark eyes fringed with kohl. '*Qdeem bezzaf*, very old,' she laughed.

The two girls kept stealing looks at Karim and whispering to one another. They hoped the handsome, green-eyed stranger was going to crack a joke or make a flirtatious remark, but Karim's thoughts were elsewhere.

He was remembering a sunny afternoon on the roof of the riad. Ayesha had finished hanging out the washing and the two of them were enjoying a favourite pastime – lying on the old mattress and spotting airplanes as they flew overhead.

All of a sudden, Ayesha jumped up. '*Shoofnee*. Watch me.'

She ran towards the end of the roof and leapt off. The last

thing he saw was her long dark hair disappearing over the side. Horrified, he dashed to the edge and stared down into the abyss.

'Coo-ee!' Ayesha was grinning at him from a roof on the other side of the alleyway. To his horror, she was preparing to make another jump. She took a few steps back and sprinted towards the edge, flying over the parapet in one gigantic, heart-stopping leap and landed on the neighbour's roof, fifteen feet below the Belkacems'. Picking herself up, she ran to the stairwell and vanished. Two minutes later she reappeared next to him. She flopped down on the mattress and pointed at a plane in the sky.

'EasyJet Airbus A320!'

Karim was coming out of evening prayers when he felt his phone vibrate.

'It's done,' said Simo. 'I've persuaded a judge to give us a search warrant. I'll pick you up at eleven.'

Buoyed by the news, Karim had a shower in the hotel and treated himself to grilled chicken and chips in the square. When Mokhtar sidled up to his table, Karim pushed him away, telling him that his information was muddled and that he wouldn't earn another dirham unless he came up with something useful.

At 11.30, a van of five commandos headed to the Free Zone, followed by Karim and Simo.

'It's nice to see proper police on a raid,' said Karim, putting on a red *Police* armband. 'I was beginning to think that

Mansouri's men did everything.' The remark sounded more disparaging than Karim intended.

'I have three hundred and eighty disciplined and highly trained police officers under my command, lieutenant. What I haven't had – until now – is lone officers prowling around like vigilantes.'

'You heard about my escapade last night.'

'As I told you, I know everything that goes on in this city. You're lucky you didn't break a leg!' Simo turned to him. 'Karim, somewhere along the way we've lost our chain of trust. I consider you my friend. I'm as keen as you are to solve this mystery. You simply have to keep me informed of your movements. Let's start again. What are we looking for?'

Karim relented. 'I saw Africans – sub-Saharans – working on the production line in the factory. It's possible that the drugs are coming through Tanger-Med, hidden in clothing, then are being packaged by *Afaraqa* too terrified to speak up. Abdou and I have come across that scenario before – Chinese cartels using African labour.'

'So how do you explain the fact that Abdou opened one of the containers from the *Pacific Star* and didn't find anything?'

'Perhaps it was a decoy container. We've seen that before as well.'

Simo frowned. 'It wasn't easy getting a warrant. Let's hope that we're not wasting our time.'

They arrived shortly after midnight and parked a short distance away. Two commandos crept around to the back of the building while the rest of the group waited by the entrance. After a few minutes, a Moroccan night manager opened up. His unflustered response to gun-wielding commandos hammering on the doors immediately made Karim suspect a tip-off.

After a cursory glance at Simo's search warrant the manager took the men into the factory, which was brightly lit and smelling of sweat. Forty or fifty sub-Saharans in casual clothes were ranged around the conveyor belts, some of the men standing, others sitting at sewing machines, while a Chinese overseer moved among them. But instead of pills and blister packs, the men were working on clothing accessories. Karim strode over to a 'Louis Vuitton' bag and held it upside down to see if anything fell out.

'Explain what it is that you're doing here,' Simo said to the manager.

'We are finishing bags and garments, inspector.'

'I can see that. Why have you got illegal immigrants working for you?'

Karim watched the manager closely. He was a middle-aged man with glasses and a moustache which lifted as he smiled.

'As you know, inspector, one of the biggest problems in Tangier is the presence of sub-Saharan migrants. We help them in return for a few hours of shift work. It's what you might call a humanitarian gesture.'

'It sounds like slave labour to me!' cried Karim.

The manager peered at Karim through his spectacles. 'Would you rather they beg on the streets, lieutenant? No one else will help these poor unfortunates.' He tapped a young man on the arm. 'Show them your back, André.'

The man lifted his shirt, revealing ugly looking welts and scars.

'Who did this to you?' Simo asked.

'*Les passeurs.* Traffickers.'

Karim thought that a more likely explanation was that the man had been beaten by the police.

Simo asked the manager a question. 'Are you aware that it is against the law to employ illegal migrants?'

The manager beamed. 'Ah, but we are not employing them, inspector. You see, we don't pay them money. Instead, we give them a hot meal and free clothing, along with food parcels when they leave in the morning. We are a company that operates according to strict sharia principles.'

After a few minutes, the two commandos returned and made a sign to the captain that they had found nothing suspicious on the premises. Karim grew impatient.

'You received a container from the *Pacific Star* on the second or third of March. Is that correct?'

'I believe so,' replied the night manager.

'What was in the container?'

'Approximately four tons of clothes! Let me explain. We receive unmarked clothing from our parent company in China – sports clothes, caps, polo shirts, shoes, handbags and accessories. We add the finishing touches.'

'I know that, by God!'

'If you please, I will explain for the inspector here. We use local women to sew on the logos. We employ forty women – more than any other company in the Free Zone, I'm proud to say! However, our women have families and they're not keen to work at night. So we have turned to migrants. They are resourceful people who are used to mending clothes.' He ran his eye over Simo's chest. 'Are you a *large*, commissioner?' He handed Simo a Lacoste shirt. 'Please take it, with our compliments.'

'Thank you,' Simo chuckled. 'But I already have one!'

Karim was brimming with rage. 'Are there other rooms in this building?'

'Over there is the packing and storage area, with lavatories and changing rooms down the corridor and, through the doors, a canteen. Up on the mezzanine we have a small suite of offices. Please, see for yourself.'

While Simo continued questioning, Karim went off to explore. In the changing rooms the locker doors were open and he found nothing apart from aprons and overclothes. The lavatories were spotless – and empty. He flicked a light in the next room: the store room. It was lined with neatly labelled cupboards and drawers whose contents were all samples or finished merchandise. It was the same with the store racks in the factory. Finally, Karim marched into the canteen, surprising two Chinese men behind the serving counter who were filling boxes with food. Karim looked in every oven, sink and drawer but the only pills he found were in a first-aid kit on the wall. He ran up the stairs and checked the offices. When he emerged on the walkway Simo and the manager were down below, sharing a joke. On his way over to them Karim questioned a young African at a sewing machine.

'*Tu es content?*'

'*Oui, monsieur, je suis très content.*'

'*Depuis combien de temps tu es là?*'

'*Trois nuits, monsieur.*'

There was something not right about this, Karim thought, as they walked through to the loading bay. He was desperate to find something, some slip or oversight, to justify the raid and propel the investigation in a new direction. A lorry was parked in the same spot as before, its doors open, half-filled with boxes. Above was the gable where he stood twenty-four hours ago. He cast his eyes over the loading platform, littered with plastic packing strips and torn clothes wrappers, then examined the markings on the container doors.

'*Gouliya*, tell me: do you use the same container that comes from China to send the clothes on to Spain?'

The manager faltered. 'Er, I believe so.'

'So it goes back out via Tanger-Med?'

'Correct.'

Karim had one last question. 'Do you use security guards?'

'Yes. A company called EDS. They're excellent. Would you like to meet our security guard?'

'That won't be necessary.'

As he escorted the team out of the building, the manager pointed to a framed certificate by the entrance.

'Last year we received an award for humanitarian relief. It was presented by Princess Lalla Salma herself!'

Chapter 6

The coast road was a blaze of yellow mimosa, interspersed with vistas of blue sea. Karim preferred it to the dull motorway with its toll. But this Friday morning he was too despondent to enjoy the view.

Noureddine once told him that the most powerful weapon a detective had was intuition. Intuition wasn't a whim or a passing fancy but a highly sophisticated response mechanism made up of all a man's experiences in life. Today, for the first time in his career, Karim started to mistrust his intuition.

He could have sworn that the factory was not what it claimed to be. Why else would it employ a guard with such a fearsome dog? And what about the migrants? The night manager's explanation was bizarre . . . but plausible. The fact remained that Abdou had checked their container three days before he disappeared. There had to be a link.

Whenever Karim felt stressed he bought a cigarette from a street-corner cigarette seller. These men – sometimes, boys – bought their cigarettes in cartons then sold them in ones and twos to passers-by. There was a *moul garro* who sat on the pavement outside the commissariat in Marrakech. Over the years Karim had bought hundreds of cigarettes from him, usually one at a time. Bouchaïb, the parking attendant, shook his head at Karim's profligate behaviour. *Why don't you just buy a packet and have done with it?* To which Karim would reply, *Ah, but if I did that I might start smoking.*

Parked on an overlook by the sea, Karim lit a Marquise he had bought that morning. The kick of nicotine and the crash of the waves made a pleasant combination. The sun was warm enough for him to open the car door and sit with his feet on the threshold. Down on the beach he spotted something pale and fleshy. *By the Seven Saints . . . it looked like a dead body!* Stubbing out his half-smoked cigarette Karim reached in the glove compartment and grabbed his binoculars. To his relief it was nothing more than a porpoise washed up by the tide.

Larbi wasn't around when he arrived at the prefecture. Instead, Karim summoned Ali.

'You told me you were an expert on the Strait of Gibraltar.'

Ali laughed. 'I've studied the Strait, it's true.'

'I have a question for you. As you know, I'm investigating the disappearance of my colleague.'

Ali heaved a sigh. 'I wish we could find an explanation.'

'Let's imagine he fell into the water and drowned. Surely his body would have surfaced by now?'

'It depends on the current.'

'Why? Which way does it flow?'

'Eastward – on the surface. The water from the Atlantic Ocean isn't as dense as the water from the Mediterranean so an upper layer of water, about a hundred metres deep, flows eastward.'

'And the lower layer?'

'Saltier and heavier Mediterranean water flowing westward into the Atlantic.'

Karim did some reckoning. If Abdou had drowned, his body would have sunk and been carried westward before decomposing and rising to the surface, where it would have floated east. But if he had been killed *before* being thrown in the water, his lungs would still have been full of air and his body would have been carried eastward from the outset. It was hard to work out. But it got even harder, according to Ali.

'There are tidal currents of up to four knots that can speed up or slow down the eastward current, depending on the tide. There's also an eddy caused by the rotation of the earth. It produces a counter current, increasing the westward flow by two knots. Add everything up and we haven't the faintest idea what happens to a dead body in the Western Mediterranean. If Lieutenant el-Mokhfi has drowned – may God forbid it – then his corpse could drift back and forth in the Strait for months. I'm sorry I can't be more help. Was that the reason you called me down here?'

'No. I would like to see the CCTV footage for the fifth of March.' Ali's face betrayed a tremor of anxiety. 'Inspector Larbi has given permission,' Karim lied.

'*Makayn mushkeel.* No problem.' Ali sat down and tapped the computer.

'Camera eight,' said Karim.

One of the wall monitors went blank for a moment, then started showing footage with the date *050313* on the counter. The camera was trained on the block of containers where Abdou had gone missing.

'Advance frame to 1700 hours.'

They watched the shadows lengthen in the storage yard. Suddenly Abdou appeared in frame.

'Stop!'

Ali let the tape run at normal speed. At 17.37:27 they saw Abdou walk across the gap between J2 and K2. He turned his head to look towards the camera then moved out of shot.

'Freeze frame and zoom in tight on Abdou.'

Karim walked up to the monitor and scrutinised the object in Abdou's right hand. There was no doubt: it was a monocular. Karim considered the implications. What was Abdou looking at? And, if he was using only one eye, how had he not managed to spot his assailant?

'I believe there's a camera on the other side of K block.'

'Yes. Camera seventeen.'

'Please bring up camera seventeen, same date and time.' The screen went black then showed footage from a different angle, this time from the other end of the storage yard. Karim pointed.

'Can you zoom into the gap between those two rows?'

The image showed the rear view of the gap between bays J and K. Half of the gap was obscured by containers but they could see a slim section at the far end. There was a blur as someone – Abdou – moved across the gap at 17.38:28. The area of the gap hidden by the containers was wide enough for a person – or persons – to steal along without being seen.

'Can you try one last thing, my brother? Stay on this camera but fast forward an hour or so.'

When the counter reached 18.30 the yard went dark, followed by the floodlights coming on. Then, at 19.57, a Sûreté van pulled up in front of the gap.

'Stop! Now play at normal speed.'

The angle of the camera meant that it was impossible to see the faces of the drivers or what was taking place at the rear of the van.

'Can you go in tighter on the windscreen?'

Karim could see a scarf lying on the dashboard. It was the same Raja supporter's scarf that the policeman had been wearing – the one who had spoken to Abdou a few hours earlier, the one who – according to Larbi – was now on holiday.

'What's going on?'

Larbi marched into the room, his face like thunder. He stopped at Karim's desk and pointed a nicotine-stained finger at the monitors.

'Who authorised this?'

Karim was unruffled. 'I've been looking at CCTV footage. And now, if you don't mind, I'd like to do some research on my colleague's computer.' He turned to Ali. 'Thank you lieutenant, *barakallufik*, God bless you.'

When Larbi and Ali had gone, Karim entered *Mohammed Mansouri* in his browser. All that came up were some business listings that gave the address of EDS Security and details of the directors and capitalisation. It was remarkable that there was almost no information on Mansouri himself, a man of sixty-three years who ran a successful business with clients throughout the northern region.

Karim's gaze wandered around the room. On the monitors were views of the train station . . . the logistics zone . . . the landscaped gardens by the Port Authority offices.

He now knew that Abdou had not been inspecting shipping containers on the night he disappeared. He had been
spying on something – or someone. The presence of the Sûreté
van at 18.57 was troubling. Karim decided that he needed to
inspect more footage from camera seventeen to see if the
Sûreté van had been at the scene earlier. If so, there was a
possibility that it had dropped off Abdou's abductor, or abductors. Karim called Ali's extension but there was no answer. At
the front desk he asked the female duty officer where he could
find him.

'Do you mean Lieutenant Hammoudi?'

'All I know is that he is on extension twelve.'

She pointed Karim to an upstairs office. The stairs, like the
rest of the building, looked tatty. Simo had told Karim that a
new prefecture was under construction, more in keeping with
the twenty-first century image of Tanger-Med. Karim walked
along a series of offices whose occupants raised their eyes as he
passed. There was no one in the last office, which was bright
and airy, with a window overlooking the sea. Karim couldn't
help comparing the spacious surroundings to the cramped
office he shared with Abdou and Noureddine. On the desk
stood a family photograph of Ali, his wife and two children.
Karim was on his way out when he noticed an article of clothing hanging from the back of the door: a green-and-white
scarf with the logo of Raja Football Club.

When Karim got behind the wheel of the Dacia his heart was
racing so fast he thought he would pass out. The mysterious

officer who Larbi claimed had gone on holiday was none other than Ali himself. He had spoken to Abdou on the fifth of March. Even more damning, he was in the van an hour after Abdou disappeared. Karim took a breath and forced himself to think clearly. It was possible that there were two officers in the Tangier Med Prefecture who supported Raja Athletic and who owned green and white scarves, but it seemed unlikely, somehow. Karim drove down the perimeter road to the APM terminal. The guard at the entrance recognised him.

'Good afternoon, sir. Are you meeting Mr El Hajjem? Or Mr Berrada?'

'Neither.'

'I can't let you through without authorisation.'

'I just need to check a detail.' Karim replied. He parked outside the barrier and grabbed his binoculars.

'You can't park there, sir!'

Karim strode past him. 'I'll only be a minute. Call Police Commissioner Larbi if you have to!'

Karim reckoned he had about ten minutes before someone at the prefecture or the security company sounded the alarm. As he hurried to the storage yard he looked in the direction of the quay. There were two ships: a medium-sized freighter and a larger vessel. He could see Faisal Berrada with his clipboard and, to his left, through the wire fence, hundreds of shiny white cars glinting in the sun.

Karim made for the area of the yard where he thought he would find camera seventeen. Sure enough, there it was, opposite a gap between two rows of containers. As he walked along the gap, just wide enough for a stacking crane to move down, the silvers and blues and oranges of the containers coalesced

into a single black trench. It took him just over two minutes
to emerge at the other end at K2, blinking in the sunshine. He
took two steps forward and saw camera nine on the perimeter
fence. His face was clammy with perspiration. He could hear
seagulls, the hum of a stacking crane and a rumble from the
quayside like distant thunder.

He raised his binoculars. To his surprise, his view of the
terminal was blocked by containers. He could see nothing
apart from the walls of J2 and K2. What, then, was Abdou
looking at? Karim circled in the other direction . . . along the
wire perimeter fence . . . over the patriotic slogan painted on
the mountainside with the words *God, Homeland, King* . . .
past the quay of the Eurogate terminal . . . *stop!* That was it!
He could see the quay through the fence! Abdou hadn't been
watching Terminal 1, but Terminal 2! He had hidden in the
blind spot to avoid being seen! Karim had a perfect view of the
ship in the quay, a Maersk vessel underneath the Eurogate
gantries, no more than two hundred yards from where he was
standing.

At that moment a seagull flew overhead and Karim looked
up. *By God!* A gigantic shadow was falling from the sky. With
a split-second reflex Karim hurled himself to the side. There
was a rush of air followed by a colossal *boom*, and the ground
shuddered as if struck by an earthquake. Karim lay on his back
for several seconds, dazed with shock, after-tremors running
through his body. Slowly, he eased himself into a sitting position. A container lay embedded in the concrete, a forty-by-
eight-foot brown monolith taking up his entire field of vision.
He stared at a giant white *M* in front of his nose. Somewhere
under the container, fused with several tons of steel and

cement, were his binoculars. A port employee came running up, closely followed by Saïd the lorry driver.

'What happened?' cried Saïd. 'Did the chain snap?'

The cradle of the stacking crane was above them, the spreader still swinging gently.

'What did the foreman say?'

Noureddine was almost speechless with shock. Karim was sitting in the Port Authority offices, rubbing his palms with antiseptic wipes, mobile wedged between shoulder and chin.

'He said that the bearings failed in one of the twist-locks.'

'Do you believe him?'

'No.'

'What about your injuries?'

Karim gazed at his torn sleeve. 'A few cuts, but otherwise OK.'

'Are you going to the hospital?'

'No. There's a nurse here who fixed me up.'

'So the blind spot – Abdou knew about that?'

'Yes. He wanted somewhere from where he could watch the Eurogate terminal.'

'And the ship that was in the terminal?'

'I haven't had time to check.'

Karim smiled at the nurse, who was hovering with a glass of water in one hand and two paracetamol tablets in the other.

'I'll do a search on the ship,' declared Noureddine. 'But it's time to get the intelligence services involved.'

'Not yet, Noureddine – please. Give me a few more days.'

'Karim, your life is in danger! I cannot allow the same thing to happen to you as happened to Abdou. He tried to handle the case on his own and look what—'

'Abdou was on to something. We owe it to him to find out what it was.'

'Tomorrow is Saturday. Return to Marrakech for the weekend and we'll talk further.'

Karim was driving along the coast back to Tangier when Simo called. The police chief seemed even more upset than Noureddine, reciting several *al-hamdulillahs* for Karim's deliverance.

'I will order an investigation! This kind of negligence is inexcusable!'

'*Maalesh*, let it go,' said Karim. 'It was an accident. Don't blame the driver of the stacking crane. Let's not do anything that affects Tanger-Med's reputation – Larbi would never forgive us.'

'Larbi? Never mind Larbi. He'll do as I say!'

Karim wanted to give Simo the impression that he had been scared off by the incident. 'I'm going to return to Marrakech for a few days.'

'Very well. But I will have stern words with the terminal supervisor. And I will take you to dinner tonight. We must drink a beer to celebrate your narrow escape!'

'God bless you, but I don't drink alcohol.'

'No matter! We'll drink Coca-Cola!'

'Thank you, Simo, but I'd prefer to go back to my hotel and rest.'

'*Fikra mezyana*, good idea. You've had a nasty shock, after all. Take a few days off. I'll call you if there are any developments.'

Karim put the phone away and stepped out of the car. Around him, the wood sorrel and gorse blossoms were a riot of yellow. He realised that his hands were trembling. He kneeled down on the roadside and gave thanks to God for saving his life.

Glory to Allah, all praise belongs to Allah, Allah is the Greatest. Blessed be the name of thy Lord, full of Majesty, Bounty and Honour.

It would be several weeks before he stopped having nightmares about falling containers.

Chapter 7

The morning was chilly. Rain dripped from the palm trees as Karim drove to the railway station. It would be a relief to get out of this dangerous city with its cold beds and obstructive people. A few nights away would help him to think straight. He felt a sharp pang as he parked the car: in leaving Tangier he was saying goodbye to any lingering hope that Abdou might still be alive. There was no urgency any more, just sadness . . . sadness and iron resolution.

He bought a *pain au chocolat* and a packet of sunflower seeds and boarded the train to Marrakech. For the first hour he stared out of the window. What was the moment, he wondered, when the cartel – because there *was* a cartel, of that he was sure – decided to kill him? Was it after the interview with Mansouri? When he asked Simo to carry out the raid on Best Century Clothing? Or when he spotted the scarf? Of all the people he had met in Marrakech, Ali was the one he would have least suspected of being corrupt. Once again, his intuition had failed him.

When the train stopped at Asilah, Karim wondered if the old lady with the thermos flask would get on. Perhaps she would read his future, examine a set of cards and tell him what had happened to Abdou. But the only passengers were a group of French tourists and a man with a crate of squawking chickens. By the time he reached Larache he was thinking of Ayesha. He wanted to talk to her – about the case, about his near-escape, about everything. As the train pulled into Kenitra he decided that to meet her after all these months would be insanity. The guard blew his whistle. Slowly, the train started to move. Karim stared at his bag. He jumped up, opened the door and leaped onto the platform.

It was four years since he had been in Kenitra and the city had changed. There were new buildings, smart shops, an Italian restaurant. He stopped at a cashpoint machine and withdrew his entire balance of four hundred and fifty dirhams. Then he called the Institut Royal de Police and left a message.

'You were lucky to get hold of me,' said Ayesha, poring over the menu in the Italian restaurant. 'Every other weekend I stay with Salma's family but she has a law exam and needs to study.'

Ayesha and Karim had never eaten *à deux* before. It felt illicit, daring, and the waiter's eyes twinkled as he handed them the menu, taking them for a courting couple. To Karim, setting eyes on Ayesha after a long interval was like meeting a different woman. She had a confidence, an assurance, that was new. The black suit and blouse suited her. Her dark hair was tied in a ponytail and, even without make-up, her eyes shone. The overall effect increased the tug on his heartstrings.

'You look well.'

'You too.' Ayesha grinned. 'Although I'm not sure about the moustache!'

Ayesha's view of their lunch date was very different from Karim's. She had lived her first twenty years in the sheltered environment of the Belkacem household where one day was much like the rest. The eighteen months that followed had been a tumult of shock and grief, ending with her moving out to look after her traumatised mother. Going to police college was the start of a new life. To be a warrior, a guardian, an athlete: those were her desires! She wanted adventures and excitement and romance! Romance . . . that no longer included Karim. She had grown tired of his constant fretting and indecision. His unfashionable clothes, the ever-serious face . . . the idea of marrying him now seemed quaint, even absurd. Her twenties would be spent chasing criminals and visiting new places. One day she would meet a man with a hearty laugh, who found life entertaining rather than challenging. They would settle down and have children, *inshallah*!

Both Ayesha and Karim had trouble deciphering the menu. Neither of them had eaten at an Italian restaurant before and when the waiter came to take their order they asked for pizza. Karim felt ill at ease. Attempts at humour came out stilted and clumsy. He told Ayesha about Mokhtar and his freezing room in the Hotel Fuentes.

'Tell me about Abdou. You will find him, won't you?'

Karim knocked over the bottle of Sidi Ali, spilling water everywhere. He dabbed at the table ineffectually with his napkin.

'Everyone claims that Abdou got trapped in a container by accident and is far away by now, possibly dead.'

'That's unlikely, isn't it?'

'Ten days have now passed without a word.'

'Don't give up, you may still find him.' Her palm felt cool on his hand.

Karim told Ayesha what he had discovered at the port. 'Simo says that Mansouri was recruited as part of a privatisation initiative and claims he only uses him outside the port when he doesn't have enough police officers. But I sometimes wonder who's really in charge, Mansouri or Simo.'

'Tell me about the night that Abdou disappeared. You believe he was spying on the Eurogate terminal?'

Karim nodded. 'He thought he couldn't be seen. Unfortunately he was wrong.' He put his knife and fork down with a chuckle.

'What's funny?'

'I just remembered something that Abdou said to his driver. *Don't look for dates in the olive tree.* Everybody, including me, assumed that Abdou was checking Terminal 1 when he was actually watching Terminal 2.'

'What do you know about the ship in the quay?'

'I didn't see the name. Noureddine is looking into it.'

'Will you investigate Terminal 2?'

'I don't know yet.'

Ayesha pointed at his half-eaten pizza. 'Are you going to finish that?'

Karim pushed his plate across the table.

'Tangier sounds like a scary place,' said Ayesha, chomping away.

'You have no idea how scary. A man was killed outside my hotel window a few nights ago.'

'My God! What happened?'

'He was a people smuggler. There's some kind of war going on between rival smugglers. There are a lot of migrants in Tangier, more than anywhere else in Morocco. They're all desperate to get to Spain. It's given rise to a wave of violence.'

Ayesha nodded. 'Did you see what happened at Ceuta? Colonel Choukri showed us the TV footage. According to him, there are lessons to be learned from the way the police mishandled the situation.'

'Let's talk about something less depressing. Tell me about college. Are you enjoying it?'

'Yes. Or rather – I was until last Wednesday. One of the boy cadets provoked me about Abderrahim.'

'What did he say?'

'He asked how I liked having a convicted terrorist for a brother.'

'What did you say?' Karim had been on the receiving end of Ayesha's quick temper and hoped, for her sake, that she hadn't lashed out.

Ayesha chose not to upset Karim. 'I ignored him.'

'Quite right! It's none of his business. If anyone asks, tell them Abderrahim is an innocent man who fell victim to police paranoia. Have you been to see him yet?'

Ayesha gave a weary sigh. 'Don't you start. I've had Lalla Fatima and Khadija on at me.'

'You must go. He's your brother.'

'You are my brother.'

'I am your *also* your brother, although I wish I weren't. You know my feelings for you.'

If Karim hoped that Ayesha would reciprocate those feelings, he was disappointed. Ayesha's mind was still on Abderrahim.

'I know I won't like him.'

'He's not an easy man. I met him on two occasions. He was very – how shall I put it? Austere.'

'They say men get radicalised in prison.'

'That is true.'

'And Kenitra is a violent place.'

'That is also true. You will see some unsavoury-looking people if you visit him. It would be good for you to see inside a prison – useful for your training. You would learn about prison conditions and miscarriages of justice. If you get involved with Abderrahim's case you might be able to help him.'

Ayesha was unconvinced. 'Maybe.'

'You know the man who runs the security company, Mohammed Mansouri.'

'What about him?'

'I saw tattoos on two men last week. One was a migrant called Joseph. The other was Mohammed Mansouri.'

'So?'

'I've only ever seen tattoos on prisoners before. Moroccan men often get tattoos when they're in prison.'

'You think that this Mansouri character was in Kenitra?'

'If he committed a serious crime – yes. Kenitra is a maximum-security prison.'

'Is that why you came to see me?' Ayesha's cheeks flushed with anger. 'You want me to grill Abderrahim for information?'

'No, I wanted to see you because I . . . was lonely. I only thought of the tattoo a minute ago.'

The waiter came with the bill and Karim counted out one hundred and eighty dirhams. He was getting through his money fast.

'The last week has been the hardest of my life. My best friend is dying or already dead ... I'm alone in a strange city ... among people who have the marks of officials but who act like my enemy ... I can't voice my fears to Noureddine in case he recalls me to Marrakech ... I have no one I can trust ...'

Ayesha was moved. 'Karim, you know I would help, but I'm in class all day!'

'I know there's nothing you can do.' Suddenly he blurted, 'I was nearly crushed to death yesterday.'

'Oh God!' Ayesha sat up in horror.

'I'm sorry.' Karim bit his lip. 'I didn't mean to alarm you.'

'What happened?'

'A container fell from a crane.'

'Surely it was an accident!'

'There have been too many accidents for them all to be considered accidents.'

'But that's ... awful! You need someone to support you.'

'Noureddine won't send another officer. It would look like we don't trust the Tangier police.'

Ayesha said nothing for a long while, toying with the corner of her napkin.

'I have an idea,' she said. 'But you've got to keep this a secret – promise?'

Karim nodded.

'I keep a second mobile phone at college.'

Karim was horrified. 'You could be expelled!'

'It's for emergencies only,' Ayesha said quickly. 'For my mother, for Lalla Hanane. You don't know how ill she is.'

'She just has to call the college! You would get compassionate leave.'

'It's not as simple as that. Lalla Hanane has panic attacks,
palpitations – if she felt that she couldn't get hold of me she
would be a thousand times worse. I told her that I would take
a second phone into college, hidden in my suitcase. She can
leave a message if she feels desperate and I call her back.
Having me at the end of a phone keeps her anxiety at bay.'

'How do you use the phone without anyone knowing?'

'I check it every evening after dinner. Salma is the monitor
for our dinner table so she helps clear away the dishes and do
the washing up. She doesn't get back to our bedroom until just
before eight. She doesn't have the slightest idea the phone is in
the room. And my mother has only called twice – it's more for
reassurance than anything. I could never have left Lalla
Hanane all alone in Marrakech without providing her with
that lifeline.'

'So what exactly are you proposing?'

'That the phone becomes your lifeline as well.'

'Absolutely not. I refuse to risk you getting expelled.'

'You're not risking anything. I'm the one taking the risk.'
Ayesha scribbled a number on the napkin and pushed it across
the table.

'For emergencies only.'

Kenitra prison was tucked away behind a housing estate, on a
hill overlooking the Sebou River. As Ayesha walked up to the
building's massive doors she thought that the French who

built the prison in the 1930s must have had an odd sense of humour, siting the country's prestigious police academy and its highest-security penitentiary in the same, otherwise unremarkable, northern city.

As she waited in a line of anxious women and grim-faced men she felt a flurry of anxiety. She had only been inside a prison once before, in Marrakech, to visit her dying father. The conditions in Kenitra were reputed to be worse.

How would Abderrahim react to her turning up out of the blue? How would he take the news that she was training to be a police officer? His views were, by all accounts, even more extreme than her father's. Abderrahim never smoked or drank and had been planning to make the pilgrimage to Mecca before he was arrested. Ayesha's own view of Islam was simple. God wanted his children to live together in peace and harmony. She said her prayers, observed Ramadan and gave what she could to the poor. Everything else was a lot of fuss stirred up by men. Nonetheless, she was glad that she was wearing a *jellaba* and blue headscarf over her suit.

When she reached the head of the line she placed her bag in the X-ray machine and waited while a sergeant wrote her details in a ledger. Seeing the toiletries and food parcels that other visitors had brought made her ashamed that she'd arrived empty-handed. After passing through a body scanner, she was manually searched – too intimately for her liking – by a male guard.

'Keep your hands where they belong!' she snapped.

'Calm down, *lalla*. It's protocol.'

The twenty or so visitors were herded together and taken through a locked gate to a cold, bare room with barred windows. Ayesha sat near the door and stared at the inmates as they came in one by one. As Karim warned, they were a rough lot, in grubby shorts and sports tops. She noticed tattoos on several men. The faces of some lit up when they saw their visitors, others were sullen and cowed. One man sat on the other side of the room, his arms folded, looking impassively at his weeping wife.

'*Salaam ou-alikum.*' The man before her was dressed in a spotless *gandora*. He was slim, with the heavy eyebrows of their father and a long black beard. He embraced her formally.

'We have been waiting a long time.'

Ayesha wondered who he meant by *we*. Himself and Lalla Hanane? The family, waiting for the estranged daughter's return? Or was he grandly referring to himself, waiting for Ayesha to visit him in prison?

'I'm sorry – I've been busy . . .'

Abderrahim ran his eyes over her. 'I remember when you left twenty years ago. Father never gave up hope of your return.'

'I saw our father before he died.'

'*Al-hamdulillah.* Mother says that you are looking after her.'

'I make sure that she is comfortable.'

Among Ayesha's other duties she acted as her mother's secretary. She had transcribed and posted dozens of letters for her mother, but had never added a personal message on the letters she sent to Abderrahim.

'She tells me that you are attending police college here in Kenitra.'

'Yes.'

'How can you do both?'

'Excuse me?'

'How can you look after Mother if you're in Kenitra?'

Ayesha was unprepared for this question. 'I go back to Marrakech most weekends.'

'And during the week? Who looks after her then?'

'I, er – I will get a posting in Marrakech when I finish college, *inshallah*, and then I will be able to look after, er, Mother. Perhaps you will be out of prison by then, *inshallah*!'

'So we will be a happy family again, is that what you're saying?'

Ayesha swallowed. 'Have you got a date when you might . . .? When do you . . .?'

'Some men have been here for twenty years.'

'Yes, but you're not a dangerous criminal!'

'I'm considered a dangerous criminal. All men in Kenitra for so-called terrorist offences are kept in solitary confinement.'

'That's terrible! I thought that conditions in prison had improved.'

One of the central missions of the Royal Institut de Police was to signal that the bad old days of an underfunded, repressive justice system had been swept away, along with bribery and torture chambers, replaced by human rights, equality before the law and modern toilets.

'Oh, there are decent cells. Tidy cells, with four beds and a flush toilet. Not mine, however.'

'What is it like?'

'Have you seen photographs of prehistoric caves? The ceiling is so low I spend my day in a permanent stoop. The floor slopes towards a hole where I squat like an animal. I have to keep my clothes in a carrier bag tied to the door otherwise they would stink of piss.'

Ayesha put her hand over her mouth. Despite her revulsion, she couldn't help being impressed that her brother had looked after himself in such dreadful conditions.

'Are you allowed out to pray?'

'Five times a day, *al-hamdulillah*, before my shifts at the kitchen and workshop. I can stand upright, stretch my limbs and perform my ablutions. I give thanks to God for this mercy. Do you see that man over there?'

Ayesha turned towards the back of the room. A hunched man in t-shirt and shorts, with thin arms and bandaged legs that made him look like an emaciated hawk, was arguing with a woman holding an infant.

'He jumped out of a window in an attempt to escape. Broke both his legs.'

'May God preserve him!'

'Men go mad in here. Some long for death. They pray for an aneurism or a heart attack to carry them off. I pray for fortitude and resilience.'

'Perhaps Karim can talk to the prison governor . . .'

'*Karim?*' Abderrahim spat out the name. 'If Karim had done his job properly I wouldn't be in in this pigsty! I would never have been arrested. Nor would my father. *Our* father. You are a Talal. Your loyalties lie with us now, not with Karim.'

Cowed by this onslaught, Ayesha mumbled something about trying to obtain permission to visit him during the week. Abderrahim rose to his feet.

'Bring food next time. And wear a plain scarf.'

ي

Karim stumbled out of the hotel into dazzling sunshine.

After prayers at the mosque he decided to take a walk. Difficult problems, he found, had a habit of resolving themselves during a walk. In Marrakech he would sometimes walk five miles to the Menara Pavilion and back when he was grappling with a particularly tricky problem. On that bright Sunday morning in Tangier he headed uphill, along winding lanes and busy thoroughfares, reciting the Surah al-Falaq to invoke the protection of Allah. By the time he reached the Grand Socco there were damp patches under his arms.

Mokhtar wasn't anywhere to be seen. It was time to find another informant, he decided, one who gave him straight answers. As for Larbi, Ali, Berrada, Mansouri and Simo, they could go to hell. The only honest Moroccan he'd met in Tangier was a lorry driver – and he was probably on the take as well.

He noticed the tower of a church looming above the square and presumed that it was the church where Joseph worshipped. Outside the church a souk was in progress. Country women in striped skirts and straw hats with pom-poms were selling chickens, eggs, fresh vegetables and produce. Karim watched one of the women weave a palm leaf around a slab of cheese.

'*Formaj?*' he asked.

'*Jben.*'

Karim asked if he could try a piece and she launched into a torrent of dialect. A passer-by, a man in a woollen *burnous*, told Karim that the woman was saying he had to buy the cheese if he wanted to try it. It was delicious, the man added; sweet and creamy, fresh from the Rif mountains. Mention of the Rif made Karim think of Mohammed Mansouri. He looked for similarities in the women, with their sunburned faces, quick patter and sturdy hands. He made a little tour of the souk, browsing piles of bric-a-brac and second-hand clothes, then peered into a forge and watched a blacksmith roast sheep's heads on long metal rods.

Just before noon the congregation of the church filed out. Despite the presence of several sub-Saharans there was no sign of Joseph. Disappointed, Karim turned along a crowded shopping street. The transition from medina to new town was abrupt: glitzy hotels and expensive shops. He sat outside a café at a roundabout watching a cavalcade as varied as that in the Petit Socco: smart young Tanjaouis, veiled women, hollow-eyed glue-sniffers, mumbling beggars and eager shoe-shine boys.

After finishing his coffee Karim strolled along Boulevard Pasteur. He took a photograph on a lookout terrace with cannons and a view of the Strait, then walked across the road to a perfume shop. Inside, he overheard a young assistant claim that the shop could replicate any scent in the world. Karim asked the youth which perfume he would recommend.

'Is it for your girlfriend?'

Karim gave a noncommittal answer and the assistant sprayed Karim's wrist.

'*L'Air du Temps*, that's very popular . . . Or Hugo Boss, it's a floral scent . . . How about orange blossom?'

Within minutes Karim's wrists and arms were reeking. He bought a bottle of Dolce & Gabbana for Ayesha and La Vie est Belle for Khadija. As he was walking out of the shop his mobile buzzed with a call from Simo.

'Are you still in Tangier?'

Karim saw no point in lying. 'Yes.'

'Can you help us? We're short of manpower and we need all available officers.'

'What's the problem?'

'Come to the prefecture and I'll explain.'

'I'll go via my hotel and change.'

'No. Come straight here.'

Hailing a *petit taxi*, Karim wondered what kind of crisis could have arisen on a sleepy Sunday afternoon. The driver remarked on the smell of perfume and muttered something vaguely homophobic.

Outside the police station, officers in commando uniform were grabbing weapons and climbing into vans. Karim hurried up the stairs to the sixth floor. Simo was standing on the landing talking to his second-in-command.

'Ah, Karim! Jibrane will fit you out with a uniform.'

Karim was taken to a locker room. All around him there were shouts and slams as men put on riot gear. Moments later Karim was bundled into the back of a crowded Sûreté van. Jibrane got in last, his uniform marked by two stripes on the shoulder. He banged the underside of the roof and the van swerved out of the parking lot. The other men gazed at Karim curiously: the vehicle stank of perfume.

'Marrakchi?' one asked.

'Yes.'

The men nodded, as if the answer explained Karim's taste in perfumery.

Another commando shouted from the back, 'You smell like a brothel.'

Everyone laughed, including Karim. He accepted a handful of sunflower seeds from his neighbour and joined in the general banter. Through the window he noticed that they were heading out of town, towards the motorway.

'*Fin ghadeeyin?* Where are we going?'

'The border.'

Karim looked puzzled and another man shouted out.

'Ceuta!'

The ride in the back of the van made Karim feel sick. The smell of perfume, combined with the twists and turns, forced him to cover his nose with his balaclava and lean forward with his hands under his knees to stop himself from vomiting. The other commandos soon lapsed into silence. After what seemed like an eternity, the van lurched to a stop. It was dark outside and Karim could hear shouts and cries. Something – a stone – smashed against the side of the vehicle. The men put on their helmets, took batons and jumped out.

It took Karim a moment to take in the scene. They were parked in a line of police vans on a hilltop, facing an eighteen-foot-high floodlit fence strung with ragged bodies. So this was it: the Ceuta wall, the frontier between Morocco and Europe, a barrier three fences deep of steel and razor wire designed to keep the African hordes from reaching Paradise. Sirens, the shattering of glass and garbled commands from walkie-talkies filled the air.

What the fuck are you doing?

Jibrane was standing ten feet away, the only commando without a helmet. Karim ran across to the wall, immediately coming under attack from missiles. The Africans were throwing broken bottles, rocks, hooks and pieces of ladder at the police, who were doing all they could to pull them down. Many of the migrants had stripped off their tops to camouflage themselves better in the darkness. A few were already astride the first fence, throwing flaming bottles onto the policemen's heads. This was a bigger and better-planned assault than the one on television and the commandos were responding as poorly as before.

Something sprayed his visor: blood. A teenage boy with short dreadlocks was draped along the top of the wire, blood spurting from a gash in his leg. The boy tumbled into no-man's land and landed with a sickening thump. Karim looked up, saw the bare foot of another climber and hit out with his baton. It seemed barbaric . . . Another *thwack* . . . now the man had his hands on the razors at the top – thank God he was wearing gloves! On the far side of the fence Karim saw the Guardia Civil rounding up any migrant who had made it over the final barrier, escorting them to an ambulance. A grappling iron clanged against Karim's helmet. The migrants with missiles were trying to hold off the police while their comrades made their escape, as if the battle plan was to sacrifice twenty men so one could get over. A muffled bang was followed by a shriek as an African dropped to the ground, felled by a rubber bullet.

Just then a wave of Africans broke cover and rushed towards an unguarded section of fence. Jibrane's voice crackled through the walkie-talkie. *Tower eight!* Karim ran along the base of the wall, thick with bodies. He climbed halfway up and wrapped his arms around a man's waist, feeling him wriggle and squirm. When the man looked around, one eye swollen shut, another commando grabbed his leg and helped Karim pull the man off the wire like a crab clinging to a fishing net. There was a thud of rubber bullets and another migrant dropped unconscious to the ground. *This is awful,* thought Karim – *armoured police commandos fighting half-naked men.* The reckless way the commandos lashed out made Karim suspect that many were Mansouri's paramilitaries. What made the savagery worse was that Jibrane was ordering them to keep hitting the Africans once they were on the ground, so they wouldn't resist being carted off to a police van.

Fucking get him! Jibrane was staring at Karim, pointing with his baton at a migrant in a puffa jacket who had nearly made it over the first fence. Quick as a flash, Karim scrambled up and wrapped his forearm around the man's neck. The man tried to grab the top of the fence but the sleeve of his jacket snagged on the barbed wire and he reached out uselessly, his bare arm caught in the floodlight. *Joseph.* Karim froze. Everything afterwards happened in slow motion: Joseph being pulled down; Joseph lying on the ground; Jibrane raining blows on his back.

'Stop!'

Karim jumped down and put a restraining hand on Jibrane's shoulder. Jibrane turned around, incredulous.

'What did you say?'

Joseph opened his eyes during this exchange but he didn't appear to recognise Karim behind his visor.

'Don't beat him!'

'Why the fuck not?'

'It's . . . inhumane.'

'*Inhumane?*' Jibrane slammed his baton into Joseph's kidneys. 'We have to beat them!' Joseph gave a loud groan and rolled onto his back. 'Hard!' Jibrane landed another blow, this time on Joseph's chest. 'Like this!' *Wham* – a final, two-handed, sledgehammer-like strike on Joseph's ribs.

He upended Joseph's bag and dozens of sunglasses fell on the ground. He ground them under the heel of his boot.

'Take him away!'

Enduring multiple levels of shame, praying that Joseph hadn't recognised him, Karim took him under the arms while another man – an EDS officer – grasped Joseph by the feet. The EDS man made no attempt to lift Joseph's body clear, leaving a bloody trail as his back dragged over the ground.

'Lift the poor fellow up!' Karim cried.

At that moment Joseph's money belt snagged on a stone and came away. The EDS officer saw the belt lying on the earth, stuffed with banknotes. He flashed a furtive look at Karim then let go of Joseph's legs and grabbed the belt. Instantly, Joseph sprang to his feet and ran into the night.

Karim returned to the hotel at two o'clock in the morning.

'Hey, mister!' A cough came from the shadows. 'You look like you've just been in a war zone.' Karim turned around to see Mokhtar sitting at the reception desk.

Karim nodded wearily. 'That is exactly where I have been.'

'What do you say we drink a nice mint tea together? The café is almost closed but the waiter is a friend of mine and he'll make old Mokhtar a *berrad atay*, a nice pot of mint tea, if I ask him! What do you say?'

'I don't drink tea.'

Mokhtar got down and waved an arm. 'Come! Come!'

In the café the barman was busy counting money at the till. He frowned when he saw the men approach but he heated up some tea.

'Can you make me a *nuss-nuss*?' asked Karim.

Muttering an obscenity, the waiter turned on the espresso machine.

Karim sat down opposite Mokhtar, too traumatised to speak. Humming to himself, Mokhtar took out his leather pouch, loosened the strings and tipped some kif on the table. He separated the stalks and seeds with the blade of a knife then, using the flat part of the blade, he crushed the kif against the table top. When he had pressed the kif to his satisfaction he began to cut it. The kif now had the consistency of a fine powder. Despite his fatigue, and his burning shame after the events of the evening, Karim found himself being drawn in by the ritual. Mokhtar slid the blade of his knife underneath the powder and poured most of it back into his pouch. The remaining kif he tipped into the bowl of his pipe. Using his finger to tamp it down, he lit the pipe and inhaled forcefully. He blew out a cloud of smoke.

'You left Tangier. Then you came back again.'

'I went to see my sister. She lives in Kenitra.'

Mokhtar sucked on his pipe. 'First Kenitra,' he said pensively, 'then Ceuta. Quite a weekend.'

Karim was startled. 'How do you know I was at Ceuta?'

'I saw it on the television. All police officers in the area had their leave cancelled.' Mokhtar succumbed to a coughing fit.

'You shouldn't be smoking with a cough like that.'

Mokhtar smiled. 'Ah, that's where you're wrong, mister. Kif cures ninety-five per cent of ailments. The other five per cent can be fixed with mint tea.'

Mokhtar opened the lid of the teapot, dropped in two rectangles of sugar and gave it a stir. He poured himself a glass of tea then added another lump of sugar for good measure.

'They said that a lot of police were injured. But not as many police as Africans, eh, mister?'

'It was a *shalada*, a fiasco.' Karim put a sugar in his *nuss-nuss*. 'I've never taken part in such an unprofessional operation.'

'The things we have to do, eh, mister? But then, the *azzis* will swamp the frontier if we let them.'

His casual insult made Karim get to his feet. 'I'm going to bed.'

Mokhtar fixed Karim in his gaze. 'You have to move out of the hotel.'

'What are you talking about?'

Mokhtar puffed his pipe. 'The hotel. It's being watched.'

'The only person watching it is you!'

Mokhtar shrugged. 'Suit yourself.' He relit his pipe with a match.

Karim wanted to drag his aching body upstairs but he was disconcerted by Mokhtar's remark and he sat down again.

'You're wrong about the hotel being watched. That kif you put in your pipe is making you imagine things.'

Mokhtar regarded him languidly. He seemed to have undergone a transformation from shifty-eyed informant to suave debauchee.

'Kif, among its other properties, makes you vigilant.'

'Paranoid, more like!'

'Are you sure you wouldn't like a puff?' Mokhtar held out his *sebsi*. 'It would help you to sleep.'

'Ugh.' Karim had never smoked kif and he wasn't going to start now. He had enough nightmares to contend with. 'Who's watching the hotel?'

'Two men. One tall, one short. I didn't get a good look at them.'

'So how do you know they were watching the hotel?' Karim wished that he hadn't drunk the *nuss-nuss*. His brain was now fully awake and anxiety had gained a foothold.

'I saw them from behind. One in a robe, one in a coat. They were looking up at your window.'

'That doesn't prove they were looking for me.'

'What else would they be doing? There's no one else staying at the hotel.'

'Where did they go afterwards?'

'Down the alley opposite. Do you know what the alley is called? *Mokhtar – Mokhtar Aharden!*' Mokhtar laughed so much that his frame shook, then he started coughing and spluttering.

Karim stood up. 'I'm going to bed!'

'You need to pay for the drinks first, mister.'

Karim slapped a coin on the table. 'Good night.'

He went upstairs and sat on the bed, his head spinning. As he unbuttoned his shirt he checked his phone for messages. There was a three-word text from Ayesha – the only good news he'd had all evening.

'*Ana wakf mak*, I'm here for you.'

Chapter 8

It was just after six in the morning and still dark outside. Salma was tying her hair in a ponytail.

'Are you going to visit him again?'

Ayesha looked at her red tracksuit in the mirror.

'Yes. I'll take food and a blanket. If he is pleasant and respectful, then I will go again. If he is disagreeable like he was yesterday, *safee* – no more visits.'

'He's probably not used to company. You're probably the first person he's had a proper conversation with for months.'

'It wasn't a conversation. He wasn't interested in me.'

'Nonetheless, I think you should keep visiting him. One day he's going to come out of prison and he may hold it against you if you haven't been to visit him regularly.'

'I suppose you're right,' Ayesha sighed, making her bed. 'Although when he comes out I have no doubt that he will want me to wait on him hand and foot, like a good Talal girl.'

'*A good Talal girl?*' Salma gave a mischievous grin. 'I didn't think there was such a thing!'

Hearing the blast of a whistle, they joined the other cadets trooping down the corridor.

'I know one thing for a fact,' said Ayesha.

'What's that?'

'If I lived under the same roof as Abderrahim I would have to wave goodbye to my career in the Sûreté.'

'Wouldn't your mother take your side?'

'You don't know my mother. Or my brother. He will rule the house with a rod of iron, just as my father did.'

'Couldn't you move away – apply for a posting in Casablanca or Fez?'

Ayesha shook her head. 'I've already submitted a request for Marrakech. I made a commitment to my mother. No – the only way I can make Abderrahim accept my choice of career is to show its advantages.'

'You mean, by trying to get him released? But what can *you* do? You're just a cadet!'

They walked onto the floodlit parade ground where cadets were already lined up in formation. A glimmer of light appeared in the eastern sky.

'Keep visiting him,' urged Salma. 'Allow him to get to know you. Keep the conversation neutral.'

'That doesn't leave much for me to talk about! I can't mention Karim, Lalla Fatima, police college, my future or my past!'

'Ask him about his childhood. Find out about your sister Amina.'

'From what I've heard he disapproved of her, too!'

'You could ask him about his faith – when he became religious. Talk about Islam.'

Ayesha gave a hollow laugh. 'Religion is a touchy subject. If I say the wrong thing he stings like a scorpion.'

As they lined up for the morning exercises she noticed Khalid Hakimi in the row in front, giving her a look of pure hatred.

'Talking of scorpions . . .'

Joseph, Jean-François and a handful of other migrants limped uphill through the eucalyptus trees. Several of the men had their hands bound in blood-soaked cloth. Two men, Louis and Franco, were supporting a teenage boy whose eye was puffy and whose head was lolling to one side. Joseph's body hurt so much that every movement was agony. He had cracked at least two ribs and had lost the hearing in his left ear. *You've been baptised*, Jean-François joked. When Joseph laughed in response, he felt a violent stab in his midriff.

Now that he'd seen the border wall at close quarters he would never try climbing it again. The raid on the camp in Boukhalef had been shocking, and he'd heard second- or third-hand accounts of police violence, but nothing approached this level of savagery. In their visors and black uniforms the commandos were like robots gone berserk. He had lost his money, his phone and his bag with fifty pairs of sunglasses and all his clothes. God only knew what had happened to the boy who fell off the fence and landed so awkwardly in no-man's land.

He wiped his hands on his jeans. The razors on top of the wall had cut through his cheap gloves like scissors through paper. His nostrils were still filled with the smell of exhaust fumes. And the noise! Guns and shrieks. That bastard police-man – the second one – had almost kicked him to death. His back felt like it had been flayed. Thank God he still had the use of his legs. His legs had carried him from Kisangani to Tangier. They were his best friend. All he needed to do was put one foot in front of another.

They had cleared the eucalyptus wood by now and were climbing through palmetto and gorse scrub. They stopped to rest and drink from the stream. Men lay on the ground or sat hunched, examining their wounds. Gazing out across the Mediterranean, Joseph could see the tops of the Spanish hills rising from the early morning mist. A sailing boat was setting out from Ceuta harbour, a triangle of white on blue. Birds called to each other from the bushes and orange butterflies floated above his head.

It felt peaceful.

ي

'We don't want to keep them out of Morocco. We just have to prevent them getting to Spain.' Simo stood at the doorway of his office addressing Karim, who was sitting sullenly at the table. 'Just a moment, my brother.'

While Simo went out to discuss some matter with an officer, Karim gazed around the room. It was a fine day with the window open and he could hear car horns from the street below. On top of a wooden filing cabinet was a portrait of Simo's children. The only thing that Karim noticed out of the ordinary was the presence of three mobile phones on Simo's desk. One for work, one for family, one for –?

'The problem wouldn't exist if Ceuta and Melilla belonged to us,' said Simo, closing the door. 'It's ridiculous – two tiny patches of Europe inside the Maghreb! Unfortunately, the Spanish have occupied Ceuta and Melilla for five hundred years so I don't expect they're going to hand them back any time soon.'

Karim was in no mood for a history lesson. 'Some of the police had batons studded with nails! That's not policing, that's sadism! Jibrane behaved like a man possessed!'

The police chief spread his arms with a look of resignation. 'We have to encourage these people to go home.'

'You'll never succeed! Home for them means poverty and war!'

'Ah, my brother, now you're talking politics. Leave politics to the politicians. Was that a sneeze? Don't tell me you've caught a cold. I'm sorry I had to pull you in to help us but we need all officers when we get word there's going to be an assault.'

'I didn't see Larbi or anyone else from the Tanger-Med prefecture,' Karim said pointedly.

'How would you know? You were all wearing helmets and visors.'

'Did you use EDS men?'

'Every man was trained in crowd control.'

'So that's a *yes*.'

Simo gave a thoughtful look. 'Personally, I have no problem with a man upping and leaving home. A man set off from here once and travelled all the way to Baghdad, then up to the Volga River and as far east as China. His name was Ibn Battuta. You can see his tomb in the medina.'

'Ibn Battuta didn't have to contend with razors and rubber bullets!'

'Rubber bullets are a last resort.'

'The *Afaraqa* will never give up trying to get to Europe. Have you heard what happens to them in Libya? They're raped and tortured by the militias and sold into slavery or sex work. Now that they've found a safer route through Tangier they're not going to be put off by a few rubber bullets.'

'I agree with you. But as long as I'm the chief of police in this city we have to try and stop them. We will be here until the Last Judgement, guarding the walls and patrolling the beaches.'

'That's a fine speech,' Karim said acidly.

'Karim – if I may say, you're being a little partisan towards the sub-Saharans. Defending the border is a huge headache for us here in the north. It's not like in Marrakech.'

'We have our own problems in Marrakech.'

'I'm sure you do. Why not go back and help your colleagues? As I told you, there's nothing more you can do in Tangier.'

'Are you worried another container might fall on my head?'

Simo paused before answering. 'I agree, that was unforgivable. I've already spoken to the terminal supervisor, who was most apologetic. There ought to be an enquiry. But you said you wanted to let the matter drop – if you'll forgive the pun,' Simo said with a chuckle.

'Do you know what Mohammed Mansouri was doing on the night of the fifth of March?'

The police chief's face clouded. 'I thought you said that you were going to take a few days off from the investigation.'

'I've changed my mind. I want you to upgrade the investigation from *Missing Person* to *Suspected Homicide*.'

'Don't tell me how to do my job! Four days ago we conducted a night raid on the clothing factory which resulted in precisely nothing.'

'They could have been tipped off.'

Simo pressed his fingertips together. 'Three rules. One: from now on, you do as I say. Two: you do not speak to anyone unless I have expressly sanctioned it. Three: step out of line and you'll be on the first train back to Marrakech.'

The survivors from *La Bataille* – the battle, as they called it – had rebuilt their camp within an hour. They were helped by the fact that the camp was exactly as they'd left it. Normally the shelters and cooking utensils would have been ransacked, salvaged by other migrants, but every camp on the mountain had taken part in the assault on the Ceuta wall.

The men's priority now was to get medical help for those in need. After helping the injured boy back to the camp, Franco and Louis took him down again when it emerged that his injuries were serious. The medical centre at Fnideq was three miles away. Late that afternoon they reappeared with the welcome news that the boy's eye had been saved. They had even managed to persuade the medical team to donate bandages and antiseptic cream for the others.

Joseph and Jean-François volunteered to cook dinner. Sitting under a juniper tree they sifted through a load of old vegetables, discarding the rotten ones and slicing the rest into a cooking pot, while they discussed the events of last night.

'You know the funny part?' Jean-François exclaimed. 'Most of the migrants in Spain are Moroccans! The country is full of them. They work in the restaurants, save up, buy a Mercedes, bring it back to Morocco and sell it for a fortune!'

'If I had a Mercedes I'd keep it,' said Joseph. 'They're the best cars in the world.'

'Teslas are better.'

Joseph chopped a carrot then picked out an onion. 'Don't you have to keep charging the batteries?'

'No. The new ones can go two hundred miles on one charge.'

'Did you ever work on a Tesla?'

Jean-François shook his head. 'You don't see many Teslas in Abidjan.'

Joseph was having difficulty chopping. He put down his knife and stared at his right hand. 'I think I dislocated my thumb when I fell off the wall.'

Jean-François took Joseph's wrist. 'Can you move it?'

Joseph winced. 'No.'

'*Un, deux, trois!*' Jean-François gave the thumb a sharp twist. Joseph howled with agony as the thumb clicked back into place.

'Did you have to be so rough?'

'*Quoi?* You would have to preferred to piss with your left hand for the next two weeks?'

'No . . .'

'Well then.'

Joseph massaged the base of his thumb. 'How many men do you think got over?'

'Eight. And a guy from the other camp told me that three were taken away by ambulance. That makes eleven.'

'Eleven! Out of five hundred!'

'*Pas mal.*'

'What do you mean, not bad?'

'Nobody lost their life.'

'I lost all my money, every dirham!'

'Then you'll just have to learn to swim, *mon ami*,' Jean-François chuckled. 'Go and fetch some water.'

Joseph gave his swollen thumb a shake and clambered through the undergrowth to the stream. The stream was the best thing about the camp. It brought mountain water, sweeter than the muck they obtained from the standpipe at Boukhalef. Amadou, the carpenter from Guinea, said that only animals slept on the mountainside but Joseph disagreed. If he couldn't be on Spanish soil then this was the next best thing, far from trouble, with the babbling of the stream and the hoot of owls to send him to sleep at night.

He filled the cooking pan in a shallow pool then cupped his good hand and took a drink. Around him, the other men were collecting firewood. Some were even singing. Where there is life, there is hope. That's what his mother used to say, before her head was severed from her body outside Kisangani.

A man in a blue work coat was criss-crossing the Petit Socco trying to change a hundred-dirham note. He tried his luck in a juice bar, then asked an elderly Englishman in a bow tie and white fedora sitting at the Central. Karim watched the Moroccan from his table outside the Tingis, where he was sitting with Mokhtar. He checked his wallet to see if he could help the man out, but decided he would need his change to pay Mokhtar.

'Did you work as an informer for my friend?'

'*Shh*, mister!' said Mokhtar. 'Keep your voice down! Yes, I helped your friend.'

'How?'

'I took him places.'

'What sort of places?'

'Restaurants, clothes shops, a *seeber*—'

'A *seeber*? An internet café?' Karim felt a flurry of excitement. Perhaps Abdou did his real research far away from the prying eyes at the Tanger-Med prefecture.

'Which *seeber*?'

Mokhtar puffed on his pipe. 'There's only one *seeber* in the medina.' He gave in to a prolonged bout of coughing, then wiped his sleeve over his mouth. 'Those fancy new mobile phones are putting *seebers* out of business.'

Karim slid a twenty-dirham note across the table. 'Take me there.'

Fifteen minutes later they were in a dark ground-floor room off Rue d'Italie. The owner looked up from his desk by the door and Karim came straight to the point.

'A colleague of mine was here two weeks ago.'

'What of it?' the owner asked suspiciously.

Karim decided that honesty was the best policy. 'My colleague was a police detective. He's missing, presumed dead. He may have done his research here, and the information could provide a clue to what happened to him.'

'By Allah!' The owner's dismay seemed genuine. 'I remember him well. He was a decent fellow.'

'Could you show us which computer he used?'

The owner led them to a desk in the corner. There were only two men in the *seeber*, both of whom were too absorbed to pay them any notice. Karim sat in front of the screen while Mokhtar and the owner stood at his shoulder.

'What day did you bring him here?' Karim asked Mokhtar.

Mokhtar scratched the bristles on his chin. 'Let me see . . . it was raining . . .'

Karim rolled his eyes. 'He went missing on a Tuesday. Was it long before that?'

Mokhtar tried to remember. 'No . . . not long . . . He bought me a mint tea, I remember . . .'

'Think! Were the banks open?'

'I really can't remember, mister – wait – one of those crazy Rif women was on the road when we came out – yes! It was a market day. So it must have been a Thursday or a Sunday.'

'The Sunday before he went missing?'

'*Momken.* Possibly . . .'

'That was the third of March.' Karim opened the browser and clicked *Show all history.* To his chagrin the browsing history ended on the sixth of March.

'That's the day after he disappeared,' said Mokhtar, trying to be helpful.

'I know!' snapped Karim. He looked at the other man. 'What happens to the browsing history?'

'It's cleared automatically,' replied the *seeber* owner. 'It stays on the computer for twelve days then it gets erased.'

'Is there any way to retrieve it?'

'*Ma arfch.* I don't know.'

Karim stared at the screen helplessly. He wondered whether to phone the IT guy at the Fourth Precinct in Marrakech. The owner made a suggestion.

'Why don't I fetch his notebook?'

'His *notebook*?'

The owner nodded. 'He left it here, don't ask me why.'

He disappeared into a back room, returning a moment with a black pocket book. Karim could hardly contain his excitement. He ran his fingers over the black plastic cover, as if to make contact with Abdou, then placed the book in his lap where the others couldn't see it, and eagerly thumbed the pages. There were lots of scribbles in Abdou's looping handwriting, ending with a list of names:

<u>Larbi</u>
Simo
<u>Ali</u>
<u>Jibrane</u>
Mokhtar
Berrada
El Hajjem
Mansouri
<u>Ben Jelloun</u>

Karim wondered why some names were underlined. On the last page, circled three times, was a name that Karim didn't recognise. He turned to the others.

'Who is *Mustafa*?'

It was 9.45 p.m., fifteen minutes before lights out. Ayesha sat on her bed in her pyjamas, watching Salma dry her hair with a towel. There were books all over Salma's bed.

'Thank you for helping me wash up after dinner,' said Salma.

'*Makayn mushkeel.* You have an exam tomorrow. You had to study.' Ayesha picked up one of Salma's books and leafed through it. 'I hope I pass my exams.'

'Of course you will!'

'I like the practical side. But the theoretical stuff . . . law, French composition, remembering the sequence of events between going before the Public Prosecutor and attending the Tribunal de Première Instance . . . it's beyond me.'

'That's only because you missed two years in high school. You'll get the hang of it.'

'It's easy for you – you like books. You were born to study.'

'*Makayn al-hroub min al-mktoub.* There's no escaping your destiny.'

Ayesha grinned. 'That's the sort of thing that Karim would say.'

'Tell me more about Karim,' said Salma, holding out a comb. Ayesha ran the comb through Salma's fine black hair.

'He's a good detective, very persistent, although sometimes he misses things that are right in front of his nose.'

'I mean – as a person.'

Ayesha thought for a moment. 'I've known him my whole life. One of my earliest memories is of him and his friends taking me to look for coins that tourists had dropped in Souk Semmarine. We found ten dirhams. We spent it on ice cream!'

'You're very fond of him, aren't you?'

'It's true. I get on better with him than with Khadija. He's my . . . soul-mate.'

'Careful!'

Ayesha lifted the comb from her friend's hair. 'Sorry, did I catch a knot?'

'No, I meant be careful of your relationship with Karim. In ancient Egypt brothers used to marry their sisters.'

Ayesha laughed. 'No chance of that! We're forbidden by the Quran, no less – we were nursed by the same mother. Besides, Karim's my best friend, not my fiancé. You must meet him some day. You would like him.'

Salma winked. 'Are you matchmaking?'

She went off to the bathroom to brush her teeth. While she was out Ayesha quickly flipped open her suitcase and checked her phone. The message was terse.

I found A's notebook & a name: Mustafa. Have u been to see Abderrahim? I need info on Mansouri.

Ayesha was so absorbed in reading the text that she didn't notice Salma had come back to fetch the toothpaste. Salma's mouth fell open.

Ayesha tried to hide the phone behind her back. 'I can explain,' she stammered.

Salma stared in disbelief. 'You're going to get expelled!'

'Salma, listen to me. Karim is in Tangier. His life is in danger.'

'You're in danger as well – of being kicked out. You've already been given a warning!'

'Salma – what we do here – this is just training. What Karim is doing – that's the real thing. His colleague is dead.

He's dealing with violent criminals and he has no back-up. I told you about MEDIHA—'

'What does MEDIHA have to do with that Nokia being in your suitcase?'

Ayesha had never seen her room-mate so angry. 'It's not Karim's fault. I keep the phone for my mother in case of emergencies.'

'You know the rules about phones.'

'I'll be careful, I promise!'

Salma shook her head. 'That's not good enough. You have to get that thing out of this room. Hand it in, throw it away – I don't care what you do, but get it out of this room. You may be happy to jeopardise your career in the Sûreté but I'm not going to let you jeopardise mine!'

Come morning, Karim took up position in the Fuentes café. With its location on the first floor of the hotel the café was more discreet than either the Central or the Tingis and, if Karim sat by the high windows, he could keep an eye on goings-on in the square. Despite rubbishing Mokhtar's story about stalkers, it had put him on alert.

He had been up for most of the night poring over Abdou's notes. He had learned that Abdou made two trips to the clothing factory, one to the security company depot and five to Terminal 1. Abdou hadn't been inside Terminal 2 – possibly because he didn't want to alert the criminals. He did, however, visit the Export Access Zone and make copious notes on the *Autorisation de Mouvement Portuaire*, the paper that lorry drivers needed to get past the checkpoints at the terminals. There were details about trans-shipment as well as a timeline of the logistics of the Best Century Clothing company, from manufacture in Guangdong to delivery in Spain.

As he sipped his glass of *nuss-nuss* Karim went through the names on the second-to-last page. He paid particular attention to the names that Abdou had underlined – Larbi, Ali, Jibrane and Ben Jelloun. Karim had already reached the conclusion that the first three men were conspirators. Larbi had been evasive in questioning, had absented himself from the tour of the port and was furious when he saw Karim examining the CCTV footage. He also claimed the police officer talking to Abdou had gone on holiday when it was actually Ali. As for Ali, he had lied about being in the terminal before and after Abdou's disappearance. What about Jibrane? The man was a psychopath. He had shown his contempt for rules at Ceuta. The only surprising name on the list was Ben Jelloun. Karim had taken him for a decent fellow – evasive, yes, but no more so than any other port official.

One item that caught Karim's attention was a paragraph on the lighthouse at Cap Spartel. Abdou had scribbled *Twelve miles* next to the name which was perplexing; the lighthouse was eight miles west of the city and twenty-five miles from the Spanish coast. When it came to the most important clue of all, the name *Mustafa*, there was no further mention.

'*Sbaeh al-khir*, O Generous One.' Mokhtar settled in the seat opposite.

'Good morning, O Unreliable One.'

Mokhtar summoned the waiter and asked for mint tea, then took his pipe from the pocket of his gown. 'I have something to tell you.'

'About Mustafa?' Karim said with excitement.

'No.'

'Tell me what you have found out about Mustafa!'

'Well now . . .' Mokhtar sparked a match and took a long, throat-scorching pull. 'One of the waiters at the restaurant in the El Minzah is called Mustafa, there's a Mustafa at the Bureau de Change in Rue Siaghine and there's a Mustafa who runs errands in the kasbah, although he's eighty-six years old and, *yanni*, you know, soft in the head.' Mokhtar gave a little laugh, followed by a coughing fit. 'There's a Mustafa who summons the faithful at the mosque by the ferry port and a Mustafa who sells eggs in the souk—'

'That's a lot of Mustafas.'

Mokhtar shrugged. 'It's a common name.'

Karim decided that it might be more fruitful to go through a list of the names of the security staff and port workers at Tanger-Med and wondered if Simo would grant permission.

'Those men were back this morning,' said Mokhtar.

'Which men?'

'The ones looking for you.'

Karim snapped to attention. 'Did you see them?'

'No.'

'So how do you know?'

Mokhtar pointed the stem of his pipe at the hotel clerk, who was sitting at his little desk just outside the door.

'They were *here*?' exclaimed Karim.

Mokhtar gave a nod. 'An hour ago, while you were at prayers.'

'By the Seven Saints! Why didn't you tell me?'

'I tried to.'

'Did they talk to—?'

'Abdelkadir? Yes. They asked him if you were in your room.'

'And?'

'He told him that you were at the mosque and to come back later.'

'Is Abdelkadir telling the truth? Do you trust him?'

Mokhtar took the pipe from his mouth and raised his forefinger to heaven. 'In this town you can trust nothing and no one, except Allah.'

'Stop wasting time!'

'One of the men was Chinese.'

Karim practically fell off his chair. '*Chinese?* What kind of Chinese?'

'You know – Chinese.'

'Well-dressed? Shabby? Tall? Short?'

'He was wearing a suit. The fellow with him was a big, ugly looking Moroccan with a harelip. He looked like he could snap you in two.'

'My God!' Knocking over the chair in his haste, Karim dashed out of the café and up to his room. Taking off his sweat top, he attached his shoulder holster and Glock 17 handgun. He bundled all his remaining clothes, along with Abdou's black bag and possessions, into his own black holdall and marched downstairs.

'Where are you going?' said Abdelkadir, rising from his stool.

Karim threw some money on the desk.

'If anyone asks I've gone to the bus station. *Fhemtee?* Do you understand?'

Abdelkadir nodded, wilting under Karim's aggressive tone.

'*Psst!* Mister!' Mokhtar was trying to attract his attention from the café. He was half out of his seat, gesturing frantically at the window. *The men were coming!* Karim leaped down the stairs and into the alley. He ran down to Tannery House Gate, then doubled back to Port Gate and zigzagged along the back streets. He located another hotel, even seedier than the Fuentes, and took a first-floor room with a window overlooking a quiet alley.

Locking the door, he took everything from his black holdall and transferred it to Abdou's black holdall. At a glance the two bags were identical. Into his bag he stuffed a grubby blanket from the cupboard, then zipped the bag shut and left it on the bed, mussing the bedcover. He opened the window, checked that no one was around, threw out Abdou's holdall and jumped down after it.

On the way to the car park he called at Samir's shop and bought cigarettes, rice, a twelve-pack of juice drinks and three cellophane-wrapped trays of *pain au chocolat*. He dashed into a produce store and told the surprised owner to bundle some mandarins, bananas, tomatoes and onions into a carrier bag. As he got behind the wheel of the Dacia the sky was heavy with thunderheads. Two minutes later, the first raindrops hit the windscreen.

Karim followed the coast road to Tanger-Med then took the N16 through the mountains. Mimosa and date palm gave way to conifer and holm oak. As he climbed, fog made visibility poor. He had the sensation of being on the edge of two vast and watery expanses, the Atlantic and the Mediterranean, their vapour cloaking everything in a mantle of white. The fog grew thicker. Just as he was thinking his dash out of town had been a bad idea, two Africans appeared out of the mist, flagging him down. He braked so fast that the car stalled. The men came up to him warily.

'*Ca va?*' Karim rolled down the window. '*Comment vous vous-appelez?*'

'Oussuman.'

'Bouboucar.'

The men were sodden, bedraggled. Their shoes had no laces and their trousers were hanging off their waists. Seeing them eye the food on the passenger seat, he gave them each a banana and they stood in the rain holding the unpeeled bananas, waiting to see what he would do next.

'Do many cars stop?'

The two men shook their heads.

'*Les Marocains, jamais,*' said Oussuman. '*Les touristes, quelquefois.*'

'You must be hungry.'

They nodded.

'Where do you live?'

They pointed to the hillside.

'*Ecoutez* – I'm looking for a man called Joseph. He's a Congolese guy with a tattoo on his arm.'

The two men exchanged glances then Bouboucar spoke.

'*Viens.*'

'*Memnoueh.* Not allowed.' The prison guard held up a tin of tuna, then a tin of sardines. '*Memnoueh . . . memnoueh . . . memnoueh . . .*'

One by one, the apples, olives, long-life milk, soft cheese, sugar, fresh mint and black tea that Ayesha had bought with her precious dirhams on were removed from the X-ray belt. In the end all she was allowed to bring in were a pillow and a towel. She made a note of the guard's name and badge number. Next time she would come with a letter from the Institut Royal de Police and shove it down his fat throat.

She was the only person in the visiting room, apart from another prison guard. Abderrahim sat down on the battered chair, dressed in a clean white *galabiyya* robe.

'Two visits in three days. I'm honoured.'

'*Kulchee bekhir?*'

'All is well, thanks to God. I read the Quran and I invoke our Prophet, may God's grace be upon him.'

'I brought you a pillow and a towel.'

'So I see.'

'The guards confiscated the food I brought.'

'You have to bring *baksheesh.* But I don't approve of *baksheesh.*'

'I understand,' said Ayesha, although she didn't understand at all.

'And you. You are well?'

'*Al-hamdulillah.*'

'Why do you want to be a police officer?'

Ayesha had rehearsed her answer. 'There is injustice in our country. Innocent people like you, who have done nothing wrong, get locked up.'

'That's because the police are corrupt.'

'There are good and bad police just as there are good and bad people in every walk of life. As a police officer I will be able to make things better. That's a desirable aim, surely?'

Abderrahim gave the faintest of nods.

'How are your lessons going?' Ayesha continued. 'Mother told me that you are learning to carve stucco.'

'Idle hands make an idle mind.'

'They say there is a lot of work for stucco-carvers in Marrakech. Rich foreigners are renovating riads and need the old skills.'

'I have no desire to work for those people.'

'Because they're infidels?'

Abderrahim gave a thin smile. 'No, because I wish to be a school teacher.'

'You will be a good teacher, I am sure.'

'*Inshallah.*'

She swallowed hard. 'I need your help.'

'You need *my* help? Shouldn't you be helping *me*? You said you could make things better. You should be helping to get me out of here.'

'When I have passed my exams I will do my utmost to get you released, by God's grace. But right now, there is a man who may have been in prison here.'

Abderrahim stiffened. His face took on a hostile expression.

'Let me continue,' Ayesha said quickly. 'I am a Talal, the same as you. The same blood flows through our veins. You can choose to help me or not. I am not here to bargain my charity for yours. I will be a good sister and come regularly, regardless of what you do or say, but I need some information.'

Abderrahim gave a grudging nod. 'Who is the man?'

'He goes by the name of Mohammed Mansouri. He comes from the Rif mountains.'

'So he is Amazigh, like us.'

'I believe so, although I know very little about my background. Mother never speaks of it.'

'We come from a proud Amazigh family.'

Ayesha seized the chance to learn more about her roots. 'Brahim Belkacem said that I was born in the Zat Valley. Is that true?'

'Yes.'

'Did you live there? As a boy?'

Abderrahim's face softened. 'It is a beautiful place, thanks to God's blessing. We had a smallholding in the mountains near Amassine. I would take Amina with me to look after the goats and we would climb trees, hunt for hawkmoths or make necklaces out of wild flowers. There was no heating in the house and no glass in the windows, but we were happy.'

'Karim and I used to climb the trees in Bab Taghzout.'

Abderrahim grimaced and Ayesha realised it was the wrong thing to say. She returned to the subject of her enquiry.

'Mohammed Mansouri runs a security company in Tangier. *Mansouri* may not be his birth name. He may have changed it when he came out of prison.'

'This information,' Abderrahim said, narrowing his eyes. 'It's not for Karim?'

'Brother of mine, listen. We have lost our sister and our father. Our mother is a frail woman who may not survive to welcome you home. We are all that is left of our proud family. Does that not count for anything?'

'Answer me. This information is not for Karim?'

'Why should it be for Karim? He's in Marrakech! Salma – my room-mate – her father runs an IT business in Tangier that deals with sensitive data. He wants to hire Mansouri to handle security, but he has heard rumours about his past – that Mansouri may have been a criminal.'

Abderrahim's dark eyes bored into Ayesha's. They both sat at the table staring at each other without speaking. Finally, Ayesha broke the silence.

'I have a class in thirty minutes. I will be back on Sunday. *T'halla frasek.* Take good care of yourself.'

Abderrahim got to his feet. 'God takes care of me.'

Despite the umbrella that he valiantly held over Bouboucar, Oussuman and himself as they trudged through the wet undergrowth, Karim's trousers and shoes were soon drenched. The men told him they were from Cameroon and had been at *La Bataille* on Sunday night.

'*Ils nous ont frappé aux mains, aux bras, aux jambes, à la poitrine, à la tête.*' They spoke in a matter-of-fact voice, as if they were running through a shopping list. 'They beat us on our hands, our arms, our legs, our chests and our heads.'

Karim saw smoke drifting through pine trees and more black faces appeared. Bouboucar spoke to another man in dialect. Several men came to stare, passing comments when they saw Karim's bags of food. When he was in the middle of the camp Karim addressed them in a loud voice so that every-one could hear.

'I'm looking for Joseph! *Où est Joseph?*'

A figure stepped from under a plastic roof. Joseph recognised Karim at once and the two men embraced. Tears streamed down Karim's cheeks while Joseph smiled awkwardly, unsure what the fuss was about. Karim, Joseph and Jean-François sat by the fire while Louis and Franco sorted through the contents of the shopping bags.

'How did you find me?' Joseph asked.

'I saw you at Ceuta. I guessed that you were hiding out in the mountains.'

'You were at *La Bataille?*'

'Yes.'

To Karim's relief, Joseph didn't ask what he was doing there. He had no idea that it was Karim who had stopped him getting over the wall.

'Were you badly hurt?'

'*Ça va.* Others had it worse.'

Amadou unwrapped a length of bandage to reveal deep red gashes on his hands. Another man was in crutches, his leg broken.

'We buried a man from Senegal yesterday,' said Jean-François. 'He died from internal wounds.'

Karim was filled with horror. 'Is there nowhere you can get treatment?'

'The clinic in Fnideq.'

'Is Fnideq close?'

'A two-hour walk. We buy our food there.'

'I have a car. Let me drive down and buy more supplies.'

Joseph put a restraining arm on his shoulder. 'Stay. Have a meal with us. We will make dinner – *tu vas voir.*'

Karim watched Franco prepare a meal from the ingredients he had brought.

'Where have you all come from?'

'*Partout*,' replied Franco. 'Everywhere.'

Karim gazed at the men, noting the difference in their features. They all dressed the same, in bedraggled puffa jackets, apart from Louis, who sported a blouson and a yellow beret.

The men started recounting tales of hardship on the road to Tangier.

'The Algerian border was the worst,' said a man with welts on his cheeks and forehead. 'I got there with my friend late in the evening . . . the guards were drinking . . . we gave them money to let us through but they saw my friend's watch and asked him to hand it over. I could see they were bad men, but my friend refused. They said they would cut his wrist off but he still refused. So they bent him over and forced the barrel of a rifle up, you know, his . . . He died of fever a week later. I buried him in Tamanrasset and made a cross with his name on it . . . I sent a photo to his family.'

A respectful silence followed. Then Louis piped up, declaring in impeccable French that the hardest thing had been leaving behind his leopard print waistcoat. Everyone roared with laughter.

'What about you, Joseph?' Karim said softly. 'Where are you from?'

'Kisangani.'

'It's in the Republic of the Congo, *c'est vrai*?'

The other men laughed.

'What's so funny?'

'I come from the *Democratic* Republic of the Congo,' Joseph explained. 'They are two different countries.'

'Yes. We don't want our guest thinking you come from a smart city like Brazzaville,' quipped Louis.

By now the stew was ready. Franco served the food in plastic bowls and gave Karim the only utensil, a battered pewter spoon.

'*Bismillah*,' said Karim. 'By God's grace.'

They ate around the fire, sixteen men in a circle in a darkening forest.

'Tell me about growing up in your country, Joseph.'

'It was hard. In DRC they don't ask you what you want to *be* when you grow up. They ask you where you want to *go*.' His answer was cut short by loud murmurs of agreement.

'And that's Europe? But how will you get there? Not the wall, surely?'

'*La mer*,' said Jean-François. 'On the sea, we have a chance, *une possibilité*.'

An argument broke out about the merits of the wall versus the sea.

'Is the sea risky?' asked Karim.

There was a chorus of voices, lurid accounts of swindles by *passeurs* and tragic accidents. Franco shouted to make himself heard.

'I tried *la mer*. Two men died, including my brother.'

'Yet you still want to try?' asked Karim, offering his cigarettes around.

'It is better than staying in our country,' said Franco.

'There's no work, nothing,' added Joseph.

Karim told them about his cousin Majid, who had left Marrakech to find work as a waiter in France. The men were curious to know more but Karim struck a cautious note.

'He says that life in the *banlieues* is hard. There is racism, and unemployment.'

'That is true,' replied Jean-François. 'We are not stupid. But now that we've left home to go to Europe we can't return and face our families.'

'At least they would have you safe and alive!'

'You don't understand. *C'est la honte.* It's the shame.'

When the night grew cold Karim rose stiffly to his feet and thanked the men for their hospitality.

'Next time I will bring more supplies. Is there anything you need?'

'Couscous!' cried one.

'Meat!' said another.

'Soap!' said Louis.

'Bring what you can,' smiled Jean-François. 'But most of all, bring yourself.'

Chapter 9

There was only one place in Tangier which Karim thought was safe.

It was almost midnight when he knocked on the door of the Widow Khoury. As far as he could tell, nobody had followed him there. Only Mokhtar knew the address. And, after days wondering if he was one of Mansouri's spies, seeing Mokhtar's name in Abdou's list of honest men was reassuring.

Abdou had put Simo's name on the same list. Perhaps what Karim had perceived as lack of cooperation was simply a lack of manpower. As for the abortive raid on the clothing factory, Jibrane, Simo's second-in-command, was surely behind the tip-off. Everything about Jibrane smelled bad. Karim decided to call Simo tomorrow to apologise for losing his temper and ask about the mysterious Mustafa.

Lalla Khoury stood in the doorway in a green dressing room. 'I'm sorry, *a lalla*,' said Karim. 'It's late, but I need your gown.'

Without a word she led him to the bedroom overlooking the courtyard. He put his bag down, threw himself on the bed and fell into a dreamless sleep.

He was woken by a phone call from Mokhtar.

'Meet me at Café Hafa.'

'Where's that?' Karim rubbed the sleep from his eyes.

'Head for the Phoenician Tombs and ask.'

Karim looked out of the window, at the sunshine and flowers in the courtyard, then padded over to a mirror on the wall. His moustache was growing bushy and his chin needed a shave. Out in the hallway he opened a few doors until he found the shower.

'Will you be back tonight?' The widow was holding a kitten in one hand and a bar of soap in the other.

'God willing.'

She was a good woman, Karim decided. A bit crazy, but honest. As he strode down the alley, feeling clean and refreshed, he thought about Joseph and the other men on the cold mountainside. He felt ashamed that he hadn't told Joseph what had happened at the wall. He would go back to Casiago tomorrow, he decided. Today he had his hands full.

It was quicker to walk to Marshan than to go all the way down to the car park and drive up the hill. A street cleaner gave him directions to Café Hafa. The café consisted of a series of open-air terraces tumbling down the hillside, each lined with a row of concrete tables, all empty.

'*Salaam ou-alikum.*' Mokhtar was tucked in a tree-covered alcove and Karim didn't notice him at first.

'*Ou-alikum salaam.* This is a good hiding place.'

Karim slid his knees under the table, so that both men faced the sea. A man appeared dangling glasses of mint tea in a wire bottle carrier.

'Do you have coffee?' Karim looked at him hopefully. '*Nuss-nuss?*'

The waiter shook his head.

'Nothing, then.'

Karim stared at the grey ocean stretching away to the horizon. Fishing boats chugged along the coast. Further out to sea were colossal ships stacked with containers like ziggurats. Karim was reminded that he still hadn't heard from Noureddine about the ship in Terminal 2 at the time of Abdou's disappearance. He gazed at Mokhtar who was puffing his *sebsi*, his body draped over the hard seat as if it was the most comfortable armchair in Tangier.

'Tell me what you have discovered.'

'I have found more Mustafas. A Mustafa Oualoulou who owns a carpet shop in the medina, a Mustafa Chaabi who lives in a house near Bab Bhar, a Mustafa who shines shoes—'

'*Safee!* Anything else?'

'I was walking past Chez Kebe yesterday after you left the hotel. The woman hailed me. Nice woman, long braids, always smiling.' Mokhtar lit his pipe again. 'So what did old Mokhtar do next?'

'I don't know. What did old Mokhtar do next?'

'I had lunch in the café.'

'Is that all you dragged me here to tell me?'

'Of course not,' said Mokhtar, languidly exhaling a cloud of smoke. 'The men came in.'

'Which men?'

'The Chinaman and the Moroccan – the brute with the harelip. They came into the café and started interrogating everyone. They asked the blacks where they were from, where they lived in Tangier – trying to intimidate them. They showed a photo and asked if anyone had seen you. Everyone shook their heads apart from the woman, who said you'd eaten there a few days ago. I told them you'd left town. They know that you're not at the Fuentes or at that other place, the hostel where you left your bag. Are you staying with the Widow Khoury?'

'Yes,' Karim admitted, alarmed at Mokhtar's knowledge.

'You should move again. Nowhere is safe.'

Karim saw an incoming call on his screen. It was Noureddine. He rose to his feet to take the call.

'The ship in Terminal 2 was the *Emma Maersk*,' Noureddine told him. 'We've done a thorough search and can't find anything suspicious. It came from Singapore and was en route to Savannah, USA. We checked its cargo, its previous journeys . . . nothing. No links with China. The ship was last at Tanger-Med eight months ago and it isn't scheduled to return. What's happening at your end?'

'I found Abdou's notebook.'

'Praise God! That's the first good news we've had.'

Karim told Noureddine about the contents, and the list of suspects. 'The final entry is the name *Mustafa*.'

'Any idea who he is?'

'Unfortunately there are dozens of Mustafas with whom Abdou might have come into contact. He jotted the name down while he was in a *seeber*. I'm going to ask Simo if I can search the employee rolls at the port.'

'Good. What else?'

'Abdou mentions the lighthouse at Cap Spartel. I'm not sure why. He also made notes about a company in the Free Zone which has a factory in Spain.'

'Do you think Abdou took the ferry to Spain?'

'It is something we should consider. One more thing: I'm being followed. A Chinese man and a Moroccan.'

'That doesn't sound good – not good at all. What were you planning to do today?'

'Drive to Cap Spartel.'

Noureddine dissuaded him. 'From what I remember, the lighthouse is remote. It's not a good place to be caught alone. See what else you can find out about Mustafa and call me tonight. Oh, and Karim?'

'Yes?'

'We think there's a trace on your mobile. Find another way to stay in contact.'

ي

Karim walked down to the car park and found a payphone from which to call Simo.

'Listen, my brother – I'm sorry I lost my temper when we last spoke.'

'You are forgiven.'

'Do you know a man by the name of Mustafa?'

'Mustafa who?'

'I don't know. I think that Abdou may have met someone called Mustafa just before he disappeared.'

'How do you know?'

Karim was going to mention the notebook but at the last minute he held back.

'An informant told me. I thought I could come into the prefecture and check the payrolls for police, security service and Tanger-Med Port Authority.'

'No. I'll get a colleague on to it. Don't do anything without my say so, do you understand?'

Karim put the phone down with annoyance. He resented having his wings clipped twice within one hour. He was standing in an esplanade of shops and noticed a ticket office for the ferry company.

'How much is a day return to Tarifa?' he asked, wandering in.

'One hundred and fifty dirhams,' replied a slim girl in a red uniform. 'There's a ferry leaving in twenty-five minutes.'

'Is it nice in Tarifa?'

'I don't know,' the girl laughed. 'I've never been there. Are you a tourist?'

'I'm from Marrakech.'

'I've never been to Marrakech, either – they say it's very beautiful.'

'You should go some day.'

'I have no one to take me,' she said coquettishly.

'All you have to do is step on the train, *lalla*,' Karim grinned.

'But who would show me around when I get there?'

'Oh, you could manage! There's a bus tour, just like the one here in Tangier.'

The girl glanced at the clock on the wall. 'If you want to catch the ferry you'd better hurry.'

Karim ran across the boulevard and joined some burly Moroccan women in a queue of foot passengers. He turned around and made a quick sweep of the area but, to his relief, there was no sign of his pursuers. As he turned back he almost jumped out of his skin: there was a Chinese man three feet from where he was standing!

False alarm: the man was a tourist. Karim heard him address a middle-aged woman in Mandarin and breathed a sigh of relief. The couple were part of a tour group. It seemed to Karim that the Chinese were everywhere in the Maghreb these days. He had noticed that the gantry cranes in Tanger-Med were made by a Chinese company and Simo had said that fifty per cent of container traffic came from China. There was a Mr Zhang in the Free Zone and now there was a Chinese man on his tail. Chinese people would have been a rare sight in Tangier forty years ago, he reflected, before the advent of mass tourism and the Line of Zero Deviation. The most exotic sights in Tangier would have been cargoes of fruit bound for Europe, or trains bringing coal and timber south to Casablanca. Now the freight had all moved east and the old port was quiet, apart from ferries like the *Ibn Battouta* in front of him.

Fifteen minutes later, the *Ibn Battouta* slipped its hawsers, sailed past a breakwater and headed out into the Strait of Gibraltar. It was only then that Karim remembered that he didn't have a passport.

It had been a busy two days at police college. Ayesha behaved like a model cadet. She attended lessons punctually, got good marks in her judo class and completed a night exercise with Salma and the others. Salma, after the stress of her law exam, had forgiven Ayesha and the phone wasn't mentioned again. On Tuesday evening, after dinner, Ayesha had crept into the library with the Nokia and a roll of duct tape. Shoving a desk against the door, she went to the *Shorthand and Typing* section and taped the phone to the back of the shelf. She stepped back: the phone couldn't be seen from any angle, even if the books were removed from the shelf.

Hakimi had left her alone, presumably because, as Salma suggested, he feared expulsion even more than she did. On Wednesday Ayesha went to see Colonel Choukri. She apologised for fighting in class and explained that the incident had come about because her brother was in prison. The colonel was sympathetic although he refused to retract the official warning. But he did grant a pass so she could visit Abderrahim, and later on that day Ayesha returned to Kenitra prison.

Once again, she was the only visitor and the prison guard took great delight in confiscating her food.

'I told you, food is *memnoueh*.'

'The only thing that is *memnoueh* is your behaviour,' retorted Ayesha. 'Put everything back in my bag and don't you dare give me a body search.'

'And why should I do that?' the guard leered, looking around to check that they were alone.

Ayesha produced the authorisation from Colonel Choukri and the guard backed away like a scolded dog. Another guard took her to the visiting room where she waited until her brother appeared.

'I brought you food. Also two woollen vests to keep you warm.'

'May God bestow his blessings upon you,' said Abderrahim. He was wearing a brown *jellaba* and his long beard was trimmed.

'How do you manage to take such care of your appearance?' Ayesha asked.

'Allah loves those who keep themselves clean and pure.'

He's worse than Karim with his proverbs, thought Ayesha. Her sister Amina, whom she never knew, sounded a lot more fun.

'Tell me,' said Abderrahim, folding his hands in his lap, 'did the Belkacems treat you well?'

'Yes. Lalla Fatima and Si Brahim loved me the same way they loved their three children. Si Brahim died four years ago.'

Abderrahim was unmoved. 'I never saw him at the mosque.'

'That's because he refused to worship at the same mosque as our father after they had their quarrel.'

'Did Brahim say his prayers?'

'Of course. He studied the prayer book of Sidi ben Slimane al Jazouli.'

This reference to a Sufi saint did not meet with Abderrahim's approval.

'A *Sufi*? Ever since the King put a Sufi in charge of Islamic Affairs this country has gone to the dogs!'

Ayesha changed the subject. 'Are you eating well?'

'The cook is a brother. He gives me extra rations.'

'*Meziane*, good.'

'So you want to know about Mohamed Mansouri?'

Ayesha sat up attentively.

'He was in Kenitra. He had a cell to himself – a special cell with a comfortable bed and a television. His name, before he changed it, was Yusuf Ben Yahmed. He was a hard man.'

'Why do you say that?'

'He lived in a remote village when he was young. He had four wives by the age of twenty-five. One was a girl from Al-Hoceima – a pretty girl of sixteen, with tattoos on her chin and forehead. One day, he was hunting with his rifle in the high country above the village. On the way home, he looked down on his house and saw the girl standing in the doorway. He decided to teach her a lesson for flaunting herself so publicly. He picked up his rifle, looked through the sight and – *bam.*' Abderrahim pressed his index finger between his eyes.

Ayesha stared in horror. 'He *shot* her?'

'He said that a woman who came out of her house like that could only be a whore.'

'Is the story true?'

Abderrahim upturned his palms with a shrug. 'That's what I've heard.'

Ayesha recoiled. 'That's horrific! I thought that kind of behaviour disappeared with the sultans!'

'There are still pockets where it survives.'

'Is that why Mansouri was thrown in prison? For shooting his wife?'

'No. His imprisonment happened years later. He was a hashish smuggler, one of the biggest in the Rif. He bought second-hand jet skis in Saïdia and strapped hashish to the sides. He hired African migrants and told them that if they made it across on the jet skis they were free to go. But one African was caught by the Spanish and confessed. Mansouri was sent here, along with the African. One day the African was found lying on the kitchen floor with his head crushed under a heavy oven. Yahmed – Mansouri – was released soon after. People say he has powerful friends. So – do you think he will hire Mansouri?'

'Who?'

'The father of your room-mate.'

'Oh, probably not,' said Ayesha, still shocked by what she had heard. 'Mansouri sounds like a monster. Don't you think?'

Abderrahim stood up, gathered his packages and shrugged. 'Sometimes women step out of line.'

It was the first time Karim had ever left Morocco. Despite lacking a passport, he couldn't help feeling a thrill as he watched the coast of his homeland recede. To the east, the cranes of Tanger-Med appeared from behind the Malabata lighthouse. To the west, where the Mediterranean opened out into the Atlantic, he could see another lighthouse: Cap Spartel, a lone sentinel on the tip of Africa.

Finding it cold on deck Karim made his way inside. As he was descending the stairs he saw a small queue of people under a sign that read *Spanish immigration*. When he was at the front of the queue he showed his police badge.

'I'm investigating a missing persons case.'

'I'm sorry, lieutenant,' the Spanish official replied. 'I need a passport or Interpol accreditation, or you cannot enter Spain.'

'*Makayn mushkeel,*' Karim replied cheerfully. 'When we arrive at Tarifa I'll simply stay on the boat and come back.'

He bought a coffee and sat at the back of the cabin. The rock of Gibraltar loomed through the window, a sign that they were already halfway across the Strait. The gantry cranes of Tanger-Med had shrunk to the size of wax matchsticks.

Karim had brought Abdou's notebook with him and settled down to read. Abdou had known about the competition between migrant smugglers. He had written down details of two suspicious deaths in Tangier, along with statistics about clandestine migration into Spain. Ever since Karim had spotted the sub-Saharans at Best Century Clothing he had wondered about the connection between African migrants and Chinese organised crime. The people smugglers were another possible link in the chain.

Before he knew it, the *Ibn Battouta* slowed and Karim went back on deck, eager for his first impressions of Spain. The houses had pitched roofs and were spaced apart, unlike Moroccan homes. Everything seemed greener and lusher, with alder trees, Aleppo pine and fields of waving barley. A solitary windsurfer was struggling to keep upright in the wind. The ferry sailed into Tarifa harbour past a statue of Jesus Christ, his hand raised in benediction above a row of anti-landing spikes and security lamps.

Karim felt a tiny rush of hope: was it possible that Abdou had made this trip? Could he be nearing the end of his search?

The cheap suitcases of the Moroccan women were no match for the ridged disembarkation ramps. They bounced up and down, one suitcase losing a wheel in the process. Karim waited until all the foot passengers had gone and the last tourist had taken a selfie, then walked up to the border post of the Policía Nacional Fronteras.

'Are you here on official business?' the policeman grunted, scrutinising Karim's ID with none of the camaraderie Karim might have expected from a fellow cop. 'If so, you are transgressing international protocol. If you're off duty, then you need a passport. Either way, we cannot let you in.'

Karim explained that he had taken the ferry in search of a missing colleague and that, if it were possible to talk to someone from the border force on an informal basis, he would be very grateful. With an impatient gesture, the officer told him to wait in the arrivals hall.

From the window Karim could see lorries, cars and motor-bikes trundling off the ferry. There were fishing boats in the harbour, although the fleet seemed smaller than the one in Tangier. To his right he spotted the ramparts of a castle. Apart from surveillance cameras, the setting was quiet, even sleepy.

'*Salaam ou-alikum! Buenos días!*'

A large man, his shirt buttons straining at his belly, strode over and addressed Karim in English. 'Raoul Gómez, at your service.' He shook Karim's hand. 'I'm with the Servicio Marítimo, the coast guard. They couldn't find anyone else to talk to you. Coffee?'

Karim was glad that he had spent the last year improving his English at night school. He followed Raoul to a coffee machine and then into an interview room. Raoul shut the door.

'What do you want to know, exactly?'

Karim explained that he was part of Operation MEDIHA and that he was looking into the disappearance of his deputy two weeks ago.

'He went missing while looking for illegal shipments at Tanger-Med.'

Raoul examined the photo that Karim had brought. 'And you think he may have come to Spain?'

'Perhaps.'

'Have you checked with immigration?'

'As far as I know, my colleague didn't have a passport.'

'In that case it's almost impossible.'

'Could he have come across secretly?'

'How do you mean?'

'If he was in a container – trapped inside?'

Raoul gave a smile. 'There are seventy thousand ferry crossings a year between Spain and Morocco. And almost as many crossings by container ships. So yes, of course, it is possible. Would you like another coffee? In fact – let's go to upstairs. It's more comfortable, and the coffee is better!'

The two men climbed to a large open-plan control room resembling the bridge of a ship. Underneath a panoramic window overlooking the harbour was an array of radar and GPS screens. A VHF intercom crackled with voices in English and Spanish. A man with a white shirt and epaulettes, whom Raoul introduced as Jorge, waved from a corner. Raoul went over to a small kitchen area and Karim watched as he put coffee into an espresso machine.

'What's your experience of counterfeit medicines? Are they a problem?'

'Not as far as I know. The drugs we have most trouble with are cocaine and hashish.'

'How do they come into Spain?'

'In fishing boats, speedboats and light aircraft. And containers, *naturalmente*. Most go via Algeciras.'

'Because the volume of traffic makes it easier to escape detection?'

'Yes.'

A call came through on a walkie-talkie. While Raoul was occupied Karim looked around the room. Ranged along the back of the room was a line of cubby holes containing folded maritime warning flags. Two men were sitting at a desk poring over a chart. Karim picked up a pair of binoculars and examined the underside. They were a cheap make but they had a powerful, 10x50 magnification. He took a look through the eyepieces.

'Looking for dolphins?'

'No.' Karim put the binoculars down with a laugh. 'I had a pair of Nikons but they were crushed by a shipping container. I was just trying yours out for size.'

'Keep them,' said Raoul. 'They're Chinese. We have at least a dozen pairs.'

Karim thanked him. 'Am I keeping you from your work?'

'Not at all! We can carry on talking as long as you don't mind following me around. We're not as busy as we used to be, not since Tanger-Med–Algeciras opened, but there still don't seem to be enough hours in the day!'

Karim watched him take a reading from a digital tides map.

'What about illegal migrants? They must be a headache for you.'

Raoul tucked his belly into his belt. '*El problem de los migrantes*... when I started this job in 2001 we caught fifteen hundred migrants a year. Ten years later the numbers had quadrupled. The Red Cross were overwhelmed.'

'The Red Cross?'

'They meet the rescue boats and give the people first aid, blankets and clothes. The worst cases are taken to hospital.'

'Where do they come from?'

'Hard to say. A few from Iraq, Syria and Afghanistan ... the vast majority come from sub-Saharan Africa but we don't know their countries of origin.'

Karim looked puzzled.

'They destroy their passports and documents,' Raoul

explained. 'There's a law in Spain that says you can't be deported if there is no proof of your country of origin.'

'So you're catching thousands of undocumented migrants?'

'That's the strange thing. For the last six months we haven't seen a single one.'

Raoul called to his colleague. '*¿Cuántos migrantes hemos visto desde julio?*'

'*Nueve.*'

'Nine migrants since July.' He called to Jorge again. '*¿Desde agosto?*'

'*Ninguno.*'

'Not one migrant since August. Not a single dinghy. Our electronic warning system has hardly been activated. The Salvamento Marítimo – the search and rescue teams – have been sitting on their hands.'

Karim was astonished. 'But we have thousands of migrants in Tangier – all desperate to get to Spain!'

Raoul grinned. 'Well, I guess that proves the success of our cross-border cooperation pact!'

'Raoul – I have one more question . . .'

'*Díga-me.*'

'There is a strong possibility that my friend drowned at sea. Can you check if any bodies have been washed up on Spanish shores in recent weeks?'

Raoul was touched. 'I tell you what, *amigo* – stay a while longer. There's a ferry that leaves at seven o'clock. I'll fetch some sandwiches and put out a request for information. I don't think we've had any bodies, but it's best to make sure.'

A strong easterly wind was blowing when Karim said goodbye to Raoul and boarded the ferry back to Tangier. Although disappointed that Abdou had never made it to Spain he was relieved that no bodies matching his description had washed up on the beaches. He felt a post-caffeine slump coming on and sat on the starboard deck, hoping the wind and spray would kickstart his brain. Two Spanish girls came up to him, the map in their hands flapping in the breeze. They told Karim that they were looking for Chaouen but couldn't find it on the map.

'That's because its full name is Chefchaouen,' said Karim, pointing to the town.

The girls smiled gratefully. 'Do you have any advice for us about travelling in *Marruecos*?'

'The best advice is to tell any man who bothers you *seer fehalek*, which means *go away*.'

One of the girls handed Karim her mobile phone and asked if he could take a photo of them with the coastline of *Marruecos* in the background.

'*Naturalmente*,' he replied, using the one word of Spanish he had learned that day.

He lined up the photo, making sure he had the white cubes of Tangier medina in the background . . . *By Allah!* His heart almost stopped. Moving slowly from left to right behind the girls' heads was the name *Mustafa*. It was painted in large white letters on a container ship sailing towards the mouth of the Mediterranean, flying the flag of Liberia, with four onboard cranes and around eight thousand containers on board.

Ayesha went to the library after dinner. She switched on the lights, sat at a computer and entered the name *Yusuf Ben Yahmed* into a browser. A news article popped up.

Drug baron sentenced to eight years

Rabat – a drug baron has been imprisoned after a month-long trial that exposed corruption in the state security services and a network of powerful interests in Morocco's marijuana-growing region.

Yusuf Ben Yahmed was sentenced to eight years in prison, with the court ordering 9,600,000 dirhams to be confiscated and imposing a fine of 500,000 dirhams.

Officers from the judicial police seized Ben Yahmed in October 2006 at the Al Ghouroub Café outside Tangier, acting on a warrant issued after a previous drugs trial.

Ben Yahmed implicated 34 members of the security services including Abdelaziz Alami, head of the Tangier judicial police from 1996 to 2003, who was sacked as head of security at Morocco's royal palaces. Alami was imprisoned for 18 months and had 700,000 dirhams seized. Two further individuals were jailed, including Ben Yahmed's brother, while nine were acquitted, including another top Tangier police official.

According to government sources, the criminals were found guilty of offences including international drug trafficking, abuse of power, incitement to illegal immigration and failing to report crimes.

The Rif region is still the world's biggest hashish producer. Traffickers hide the drug in shipping containers or use powerful speedboats and jet skis to carry it to Malaga, Barcelona or Marseille.

Ayesha stared at the screen for a long time. This was what Karim was after! It gave him a springboard to start investigating the links between Mansouri and the police. She went over to the *Shorthand and Typing* section and reached behind the shelf. To her surprise, she couldn't feel the outline of the phone. Maybe she hadn't reached far enough. She peered into the gap then rolled up her sleeve and tried again. Nothing. In a panic she pulled the books out and ran her hands along the back of the bookcase. The phone could have fallen, she told herself. She looked underneath the bottom shelf. Next she attempted to pull the wooden bookcase away from the wall but it was too heavy. She swept all the books onto the floor then placed her shoulder against the side. Using all her strength she managed to slide the bookcase forward by two inches. Almost unable to look, adrenalin coursing through her system, she kneeled on the floor. Lying in the dust and dead flies was the curled-up strip of duct tape. There was no sign of the phone.

'Let me through! *Policia!* Police!'

The passengers clogging the stairwells of the ferry stared at Karim but didn't move. Directly in front of him a tourist was blithely adjusting the hour on his watch. Karim shouted in Arabic at a female crew member but she held up her hands to signal that there was nothing she could do. Balancing on the balls of his feet, Karim waited until the ship had docked then fought his way through the passengers onto the car deck, nearly colliding with a woman opening a car door. He sprinted through the terminal building, flashing his *carte nationale*.

Outside, night was falling. Karim ran along the busy boulevard, jumped the low rope of the car park and got behind the wheel of the Dacia.

Within two minutes he was on the Merkala road, heading west. He stared out into the darkening Strait, anxiously checking for the ship's lights. He left the seafront and followed the road inland, up the Old Mountain, past the walled estates and into the Perdicaris forest. After fifteen minutes he swerved right along a woodland track. He nearly hit a wild boar, frozen in the glare from the headlamps.

There was one thought in his head: was Abdou waiting for the *Mustafa* on the night he disappeared?

Just as he was coming out of the forest, the engine spluttered and died. He realised that had forgotten to fill the tank. Before him was a grassy promontory overlooking the sea. To his left was the silhouette of Cap Spartel – the last lighthouse on the African mainland.

Grabbing his binoculars he hurtled down the hill, slithering on loose stones, keeping an eye on the *Mustafa* slowly sailing across the moonlit sea. The lighthouse was surrounded by palm trees, its square tower white against the dark sky. Parked nearby was a solitary car. Could there be a lighthouse keeper? Karim crept along the wall of the lighthouse and lifted his binoculars. *There it was*: a mid-sized ship with four cranes and the name *Mustafa* on the stern. The ship was moving so slowly, and the sea was so wide, that it was impossible to determine its direction.

In the foreground a silhouette merged with the dark foliage. Karim held his breath. A terrifying realisation. There was another man below him! Good God, he was also looking through binoculars! Karim gave an involuntary start and the man turned around: *Simo!*

When Karim thought about it afterwards, Simo didn't register the slightest surprise at seeing him. It was as if the police chief considered Karim's presence at a lonely lighthouse on the north-westernmost point of Africa the most natural thing in the world.

'Ah, Karim,' he said, walking up towards him. 'A chance meeting is worth a thousand appointments, as they say!'

Karim was paralysed with fear. Right now, there was an extremely high chance that Simo would put a bullet in his brain or dash his head on the wall. The police chief was a big man, four inches taller than Karim. And Karim had left his gun in the Dacia.

'Fascinating, isn't it?' Simo said, facing the sea. 'This is the point where the Mediterranean and the Atlantic meet. There's a sign on the road if you look for it.'

Karim remined silent, his eyes locked on Simo.

'The harbour master saw the ship arrive at Tanger-Med,' Simo continued. 'I tried to call you but you didn't pick up. Where were you?'

'Tarifa.'

'Ah, that explains it.' Simo looked through his binoculars again. 'There's nothing we can do now. The *Mustafa* will be outside territorial waters.'

'What?'

'It's twelve miles away – outside Moroccan jurisdiction. Don't worry, we'll find out its course and other details tomorrow. Where's your car?'

Karim faltered. 'It ran out of petrol.'

'You're in luck, my friend! I carry a spare can. You'll be asleep in an hour, *inshallah*, ready to make a fresh start in the morning!'

In fact, it was well after one o'clock when Karim finally got back to the Widow Khoury's house. Lying in bed with some food he had picked up at a late-night *hanout*, Karim checked his phone for calls. Then he stared at the ceiling for half an hour and came to the conclusion that Simo was a member of the criminal cartel.

Chapter 10

'The Petit Socco is restless.' Mokhtar gave a hacking cough. 'It's the east wind. It makes everyone out of sorts.'

They were sitting in the alcove at Café Hafa. Mokhtar was drinking mint tea with a sprig of wormwood and smoking his pipe. A seagull glided, almost stationary in the headwind, before wheeling away towards the shoreline. Below, there were white crests on the waves. Karim had slept poorly. If Simo was corrupt, then he had got Abdou's names the wrong way round and the unmarked names were the men that Abdou distrusted. Abdou was a shrewder judge of character than he was, rarely wrong about liars or criminals. But Mokhtar's name was on the same list as Simo. Therefore Mokhtar couldn't be trusted. And if Mokhtar couldn't be trusted, what was he, Karim, doing sitting there with him?

'What's the matter, mister? You seem lost for words.'

'That cough sounds like it's gone to your chest.'

'It's damp where I live, mister. You should see the place!' He blew a puff of smoke and watched it waft away. 'I can tell you're jittery. Your mind is elsewhere. Or maybe it's the east wind. When the east wind is blowing I don't feel like eating food or going with a woman.'

Despite his suspicions, Karim couldn't suppress a smile at the thought of Mokhtar having sex.

'What's so funny?' croaked Mokhtar. 'Ask your friend the chief of police. He'll tell you that most crimes occur when the *chergui* is blowing.'

Karim was much more interested to know why Simo didn't kill him while he had the chance.

'Is that so?'

'Yes! The police have closed Chez Kebe and rounded up the *Afaraqa*. Maybe it's because of the gangster who was shot.'

'Any sign of the men following me?'

Fortunately, Mokhtar hadn't seen them. 'Not for two days now. I'd know the Moroccan bastard a mile off, he's over two metres tall. It gives me the creeps just thinking about him. Have you found out about Mustafa?'

Karim refused to say.

'Hey mister! You don't trust me? I'm exposing myself to danger, being with you!' Mokhtar gave into a prolonged attack of coughing which finished with him producing a gob of slime.

Karim made a face. He placed a fifty-dirham note under Mokhtar's glass. 'Go to a doctor.'

'Doctors are all liars and thieves,' said Mokhtar, taking the note and folding it carefully in his pouch. 'No doctor can help against the east wind. You need to cast a spell or eat cannabis jam. Have you tried *majoun*? I'll give you the recipe, if you like.'

They walked down the hill, Mokhtar gabbling and spluttering, until they reached the *seeber* and parted company.

When Karim entered the internet café the owner greeted him like an old friend. Within minutes of logging on Karim had found a website that allowed him to track the movements of any container ship in the world. The *Mustafa* was currently at Cadiz. It had called at the Eurogate terminal at Tanger-Med at 17.50 last night and at 18.28 on the night of Abdou's disappearance, docking after the *Emma Maersk*. During March it had called at Terminal 2 every few days, on the fifth, tenth and seventeenth of the month, between 17.50 and midnight. The *Mustafa* was planning to do something once it was out of Moroccan waters. But what?

Karim looked around the *seeber*. Apart from the owner, and three teenage boys sniggering at a computer, the room was empty. He noted the dates and times of the *Mustafa* in Abdou's book – it felt good continuing Abdou's notes – then went outside and looked around carefully. A fruit seller, bundled against the wind, was trying to stop mandarins rolling off his barrow. A girl trotted to the neighbourhood oven with a platter of dough, her hand on the flapping cloth cover. Apart from the wind, everything seemed normal. He zeroed in on two men outside a garment shop, their faces hidden by a row of hanging football jerseys. A gust of wind caught a *Messi 10* shirt and Karim locked eyes with a Chinese man and a tall Moroccan with a twisted grimace.

Instantly, Karim turned on his heel down the alleyway. *Son of a bitch!* He ducked under the displays of sports tops and jogging pants. The clothes shops were ranged down one side of the alley so that if he hugged the right-hand side his pursuers couldn't see further than the hanging clothes directly in front of them. He weaved in and out of the shoppers, past tailors' shops and hole-in-the-wall cobblers, through a gaggle of tourists listening to a guide, past barrows of strawberries and sheaves of mint. As soon as the ground started to slope he followed it down in the direction of the sea. He knew the city and its labyrinthine alleyways by now. He reached the barber's shop he had visited with Mokhtar and, with a backward glance, darted inside.

'*Ajee!* Come on!' Salma was standing in the parade ground dressed in her fatigues. 'We'll be late!'

Ayesha walked morosely towards her. All her troubles up to this point paled in comparison with the enormity of losing the phone. She didn't dare tell Salma what had happened. She had replaced every library book one by one, just to make sure that the phone hadn't fallen underneath or become wedged between the pages. Someone had been in the library when she hid the phone, it was the only explanation. She could kick herself for not checking. She considered what was on the phone . . . four phone calls to or from her mother, a text to Karim promising her support, and one highly incriminating text from Karim, mentioning Mustafa, Abderrahim and Mohammed Mansouri. *Oh God.*

The rest of their classmates were already waiting for them at the obstacle course. It was a tough course requiring a lot of stamina. Daoud, the young instructor with the crooked nose, blew his whistle and the two girls lined up on the start line. The obstacle course was staggered, one cadet starting every fifteen seconds, with the women setting off first. Once Salma was halfway along the monkey bars, Ayesha followed. The obstacle course absorbed all her concentration and for the next eighteen minutes her only thought was getting to the end. Rain and sweat had made the bars slippery but Ayesha's grip was firm and she quickly caught up with Salma.

'Faster! Cycle your legs!' shouted Ayesha. 'Rock back and forth, like this!'

When Salma had safely made it to the end of the bars they ran to the triple hurdle, which both girls vaulted easily. Then came an eight-foot-high angled wall. Salma tried to pull herself over but she lacked Ayesha's upper body strength. The instructor, running alongside, blew his whistle, indicating that Salma should leave it and move on to the next obstacle. Ayesha hooked her heel over the wall in a single fluid motion, rolled her body over, jumped to the ground and darted to the lattice of barbed wire. She flattened herself to the ground, using her elbows to propel herself forward. Salma's fatigues snagged on the wire and she stopped to free herself. Behind them, the girls could hear the grunts of their male classmates. The instructor gave three sharp whistles to urge the cadets along.

The last obstacle was a twenty-foot wooden wall with knotted ropes on either side; a severe challenge for aching arms. Ayesha was determined not to give the men the satisfaction of lapping them. She shimmied up the first rope, cleared the wall and dropped down the second rope, then sprinted to the finish line. She turned around and shouted encouragement.

'Come on, Salma!'

Salma forced her tired body up the first rope. She was utterly spent.

'Come on – you're nearly there!'

Salma swung her legs over and descended the rope, knot by knot. With ten feet to go she jumped to the ground, tumbling over. She picked herself up and stumbled to the finish line, high-fiving Ayesha just before the first of the men arrived. They waited for the other cadets to complete the course then Daoud gave a long blast on the whistle and Ayesha formed a line with Salma and four colleagues, the remaining cadets in two rows behind them. As Daoud read out details of the next day's track event Ayesha felt a nudge in her back. Hakimi was standing directly behind her. She followed his gaze downwards: cupped in his palm, visible only to her, was her black Nokia.

Karim flung himself into the nearest swivel chair, eyeing the shop window in the barber's mirror.

'Lather my face – now!'

The barber with the hunched back was taken by surprise.

'But—'

'Quickly, do it!' barked Karim.

Wordlessly, the man spread the cloth over Karim, buttoned it at the neck and started heating water in his kettle.

'Don't worry about warm water!' Karim hissed. 'Just get some foam on me!'

The barber used his fingers to dab shaving cream on Karim's neck and cheeks then started lathering with his brush. As the lower part of his face disappeared under a layer of lather, Karim started to relax. Anyone passing would see an innocuous-looking man having a shave.

While the barber was still lathering, another barber came in from an errand, said something to the first man, then took over.

'This is my chair,' he explained.

Karim nodded. Each barber in a *coiffeur* had his own chair and they were touchy about the others taking their customers. The second barber seemed like an affable fellow, with oiled hair and a toothy smile.

Karim turned his thoughts to his next move. Thank God, he had lost the two men. They hadn't worked out that he was staying at the Widow Khoury's – not yet – but Mokhtar had. *Mokhtar!* He should never have trusted the miserable wretch. Mokhtar, with his stupid pipe and his oily grin. Mokhtar knew that he drove a blue Dacia and that it was parked below the Continental.

The barber tilted Karim's head to one side. Spreading the skin below his lip with his forefinger and thumb, he cut the foam-softened hairs with the precision of a surgeon. Karim had a moment of alarm – natural when you expose your neck to a man with a cut-throat razor – but the barber made two careful passes with the blade before wiping Karim's neck and cheeks with a damp towel. He picked up a pair of long scissors.

'Moustache trim?'

Karim nodded. He decided to call Noureddine and tell him what he had learned about the *Mustafa*. There was a payphone by the car park. Payphones, like *seebers*, were a vanishing species. It was all very well for Noureddine to tell him to use other means of communication but what were you supposed to do if you couldn't find a payphone, or – even rarer – a *téléboutique*?

Aargh! He was aware of a sudden blinding pain, as if the top of his nose had exploded. The barber had shoved the long scissor up Karim's right nostril. Karim managed to stay the barber's hand just as the tip of the scissor was about to puncture the bone between his nose and his brain. Blood spurted everywhere. Karim jerked backward, one hand holding tight on the barber's wrist, the other flailing at the man's collar. He forced the man's hand down, millimetre by millimetre, until the scissor came out from his nasal cavity, bringing a cascade of blood and gristle. He managed to raise himself from the chair, one hand still on the barber, and shoved him against the glass shelves, sending bottles of aftershave crashing to the floor.

Giant bursts of pain were shooting from Karim's nose to his testicles. The barber scoured the shelf and his hand lighted on the still-open razor. He made great sweeps of his arm, trying to slash Karim. There was no sign of the hunchback or anyone who could come to Karim's rescue. He was desperate to staunch the haemorrhage from his nose but he needed both hands free. The men were circling now, looking for an opening. With a snarl the barber lunged forward. The blade slit through Karim's hoodie and a line of red appeared on the grey cotton. The barber made another sweep with the razor but his foot slid on the blood-slicked floor and he lost his footing. As he fell, Karim grabbed the barber's head with both hands and smashed his chin on the edge of the sink, then shoved him face-first into the mirror, causing a spider's web of cracks.

Clutching his nose, Karim staggered out into the alley.

'In the name of God! What happened?'

A second voice: 'We need to get him to the hospital!'

Karim sank to his knees. He was aware of someone pressing a sheaf of paper tissues to his nose. Three or four men were standing over him, one of whom offered to call the police.

'No!' gasped Karim, holding the tissues to his nose. 'Just get me to the hospital!'

'I have a car!' the first man said.

While he ran ahead the others helped Karim to the end of the alley. They bundled him into the passenger seat and placed a box of tissues on his lap. He managed to insert a plug of tissue in his nostril. He closed his eyes and thought he was going to pass out with the pain.

'Keep your head raised!'

'May God protect you!'

Karim felt the car pulling out. He lost consciousness for a few minutes then recovered for long enough to notice that they were driving into the new town. The driver kept casting anxious glances at him. The next thing Karim knew, they were pulling up outside the hospital. The pain had shifted gear to a head-splitting throb.

'Keep your hand pressed on your nose,' cried the man as he helped Karim out of the car. 'No, not like that! Where are you going?'

Karim was scanning the street to see if they had been followed. Fearing that Karim had become deranged with pain, the man put his arm around him.

'Come with me, my brother! There might be a queue in the Emergency Room!'

When he had dismissed the class, Daoud asked the girls if he could have a brief chat. He was a good-hearted man and wanted to check that the girls were coping with the physical demands being placed on them. Ayesha was itching to leave but Salma got into a long conversation about diet and nutrition and, by the time she'd finished, Hakimi was nowhere to be seen. Just before lunch Ayesha tracked him down to the television room. He was playing table football with a fellow cadet.

'Give it back!' she said in an undertone.

'Give what back?'

Ayesha glanced around. A few of the men were watching television but most of them were staring at her. The television room was a male domain into which few women ventured.

'Give it back!' she repeated.

Hakimi gave a violent spin of the handle.

'My affairs are nothing to do with you,' she said, her lip quivering.

Hakimi let out a whoop as he scored a goal.

'Who have you told?' she asked. 'What do you want?' Tears of frustration welled in Ayesha's eyes. If Hakimi handed in the phone, or mentioned it to another cadet, her career was over.

'What do you want?' she repeated, all pretence at being in command of the situation gone. Her forehead was glistening and her legs felt weak, as if she might collapse at any moment.

Carefully manoeuvring one of his six-inch high players behind the ball, Hakimi rotated the handle slowly through ninety degrees then, with a flick of the wrist, thwacked the ball into his opponent's goal.

'I haven't decided yet.'

Mohammed V Hospital was much like any other resource-starved hospital in the kingdom. A decrepit ambulance stood outside a crowded waiting area filled with pregnant women and wailing children. There was a man whose face looked even more smashed-up than Karim's and several individuals were leaning on crutches or moaning in wheelchairs.

I beseech you, I'm dying! I'm about to give birth! Please look at my little girl! May God bless your parents! Give me something to take this pain away!

As every seat was occupied, Karim and his saviour, whose name was Ahmed, stood by a window that was missing two of its panes. By now the bleeding from Karim's nose had stopped. In its place was a throbbing ache that seemed to repeat with each beat of his heart. Ahmed had managed to get hold of four paracetamol tablets and a cupful of water. A harassed-looking nurse and a man in a white coat were moving among the patients, doing triage. If he'd shown his police badge Karim could have pulled rank, but his injuries weren't life-threatening so he waited his turn like everyone else.

Over the next few hours Ahmed told Karim his life story. He lived on Charf Hill with his wife and two children. The first child had been born in this very hospital. Despite a bribe to the midwife, he related bitterly, the delivery had been botched and his wife couldn't conceive for the next fourteen years. Their second child was now ten months old, *al-hamdulillah.*

When the doctor finally got around to shining his pen-torch in Karim's nostril, Ahmed had gone home for dinner. The doctor confirmed there was no damage to the septum or ethmoid bone, but predicted that Karim wouldn't be able to breathe through his right nostril for a week. The wound would mend without the need for cauterisation as long as Karim maintained a daily regime of nasal rinses with salt. Karim refused antibiotics and came out of the hospital clutching nothing more than a tube of antiseptic cream, a bag of cotton wool plugs and fifty paracetamol.

He hailed a taxi and returned to where his car was parked by the marine boulevard. Flipping down the mirror he examined his black eye and swollen nose. *May God curse his enemies!* He swallowed four paracetamol then drove through town to Casabarata and parked outside Simo's front door. He had survived being crushed by a container and stabbed with scissors, there was a trace on his phone and his best friend was dead. The time for heroics was over. After tonight, he would let the Secret Police take charge. There was one last thing he must do: confront Simo. He would have it out with the police chief, once and for all.

Removing the SIM card from his mobile, he switched the phone back on and scrolled down until he found Simo's number. Then he stepped from the car and found the nearest payphone. As he was putting a coin in the slot, the payphone sounded with a loud ring. Karim was so startled that he stared at the receiver for several seconds before lifting it from the cradle.

'Yes?'

'Karim? It's Simo.'

'How – how do you know where I am?'

'Never mind. Listen carefully. Drive along the road from my house towards the *centre ville*, then turn left at the crossroads. Take the second street on the right and you'll see a sign

Hammam Tingis. Meet me inside at nine o'clock. I'll tell you everything.'

It was the worst day in the history of the universe. One minute she burned with resentment at Khalid Hakimi, the next she blamed herself for not checking that the library was empty when she hid the phone. As the afternoon sped past, Ayesha was plagued by a new and terrifying thought. She had no way of contacting Karim, of telling him what had happened. Sooner or later Karim would send a text, giving Hakimi more leverage over her. Awful as it seemed, she had to rely on Hakimi being a blackmailer rather than a snitch.

During mid-afternoon class Hakimi caught her eye and gave his trouser pocket a light pat. He obviously enjoyed seeing her squirm. Several times during the day Salma asked her what the matter was. Finally, Ayesha confessed. Salma listened with horror.

'You must go to Choukri – admit to having a phone! Tell Choukri that your mother has a terminal illness and that you have to be in constant contact!'

'I can't,' said Ayesha, swallowing hard. 'He'll read the messages and see that I was in contact with Karim as well.'

'Let's think this through carefully,' said Salma. 'Hakimi isn't the brightest of students. We know his fingerprints are on the phone. Apart from the names you mentioned, and the two phone numbers, is there anything on the phone that ties it to you?'

Ayesha tried to remember if Karim had used the name *Ayesha*. She thought not.

'There you are!' exclaimed Salma. 'No one can prove that the phone is yours or that you know those men, Mansouri, Abderrahim and Mustafa.'

'But Abderrahim is my brother!'

'*Thennay*, relax. There are lots of Abderrahims, just as there are lots of Mustafas and Mansouris. As for Karim, well, who's to say that Hakimi doesn't know Karim?'

'What about my mother's number?'

'Yes. That is a problem. You have to go to Choukri,' Salma said finally. 'Choukri is a decent man. You have to throw yourself on his mercy. Tell him your entire family history if you have to. What's the alternative? Hakimi could prolong the agony for days, even weeks. God forbid, he might force you to have sex with him! And then, when you are utterly shamed and humiliated, he might still hand the phone in to the principal – you would have lost everything!'

But Ayesha refused. For the rest of the afternoon, she kept Hakimi in her sight, looking for an opportunity to catch him on his own. At 5.30, when lessons were over, she found her chance. Hakimi peeled off from his friends and returned on his own to the accommodation block. Ayesha followed at a safe distance. She crept down the corridor and watched him go into the men's shower room. Without pausing to think through the consequences of being caught, she followed him inside. She was in an L-shaped changing area, larger than the one in the women's shower block, with wooden benches, frosted windows and an A-frame ceiling with cross-beams. On the right was a row of showers; to the left stood a line of toilets. Apart from a locked lavatory cubicle the place was deserted. Ayesha moved silently into the cubicle next to

Hakimi's, sat on the toilet seat and, with infinite care, looked under the partition. Hakimi's trousers were around his ankles. The combat fatigues issued to cadets were made of heavy, baggy material with wide belt loops and the way Hakimi's trousers had gathered on the floor meant that the pocket was directly under the partition, the opening facing towards Ayesha.

Holding her breath, Ayesha kneeled down beside the toilet bowl and reached out two fingers. She probed the material gently, so as not to disturb the creases on the pocket. Perspiration beaded on her forehead. Her finger nails touched something, there it was – a hard shiny surface – *al-hamdulliah*, she had the phone between her fingers! Just as she was about to retract her hand she felt a sudden, vice-like grip.

She tried to yank back her wrist but it was caught fast. A second later Hakimi gave it a violent tug, slamming the side of her face against the partition. She caught a powerful smell of urine from the toilet bowl next to her head.

Grasping her wrist he bent her index finger backwards with his right hand. He was going to break her fingers! She had tears in her eyes but she was determined not to plead or cry out. Then, just as quickly as it had started – as if Hakimi had planned the whole thing and then grown bored – he let her go. Ayesha pulled her arm back, staring at her fingers. There was a flush from the toilet and the sound of the next door opening. She heard Hakimi wash his hands, press a hand dryer then open the door of the washroom. Ayesha got to her feet, smoothed her uniform, and fled.

'*Labas?* Everything all right?' Salma whispered as they sat down in the refectory for dinner.

Ayesha shook her head miserably. Hakimi was sitting on the other side of the canteen, laughing with his friends. Ayesha didn't touch the salad of lettuce, tomato, boiled egg and onion. The *seffa* chicken with cinnamon came and went. Salma was talking to one of the other boys about a night exercise. Ayesha was glassy-eyed, her mind already running through the consequences of dismissal from police college; the shame of returning to Marrakech and confessing to Lalla Fatima and her mother; the need to look for some awful dull job like Khadija's; the satisfaction on Abderrahim's face when she told him. And Karim! He was utterly compromised, with no way of warning him.

Then, halfway through chocolate pudding, the unthinkable happened.

Brrinnnng.

The entire hall stopped talking. No one moved. Then there was a flurry at the far end as Hakimi pulled the phone from his pocket and flung it, horror-struck, on the table. Ayesha realised two things at once. When Hakimi groped behind the bookcase he must have inadvertently slipped the ringer to *on*. And, secondly, if Karim was calling her then it was an emergency and his life was in extreme danger.

'Well, Cadet Hakimi? Aren't you going to answer it?'

The voice was that of Colonel Lalami. He was the firearms instructor, a man feared and hated by all the cadets. Even Karim, who had come top of his year in marksmanship, had disliked Lalami. The colonel never smiled, never gave praise or encouragement.

Hakimi fumbled with the phone, turning the ringer to *off*. Ayesha's initial panic eased slightly as she realised that there would be more of Hakimi's fingerprints on the phone. It was

19.40 according to her watch. Dinner had started late. Karim must have thought she would be in her room.

Colonel Lalami rose from the officers' table. He walked over to Hakimi's table, picked up the Nokia – more finger-prints, thought Ayesha – and signalled to Hakimi to follow him out of the hall. As Hakimi did so he stared in Ayesha's direction. It was impossible to tell whether his look was one of despair or triumph.

Ayesha's number kept ringing but she didn't answer. Karim wanted to hear her voice: deep down, he had a feeling that this night might be his last. With a heavy sigh, he replaced the handset and went back to the car. It was 19.45. His nose was throbbing, a dull ache that seemed to have sunk into his soul. Feeling sleepy from all the painkillers, he switched on the car stereo and listened to the CD he had bought, to Fairouz's soar-ing laments.

After half an hour had passed, he reversed from Simo's gate and drove slowly down Avenue Moulay Abdelhafid. He stopped at a petrol station, filled up the car and drank two *nuss-nuss* coffees in the cafeteria. Taking a left off Avenue Moulay Hafid he saw the sign for the bathhouse and parked outside. He flipped down the mirror and gently extracted the bloody cotton wool plug from his nostril, then inserted a fresh one. He gulped two more paracetamol, checked the safety catch on his gun and stepped out of the Dacia.

On the wall by the *hammam* was a crudely painted sign with the profiles of a man and a woman. Customers were coming from the men's entrance with towels wrapped around their heads and plastic buckets in their hands. Karim paid twelve dirhams to the attendant in the vestibule, along with five more for a towel.

'*Kisk? Sabon?* Glove? Soap?' The attendant's gaze lingered on Karim's swollen face.

'No, God's blessing on you.'

Karim stepped into a small changing room with wooden decking. He sat on a bench and undressed, his senses alive to every sound and movement. The room smelled of talcum powder. Two men were chatting about recent gains by the Islamist party while a third man, tall and lanky, was standing in a pair of white Y-fronts, spraying his armpits. An elderly man asked Karim for help with the combination on the padlock for his locker. Apart from the old man, no one paid Karim the slightest attention.

Karim stripped to his undershorts. He went back to the attendant and bought an exfoliating glove. Tucking his gun inside the glove he arranged the rest of his clothes on the bench. With his head swirling from nausea and fear, he pushed aside the plastic flaps and plunged into the interior.

The first room was a sort of anteroom, tepid and empty, with a slippery white floor. So intense was the heat in the next room that his nose erupted in a scalding jag of pain. He put one hand over his nostrils to shield them against the steam and groped his way towards two rubber buckets against a wall. Placing the weighted glove in one of them, he filled the other from a hot tap. When it was full to the brim he carried both buckets through to a third room where the clouds of vapour were even thicker.

As he sat down on the floor, his back to the wall, he was aware of two other men opposite. One was lying on his back with his legs splayed and eyes closed. The other sat by the entrance, facing Karim. He had a gym-toned torso and massive arms. The only sound was a tap dripping into a basin of water. The first man sat up and upended a bucket over his head, sending a cascade of hot water across the tiles towards Karim. The large guy stared at Karim impassively, scratching his pectorals. There was no way he could fight these two gorillas. They would overpower him in a minute.

Billows of steam rolled over the floor and Karim edged along the wall to keep the men in sight. By now, his body was coursing with sweat. He splashed water on his face, ignoring what the doctor had said about the risk of infection. His nose throbbed. He felt like his brain was being pulled through his nasal cavity on the end of a pick, like an Egyptian pharaoh being prepared for mummification. He had enjoyed studying the pharaohs in high school. Those noble figures were the ancient inhabitants of North Africa, Amazigh like him. Sometimes when he looked at Ayesha, with her full lips and large eyes, he imagined he was gazing upon Cleopatra herself.

By the Seven Saints! The two men were no longer opposite. Where had they gone? He grabbed his gun and jumped to his feet, waving the steam aside, expecting the men to leap out at any minute. He looked in the ante-room. There was no doubt – they had left. In the dressing room towels and mittens were scattered, as if everyone had left in a hurry.

Holding his gun with both hands he ventured back into the steam room and sat down to wait for Simo. He closed his eyes and recited the 108th sura for protection from his enemies.

When he opened them again there was a filament of red water between his legs. He put his finger to his nose, worried that the plug was leaking, then lifted his bottom, fearing some other awful injury. But the blood on the floor was flowing towards, not away from him. He followed the tributary across the floor as it grew wider and redder, turning into a stream of blood. It seemed to be coming from the base of the wall with the water tap – no, it was flowing *around* the wall. Wafting the steam with the gun, he saw that there was a fourth room that he hadn't seen before. The steam made it impossible to see beyond a small section of floor, which was bathed in blood.

'Simo?'

Where the red was thickest a wooden bench rose into the mist, and on the bench sat a naked man. Even with his back to Karim he knew it was Simo. Karim rounded the bench. Simo was slumped against the wall with his eyes open. The slit in his neck stretched from ear to ear.

Without bothering to shower Karim dashed to the dressing room, threw on his clothes, fled to the car and pulled away from the kerb, tyres screeching.

It was a cold night on the mountainside. The men were sitting in a circle around the fire eating a mishmash of chickpeas and lentils.

Franco, who had cooked the meal, was talking about his favourite subject: what he would do when he got to Spain. He was going to Madrid where he would work as a waiter – day and night if necessary – until he had enough money to open a place of his own. He would marry a Spanish girl with large breasts and take his son to watch Madrid play Liverpool.

Then Louis spoke. Louis prided himself on being a *sapeur*, a dandy; his stamping ground had been the nightclubs of Brazzaville. He kept a pair of crocodile-skin shoes in his sleeping bag, ready for the day when he would step out on the boulevards of Paris and dazzle the *mademoiselles*. He now got to his feet in his ochre-coloured beret and boasted that he would command a high price as a gigolo in the Bois de Boulogne.

'French women love stylish African men,' he said, gyrating his hips. 'Especially on the Rive Gauche. That's where the cool women hang out. You just have to look them in the eye. *Come to me, chérie,*' he said, beckoning to an imaginary partner.

The others laughed with delight.

'You'd be arrested if you did that!' Jean-François exclaimed, rising to his feet. 'Do you want to know how to approach a French woman?' Everyone clamoured in assent. He gave a sweeping bow and extended his hand. '*Mademoiselle – vous avez les yeux d'un ange.* You have the eyes of an angel.'

Louis pushed him aside. '*Non, non, non!*' He addressed the imaginary girl. '*Mademoiselle, j'ai un problème avec mon portable – il manque ton numéro!*'

A fourth man, a diminutive seventeen-year-old from Senegal whom everyone called *Le Gosse*, leaped to his feet and played the part of the girl, holding the ends of his hoodie like a dress and fluttering his eyelashes. '*Ah, monsieur, t'es trop charmant!*'

A headlamp beam fanned across the group.

'Relax,' Jean-François reassured them. 'It's only a truck.' They heard the grinding of gears as an overloaded lorry crawled up the mountain road. The men sat down and silence descended once more.

'I heard of a way to get across,' said Amadou, who had been quiet up to this point. 'I'm not sure if it's for real.' The other men regarded him intently.

'A guy in the other camp told me. There's a factory outside Tangier in a place called the Free Zone. They make t-shirts and bags. They need workers for their factory in Spain. You have to go to the Free Zone so they can check you out and make sure you can do the job. Then they ship you over to Cadiz. The factory in Spain has a dormitory and everything. You have to work for them for three months then they give you back your passport and you disappear.'

'They make you hand over your passport?' asked Franco.

'If you have one,' Amadou nodded. 'But you get it back at the end.'

'How do they take you across?'

'In a shipping container. They fill the front half with clothes and fit you in the back half, behind a false wall. Once on the Spanish side the container is taken to the factory.'

There was a moment's silence, then everybody spoke at once. *They've got scanners at the port! They check containers! The dogs will sniff us out!*

Franco appealed for calm. 'Maybe they've bribed the security guys. Or the containers are marked somehow and the officials are told to let them through.'

'How do we know the containers won't be checked at Cadiz?' asked Joseph.

'Less than two per cent of containers get checked, that's what I've heard,' said Louis.

Jean-François was unconvinced. 'I don't like the sound of it. We should try our luck in Agadir, get a boat to the Canary Islands.'

'Agadir!' snorted Franco. 'What makes you think we'd have better luck in Agadir? My friend was in Agadir, he says all the boats have been destroyed and the *passeurs* have been killed!'

Another man spoke up. 'What about Melilla?'

Franco frowned. 'The wall is worse than the one at Ceuta.'

Amadou kept trying to persuade them. 'We wouldn't have to wait for a calm sea or moonlight. Container ships sail whatever the weather. We wouldn't even get our feet wet.' He held us his bandaged hands. '*Les mains non plus.*'

'Do the containers have ventilation?' asked *Le Gosse*.

'Yes,' replied Amadou, 'and they give you water.'

'It must be a long journey.'

'Eight hours.'

'Louis will need to take his silk dressing gown!' joked Franco, and the group erupted with laughter.

Finally, Jean-François declared, 'I think it's worth a try.'

Karim drove back through the city streets, eyeing the police radio on his dashboard. The chief of police of Tangier had been murdered, his throat slit in a *hammam*. A *hammam* was second only to the mosque as a place of safety and community. Even if the local Sûreté was riddled with corruption it was his duty to report the incident. He pulled over on Boulevard Mohammed VI and switched on the radio. Before he could figure out how the receiver worked, an operator's voice broke in.

'The suspect is driving an unmarked blue Dacia, registration number 69214-alef-40, approach with caution.'

Karim's jaw fell open. The operator was referring to him! His thoughts flashed back to the old man at the *hammam*. Karim had helped him open his locker . . . his prints would be on the lock, and inside, no doubt, would be the knife that slit Simo's neck. Karim gritted his teeth and swerved off down a side road, taking a circuitous route towards Bab Kasbah. He drove slowly down narrow streets not meant for cars. All was quiet, *al-hamdulillah*. At Jnane al-Captane he turned the engine off and let the car roll gently down downhill, braking at the entrance to the blue-and-white alley. *By the Seven Saints of Marrakech and All Who Revere Them!* A police patrol car was parked outside the Widow Khoury's house.

Karim turned the ignition and reversed back at speed along the alleyway, executing a three-point turn into the shutters of a shop then accelerated back up the hill. The patrol car was behind him, lights flashing. Karim made a sharp right along an alley at high speed, scraping the sides of the car and losing both wing mirrors. He turned right, then left, emerging in the tiny Rue Dar Baroud, past the Hotel Continental, the Dacia juddering as it made one final metal-shearing scrape, before emerging from the medina. He didn't lift his foot from the accelerator until he was on the coast road to Casiago.

Dawn was breaking when he turned off the N16. He parked under a pine tree and leaned back in his seat. Below, he could see the lights of Ceuta. Spanish families were still asleep in their beds while, at the border crossing, hundreds of Moroccan maids and chauffeurs stood in line, preparing for another day of cooking, cleaning and driving their employers' children to school.

A dull throb radiated from his forehead and right eye. He swallowed two more paracetamol and replaced the bloody cotton wool plug in his nostril. Then he covered the car with a tarpaulin from the boot, took out his binoculars and started walking.

When he finally located the camp he found Joseph sleeping beneath his makeshift plastic roof. Karim covered his aching head with his hoodie, lay on the ground next to him and fell asleep.

Chapter 11

It was quarter to six on Friday morning and still dark in the girls' bedroom. Ayesha hadn't slept all night. She would have given everything she possessed to turn the clock back and hide the phone elsewhere. As soon as the whistle blew for reveille she was at Salma's bedside.

'What shall I say if Lalami asks to see me?'

Salma propped herself up, squinting. 'What time is it?'

'Lalami's in the building! I can hear his voice in the corridor!'

'So what?'

'What about Karim?'

'*Blesh*, forget Karim! It's you that we have to worry about!' Salma disappeared into the bathroom. When she came out a minute later she continued. 'Tough it out. Stand your ground. It's Hakimi's word against yours. Everyone in the class saw the two of you fighting, including Colonel Choukri. Our class-mates will testify that Hakimi had a grudge against you if he claims that the phone is yours.'

'But the phone *is* mine!' Ayesha wailed.

'You have to stop thinking that! It's nothing to do with you – that's your story!'

Salma's exhortations failed to convince Ayesha. Morning rollcall would take place in ten minutes with the entire cadet corps, nine hundred cadets, on the parade ground. If one of the men had forgotten to shave, or tied their shoelaces incorrectly, they would be hauled to the front and made to perform sixty press-ups. Women who contravened regulations were not spared. Hafida, one of the other girls in their year, had forgotten her beret a fortnight ago and was made to run five times around the parade ground while the others did their exercises. If that was the penalty for a missing beret, what was the punishment for one of the most serious offences at the Institut Royal de Police, smuggling a mobile phone?

Ayesha knew that she would be able to read her fate in Hakimi's face. One glance, and she would tell if he had succeeded in pinning the phone on her.

The girls dressed in their red tracksuits and tied their hair, Ayesha fumbling with the hairbrush. As they stepped out of their room they heard a commotion. Someone ran past. A crowd of male cadets was standing at the other end of the corridor. Ayesha had a sixth sense that the disturbance involved Khalid Hakimi.

'What's going on?' Salma asked a distraught boy in a green tracksuit.

He swallowed and mumbled something about *showers*. Ayesha and Salma exchanged glances. Someone shouted for first aid. Ayesha pushed past the boys in the corridor and ran into the men's wing. Dozens of cadets in green, yellow and red tracksuits were peering through the doorway into the shower room – the same room where Ayesha had gone after Hakimi yesterday. She barged her way through, looked around, didn't see anything at first. Then she looked up. Khalid Hakimi was hanging from a beam in the ceiling with a belt around his neck. His tongue was an odd shade of blue.

Karim, Amadou and the other Muslims performed *salat* on the edge of the camp, ending their prayers by turning to each other with the words *Peace and God's mercy upon you.* Afterwards, Karim joined Joseph in his lean-to, drinking tepid chicory coffee. Karim's face was swollen and his eye socket had turned black but no one asked him about his injury. Bruises and cuts were a given in migrant camps.

At midday he walked up to a high ridge. From here he could see Tanger-Med through his binoculars. The day was bright and sunny with a promise of spring. A flock of goats was grazing a mile away and he could see other camps dotted over the mountainside. He scanned the boats out at sea. The pattern established by the *Mustafa* suggested that it would be back within six days. Every afternoon and evening, he decided, he would climb to the ridge and check its whereabouts.

When he returned, the men were pooling the meagre amount they had made from begging by the roadside. Two migrants volunteered to make the trek to Fnideq for rice and vegetables and Karim gave them some money, adding a request for paracetamol.

The afternoon was spent collecting firewood – no easy task after such a wet month. Most logs and branches were too sodden to burn. When the sun was low in the sky Karim climbed back to the ridge, stripped off and washed in the stream. As the call to prayer drifted up the mountainside he turned towards the east and prayed.

He didn't tell anyone, not even Joseph, what had happened the previous day. He realised that, for the first time since arriving in Tangier, he felt safe, even happy. No one would find him out here among the woods and streams, sleeping under the stars. What were those lines of the poet Kahlil Gibran that Fairouz sung?

> Did you, like me, choose woodlands, not palaces as your
> 　home?
> And did you follow the streams and climb up the rocks?
> Have you, like me, slept on the grass at night
> And used the sky as your blanket?
> Have you bathed in perfume and dried yourself under the
> 　light of the sun?
>
> Give me the flute and sing
> Because singing is the secret of existence.

The girls returned to their bedroom just before midday prayers.

The dawn exercises had been cancelled and the cadets had eaten their breakfast in silence. No one at Ayesha's table had any appetite. At the end of rollcall the principal made a short announcement that Khalid Hakimi had taken his life 'in a regrettable incident', and that his family had been informed. Among the cadets it was agreed that Lalami had ordered Hakimi's expulsion and that Hakimi had killed himself out of shame.

'God preserve us in these difficult times,' said Salma, throwing herself on her bed.

Ayesha said nothing. She changed into her suit then took out her overnight bag and packed a tracksuit, a *jellaba* and a turquoise patterned headscarf that Karim had given her for her eighteenth birthday.

'What are you doing?' asked Salma.

'Leaving.'

'What do you mean, leaving?'

'I'm going to Tangier.'

'Are you crazy? You can't just walk out!'

'Karim needs me.'

'Karim? Don't you think you should spare a thought for Hakimi? If it hadn't been for your phone the poor fellow wouldn't have hanged himself!'

'Hakimi did not hang himself.'

'What are you talking about?'

Ayesha stared at her room-mate. 'Did Hakimi strike you as the sort of man who would kill himself? He would have asked for an investigation – at the very least, he would have demanded that the phone be brushed for fingerprints. He would have done everything in his power to prove it was my phone. He wouldn't have hanged himself, not out of shame and certainly not so soon after the phone was discovered.'

'You're crazy!'

'The organised crime group in Tangier kill people who get in their way.'

'I don't understand! Hakimi wasn't involved in Karim's investigation!'

Ayesha went up to Salma. 'That's just it, don't you see? They think he *was* involved. They put a trace on Karim's phone. When the Nokia rang during dinner, Hakimi's fate was sealed.'

Salma stared at Ayesha in dumb astonishment.

'If Hakimi hadn't taken my phone,' Ayesha went on, 'I would probably be dead by now. I owe my life to Hakimi. Don't think I'm unaware of that. I'm also aware that if they killed the person who received the call, they will also kill the person who made it.'

'But that means they must have someone here at the college,' said Salma. 'Someone on the inside who carried out Hakimi's murder.'

Ayesha said nothing. She embraced her room-mate.

'May God watch over you,' Salma breathed.

As she hurried to the gatehouse Ayesha felt a lurch in her stomach. Colonel Lalami was talking to the guard. She hung back and waited but the minutes passed and the colonel showed no sign of leaving. This was going to be difficult. Cadets were not allowed leave of absence during the week except in exceptional circumstances. Moreover, the college had been placed in lockdown following Hakimi's death. She still had Choukri's letter authorising leave of absence 'for compassionate reasons'. As she walked up to the gatehouse she clutched the letter tightly.

'*Salaam ou-alikum,*' Ayesha said brightly.

'*Ou-alikum salaam.*' Colonel Lalami was suspicious. 'Where are you going?'

'Leave of absence, sir!'

Lalami turned to the corporal. 'Go to lunch. I will handle this.' When the guard had left, Lalami told Ayesha to step inside the gatehouse.

'Has your hurry to leave got anything to do with the unfortunate incident involving Cadet Hakimi?'

'No, sir.'

'He stated that the mobile phone belonged to you,' Lalami said, monitoring her reaction.

'That's ridiculous! Cadet Hakimi and I had a *disagreement* last week, sir – in Colonel Choukri's class. I'm sure that Colonel Choukri would corroborate.'

'Were you and Hakimi having a . . . *relationship?*'

Ayesha was outraged. 'No, sir!'

'He told me that you have a brother in prison on terrorism offences. Is that true?'

'No, sir!'

'Are you going to visit him?'

'No, sir!'

'If the college had known you had a terrorist for a brother we would not have given you a place. I mean, *yanni*,' he sneered. 'We ask women to apply, but we're not that desperate!'

'My brother is a detective with the Marrakech Sûreté,' Ayesha said hotly. 'He graduated from this college with a merit! He was top of his year in firearms!' *Stay calm*, she told herself.

'Talal, Talal . . . I don't remember any cadets with that name.'

'That's because I was adopted! I have a different name to his!'

'It sounds like a lie to me. Far more likely is that you have a terrorist for a brother.'

'I told you – my brother is a police lieutenant! His name is Karim Belkacem and he's on assignment in Tangier—'

The instant Ayesha uttered the words she knew she had made a terrible mistake. Lalami crossed the room and bolted the door, then lowered the slats over the window. Ayesha backed against the table.

'I just want to sign out for a day or two,' she said in terror. 'I don't want any trouble.'

Colonel Lalami undid his tie without taking his eyes from her. Angry tears welled in Ayesha's eyes.

'Are you going to strangle me, like you strangled Cadet Hakimi?'

'If anyone is to blame for Hakimi's death, it's you. It would appear that he was telling the truth about the phone.'

'Two dead cadets in twenty-four hours?' Ayesha said, putting on an air of bravado. 'That's not going to look good.'

Lalami advanced on her, fists wound around either end of the tie. 'You will never be found,' he murmured. 'The story will be that you vanished after the suicide of your sweetheart.'

Ayesha crouched and turned slightly, as if making herself a smaller target. Then with lightning speed she spun around and aimed a judo kick at Lalami's chin. But the colonel was too quick for her. He caught her by the ankle and twisted it so that she fell to the floor with a cry. Still clutching her ankle, he reached down to grasp her other foot. Ayesha drew back her left leg and kicked him hard in the shoulder, causing him to let go. She sprang to her feet and raced to the door. His fist came at her but she swerved and let fly with a punch of her own. As Ayesha followed through, driving her knuckles into his belly, he wrapped his arm around her neck.

She was caught. She gasped for breath, her hands flapping uselessly.

What had Daoud taught them about a rear choke hold? *The most important thing is to close your chin.* She did so now, preventing Lalami's forearm from getting contact with her throat. He forced his other arm against the back of her head, trying to increase the pressure of the lock. Ayesha bent forward and jabbed her elbow into Lalami's groin, then, when he sagged, turned and jabbed both hands with fingers extended into his eyes. Clasping her hands together she brought them down on the back of his head, simultaneously bringing up her knee and slamming it into his chin. It was not an elegant move, not part of the repertoire at the royal police college. As Lalami teetered, she slammed her elbow up into his windpipe. His legs buckled and he sank to the floor like a building that has collapsed in on itself.

Ayesha ran to the filing cabinet, pulled out a drawer full of mobile phones and seized her Samsung. She turned on the phone then calmly walked to the door and slid the bolt. Lalami raised himself on one elbow, rubbing his windpipe.

'You're finished, Talal,' he rasped. 'You'll be dead as soon as you step off the train.'

Ayesha paused, then walked back to where he was lying.

'Your colleagues in Tangier will kill me the same way you killed Cadet Hakimi, is that right, Colonel Lalami?'

'That is correct.'

She held up the Samsung. 'I have recorded what you just said and will upload it to the college Facebook page if I have the slightest suspicion that I'm being followed.' At the doorway she turned around. 'One more thing – I want you to sign me out for a one-week leave of absence on compassionate grounds. Is that understood?'

The colonel stared at her, rage and confusion on his face.

'Yes,' he croaked.

ي

The air felt damp on Ayesha's face when she arrived in Tangier. Karim had told her that he was staying at a hotel with a Spanish-sounding name – Figaro? Fuenta? She asked a taxi driver.

'The Fuentes!'

Ten minutes later he dropped her at Tannery House Gate and gave her directions to the hotel.

'First two Marrakchis, now a Marrakchia!' grinned the clerk. 'We should change our name to the Red City Hotel!'

'Is Karim Belkacem still here?' she said, contemplating the peeling walls and the faded poster. After the pristine accommodation in college this place looked like a dump.

'I fear that Mister Belkacem has moved on, *lalla*. I don't know where he is now.'

There was a cough from the end of the passageway and Mokhtar walked towards them. 'Put the key away, Abdelkadir.'

Ayesha looked at Mokhtar with surprise. She could smell kif seeping from his pores.

'Peace be upon you, *lalla*,' said Mokhtar. 'And the mercy of God and His blessings! Shall we take some refreshment in the square?'

He picked up her bag and slung it over his shoulder,

descending the stairs and heading along the same alleyway she had just taken.

'Hey! I thought we were going to the square!'

'Not safe, *lalla*. The Fuentes not safe. Mobile phones not safe. My name is Mokhtar.' He gave way to a coughing fit. '*Sharaf liya*. A pleasure to meet you!'

They made a wide detour around the city walls, past the Jewish cemetery. It was growing late and dark clouds were rolling in from the Atlantic.

'Where are you taking me?' asked Ayesha. If Karim hadn't mentioned Mokhtar's name when they were in the Italian restaurant she would have seized her bag and fled.

'Not far now, *lalla*.'

After twenty minutes of strenuous walking, interspersed with pauses for Mokhtar to catch his breath, he led her into a Spanish-style tearoom.

'Why have we come here?' Ayesha asked, taking in the tiles and frilly tablecloths.

'It's the last place anyone would look for old Mokhtar,' he said with a grin.

Ayesha was still unsure whether to trust him. 'Where is Karim now?'

'Ah! Everyone would like to know that.' Mokhtar lit his pipe and let out a cloud of smoke, coughing violently. 'The chief of police was found dead last night.'

'Simo Layachi? *Dead?*'

'On the television news they said he was a good policeman. If you ask me, his snout was the deepest one in the trough. He was found at a *hammam* with his throat slit. The police have put out a warrant for Karim's arrest.'

'Karim is being framed for Simo's death?'

'Yes.'

Ayesha was speechless. At that moment, the waitress came up to their table and asked Mokhtar to put his pipe away. Mokhtar nodded and turned to Ayesha.

'You can stay at my place.'

Ayesha pursed her lips in distaste. 'Why would I do that?'

'The Chinese are on Karim's trail. They'll work out that you're his sister. And when they do . . .' He mimed a gun being pointed at his temple.

'Why shouldn't I just find another hotel?'

'Nowhere in this town is safe, *lalla* . . . nowhere that has a door or windows.'

Fifteen minutes later they were climbing down a flight of steps below Boulevard Pasteur. Mokhtar led the way, carrying her bag on his head. As they got further from the street lights it became hard for Ayesha to see where she was putting her feet.

'Never fear, *lalla*!' Mokhtar said in a husky voice. 'The steps are dark but the welcome is warm!'

It wasn't the steps that alarmed Ayesha. They were heading towards a building that looked truly sinister. It had a crumbling stucco facade, boarded-up windows and a row of half-broken statues on the roof, from which creepers dangled. Mokhtar climbed through a gap in the fence near an ancient sign: *Danger – Défense d'Entrer*. He turned and beckoned. Again, Ayesha hesitated. But she had defeated a highly trained colonel earlier that day and the man in front of her looked so weak that he might expire at any moment. Gingerly, she clambered over the rubble and debris. From what she could see of the outside, the building dated from colonial times.

'What is this place?'

'My home!'

Mokhtar took a key from around his neck and opened the padlock on a flimsy door. He shone the torch from his phone and gestured to Ayesha to enter. The interior had the chill of a large space and Ayesha could smell mildew and damp. Mokhtar switched on a hanging light bulb. They were behind what looked like the stage of an old theatre. The floor was strewn with plaster and animal droppings. Taking care to avoid the loose parquet Ayesha peered behind the proscenium arch.

The auditorium stretched away into darkness. It had a barrel-shaped vault with a gaping hole through which she could see roof timbers. The ceiling sagged in the middle and were it not for a hole that allowed water to enter, the vault would have collapsed long ago. With the faint glow from her mobile phone she could make out the first few rows of battered seats. More seats were piled on the stage, draped by a dusty velvet curtain. Mokhtar came and joined her.

'Enrico Caruso sang here. Does that name mean anything to you – Caruso, the great Italian tenor?'

Ayesha shook her head.

'The place was built by the Spanish. It hasn't been used for years. Except by old Mokhtar! Come and have some tea.'

He led Ayesha over creaking floorboards into a wing where the former dressing rooms were located. Mokhtar flicked another light. The first dressing room was narrow, furnished with a divan, low table and sateen cushions. The wall dividing it from the next room had been knocked through or had simply disintegrated with age. Ayesha followed Mokhtar into a kitchen where he put a kettle on to boil.

'How long have you lived here?'

'Since before you were born, *lalla*! I receive a small stipend and in return I take care of the place.' He gave a little chuckle which turned into a lengthy coughing. 'That is to say, I try to stop it falling down completely.' He pointed at a doorway leading into a third room. 'Now, *lalla* – I propose you take the bedroom and I take the divan.'

Ayesha peered into the room. There was a double bed with a green counterpane and a small bedside table. A pine wardrobe stood next to a boarded-over window. The room smelled of sweat and kif.

'No,' she said firmly. '*I* will take the divan.'

Mokhtar left the kitchen with two glasses and returned, water dripping from the rims. Humming a tune, he arranged the glasses and a teapot on the table, pulled up two chairs and took the pouch from his *jellaba*. He started cleaning his kif with a penknife.

'Where's the bathroom?' asked Ayesha.

'The only one that works is on the other side of the stage. Here,' said Mokhtar, giving her a candle. 'Save your phone battery.'

Ayesha ventured out in the passageway holding the candle at arm's length, more concerned about the risk of fire than anything else. There was a path through the debris, as if Mokhtar periodically swept the floorboards and left the dust and dirt in little banks on either side. She turned past the stage door, shielding the naked flame with her hand. Among the creaks, and distant coughs, she could hear cats meowing. The candlelight picked out a set of stage screens, behind which a staircase led down into darkness. At the top of the staircase was an arrow and *Taller*, which Ayesha guessed must be a Spanish word.

She turned left until she came to a door marked *Baño*. Taking a breath, she pushed the door open. Even by candlelight, the room was impressive. On her left was a row of huge *art nouveau* basins fitted with gold-coloured taps. The walls were decorated in blue-and-gold tiles depicting scenes from Don Quixote. To Ayesha they meant nothing but she stared with curiosity at the tall, spindly figure on his equally spindly horse. She was relieved to see that Mokhtar had kept the toilets reasonably clean and there was even toilet paper in one of the cubicles. She wandered over to a sink and rested the candle on the porcelain. She looked at herself in the cloudy mirror and thought what an extraordinary day it had been, starting with the suicide of a police cadet and ending with her sleeping in an abandoned theatre with a kif addict.

Chapter 12

The days passed.

Living among the men was a lesson in geography. Karim learned that there were three countries called Guinea in addition to two named Congo. It was discomfiting to think that he lived on the same continent as these men and yet was so ignorant of their countries of origin.

Five times a day he performed his prayers with the other Muslims. Louis lent him a gilet and a pair of trousers. The men never questioned why he was living among them, and he never volunteered. Nor did they press him for transport, despite the journey to Fnideq taking four hours on foot. The pain in his nose subsided, and after a few days he stopped taking paracetamol. He was anxious to re-establish contact with Noureddine and Ayesha, to reassure them that he was safe, but none of the men had a charged mobile and he didn't dare use his own.

On Thursday morning, six days after arriving, Karim invited Joseph to accompany him to the ridge. The sun was overhead and climbing over the rocks was hard work. Finally, they stopped and took a drink. Karim handed Joseph the binoculars.

'*Regarde-la, cette montagne.* That's Gibraltar.'

Joseph looked across the Mediterranean. 'I see it.'

'Now take a look down there at Ceuta.'

'Uh-huh,' nodded Joseph. '*Je le vois.*'

'*Veux-tu savoir quelque chose?*'

'*Quoi?*'

'The mountain over there, where Spain is meant to be, belongs to Great Britain. And Ceuta down there, although it's in Morocco, is in Spain.'

Joseph laughed. 'Borders are fucked up.'

'*Besahh.* Indeed they are, my brother.'

They sat in silence for a few minutes, then Karim spoke. 'Why do you have your name tattooed on your arm?'

'I destroyed my passport.'

Karim remembered what Raoul had told him about undocumented migrants being able to claim refugee status.

'I have no proof of who I am. There are hundreds of men like me, men without papers, lying in unmarked graves in Tarifa and Tangier. Nobody knows where they came from or who their families were. I don't want that to be my fate. I'm ready to die but I want people to know that I once lived.'

'*Al-hamdulillah.*'

Karim gazed over the Strait and wondered at the lengths men would go to in order to reach Europe. Joseph and his friends were no different from his cousin Majid, or Abderrezak – Khadija's ex-fiancé, married to a Parisian woman – or the footballers who left the Maghreb to play for the great European clubs like Bayern or Paris Saint-Germain. They all dreamed of reaching that fabulous land where the streets were paved with gold.

They watched the container ships for a while. Every so often Karim lifted his binoculars to check the names on the side.

'The strange thing,' Joseph said suddenly, 'is that I'm ashamed of my name.'

'How so?'

'I was named after Joseph Kabila – *le président de mon pays*. What a joke! Eleven years ago, his soldiers overran Kisangani. They went from door to door, drunk on gin. One soldier came to our house. My mother said she was a Kabila supporter, but the man caught sight of my sister in her white dress.' Joseph threw a stone down the slope and watched it ricochet off a rock.

'My mother pleaded with him, begged him to take her instead. But he refused. When he had finished he came back downstairs and told my mother to stop crying. There would be other soldiers, he said, but at least my sister couldn't lose her virginity again. A short while afterwards, my mother took my sister and me to stay with my aunt. My mother went out one evening to buy cassava. We found her at the railway track, with her head on one side of the rail and her body on the other.'

Karim was deeply moved. 'May God have mercy on her! Is your sister still living with your aunt?'

'No.' Joseph shook his head. 'My aunt died from Ebola. My sister is living in a hut outside Kisangani. She takes in washing. Her name is Gloria.'

Karim stared at Joseph. He wanted to embrace him, or kneel at his feet and clasp his ankles, but instead he perched next to him on the rock.

'Joseph . . . I was the policeman who stopped you at Ceuta. Not the second one – the one who dragged you off the fence and beat you, but the first one – that was me.'

The pause stretched out for what seemed an eternity. Then Joseph raised his hand in the air. At first, Karim thought Joseph was going to strike him but instead he rested his palm on Karim's knee.

'*Makayn mushkeel.* No problem. Isn't that what you say in Morocco?'

Something inside Karim shifted and his eyes pricked with tears. 'Thank you.'

'That second policeman . . . he was a son of a bitch.'

'Yes, he was.'

'I've seen him before.'

'Where?'

'He raided our camp in Boukhalef.'

For a while nothing more was said. A falcon hovered above them, then swept down from the ridge before soaring up again and away over the mountain. Joseph tossed another stone and watched it disappear in a ravine.

'We're going to try a new route. A crossing. By container.'

Karim felt as if he'd had the breath knocked out of him. *Was this the secret that had eluded him for so long?*

'Joseph, listen to me. Those containers – they're not safe. The ship is called the *Mustafa*. I'm not sure what awaits you when you arrive in Europe . . . you could be sold into slavery or used as guinea pigs for drugs!'

Joseph shrugged. 'It's no worse than what we put up with here.'

This time Karim kneeled before Joseph and stared into his eyes.

'Promise me you won't make the crossing until I've found out what's going on. Give me your word. *Donne-moi ta parole.*'

'*D'accord,*' Joseph said finally.

Karim spent the afternoon asking the men about the crossing. Amadou added little to what Joseph had said. He mentioned the clothing company in the Free Zone, and said that the men were to assemble there on Sunday afternoon. *Was this a state-sponsored people-smuggling operation?* Karim wondered. *A wholesale transfer of sub-Saharan Africans from one side of the Mediterranean to the other?*

When the sun started sinking Karim climbed to the ridge again. The wind had a melancholy sound. He looked westward through his binoculars towards Tanger-Med and felt the hairs rise on the back of his neck. The *Mustafa* had returned. He recognised the four cranes on the ship. It was berthed, as he had expected, in Terminal 2.

He scrambled down the hillside and shouted to Joseph that he would be back by midnight. Racing to the road, he pulled the tarpaulin from the car and got behind the wheel. An hour later, with dark descending, he reached Tanger-Med. He parked the Dacia some way from the port, covered it with the tarpaulin and put up his hoodie. Then he walked along the edge of the Logistics Zone to the passenger terminal. A glance confirmed that the *Mustafa* was still in its berth.

Once in the terminal building he was acutely aware of security cameras. How long before someone spotted him? It was evening and there were not many people about: two cleaning ladies, a uniformed security guard, a Moroccan family and ferry company representatives at their counters. Outside the entrance to a coffee shop a female tourist was reading a book, not far from a payphone. Karim went to the café and ordered a *nuss-nuss*. The barista stared and Karim realised that he must look a mess, unshaven, with a black eye and filthy clothes. He took the *nuss-nuss* to the payphone and called Noureddine.

'Where have you been?' Noureddine exclaimed. 'The police are looking for you. They say you killed Simo!'

Breathlessly, Karim relayed what had happened. 'I can't talk for long. I'm at the port. The *Mustafa* is a ship. It's in Terminal 2 at this moment. You need to—'

Karim left the phone dangling. Three EDS guards in hi-vis jackets were walking towards him, one with his hand on a gun holster. Karim darted his eyes. The fourth security guard had already moved to cover the exit at the far end.

Karim threw aside his coffee and raced for the stairs to the train station, taking them five at a time. A train stood in the empty platform with its doors open. Tanger-Med was a rail terminus, running a regular shuttle service to the city. When Karim's pursuers ran onto the platform a few seconds later Karim was nowhere to be seen. They walked along the train, checking every carriage. One of the men ran ahead to check the buffer tunnel.

On the stroke of midnight a tannoy announced the departure of the train and the doors started to close. The three guards exchanged glances then leaped aboard. As the train set off, Karim slid down from the roof of the train onto the platform. His chest and legs were caked in soot but he had the satisfaction of seeing the thugs disappear into the tunnel en route to Tangier. God was merciful. *Al-hamdulillah.*

He turned his hoodie inside out, walked up to the main concourse and out through the entrance of the building. He made his way back to the Dacia, averting his face every time a car went past. He cocked an ear: the only noise was the distant hum of the container terminals. He peered through his binoculars. *Great God!* Terminal 2 was empty. The *Mustafa* had sailed! He looked frantically out to sea, but there was no sign of the ship with its four onboard cranes. No matter, he would follow it in the car, all the way to Cap Spartel if necessary. This time he would find out what it was up to!

He scurried along the perimeter fence, turned the corner and froze: a police patrol car was parked alongside the Dacia, two officers gabbling into their walkie-talkies. Karim turned around and headed back to the station. He would hail a taxi outside the Gare Maritime, that was the only possibility. But even as he approached the passenger terminal he saw the three guards reappear on the steps, shouting frantically. They had probably already thrown a cordon around the port.

He looked through his binoculars in desperation and spotted a wharf with a grey frigate and a patrol boat of the Marine Royale. With a *bismillah*, he put his hands on the wire mesh of the perimeter fence and clambered over.

'*Salaam ou-alikum!*'

Karim hoped the officer in the waterfront building wouldn't pay attention to his inside-out hoodie and soot-blackened jeans. The naval officer had crease lines on his cheek, as if he'd been asleep on his desk when Karim entered.

'Peace be upon you, and the mercy of God and His blessing!' Karim said. 'Listen, my brother, I'm in a fix. There's a
boat out in the Strait that I'm supposed to be on. I fell asleep
and they've gone without me.'

'So what?'

'God have mercy on your parents! Can you take me out to
the boat? I'm going to be in such trouble – I'm the second
officer, you see!'

'Talk to the harbour master's office,' the officer grunted.

'They told me to phone the captain. Ha! As if he's going to
stop the vessel! Do you know how long it takes to stop one of
those things? Half an hour at least! And time is money! With
your patrol boat we could catch it in ten minutes.'

'Fuck off.'

Karim tried one last gambit. 'It's the *Mustafa*.'

'The *Mustafa*?' The effect on the officer was electric. 'Why
didn't you say so?' He took a key from his drawer.

The two men strode out onto the shorefront, the officer
speaking over his shoulder.

'What happened to your clothes?'

'Hey brother, go easy!' said Karim, jumping onto the deck
of the launch. 'I ran all the way here! I fell in that cursed ditch
– I couldn't see it in the dark!'

The officer opened the throttle and the launch moved off,
rounding the wharf at a terrific speed.

'How fast does this thing go?'

'Over forty knots.'

Karim made a calculation: if the *Mustafa* had left when he
was inside the passenger terminal then it had an hour's head
start. A container ship averaged twenty-one knots so they

would overtake it in around thirty minutes. He didn't have the faintest idea what he was going to do when they intercepted the *Mustafa*. At least he had his gun. The Glock 17 was the best gun he had ever used, light and reliable, with a capacity of seventeen rounds. He had tried out all the handguns when he was at police college, a recollection that made him immediately think of Ayesha. He longed for a cigarette. He could have bought cigarettes in the station. He could have called Ayesha as well, when he had the chance. The officer shouted.

'How many have you got on board?'

'What do you mean?' asked Karim.

The officer turned around. 'You know – livestock.'

Karim tried to disguise his excitement. So there *were* people in the containers! He plucked a figure from the air.

'Forty-three.'

The officer sneered. 'Hardly seems worth it.'

Karim sat at the stern working out a plan of action. The other man was also wearing a gun. If Karim tackled him and it went badly he could end up dead. He assessed the merits of a rear choke hold – tricky, given that the officer kept staring at him in his mirror.

The launch was now level with the Malabata lighthouse and Karim saw the glittering necklace of Tangier bay come into view. He peered through his binoculars. There were three container ships ahead of them. Two were small vessels: the *Janina* and *Africa Two*. Further away, like a distant constellation, were the lights of a much larger ship, the *Mustafa*.

'How far is it?' the officer shouted over his shoulder.

'Maybe seven miles.'

They sped past the two lumbering container ships like a cheetah overtaking elephants. They had already left the Spanish coast behind and the ocean yawned ahead. The Cap Spartel lighthouse was the last marker on the port side. The officer was gunning the throttle, raising the noise of the engine to a high-pitched whine.

'What happens if we don't get there in time?' the officer shouted.

'In time for what?' Karim shouted back.

The other man gave him a dark look.

They were closing on the Mustafa. Instantly recognisable were the four onboard cranes, with lights on top. He could see the name *Mustafa* on the stern and below, in smaller letters, Monrovia. Karim counted ten rows of containers across the beam, four behind the accommodation tower and another thirty or so behind the tower. There was someone in the cabin of the forward crane. The jib of the crane started moving to the port side. It came to a halt and the spreader descended to the stack of containers. The next second a container rose into the air. Karim watched with mounting incredulity. *What in the name of God was the crane operator doing?* The jib swung through ninety degrees until the container was suspended over the ocean. There was the faintest of clicks and the container dropped into the water. At a distance of five hundred yards the splash was like a cannon firing.

Karim's view of the container was obscured by the waves and he jumped onto the side of the launch to get a better look. So intent was he in trying to see what was happening that he didn't notice that the naval officer had cut the engine of the patrol boat and was standing below, staring at him.

'Who the fuck are you?'

Karim felt a violent impact as something slammed into his side. He was aware – too late! – that there was nothing to hold on to. His shins hit the railing and, almost before he knew it, he was in the ocean. The drop in temperature was sudden. A wave covered him, then another. He swallowed salt water. He could see the launch receding and raised his arm for help. Another wave covered him and he was gasping for air, his throat clogged with water.

Chapter 13

On Friday morning Ayesha was woken by a distraught phone call from Mokhtar.

'Come quickly!'

She threw back her blanket and sat up in the windowless room. She checked her phone: 7.36.

'What's wrong?'

'*Ajee!* Come quickly!'

'Where?'

'To the beach! There's a body – a corpse!'

Ayesha was wild-eyed. 'Is it – Karim?'

'I don't know . . . his face is gone . . .'

'What do you mean, *gone?*'

'Please, *lalla* – you must get here before the police arrive! I'm on the beach just past the marina!'

Ayesha threw on her tracksuit and trainers and stumbled into the dark corridor. She crossed the rubble-strewn garden, pushed her way through the gap in the fence and started running. There was a streak of light in the sky and the street lamps turned off as she sped past, as if synchronised with her movements. She was on the marine boulevard in three minutes, overtaking another person in a tracksuit. The muezzins started calling the faithful to prayer. Ayesha prayed aloud as she ran. *In the name of Allah, the Beneficent, the Merciful, let it not be Karim!*

Directly after the marina she took a left across the sand. There were two men at the water's edge, one of whom was Mokhtar. At his feet, gently lapped by the waves, was a body, deathly pale. The clothes were fragments; a faded t-shirt and shredded black trousers. The skin of the corpse had burst open in places, and there were holes where the eyes had been. Ayesha kneeled down on the wet sand.

'It's Abdou,' she said at last.

Karim kicked, surfaced, gasped, inhaled water, sank again.

He rose up with a crest then the trough sent him under. He could see the lights of the *Mustafa*, now a mile distant, surrounded by boundless black ocean. He kicked off his shoes and tried to swim. At least the oxygen had reached his muscles.

What was that – an object some way off, a buoy glinting in the pale moonlight . . . no, it was too geometrical to be a buoy. A wave swelled, blocking his view. When he looked again the object had disappeared. No, there it was . . . He started swimming towards it, a feeble breaststroke. Just a few more feet . . . He reached out and grasped the side, struggling to get a grip. The object was extraordinary in its solidity. He realised that it was the corner of the shipping container, most of its bulk submerged, iceberg-like, beneath the surface. With a supreme effort he pulled himself up so that he was draped over it like a cloth. Gripping a slot with his fingers he drew up his knees so that they were clear of the water. He spewed cold vomit. He had cramp and he was drifting in and out of consciousness.

To keep himself awake he recited the ninety-nine names of Allah.

The Compassionate, the Merciful, the King, the Holy, the Source of Peace, the Guardian of Faith, the Protector, the Mighty . . .

Time passed . . . *the Compeller, the Majestic, the Creator* . . . A distant voice . . . *the Forgiver, the Subduer, the Bestower, the Provider* . . . the names were like an echo. He moved his lips: *The Withholder, the Extender, the Reducer, the Exalter* . . . That echo again: *the Honourer, the Dishonourer, the All-Hearing, the All-Seeing* . . . It was an echo but the words were different.

'*Help us.*'

I can't help you, help comes from Allah alone. Glory to God. Allahu akbar.

'*Help us.*'

A cold wave swept over Karim and he opened one eye. The moon was lower in the sky. He had no idea where he was or how far the container had drifted.

'*Au secours, au secours, à l'aide.*'

This time, Karim propped himself up and looked around him.

'Who's there?'

There were no lights, no sound of an engine.

'*Here,*' said the voice.

Where?

'*Here!*'

The voice seemed to be coming from the very tip of the container. Karim groped, then he felt it: a vent, on the far side of the container, just above the waterline. He lowered his face so that it was level with the vent.

'Is there somebody there?'

'*Oui, on est là!*' It was a man's voice, speaking with difficulty. 'We are alive!'

'What . . . *quoi*?' Karim ran his numb fingers over the grille.

'We are three people . . . there were seventy of us . . . the rest are drowned. Please – help us get out!'

'I cannot remove the grille,' cried Karim. 'It is *attaché*, bolted to the side!'

'Please, *monsieur*, hurry! The water is rising! We only have a little pocket of air!'

Karim's foggy brain grasped that the ventilation grille had kept the men alive, but every time a wave hit the container, or the box dipped below the surface, more water entered and the container sank lower. Karim clawed and tugged at the vent. He peered in but could see nothing. There was the sound of gasping.

'Put your hand on the grille!' He touched a man's fingertip.

'*Comment tu t'appelles?*

'Karim. *Et vous?*'

'Sidiki. And Ismael. And Askanda. Are we going to die?'

'I don't know,' said Karim. 'God is Merciful.'

'Are we near to land?'

'*Je ne sais pas.*' Karim looked around him at the ocean, vast and silent. 'It will soon be morning, someone will see us.'

'Were you on the *Mustafa*?'

'No.' There were whispers, then another voice spoke.

'How did you come to be in the sea?'

'I was following the *Mustafa*, Sidiki.'

'No, I am Ismael.'

'Where is Sidiki?'

'Sidiki . . . he is gone.'

Karim saw lights from a container ship. 'There's a boat coming!'

'Is it the coastguard?'

'No. It's a big ship, very big.' Karim levered himself upright and waved his arm. 'Hey! Hey!' He kept waving as the ship came towards them.

At the last minute the ship steamed past, a black leviathan that seemed to go on forever.

'Help!' Karim shouted. '*Au secours!*'

Then he saw the wave. A wash of water sent out by the boat, a veritable tsunami. The next moment it had engulfed him, tossing him from the container and flinging him back into in the water. He choked and spluttered, taking great gulps of air as the tsunami subsided. He looked all around him. There was no sign of the container, nothing but the slow swell of the ocean and the receding black hull marked *Valletta*. His three friends had gone, and with them his lifeline.

He trod water, thinking of the container sinking through the depths below him, and was seized with a fierce will to live. Discarding his hoodie he started to swim in the opposite direction to the ship, using the smooth waters of its wake as a guide. He breathed rhythmically, a slow steady breaststroke, spitting out the briny water, reciting the names of God once more in his head. *The Giver of Life, the Bringer of Death, the Living, the Independent.* With every stroke, he told himself, he was moving towards warmer water. He imagined thermal currents, azure-coloured slipstreams warmed by the sunny shores of Egypt and Palestine. *The Magnificent – the Unique – the Indivisible – the Eternal* . . . Overhead, the firmament turned charcoal, then grey. A new day was dawning. *The First – the Last – the Evident – the Hidden* . . . *There were other names, human names, that he must never forget – Sidiki, Ismael, Askanda* . . .

He could see land, a pencil of black far away to his left. He turned towards it, swam some more then stopped to tread water. The land looked as far away as ever. He kept swimming for what felt like hours. Then he was under again. This time he sank faster. He struggled to breathe, drops of water entering his lungs like molten lava. It took a super-human effort to break the surface and gasp for air. He could no longer feel his fingers and his legs were like weights dragging him down. A dawn breeze had started to blow and waves smacked his face. The coastline was the merest slick, barely visible above the white crests. He would never reach it. He turned over and floated on his back, the breath ebbing from his body, gazing up at the last pinpricks in the sky, at Venus, Arcturus, the North Star, the *Njma Shamal*. How often had he and Ayesha gazed at them from the roof of the riad! He thought of his mother, and his father and his sisters. He felt strangely calm about dying. He had lived a life of submission to God. He had known what it was to love, and to be loved. He saw Ayesha's face and her tumbling, argan-scented hair. They had loved without transgressing God's law. He spoke aloud to the waves: *There is no god but Allah . . . I seek forgiveness from Allah for all my sins and turn to Him . . . To Allah we belong and to Him we shall return. I testify that there is no god but Allah and Muhammad is his messenger.*

Like harbingers of the angel of death a flock of cranes appeared in the sky. They seemed so sedate, so leisurely, flying in perfect formation. Where they were going, these graceful long-necked creatures? How did he look to them from on high, the merest speck in an infinitude of ocean?

He heard the sound of an engine and glimpsed another, darker, shape coming towards him. He turned on his front and raised his hand, immediately swallowing a great mouthful of water. He heard voices, then he was grasping an orange lifebelt and being pulled towards a row of anxious faces. They were gabbling to each other in a language he couldn't understand but which he knew must be Spanish.

'*Està bien?* Do you speak English? *Français? Es-tu le seul survivant?*'

He was being wrapped in a reflective sheet. A cup of hot liquid was thrust in his hands but his fingers were so numb that he dropped it.

'Water!' he gasped. '*De l'eau.*'

A man in a life vest marked *Salvamento Marítimo* handed him a water bottle.

'*Tu viens de quel pays?*'

'Maroc.'

'Where is your boat? Were there others with you?'

'There were others . . . they were in a container . . . it sank . . .'

A woman spoke gently. 'You made the crossing in a container?'

'*Je ne faisais pas la traversée.* I did not make the crossing. My feet, they're so cold.'

A man found another silver sheet and wrapped it round Karim's lower legs. The man looked concerned and said something to the others about *azul*.

'You weren't making the crossing?' another man asked. 'What do you mean?'

'I am not *harraga*. I am not a migrant.'

'You're not a *migrante*?'

The crew exchanged looks again. The first man asked, 'What were you doing in the sea?'

'I'm a police officer . . . with the Sûreté.' Karim searched for his wallet but it was gone. Instead he showed them his gun, still strapped in his holster. The rescue boat was lurching through the waves and he felt nauseous. The shipping container . . . had he imagined the conversation with Askanda, Ismael and Sidiki?

The crew conversed with each in rapid Spanish, then the girl addressed him again. 'We will get you medical attention. *Ne t'inquiète pas.*'

It wasn't until they arrived in Tarifa harbour that Karim managed to persuade the crew that he wasn't a migrant.

'I see,' said Noureddine.

Ayesha was in the *seeber* talking through a headset. She had known Noureddine for two years. It was his endorsement that had won her a place at Kenitra. Now it was Ayesha who broke the news that Noureddine had been dreading.

'The dead man is Abdou's age and height. I could make out the legend *Ourika* on his t-shirt. According to the police doctor the body has been in the water for over two weeks but he cannot judge the cause of death with any certainty. We will have to wait for the autopsy. I am sorry, sir.'

Noureddine heaved a sigh. 'To God we belong and to Him we shall return. What are you doing in Tangier, Miss Talal?'

'I have come to look for Karim.' It was a week since Ayesha had heard from Karim and the discovery of Abdou's body had, if anything, increased her concern.

'I spoke to Karim yesterday.'

Ayesha was overwhelmed with relief. 'God be thanked!'

'You should not be in Tangier,' Noureddine said crisply.

'I have been given leave of absence.'

'Even so, I cannot allow you to remain in Tangier. You are not yet a police officer and you do not have a licence to carry a gun.'

'Please – at least tell me where Karim is.'

'He called me last night from a payphone at Tanger-Med but he hung up suddenly.'

Ayesha felt a fresh wave of alarm. 'So he could still be in danger?'

'Yes. But the situation in Tangier is out of our hands. The Directorate of Territorial Surveillance has taken charge.'

'With the greatest respect, sir, I think I will be able to track down and help my brother faster than the intelligence services. I have been trained in undercover work. As a woman I can find out what's going on without arousing the same level of suspicion as a man.'

'The decision is not for you to make.'

Ayesha threw caution to the winds. 'May God spare you – please, sir, I cannot return to Kenitra. The organised crime group has infiltrated the college. I barely escaped with my life.'

There was a long silence at the other end of the line.

'The corruption in this case is widespread, sir. You need someone in Tangier you can trust. That someone is me.'

'Very well,' Noureddine replied eventually. 'Last night Karim spotted the ship that Abdou was waiting for when he was ambushed – the *Mustafa*.'

'The *Mustafa* is a ship?'

'One moment, please.'

Ayesha could hear talking in the background which went on for several minutes. Finally Noureddine came back on the line.

'God is merciful. Karim has been found.'

'My poor man! What happened?'

Raoul's bulky figure filled the doorway of the reception area at the Centro de Internamiento de Extranjeros. Booklets from a migrant support organisation were spread across a table.

Karim was lying on a stretcher having his blood pressure taken by a nurse. He was burning with fever and wanted to tear off the clothes and socks he'd been given by the Red Cross. The nurse said something to Raoul who pulled up a chair.

'They want to send you to the hospital in Algeciras. You have hypothermia.'

'How does my nose look?'

'Your nose?'

'It was almost cut in half a week ago.'

Raoul exchanged words with the nurse and grinned. 'Apparently that's one of the few parts of your body that's in reasonable shape. Salt water is good for wounds.'

Karim managed a painful smile.

'It's hard to know what to do with you, my friend. You are not a migrant but, because you have no documents, we have to classify you as one. That means that if you go to the hospital we will have to place you under police guard.'

Karim was rather taken by the idea of being looked after in a Spanish hospital protected by Spanish police; it was probably the safest place on earth right now.

'I will be all right . . . I just need to . . .' Karim lost consciousness. He had strange dreams, of water and falling containers. Always falling containers.

When he woke a full day had passed. He was in the Centro de Salud, a bright modern building in the centre of Tarifa, with a drip attached to his arm. Raoul was sitting by his bed, along with a younger man in a white short-sleeved shirt with epaulettes.

'*Ola!*' said Raoul. 'This is Fernando Villa, an officer with Frontex, the border agency. How are you feeling?'

'Sleepy.'

'No pain or discomfort?'

'No.'

'Can you feel your toes?'

'Yes.'

'*Muy bien.* I managed to get hold of your colleague Noureddine Serghini in Marrakech and told him you're safe. I said I would send an update after I'd had a chance to speak to you.'

Karim nodded. 'Raoul . . . when I was in the ocean . . . how did you know to send help?'

'I told you about our wonderful electronic warning system, no? We saw a speedboat – it's very unusual for a speedboat to stray out of territorial waters. But it took us four hours to find you. How did you survive for so long? It's *un milagro*, a miracle!'

'I – I seem to remember holding on to a container. There were . . . people inside the container, sub-Saharans.'

'Stowaways?'

'I'm not sure. Can you see containers on your warning system – ones that fall overboard?'

Raoul nodded. 'If they're not obscured by a ship.'

It was Fernando's turn to speak. 'Containers fall in the Strait all the time. Some float, others sink. It depends what's inside. The ones that float are the problem – the shipping lanes are only two and a half miles wide. If a ship hits a container . . . *boom*. The impact can rip the hull.'

'It wasn't meant to float, it was meant to sink.' Karim's eyes took on a faraway look. 'Ismael, Askanda and Sidiki.'

'What?'

'Those were their names. The men in the container. It will be on the seabed. Can you send a diving team to locate it? There may be others down there.'

'There undoubtedly are other containers on the seabed,' said Fernando. 'How would we know which ones had migrants in them?'

The two men chatted briefly and Karim heard the word *sueño*.

'It wasn't a dream!' he protested.

'Hypothermia can cause hallucinations.'

'It was not a dream!'

'Karim, *amigo*,' said Raoul. 'The ship was outside territorial waters. If it did drop a container it would take years to set up a marine salvage operation. Can you imagine how much money it would cost? It would also require international agreement!'

A nurse came to shoo out the detectives. 'Señor Belkacem needs to rest.'

'There's no need,' Karim said, pulling the drip from his arm. 'I'm leaving.'

Chapter 14

When Karim disembarked from the Tarifa ferry on Saturday afternoon two familiar figures were waiting for him.

Ayesha flung her arms around Karim's neck. All their pent-up adrenalin and emotion came out in floods of tears. They sat on a bench, holding each other and weeping. Mokhtar stood a little way off, looking awkward, so Karim sent him in search of a *nuss-nuss*.

'When did you get to Tangier?' he asked Ayesha.

'A week ago.'

'You've been here a week? You should be at college!'

Ayesha answered between sobs. 'How was I supposed to attend classes when I didn't know if you were floating upside-down in the Mediterranean?'

She didn't mention Hakimi's death or the altercation with Colonel Lalami. There would be time for that later.

'I know about the *Mustafa*.'

'You do?'

'I went to the *seeber* this morning. I did some research into the ship's movements. It left Tangier on the seventeenth of March with 8,345 containers. It arrived in Cadiz the following day with one container fewer. I've looked through the last thirteen sailings of the *Mustafa*. Each time there is a difference of one – sometimes two – containers between the ship's manifest on departure from Tangier and on its arrival in Cadiz.'

'It was horrible. I saw the container being dropped! It made such a crash . . . it floated at first . . . ' Karim started to choke up. 'How many sailings did you say?'

'Thirteen. The discrepancies started last September.'

'They've been doing it for six months!'

'Doing what?'

'Drowning migrants!'

Ayesha's eyes widened. '*Ya Lateef.* Dear God. But that's . . .'

'Murder. Or genocide. Take your pick.'

Mokhtar pressed a cup of coffee into Karim's hand, accompanied by a hacking cough. Karim wiped the rim of the cup with his sleeve.

'Your cough sounds worse, Mokhtar.'

'Don't worry, mister. Right now I'm looking after Lalla Ayesha. Then I will visit the doctor, God willing!'

He took out his *sebsi* pipe but Ayesha shook her head and Mokhtar put the pipe back in his *jellaba*. Karim smiled at the sight of the old rogue up to his usual mischief.

'Thank you for looking after my sister.'

Mokhtar bowed. 'It was an honour to have her staying with me.'

Karim turned to Ayesha. 'You've been staying with Mokhtar?'

Ayesha nodded. 'For a whole week! He's the caretaker of an old Spanish theatre where Enrico Caruso once performed.'

'Who?'

'Enrico Caruso – the famous opera singer.' Ayesha winked at Mokhtar. 'Really, Karim! You mean to say that you've never heard of him?'

The last of the passengers had disembarked from the ferry and the arrivals hall was empty. Mokhtar was starting to get agitated.

'We should leave.'

'One moment,' said Ayesha, unable to put the news off any longer. 'Karim . . . we found a body on the beach. A man. The corpse was badly decomposed but he was wearing an *Ourika* t-shirt.'

Karim stared at her for a moment. He hooded his eyes with his hand and pressed his thumb and forefinger against his eyelids. Tears rolled down his cheek.

'Come on mister, drink your coffee!' urged Mokhtar.

'We're not sure if it is Abdou,' said Ayesha. 'We have to wait for the autopsy.'

Karim ran his sleeve across his nose, causing a momentary stab of pain.

'It will be Abdou. They threw him in the sea. Maybe they drugged him first.'

'The toxicology report will tell us that,' Ayesha said softly. 'So what do you think happened on the night Abdou disappeared?'

'He was watching the container. Maybe he saw it arrive by lorry. The *Mustafa* docked at Terminal 2 at 18.28. He must have been waiting for the ship to load so he had proof that ship and container were connected. But they got to him first.' Karim's eyes took on a faraway expression. 'What baffles me is why a Liberian-registered ship is drowning African migrants. It doesn't make sense.'

'We should leave,' Mokhtar said, now panicking. 'The ferry people are giving us stares.'

Ayesha pushed him away. 'I know why,' she said to Karim. 'You do?'

She stood up and helped Karim to his feet.

'The *Mustafa* is registered in Liberia. But that's just a flag of convenience. The ship is owned by a company registered in Guangdong, China.'

That night Karim paid a visit to the Widow Khoury.

'Mister Belkacem! I don't understand . . . you left your bag and then . . .'

'I know,' he said, striding past her. 'It's all very peculiar.' He went to the bedroom and picked up the holdall with Abdou's clothes. He stopped on his way out and placed a hundred-dirham note in the widow's hand.

'Thank you.'

She stared as Karim marched off down the alley. Ten minutes later he joined Ayesha and Mokhtar at the *seeber* off Rue d'Italie.

'Those guys who chased you, Mister Karim,' said Mokhtar. 'I had nothing to do with them. You know that, don't you?'

Mokhtar was like Simo, Karim decided: a man who kept tabs on everything that happened in Tangier and who had a hand in many of them. But on this matter, at least, Karim believed him. 'Yes,' he replied.

'You shouldn't have gone to pick up the bag. It's not safe.'

Karim gave him a sharp look. 'They're the last possessions

of my dead friend. If you're so worried about my safety then I suggest you stay by the door and keep a lookout.'

Ayesha was at a computer. She looked up as Karim came over.

'Have you heard about the cross-border policing agreement between the Europeans and Morocco?'

'I saw it with my own eyes at Ceuta.'

'*Shouf,* take a look at this.' She swivelled the screen towards him. 'It's a speech that a European politician gave last September.'

The recording, with Arabic subtitles, was of a session of the European Parliament. A politician was angrily denouncing the policy of outsourcing border control to Morocco.

'We pay Morocco millions of euros,' he thundered, 'for what? Night after night our televisions show scenes of overloaded boats, bodies washed up on our beaches, the walls of Ceuta breached as easily as a picket fence. We need a change of policy. We have to stop offering the carrot and start applying the stick. Here's what I propose: for every migrant that reaches European soil we cut funding to Morocco. That would produce results! If Morocco realises that its precious subsidies are at risk they'll soon stop sub-Saharans arriving on Spanish territory. Problem solved!' He sat down to applause and shouts of agreement, as well as cries of 'shame'.

Ayesha stopped the video and turned to Karim. 'What do you make of it?'

'He's a right-wing politician. They spout that kind of filth.'

'But what if his speech caused alarm in Rabat? Transportation of migrants wasn't working . . . they hadn't been successful in breaking up the people smuggling networks. So someone high up gave orders—'

' —to start killing the migrants.'

'Yes! It was too risky for the police to do it themselves. So they gave the job to their security contractor Mohammed Mansouri—'

' —and Mansouri, in turn, went to the drug cartel. They agreed to dump the migrants on one condition: unhindered access for their drugs.' Karim considered the implications, then ran to the door.

'Mokhtar, how can we get to Casiago?'

'There's a taxi driver, he's from my family . . .'

'Is he trustworthy?'

'In this town you should only put your trust in Allah.'

Karim's face took on a determined expression. 'I know someone who can take us.'

In the camp the men were in good spirits. They had all signed up for the voyage on the *Mustafa* tomorrow evening. Better still, they didn't have to go all the way out to the Free Zone: the container was now departing from a depot on the Tetouan road. They would leave Casiago during the night for the twelve-hour walk to Tangier.

The camp had been swelled by three new arrivals: two brothers from Mali and a Congolese teacher by the name of Yannick Lumumba. The trio were exhausted after walking from the Algerian border and decided they would stay in Casiago until it was time for the next crossing on the *Mustafa*. After dinner Yannick switched on his portable CD player and the men danced to 'Marie-Louise', a song they all knew.

'Hey, Franco!' Louis teased. 'Are you going to miss Marie-Louise when you get to Spain?'

'No,' laughed Franco.

'Why not? Are you going to get yourself a nice Spanish *seen-yor-eeta?*'

'You'll find out tomorrow!'

Joseph was the only one not dancing. He sat in his shelter, racked with indecision. He had promised Karim not to make the crossing until Karim had found out what was going on. But Karim had been gone for forty-eight hours and the sailing was about to happen. Tomorrow was Easter Sunday: a propitious day for a Christian to make a journey. He made up his mind to attend the eleven o'clock service in St Andrew's Church. God would give him guidance on what to do.

The men celebrated around the campfire until rain started falling. They packed their belongings. Then, with Joseph, they started the long walk west.

Lightning flashed and heavy raindrops hit the windscreen as Hicham, the police driver, drove through the *centre ville* with Mokhtar beside him and Karim and Ayesha in the rear. Mokhtar was coughing into a rag.

'You shouldn't be out in the storm, Mokhtar,' said Karim. 'You're not well. You should go home.'

'Don't worry about me.'

Karim and Ayesha exchanged glances, then Karim turned to the other man.

'How's your son, Hicham?'

'He is well, praise God,' said Hicham. In a small, timid voice he added, 'Your face is on *Wanted* posters at the prefecture.'

'I didn't kill Simo.'

'I know that, sir.'

'There are rotten apples, *temrat fasadin*, within the police force. When they have been removed life will get better, *inshallah*. For now, they think I'm dead. That's all that matters.' He put his hand on Hicham's shoulder. 'Stop here!'

Hicham turned around in surprise. 'But we're only in Malabata!'

'I've changed my mind. There's a roadblock after Malabata. The police will search a car with four adults inside. Can I borrow the car?'

'Of course, sir.'

'You and Mokhtar go back to town. It's better for you, Mokhtar – you need to look after yourself. Ayesha can drive and I'll hide in the boot.'

Ayesha wasn't sure about the plan. 'I've only just learned to drive!'

'It's only a short distance. You'll manage.'

'Are you going to come back to Tangier afterwards, Mister Karim?' asked Mokhtar. 'My home is not luxurious but the welcome is warm and Lalla Ayesha knows how to find the entrance.'

Karim looked through the window. The rain was getting heavier. 'I don't know yet.'

'You can't stay at Casiago. You'll be soaked!'

'There's a hotel at the port, the Al-Majaz,' Hicham pointed out.

'Very well. If the storm is bad we'll stay there for the night.'

Ayesha whispered. 'Karim, we haven't any money!'

Mokhtar reached into his *jellaba*. For a second, Karim thought he was going to pull a knife. Instead, he took out two blue banknotes and slipped them into Karim's hand. Karim looked at the money with confusion.

'Take it,' grinned Mokhtar. 'It's money I made selling kif to tourists.'

Karim was overcome. 'Thank you, my brother.' He turned to the driver. 'Thank you, Hicham.'

'May God keep you safe.'

'A bus is coming. Jump out and you'll catch it.'

Five minutes later, Ayesha approached the checkpoint, glancing nervously at the spike strip beside the road. A gendarme peered through the window then waved her through. Ayesha stopped the car a mile down the road and Karim took the wheel.

'We're going to have to do this again in half an hour. The road to Casiago leads through Tanger-Med and there will be police at the port looking for me.'

As it turned out, there wasn't a roadblock at Tanger-Med, but Karim ducked below the window, just to be sure.

'There was no one about,' said Ayesha when they had left the port behind. 'Just some migrants on the road. They must be soaked through, poor things!'

They took the N16 up into the mountains. Even with the headlamps on full beam all they could see were rods of rain and cascades flowing down the road.

'I'm glad you're doing the driving,' said Ayesha, holding on to the grab-handle beside her seat. 'The instructor at college didn't cover these conditions.'

'He does if you opt for the advanced course,' Karim grinned.

He peered at every bend until they came to the corner where he had first spotted Oussuman and Bouboucar. He ran the short distance from the road to the forest. Five minutes later he returned, sodden and out of breath.

'They've gone. There were only three men in the camp whom I didn't recognise. They said the others have gone to Tangier. The *Mustafa* sails tomorrow!'

The descent proved even more difficult than the climb. The tyres on the Dacia were no match for the slippery bends. At one point, Karim lost control and they skidded into a tree. The impact left them both shaken.

'What day is it tomorrow?' asked Karim.

'Sunday.'

'There's no point trying to get back to Tangier tonight. Joseph goes to the English church on Sunday mornings.'

'You can't show your face in daytime! The police will be looking for you.'

'There's a train.'

'Are you crazy? It's far too dangerous!'

'For me, yes. Not for you. You must take the train to Tangier and meet Joseph at the church. The service starts at eleven.'

A few minutes later the car slowed into the car park of the Al-Majaz Hotel. The reception area was modern, with marble floors and sleek-looking sofas. Western pop music was playing softly in the background as they walked in. The clerk behind the desk greeted the bedraggled couple.

'*Salaam ou-alikum*, what a night!'

Karim asked the price of accommodation.

'One hundred and eighty for a twin room,' said the clerk. 'Two hundred and sixty for two singles.'

Until that moment Karim hadn't given any thought to sleeping arrangements.

'We'll take a twin,' said Ayesha. As they climbed the stairs she whispered, 'We can't afford to waste money.'

The beds in the room were arranged next to each other. There was a wall-mounted television, a little balcony and an *en-suite* bathroom. If Ayesha was awestruck by her first stay at a hotel she didn't show it.

'I'm going to take a shower. Do you have a spare t-shirt?'

Karim threw her a red-and-green Moroccan football shirt from Abdou's holdall. When she was in the bathroom he put on his jacket and went out in the rain. He found a payphone outside a row of closed shops and called Noureddine. They spoke briefly about Karim's rescue. Karim explained their theory about how the port was letting in fake drugs in return for the cartel dealing with the migrant 'problem'.

He could hear a sharp breath at the other end.

'You may be right. We found a correlation between the deaths of people smugglers and the decline in seizures at Tanger-Med.'

'Noureddine,' Karim asked. 'Who asked us to send an officer to Tangier, back in February? I know that it wasn't the Tangier police.'

'I wondered that myself. According to Badnaoui, the request originated from the Chinese government. They monitor the fake drug trade – as you can imagine, they're embarrassed that the drugs originate in China – and the fall in inspections at Tanger-Med aroused their suspicions. Tell me – where are you now?'

'At Tanger-Med, staying in a hotel.'

'Is that safe?'

'For one night, yes.'

'Where's Miss Talal?'

'She's with me.'

'She's staying with you at the hotel?'

Karim squirmed. Would Noureddine think he was having sexual relations with Ayesha? No, that was crazy! Why would Nour think that?

'I want her out of Tangier. There's nothing more for her to do there. She's risking her life. Make sure she's on the first train to Kenitra. You need to stand down as well, Karim. Wait until the autopsy results come through, then return to Marrakech.'

'What about the *Mustafa?* It's due in port tomorrow!'

Noureddine gave a sigh. 'Karim, you are a lieutenant in the Judicial Police in the fourth precinct of Marrakech. This case has outgrown you – and me. It is now a national security matter, possibly an international matter. It's for the Directorate of Territorial Surveillance to decide what to do next.'

'But what if the intelligence services are involved with the cartel?'

'We will have to take that risk.'

With that, Noureddine brought the conversation to an end.

Mokhtar was in his candlelit kitchen in the Teatro Cervantes. He had changed from his wet *jellaba* into a clean cotton robe and was waiting for the teapot to boil. He had already filled it with a generous sheaf of mint, a handful of black tea and three rectangles of sugar. He coughed into a handkerchief. When the teapot was piping hot, he lifted the handle with the handkerchief and set it on the table, then sat down and started tamping his *sebsi*.

A voice came from the shadows.

'Where are they?'

Mokhtar was so surprised that he dropped his pipe. He started groping under the table, then saw the pipe trapped under the steel-capped boot of his visitor. He retreated and settled unhappily in his chair.

'Who? The Ma – the Marrakchis?'

Mohammed Mansouri spoke in a low voice loaded with menace. 'Of course, the fucking Marrakchis.'

'They've gone to warn the migrants in Casiago.'

'How are they getting there?'

'I don't know.'

Mansouri brought his foot down on the pipe, producing a loud *crack*. Mokhtar shrank back, terrified.

'They took a police car, a Skoda.'

'Whose?'

'A driver, I think his name is Hamid.'

Mansouri picked up a strip of pills from the table. 'What are these?'

'Antibiotics.'

'Antibiotics?'

For a brief moment, Mokhtar thought Mansouri was going to ask if he was ill.

'You fucking idiot.' Mansouri leaned down with his mouth next to Mokhtar's ear. 'They're fake. Useless. U-s-e-l-e-s-s.' He enunciated the word slowly, as if talking to a simpleton. Then he stood up again. 'Aren't you going to offer me tea?'

'Er—'

Mansouri took a spoon from the table and gave the pot a stir. 'What's the Marrakchi planning to do in Casiago?'

'I – I don't know. Maybe stay in the camp with the blacks.'

'The blacks are already on their way back to Tangier so he's not likely to do that, is he, cuntface?'

'No.'

'And I don't think the Marrakchi would want to camp out in this weather with his girlfriend, would he, arsehole?'

'No.'

Keeping his gaze on Mokhtar, Mansouri used his sleeve to lift the hot teapot in the air.

'So . . . where are they staying?'

Mokhtar made a croaking sound but no words came. Mansouri moved the teapot over Mokhtar's lap then started to pour. Mokhtar screamed as the scalding liquid burned his flesh.

'Where are they?' demanded Mansouri.

Mokhtar clutched at the table in agony.

'Where are they?' Mansouri repeated, tilting the teapot further.

'In the hotel . . .' Mokhtar gasped. His genitals felt as if they had melted in a blaze of pain.

'Which hotel?'

'The – the Al-Majaz.'

When Karim returned to the room Ayesha was lying on one of the beds, watching television. The football shirt came half-way down her slim legs.

'*Labas?* All good?' said Karim.

'All good.' Her cheeks were glowing.

'Ayesha . . . you have to go back to Kenitra tomorrow.'

A shadow crossed Ayesha's face. 'Don't joke with me.'

'I'm not joking. This is where it ends.'

'Where what ends?'

'You and me, fighting the cartel. It's too big for us to handle.'

'What has changed since twenty minutes ago?'

'I called Noureddine. He told me you have to get on the train.'

'And what about Joseph?' Ayesha said, turning off the television. 'What about the migrants you call your friends?'

'I will find Joseph and make sure he doesn't get into the container. After that, the intelligence services will take over.'

'The intelligence services? How do you know they're not implicated? The cartel is everywhere! I haven't told you what happened in Kenitra, the night you called me.'

'Nothing happened. You didn't reply.'

Ayesha shook her head. 'Everything happened.'

'I don't understand.'

'Listen to me! Salma saw the phone a few days earlier. She wanted it out of the room so I hid it in the library. Unfortunately, Hakimi – that boy I told you about – found it.'

Karim stared at Ayesha with mounting horror.

'He taunted me all day, threatening to blackmail me. When you called I was still at dinner. Unfortunately, so was the phone – in Hakimi's pocket. The phone went off in front of everyone in the dining room. The next day Hakimi was dead. They made it look like suicide. I was the only one who understood what had happened. They traced your call.'

Karim stared, trying to grasp the enormity of the disaster he had set in motion. Ayesha consoled him.

'What's done is done. At least the cartel have no reason to suspect me.'

Karim shook his head. 'They have every reason to suspect you. They know who you are. They know everything. That's why Noureddine wants you out of the city. The cartel know that you're my sister.'

'But I'm not your sister!'

'What are you talking about,' asked Karim, growing heated. 'You are my sister. Just because I'm a Belkacem and you're a Talal that doesn't change the fact that you're my sister.'

'I don't think Lalla Hanane would see it that way. Nor Abderrahim.'

'Ayesha—'

'You *were* my brother, once upon a time, when we were growing up. I had no one else then. It's different now. I have a brother, Abderrahim.'

'Why are you saying this now?'

'Perhaps meeting Abderrahim has clarified things in my head.'

Karim stood up. 'If we are not brother and sister then we are committing an act of indecency sharing a hotel room.'

'Goodness, Karim! We can *pretend* to be brother and sister if that makes you feel more comfortable.'

'Merely because you have left to live with Lalla Hanane, you cannot break the ties that bind us.'

Ayesha laughed. 'Look at your face and look at mine. My skin is brown and yours is pale. My eyes are dark and yours are green. We're as different as black and green olives!'

'We were nursed by the same woman! We are the same, don't you understand?'

'You think we're the same?' Ayesha's voice trembled. 'You were born into a loving family and have a healthy mother and two healthy sisters. I was adopted, my father is dead, as is my sister, my mother is eaten up by despair and my brother is a man who believes that sometimes it is right to shoot a woman for misbehaviour. We are not the same.'

'It is God's law. We all have ties. You with Abderrahim. Me with you.'

'Yet you want to put me on the train back to Kenitra!'

'No, I said that Noureddine wants you on the train back to Kenitra. I didn't say I was going to put you on the train.'

Ayesha sat on her knees, her eyes shining. 'I can stay?'

'If you get on the train to Kenitra you will be killed as surely as Hakimi was killed. I cannot allow that. What's more . . . I need you.'

Ayesha clapped her hands with glee. 'I need you, too. More than I can say.' She kissed Karim on the cheek. 'Do you think it's safe to stay in the hotel tonight?' she added in a small voice.

'Yes,' Karim replied. He said the word with a certainty that he did not feel.

Ayesha smiled and closed her eyes, utterly spent. Within minutes she was asleep. Karim gazed at her for a long while.

They inhabited a realm of their own, he decided, beyond the everyday world of affection and desire, neither siblings nor lovers but something else entirely. As the rain beat against the windowpane he lay alongside Ayesha, his arm around her, his gun between them, listening to her sleep.

Chapter 15

Karim woke next morning to the sound of a cock was crowing. He got up and looked out of the window. The rain had stopped but there were heavy grey clouds over the Strait.

After dressing and saying his prayers he closed the door quietly, so as not to wake Ayesha. There was no one downstairs other than the clerk, who told him that the dining room was across the forecourt and up a flight of steps.

Karim's feet echoed on the tiles. It was a vast room, with a panoramic window and a chandelier hanging from the ceiling. He scanned left and right but the room was empty apart from a single table, laid, at the window.

'*Sbaeh al-khir!* Good morning!'

The waiter arrived carrying a tray with *msemmen* pancakes, a triangle of Laughing Cow cheese, a pot of mint tea, a croissant and a little pot of honey. As he placed them on the table Karim put his hand on his arm.

'A *nuss-nuss* please, my brother.'

The waiter smiled. 'Not a problem. I'll have to get it from the kitchen downstairs.'

Karim sat opposite the window to detect any comings and goings to the hotel. Container trucks thundered past on the highway. On the far side he could see diggers clearing the construction site of Tanger-Med 2. Work had started over a year ago but it looked like there was still a long way to go. He devoured one pancake and was already on his second when he heard the footsteps of the waiter behind him. *Al-hamdulillah!* The day was going to be fraught and he needed a short, sharp *nuss-nuss* to wake him up.

'Detective Belkacem?'

Karim twisted around and the blood drained from his face. Standing next to him was the Chinese man who had trailed him in the medina. Karim felt a lurch, as if he was falling. He fumbled at his holster then realised he had left the gun in the bed next to Ayesha.

'Relax, detective,' the man said in English. 'May I sit down? My name is Lee, from the Shanghai police.'

Karim faltered. 'You – you're a police officer?'

'Indeed! I'm with Interpol.' Lee was a tall, slim man in a grey raincoat, who wore his hair with a centre parting. 'I'm attached to the Chinese intelligence services.'

Karim was caught between surprise and relief. 'I knew the Chinese were involved in this investigation but I wasn't aware that they had sent someone here.'

'Indeed! When your associate – forgive me, what was his name?'

'El-Mokhfi.'

'When Lieutenant el-Mokhfi disappeared, our intelligence services notified us that you were in the city. We tried to establish contact with you in the Petit Socco, and later in Rue d'Italie, but you kept giving us the slip.' He gave a little laugh.

'And the Moroccan man?'

'Is our contact with the Moroccan Ministry of the Interior. He's a policeman, like you and me.'

'So you know about the *Mustafa*?'

'Yes.'

'You could have prevented the loss of dozens of lives! Why didn't you impound the ship?'

'For the same reason as your late colleague, Lieutenant Mokhfi. We were not ready. We have to cut off both heads of the snake.'

'But you will impound the *Mustafa* tonight?'

'I cannot tell you that. But whatever we do, we will not require your services. Thank you for your efforts so far, but we must ask you to desist.'

'I am happy to do so. Excuse me.' Karim mopped his mouth with a paper napkin and stood up.

'Where are you going?'

'Tangier.'

'Sit down, Lieutenant Belkacem. We cannot have you running around in Tangier. Right now, the cartel think they have eliminated the biggest threats to their operation, namely yourself and Simo Layachi. Let's keep it that way.'

A second Chinese man came up to their table, his lips tightly drawn. He whispered something in Lee's ear, whereupon Lee turned to Karim.

'Where is your girlfriend, Lieutenant Belkacem?'

Ayesha was watching from behind a pillar with mounting alarm. She had woken a few minutes earlier to find the gun in the bedclothes and Karim gone. When she saw the Chinese man talking to Karim in the restaurant she feared a trap. Karim had now reached the same conclusion.

'Tell me, Mister Lee – you referred to my girlfriend just now. But if you were really working with the intelligence services, you would know that she is my sister.'

At that moment footsteps echoed across the floor: the waiter was returning with Karim's *nuss-nuss*. He stopped short of the table and stared, sensing that something was wrong. With the slightest of movements the tight-lipped Chinese pulled out a gun with a silencer and the waiter fell to the floor, a hole in his cheek.

Before Karim could react, Lee pushed a syringe into Karim's thigh and pressed the plunger. The other man grabbed Karim's arms and pinned them behind his chair. Karim struggled to free himself but he was already getting woozy.

'Did you use that to kill my friend?' he said in a low voice.

'This is liquid ketamine. It doesn't kill people.'

'But you *do* kill people, don't you? Container-loads of them.'

'Nobody wants them, lieutenant! Europe doesn't want them. Morocco doesn't want them. They're like black rats. In China, we kill rats.'

Two shots rang out. The first one hit Lee in the shoulder, the second hit the gunman's chest. The gunman fired back and bullets ricocheted off the pillar. Ayesha kept her finger on the trigger until the magazine of the Glock had run out and both Chinese men lay dead on the floor. Karim pulled the syringe out of his thigh, swayed slightly and sat down again.

Ayesha looked at the bodies. 'I killed them . . .' she said, half in amazement, half in fear.

'You haven't killed anyone – not officially,' said Karim, taking his gun from her and wiping it clean of fingerprints.

'Are you all right?'

Karim tried to get up again. 'We have to . . .'

'You've got the drug in your system!'

'We cannot stay here . . .'

Ayesha ran out of the restaurant. Two minutes later she returned in her *jellaba* and headscarf, carrying Abdou's holdall with their few possessions. Karim had collapsed onto the floor.

'Karim! Wake up! We've got to get to the road. Come on, get up.'

Ayesha placed Karim's arm around her shoulder. They staggered outside, Karim's feet dragging like a zombie's. Ayesha cast around in a panic, then hauled Karim towards a bus stop. A group of Port Authority workers were waiting for a minibus back to Tangier. They stared at Karim.

'He had a late night,' Ayesha said with an apologetic smile.

To her consternation, the bus was crowded. She helped Karim down the aisle. The workers in the back seat shifted along, regarding Karim with alarm. The bus had hardly gone a hundred yards when Karim fell against his neighbour, a middle-aged woman in a cleaner's uniform. He opened his eyes and exclaimed.

'Khadija! What are you doing here?'

The woman edged back in fear. 'What's wrong with him?' she asked Ayesha.

'Are we going to the seaside?' said Karim dreamily. 'Fantastic . . . *mezyan bezzaf*!' He looked at the cleaning woman for a moment, then suddenly jerked forward and vomited on the floor.

Everybody on the bus jumped up. Ayesha was beside herself with panic.

'Get up, Karim!'

'Are we there?'

Someone asked the driver to stop. Ayesha did her best to support Karim and the two of them wobbled to the door.

'Sorry!' she said to the driver. Fortunately he was a kindly man, and he helped Ayesha take Karim off the bus. The doors closed and the bus drove off, the passengers' faces pressed to the windows.

'This is bad, Karim!' Ayesha said, Karim's arm around her shoulder. 'Very bad! What if they tell the police? Stand up! Stand up properly!'

Vehicles thundered past on the road. Desperate to get to safety, she helped Karim across the highway – an operation which required all her strength. They shuffled down a track to the construction site of Tanger-Med 2.

'Come on, Karim! You've got to help me!'

'Where's Lalla Fatima?' he drawled, his eyes half-closed. 'We've gone without her.'

Spotting a freshly dug concrete culvert, Ayesha lowered Karim onto the embankment. She crouched in the entrance of the culvert, placed her hands under Karim's arms and pulled him inside. Then she sat with her feet against the wall and rested Karim's head in her lap. He was breathing heavily.

'We studied Toxicology in college. Ketamine doesn't stay in the system for more than a few hours. It's not like Fentanyl, it doesn't have lasting effects. You'll be all right . . . but Karim! I killed a man!'

She might as well have been speaking to the wall, for all that Karim could hear.

'I killed a man . . . I'm not even twenty-two years old and I killed a man! *Two men!* Oh, God forgive me, what have I done? *You're not authorised to use firearms*, that's what Noureddine said! Did you see the blood on the floor? Have you killed a man, Karim? Please tell me that you've killed someone . . .'

Karim was unconscious. Ayesha shook him twice in desperation, then her face took on a different expression. Doing her best not to disturb Karim, she placed the holdall under his head and eased herself out of the culvert.

Mokhtar's face was grey as he peered from the back door of the old Cervantes theatre. He coughed, a low rattle that came from his chest. He scanned left and right then pushed the door shut. He climbed the steps up to Boulevard Pasteur with difficulty. As he did so another man, tall and thin, his mouth misshapen by a cleft palate, emerged from a doorway on the far side of the street.

A short distance away, at St Andrew's Church, white lilies had been put out for Easter Sunday. Joseph sat at the back of the congregation, exhausted after his overnight trek from Casiago. He mouthed the words of 'Christ the Lord is Risen Today' while Agnes, the elderly Englishwoman he had met eleven days ago, pounded out the tune on a battered harmonium. Most of the other men in the congregation were Nigerian, with a scattering of Ivorians, Guineans and Congolese. Many of them would be travelling with Joseph on the *Mustafa*, carrying the hopes of their wives and parents, brothers and sisters.

The priest was a short-statured Nigerian who preached that the message of Easter was one of hope: the story of Jesus Christ ended not with a dead body but with resurrection. When the time came to pray, Joseph asked God to see him safely to his new life. He would work hard in the factory, save every euro and, with God's grace, in six months' time he would make his way with Jean-François to Barcelona.

Outside St Andrew's the Sunday souk was in full swing. Along the walls, Riffian women in their striped garments and broad-brimmed hats were bartering over eggs and vegetables while fruit vendors called out, 'Strawberries three dirhams a kilo!' On the other side of the street stalls were doing a brisk trade in tagines, bric-a-brac and kitchenware.

A turquoise *petit taxi* inched through the crowd, Ayesha in the back. She gave a start when a pedestrian banged on the bonnet. The taxi driver laughed.

'It's chaos isn't it, *a lalla*? The flea market on one side, those crazy Berber women on the other! The authorities should make this a one-way street, at least on Sundays!'

'*Fin al-kanisa?* Where is the church?'

'It's straight ahead, you can see it above the palm trees. I will have you there in a minute, *a lalla*! Better safe than sorry, as they say! *Llahumma slama wala ndama!*'

But he was addressing an empty seat. Ayesha was already pushing her way through the crowd.

Pressing through the crush from the other direction was Mokhtar. He had to stop every few feet. The coughs that shook his frame were deep and racking. Leaning with one hand against a shopfront, he looked up at the tower of St Andrew. He remembered what the *Afreeqee* had said about attending the church on Sundays. A squawking chicken flapped its wings in Mokhtar's face before being hustled away by its owner. Suddenly, he saw the Africans coming out of the church. He tried to get closer – *there he was*, Joseph, shaking hands with another man outside the gate – he could see the name on Joseph's arm!

Ayesha too, saw the tattoo. She was only twenty feet from Joseph but her path was blocked by veiled women carrying heavy bags of vegetables and a blacksmith pushing a barrow of charcoal. With a gasp, she spotted Mokhtar to her right, trying to get to Joseph. *What was he doing?* She redoubled her efforts to reach Joseph. Then she saw a third person: a tall man in a robe, rising above the crowd as he weaved his way to the point where Joseph and Mokhtar's paths would intersect. Mokhtar was there first and he flung himself on Joseph's neck.

'*Tu vas mourir!* You will die!'

'*Quoi?*'

'I am Mokhtar, friend of Karim! You remember me? It's a trap. They're going to kill you! They're going to drown you!'

Terrified, Joseph looked to left and right. '*Où est Karim?*' Mokhtar's gesticulations were drawing attention. A shawled woman was trying to peddle her cheese, pushing a basket under Joseph's nose.

'*Jben! Jben!*'

'*Non, non!*'

'*Fais attention,*' said Mokhtar, giving way to a fit of coughing.

'*Jben! Jben! Jben!*' went the woman.

Joseph cast around in panic.

'Stay away,' gasped Mokhtar.

'*Jben! Jben! Jben!*' went the woman.

'What?' cried Joseph.

'Look for the—'

Out of nowhere came a flash of steel. There was an exhalation from Mokhtar and his eyes enlarged, as if he had just realised something. His grip loosened and his hand fell away.

Ayesha, only three feet away, saw it all: the tall man had thrust a machete deep into Mokhtar's stomach, then pulled the blade out, tucked the machete under his robe and turned on his heel. If Joseph hadn't been holding on to him, Mokhtar would have collapsed.

'Mokhtar! I'm here, it's me – Ayesha!'

She reached Mokhtar just as his body crumpled to the ground. The crowd had noticed that something was wrong. 'He's been stabbed!' someone shouted.

Joseph was frozen to the spot. Kneeling down among the forest of legs, Ayesha cradled Mokhtar's head and stared up at Joseph, wild-eyed.

'Don't get in the container! It means certain death!'

A voice cried. 'It was the *azzi*! The negro did it!'

Ayesha screamed. 'Run!'

Joseph sped off down Rue d'Angleterre, pursued by shouts. '*Shedd al-azzi!* Stop the negro!'

Ayesha shook Mokhtar, trying to staunch the flow of blood with her hand. 'Don't worry Mokhtar, you'll be fine, an ambulance will be here!'

'Red Cross . . .' he whispered.

'The what? What are you talking about?'

'Red Cross . . .'

'Why do you want the Red Cross?'

'Paint . . . *Tahyer, tahyer* . . .'

'What's *tahyer*? I don't understand!' She held him tight. 'You've been stabbed in the belly, that's all! The hospital can fix that!' She noticed that his eyelids were no longer fluttering. 'Mokhtar, pray! Recite the *shahada*! *Laa ilaaha ill-Allah!* There is no god but Allah!'

But it was too late. Mokhtar was dead.

That Sunday, the Terrasse des Paresseux – the lookout terrace on Boulevard Pasteur – was busier than usual. If the people admiring the view had looked downwards they would have seen a woman in a taupe-coloured *jellaba* and patterned head-scarf walking down a flight of steps and through a gap in a fence.

The back door to the Teatro Cervantes was unlocked and Ayesha felt inside for the light switch. She crept carefully over the rotten planks. Stray cats rubbed themselves against her shins. Her eyes went to the word *Taller* on the staircase down to the basement. *Taller, tahyer.* Maybe that was how the word was pronounced. Activating her phone torch, she descended slowly into the darkness, the steps creaking as she went. The basement smelled of mould. It was inky black ahead of her and she wondered if the basement extended under the stalls. She could distinguish piles of wooden chairs and old costumes draped over a table. Holding her phone aloft to increase the circle of light, she saw the outline of a door in the wall. She groped towards it and shone her light on a sign: *Taller.* The metal clasp on the door was stronger than she expected. She gave the door an experimental push, then tried kicking it. Leaving her phone light propped on the table, she went back upstairs to the stage. She tugged at the velvet curtain, producing a shower of dust. She pulled harder. More dust, and a few pigeon droppings. Finally, she gave it a violent yank. This time the curtain fell, bringing down a heavy wooden pole that smashed into the floorboards and sent a cloud of dust billowing across the auditorium. When she had recovered from coughing, Ayesha lifted the end of the pole with both hands: it would make a fine battering ram.

She dragged it down the staircase. When she reached the bottom of the steps the other end of the pole was still at the top. She worked the pole through her hands until the top end had thumped down into the basement. Holding the pole in the middle, its full weight in her arms, she stood a few feet back and lunged at the door. The door shuddered and paint flaked from the panels. She picked up the pole and tried again. This time the door gave way.

Inside was a workshop, far larger than any of Mokhtar's rooms. A faint light came from a window, the panes so dirt-encrusted that the light could only get in through a small gap where the glass was missing. Directly underneath the gap, on the stone floor, was a pyramid of pigeon droppings. Ayesha could hear the faint noise of traffic from the Boulevard Pasteur. She flicked a light switch. The room seemed to be in better condition than the rest of the theatre. Against one wall was a bench equipped with clamps and woodworking machines. Facing the window was a row of chests and a large clothes cupboard. She opened the cupboard, ran her hand along ball-gowns, military uniforms and cloaks so moth-eaten that they fell apart under her touch. A heavy trunk in the corner contained theatre props. She took out a heavy sceptre, the orb encrusted with coloured glass, then turned her attention to five large wooden trunks. Unlike the other parts of the theatre, the surfaces of the trunks were free of dust, as if they were opened regularly.

She looked in the first trunk. It was filled with passports and identity cards. She picked up one, marked *Republic of Ghana* . . . a black face stared at her. All passports must have a value, she decided, even African ones. She opened another trunk, containing numbered metal seals for shipping containers. She went through the next trunk and found mobile phones – hundreds of them. Finally, she found what she was looking for: canisters of red spray paint.

Just then there was a creak from the staircase. Ayesha quickly turned off the light, picked up the sceptre and pressed herself against the wall, holding her breath. A cat meowed just outside the door. A few seconds later, a gun broke the outline of the doorframe. The toe of a shoe appeared on the threshold and, just under the lintel, the profile of a man's face. He remained motionless for what seemed an eternity, listening. Then, just as Ayesha's lungs felt they were going to burst, he switched on the light. In the same instant, Ayesha sprayed the aerosol directly into the man's face, following through by smashing the heavy sceptre into his jaw. He fired the gun, but missed. She dashed past him, up the stairs and out of the theatre. She didn't stop running until she had reached the railway station.

'No children.'

A group of sub-Saharans, around a hundred in all, were standing in two lines in the EDS depot, being supervised by guards with walkie-talkies. Following the police raid on Best Century Clothing, the departure point had been switched from the clothes factory to the hangar of the security company.

'You were told not to bring children,' said a guard with a grizzled face and the harsh accent of a Riffian Berber.

'Please!' begged Marie-Louise. 'They won't make any noise.' She pointed to the bundle on her back. 'This one's always asleep!'

'No children.'

Marie-Louise clasped her hands. 'Please sir, I am a widow. Look at my children – they have nothing to eat, they eat banana skins from the gutter!'

'Children cannot work in the factory! Get them out of here! *Amenez-les!*' The security guard looked around, then hissed at Marie-Louise. 'Go! It's for your own good!'

Franco, who was standing behind, unzipped his belt. He extracted a fold of money and placed it in the guard's hand.

'This is everything I have. Let the woman and her children through.'

Before the guard could answer, Franco pushed the little group forward.

'Thank you, sir. God bless you.'

The mood among the migrants was cheerful. The official-looking guards, the security company vehicles and the strict embarkation procedure reassured them that the operation was genuine. Their previous attempts to get to Spain had been on flimsy dinghies or over fences topped with razor wire. A journey in a container, sitting on sandbags and supervised by men in orange vests, was like travelling first-class.

The prevailing optimism made it hard for Joseph to convince Jean-François and Amadou of the danger.

'He was standing no further from me than you are! Stabbed with a machete!'

'Probably a private vendetta,' said Amadou. 'Nothing to do with us.'

'You say he smoked kif,' said Jean-François.

'Yes.'

'And the attacker? What did he look like?'

'A tall guy, thin as a rake, with his mouth all twisted. And there was a woman in a big hat with coloured pom-poms.'

Amadou laughed. 'Are you sure you haven't been at the kif as well, *mon ami*? Has it made you a bit crazy?'

'I'm not joking. *Je déconne pas!*'

'Listen, Joseph, even if you saw a nasty accident—'

'It was not an accident!'

'—the port is covered with security cameras. The Strait of Gibraltar is as busy as Kinshasa on Saturday night. Do you think they'll drown us with so many boats watching?'

'Maybe they wait until they're out in the ocean!'

Amadou gave an impatient sigh. 'If we stay here we will starve. We will get beaten up and shipped south. Is that what you want?'

A stout guard with a moustache called out. 'One suitcase each! *Une valise, une valise!*'

'We need to take all our clothes!' one of the migrants protested.

'Why? You're going to work in a clothes factory. You can have all the clothes you want! Take one change of clothes – *safee!*'

A woman asked about the crossing. 'What if we need the toilet?'

'There are buckets.'

'Buckets?'

'What do you expect – an *en-suite* bathroom?' The guard looked at a colleague and they both laughed.

'Hurry along, now! *Dépêchez-vous!*'

Louis had refused to jettison any of his precious clothes and he looked like a Michelin Man, dressed in layers of shirts and trousers.

'If you have no identification, move to the left!' said a guard. 'If you have a passport, move to the right! *Si vous avez un passeporte, passez à droite!*'

Jean-François had held on to his black Congolese passport through four years of beatings and searches, and it was a wrench to hand it over.

'Don't worry,' said the Chinese man who took it. He sat behind a desk flanked by two EDS security men. 'You will have it returned. It's just a precaution, to make sure you don't abscond when you arrive in Cadiz. Your phone, too. Switched off.' He attached Jean-François's phone to his passport with an elastic band and added them both to a pile. 'Next!'

In the row of non-passport holders, Louis was cracking jokes with Franco.

'The first thing I'm going to do is buy a Spanish mobile.'

'I thought you said the first thing you were going to do was find a *señorita*.'

'That's the second thing. I need to be able to give her a phone number.' Louis gave a theatrical sigh. 'You have so much to learn, *mon ami*.'

Joseph stared at the crowd in the hangar. It seemed as if several camps had been rounded up for the exodus. Once the migrants had been processed they were shepherded into the forecourt, where a container lorry was waiting with its doors open. The migrants who were already standing or sitting inside were beckoning to the others like school children on an outing. Amadou and Jean-François climbed into the back of the lorry. But when Joseph reached the ramp he stepped aside.

'I'm not going.'

Amadou and Jean-François looked at him in dismay. The container was now almost full and the guards were ushering the last of the migrants forward.

'What's going on?' asked Franco, coming to the edge of the container.

'Joseph doesn't want to go.'

'Why not?'

'He thinks they're going to kill us.'

'That's crazy!'

'That's what we told him.'

'*Ecoute*, Joseph,' said Franco. 'If they were going to kill us would they give us air vents to breathe? Would they give us water to drink? Would they give us sandbags to sit on?'

Jean-François tried a different approach. 'We're cheap labour! We're young and fit and never go on strike! Why would they want to get rid of us?'

'Look around!' hissed Joseph. 'There are no Arabs here – no Syrians, no Iraqis. Doesn't that tell you anything?'

'There are a hundred Africans to every Syrian in Tangier. Stop worrying!'

The rest of the queue were trying to get past. 'You're blocking the way!' someone complained. A guard closed the first door of the container.

'*Viens.*' Jean-François held out his hand. 'The trip will be over before you know it.'

'I'm not going,' Joseph said flatly.

The guard asked in an aggressive voice what he was doing. '*Qu'est-ce que tu fais?*'

'I've decided not to go.'

'Listen, *azzi*, you're going whether you like it or not!'

With a curse he pushed Joseph inside. The sight of Joseph being manhandled into the container unnerved the occupants and some of those sitting down got to their feet. But the door slammed shut, the interior went dark and there was a loud *clank* as the bolts slid into place.

It was impossible to see a thing but Karim was aware of others around him. The floor was hard and cold, wet with condensation. There was a noise – a clanking, then a whirring, followed by the hush of people holding their breath. Karim listened, his senses on full alert. Suddenly the floor dropped and there was a sensation of falling, like being trapped in a plummeting lift, followed by a tremendous, bone-shattering impact. Bodies were flung around like rag dolls. Water started pouring in from the vents, slowly at first, then in torrents. The container tilted, sending the occupants tumbling into one corner. As the water level rose, there was a frantic struggle to get to the surface. There were prayers and moans. The water level was soon high enough for Karim to reach the vent. Groping in the blackness, he tugged at the steel louvres. His face was just above water. He pushed frantically at the roof of the container, pounding it with his fists while others clutched his legs, dragging him down.

'Wake up!' Ayesha was shaking his legs. 'Wake up!'

Karim was lying in the culvert, his body soaked with sweat, his hands bloody from battering the concrete above his head. He peered at Ayesha.

'Where . . . What . . .?'

'It's all right,' she reassured him. 'You're safe. Take your time. When you feel ready, come out.'

Ayesha sat back on the embankment. The sun was low and work had finished for the day on the construction site. She took a drink from a plastic water bottle and gathered her thoughts. On the train back to the port she had sat with her hood up, taking furtive glimpses when a guard came past. There were few other passengers, mostly Western tourists or middle-class Moroccans taking the ferry to Algeciras. Once or twice she felt the canister in her *jellaba* pocket, but she had been too scared to look at it.

Karim crawled out of the culvert, pale and disorientated. 'Is that blood on your *jellaba*?'

'It's not mine.'

'Joseph?' Karim asked fearfully.

'No – Mokhtar . . . Oh, Karim! Mokhtar is dead!'

With gulps and tears she recounted how Mokhtar had died in her arms. Karim stared vacantly.

'*Llaherhamou*, may God have mercy on him . . . The tall man with the hare lip – I've seen him before. Where is Joseph now? And his friends?'

'I don't know. But you – how are you feeling? Can you stand?'

Karim rose unsteadily and immediately went down again, his right leg unable to bear his weight.

'What time is it?'

Ayesha shaded her eyes at the sun. 'Around five o'clock.'

'We have time. The *Mustafa* won't leave just yet.'

'But Karim! How are we going to get into the port? The place is crawling with police. I saw commandos with machine guns at the station!'

'Take off your *jellaba*. No – on second thoughts, keep it on. Leave the holdall.' Karim got down on his hands and knees. 'Follow me.'

Everyone sat down once the lorry started moving. There was just enough light to see but the occupants could only stretch out a leg if they rested it on the leg of their neighbour, which provoked a lot of good-humoured banter. Marie-Louise's infant started crying and a man piped up.

'Can't you feed him?'

'Joseph? Is that you?' asked Marie-Louise.

'No, I'm over here.'

'Keep the baby quiet!'

'Let it cry. We don't have to worry about babies crying,' said another voice.

'You always have to worry about babies crying. What if the police hear it?'

'Never mind the police!'

'*Où sommes-nous?* Where are we?'

'I think we're coming to the end of the motorway,' said Joseph.

'Joseph, *mon ami* – do you have any water?' This time it was Amadou.

Joseph groped in his bag for a bottle.

'It's hot,' said Marie-Louise.

'It will get colder when the sun goes down.'

'I need a pee,' cried a woman.

'Go ahead, Fatoumata, we can't see anything back here.'

'I'm not worried about that – with the lorry moving I might fall over.'

Everyone laughed. Amadou started humming a rumba tune. The others joined in, clapping their hands until the lorry stopped suddenly and someone got out of the cab. They banged on the side of the truck and told the migrants to keep quiet. Then the lorry started moving again.

Apart from being pitch black, the culvert was so narrow that Karim couldn't turn his head to check on Ayesha's progress. The trough under his hands and knees was filled with mud and rainwater. The rank air, added to the ketamine still in his system, made him want to puke.

'Have you killed a man?' Ayesha panted.

'What?'

'Have you ever killed a man?'

'No.'

There followed several minutes of silence. All Karim could hear was Ayesha sloshing behind him.

'Your father once told me that if you kill a man it's as if you killed all mankind.'

'My father wasn't a policeman.'

'Is it a quote from the Quran?'

'Yes.'

'Will I be punished?'

'Punished by God, you mean? No. The Quran says killing is justified in retaliation for murder. The Quran also says that if anyone saves a soul it would be as if they saved all mankind.' With a catch in his voice, he added, 'You saved my life.'

'I couldn't save Mokhtar's life.'

'Mokhtar was ill. If he hadn't died from the machete, he would probably have died from pneumonia.' Karim paused to wipe sweat from his eyes. '*Labas?* You OK?'

'*Labas.* I feel a little sick, but it could be the tunnel.'

'Ayesha . . .'

'*Nam?* Yes?'

'I'm proud of you. The college would be proud of you.'

He could hear Ayesha give a little sniff. When they had gone another fifty feet they heard running water. Another tunnel joined theirs, curving away to the left. Their hands and knees were now three inches deep in water. Keep crawling downhill, Karim told himself. *Downhill leads to the sea.*

'Who's your favourite instructor?' Karim asked, in an attempt to keep up Ayesha's sprits.

'What? Oh . . . Daoud, I suppose.'

'He used to be a professional boxer, did you know that?'

'Is that how he broke his nose?'

'No. He was a boxer for four years before going into the Sûreté. His first job as a police officer was in Aïn Sebaâ. One night he was sent to break up a fight outside a supermarket. An old man got angry because Daoud wouldn't let him buy any alcohol and the old man ended by punching him on the nose. Imagine – he spent years as a boxer and ended up getting his nose broken by a drunkard in a supermarket car park!'

'Karim . . .'

'*Nam?*'

'Is it much further?'

'No.' Karim didn't know if it was ten yards or a mile, but he kept his thoughts to himself.

'Only . . .'

'What?'

'I feel claustrophobic. I feel like I've been buried alive.'

At least we'll be buried together, Karim thought. 'You're doing well. It won't be long now.'

'How did you find out about this tunnel?'

'Mansouri told me. He told me that some sub-Saharans got into the terminal by crawling along a culvert.'

'*This* culvert?'

'I think so. I saw a map of the port at the Port Authority offices.'

They continued for a few more minutes. '*Reed baalek.* Watch out,' Karim said.

'What is it?'

'Something just brushed past me. I think it was a rat.'

'*Aieeee!* I felt it!' There was a scuffle behind him then a sloshing, as Ayesha lifted her hand away. A few minutes passed.

'My hands are sore,' Ayesha said.

'Mine too.'

'I'm thirsty.'

'Me too.'

'I'd like an ice cream.'

'Have you been to that place in Kenitra? On the crossroads?'

'You mean Delicia? The best place for ice-cream is Patisserie Camilia, on Rue Sebta.'

'Who took you there?' Karim remembered taking a girl for ice cream when he was at college. Going into town for ice cream was a popular Saturday afternoon activity for cadets.

'A boy.'

Karim felt a pang. 'Seriously?'

Ayesha laughed. 'No, silly – I went with Salma. We've only been once. It's too expensive.'

Karim was starting to get worried. What if there was a grille at the end of the tunnel? It would be physically impossible to turn back. Once again, he kept his thoughts to himself.

'You said you went to see Abderrahim.'

'Yes.'

'And?'

'He told me that Mansouri was in Kenitra, as you suspected. He used to be a hashish smuggler. He was indicted by a court in Casablanca, along with several members of the Tangier police.'

'That explains a lot.'

'Yes.'

'Are you going to keep visiting him?'

'I suppose so – he's my brother, after all. But I'll only visit him on Sundays. And only if I'm not in Marrakech. You're never around when I come to Marrakech. Will I see you next time I'm there?'

Before he could reply, Karim felt cool air on his cheeks and he gave a cry of delight.

'We're coming out!'

It was painful to stand up so they leaned forward, taking great gulps of fresh air and giving thanks to God. Ayesha looked around.

'Where are we?'

Karim twisted from the waist a few times to massage his back, then stood fully upright. Night had fallen and it took him a moment to get his bearings.

'We're above the ferry port. See that frigate down there? It belongs to the Marine Royale.'

Facing the frigate was the building where he had started his ill-fated pursuit of the *Mustafa*. They sat down out of sight and huddled together for warmth.

'That was the worst experience of my life,' said Ayesha. A minute later she added: 'Do you think we can fight the cartel? Just the two of us?'

'I don't know.'

'Will the intelligence police send reinforcements?'

'I don't know that either. I've been waiting for them to contact me.'

'How could they contact you? You don't have a mobile and mine is switched off.'

'True.'

'What do you think the chief of police was doing that night at the lighthouse?'

'Simo? He was checking that the crew had dumped the container. Presumably that was his job – to check they dropped it.'

'Was he part of the cartel?'

'I'm still not sure. I think he may have been blackmailed. He has young children.'

'And Mokhtar?'

'I'm almost certain he was an informant for Mansouri. Mokhtar was a scoundrel, but he also walked the path of righteousness. He was like Simo – caught between two worlds.'

'And the others – the customs officers, the police?'

'They do as they're told. The same goes for the men at Ceuta and the seamstresses at Best Century Clothing. They follow orders. They don't realise they're part of a bigger operation.'

'Masterminded by Mansouri?'

'Mansouri is just the executioner.'

'So who's the mastermind?'

Karim shivered in Abdou's hoodie. 'I doubt we'll ever know.'

Chapter 16

An hour later, when a three-quarter moon was above the Strait and Ayesha was asleep on Karim's shoulder, a container ship with four onboard cranes slid out from behind the breakwater. Karim woke Ayesha. The pair got to their feet and stole down to the low building by the wharf. The sound of a radio drifted from the open doorway.

While Karim hid behind an oleander bush Ayesha removed her filthy *jellaba* and smoothed down her red tracksuit. Karim gave her a nudge and she walked across the courtyard into the door of the Marine Royale. Her legs felt like jelly.

There were two men inside, smoking. One was reading a newspaper. The hands on the clock on the wall stood at quarter to midnight.

'Good evening, gentlemen!'

The men exchanged glances and the older man's face broke into a smile.

'*Good evening!* Are you lost, *a lalla?*'

'No,' said Ayesha, running her hand along the counter. 'I'm staying at the Al-Majaz Hotel, up on the highway. I couldn't sleep so I decided to come for a walk.'

The two men looked at each other again. Ayesha cast around the room so they wouldn't see the nervousness in her eyes. She noticed a poster with a mugshot of Karim. The younger man followed her gaze.

'Dangerous ruffian. Killed the chief of police.' He ripped the poster from the wall and scrunched it up. 'But you don't have to worry, *lalla*,' he laughed. 'My colleague here – he dealt with him.'

'Oh, that's a relief!' Ayesha was afraid of saying the wrong thing but she remembered from her exchanges with the men at college that flattery was usually a good tactic. She smiled at the older officer. 'Do you mean to say you actually caught the man yourself?'

The man leaned over the counter. 'Indeed! We had a fight but he was no match for me. I tossed him off the boat.'

'The boat outside?'

'That's the one!'

Ayesha waited a couple of beats then said, 'It looks very fast.'

'Would you like to go for a ride?'

Ayesha felt a surge of adrenalin. The man had fallen for it! Now she had to act apprehensive, so the officer could take charge.

'Is that allowed?'

With a smirk at his colleague, the officer plucked a key from a drawer and came out from behind the counter. He put his hand on the small of Ayesha's back and they stepped from the building. Ayesha was so nervous that she almost collapsed.

Once on the speedboat the man slipped the painter and turned the key in the ignition. Karim suddenly appeared out of the darkness. He leapt onto the deck and charged into the other man, who fell backwards in surprise. Ayesha grabbed the controls.

'Turn the slider forward,' Karim shouted, his hand on the officer's chest. 'That's it! Now open the throttle – the one on the right!'

The boat swerved violently, then sped out of the harbour. The officer took advantage of the jolt to reach for his gun.

'I thought I finished you off the first time,' he growled.

Before he could shoot Karim slammed the officer's hand against the floor and jammed his forearm against his windpipe.

'Who do you take your orders from?' Karim demanded. 'Mansouri? Or someone else?'

'Go to hell,' the man choked.

Karim regarded him with contempt. 'The longer you take to reply, the further you'll have to swim.' Fear came into the man's eyes. Keeping his hands on his windpipe, Karim looked at the receding harbour. 'We're now about four hundred yards from the shore . . . four-twenty . . . four-thirty . . .'

'They'll kill me if I tell you!'

'Four-fifty . . . four-eighty . . .'

'Mansouri is on the *Mustafa*, that's all I know!'

Karim pulled the man up by the scruff and flung him over the side. He took the controls from Ayesha, who laughed with relief.

'Where did you learn to fight like that?'

Karim grinned back. 'Where did you learn to *flirt* like that?'

The container walls vibrated gently with the noise of the ship's engines. Joseph found it hard to sit comfortably. He was too broad-shouldered to lean between the ribs of the steel wall so had to sit upright with his arms around his knees. An icy draught blew from the vents and he put on his puffa jacket. The only other things in his carrier bag were a pair of trousers and a photograph of his mother and sister. Everything else he had lost at Ceuta.

A fleeting matrix of light from the vent: a lighthouse, perhaps, or a passing ship. A tang of urine wafted around the interior. After the argument with his friends on the ramp of the EDS depot Joseph had largely remained silent. What was the point of adding to everyone's fears?

There was a whimpering that sounded like it came from Marie-Louise. She had been sick and Joseph could hear Franco murmuring words of comfort. A thought: perhaps Marie-Louise was pregnant. She had been overjoyed when Franco showed up with the other men earlier. He had kissed and hugged the boys, calling the infant 'little man' as if he was his father. Maybe he had fathered all the boys.

Nobody around him spoke. Those who weren't asleep were thinking of loved ones or their future in Spain. Today was Easter Sunday. Or was it Easter Monday? In Kisangani the family used to dress up for Easter Sunday. Gloria wore a yellow dress with a bow. She didn't wear the white dress again after what happened.

Who was the girl who told him to flee earlier, outside St Andrew's? She looked too young and pretty to be a friend of the drug addict. One day in the camp, when Karim and Joseph had been washing the dishes, Karim had mentioned that he had a sister, like Joseph. But the girl outside St Andrew's didn't look like Karim.

He hadn't seen Karim since he left the camp three days ago. He had disappeared, just like his neighbour from the first camp at Boukhalef. Perhaps they were both lying dead at the bottom of the ocean. But he, Joseph, was alive. And as long as there was life there was hope.

Franco and Marie-Louise fell silent. Now there was just the drone of the ship's engines, accompanied by a high-pitched hum from the refrigeration units.

Once the Cap Spartel lighthouse came into view Karim turned into the wake of the *Mustafa*, hoping to avoid detection by the ship's radar. Five minutes later he brought the launch along the flank of the ship, a minnow alongside a whale. Ayesha could see the rivets on the hull glinting in the moonlight.

Karim tethered the boat to the pilot ladder and climbed the rungs. He put one hand on the gunnel of the *Mustafa* and peered over the side. A hundred feet to his right was the accommodation tower with *NO SMOKING* in giant letters. Thank God, there was no one standing at the bridge window. To his left, separated by thousands of containers, was a port-side crane. After checking that the passageway was clear, Karim eased himself over the side of the vessel and into a cubby hole. Ayesha joined him a moment later. They crept along towards the bow, counting the bays. In the first thirty-four bays were dry goods containers, followed by nine bays of refrigerated containers, then a bay of hazardous goods containers, their doors covered with warning signs. Beyond the crane, at the bow, stood five final bays. Karim whispered to Ayesha that on the previous occasion the jettisoned container had been positioned in the last bay but one.

They were near to the crane when a shaft of light fell in front of them. Karim and Ayesha quickly pressed themselves behind an air duct. Disaster! Two Filipino crew members in white hard hats and blue jumpsuits came out onto the walkway. Karim couldn't understand what the men were saying but he feared that one of the men was the crane operator and that any moment he would climb up to his cabin. They had to try and get to Joseph's container from the other – starboard – side but the only crossing points were in full view. Karim whispered to Ayesha.

'Can you run around the ship?'

'You're crazy!' Then she added: 'How far is it?'

Karim pointed at a sign on the gunnel giving the length of the walkway in both directions. It measured one hundred and eighty metres to the stern and one hundred and forty metres to the bow. Karim made a guess.

'Four hundred metres.'

She gave him an odd look, then took off at full pelt along the passageway. Karim followed her red tracksuit as she sprinted up the steps to the stern and disappeared from sight.

Ayesha dodged the capstans and lashing bins, skidding into a pillar. Barely stopping to catch her breath, she took the down stairs in one bound and hared along the starboard side. Obstacles stood in her path: struts, pulleys, cages, lifebelt posts. Dodging and leaping, she raced up the steps at the fore end and came to an abrupt halt – there were ten crew on the foredeck, one of whom was holding a semi-automatic rifle.

She was in the shadow of the penultimate bay, separated from the port side by nine rows of containers, five or six tiers high. She spat on her hands and reached up to the lashings of the nearest container, grabbed the locking rods and, with her trainers planted against the door, pulled herself up a tier. Using the door cams and handles, she climbed up the containers like a rock climber scaling a vertical face, finally reaching the roof of the final container. To her relief, the containers in the bay had all been loaded to the same height. She ran along the rows, jumping from one container to the next, continually checking the crane cabin for signs of activity.

By now, the *Mustafa* had left the coast of Africa far behind. Over on the port side Karim had noticed that one of the two crew members had disappeared. One man tilted his head back, suggesting that the other was scaling the crane ladder. If Ayesha was to have any chance of locating the container and freeing the occupants she would need more time. Karim grabbed an orange waistcoat from the back of the air duct.

'Hey there!'

He greeted the Filipino crew member in English. Before the man could reply, Karim looked up at the crane operator, who was just about to get into his cabin.

'Come down, my friend!'

The crane operator stopped and looked down. 'Who the fuck are you?'

It was the second time in a week that he had been asked that question.

'The captain wants me to operate the crane.'

The man on the walkway stepped between Karim and the ladder.

'Who did you say you were?'

'I'm with EDS.' At the mention of EDS the two crew shot a glance at each other. 'Call the captain if you don't believe me.'

Out of the corner of his eye Karim saw a flash of red above his head – Ayesha! He carried on talking.

'However, I don't think the captain would appreciate being interrupted right now. He's got the Spanish coastguard on his tail.' Karim put his hands on the bottom rung of the ladder and looked up. 'Come on, my friend. Let's get this done.'

'Stay there,' growled the man beside him. Keeping his eyes on Karim he pressed the walkie-talkie attached to his jacket.

'We have an unknown person on board! Repeat, unknown person, portside Bay Fourteen.'

Karim heard a volley of swear words over the walkie-talkie, finishing with 'kill him'. Without waiting he sped off down the passageway towards the bay where he had seen Ayesha. As he tilted his head and scanned the silver-grey containers, he failed to see three men in jumpsuits blocking his path. The next thing he knew the air had been slammed from his lungs and he was toppling onto the deck. More members of crew ran up and surrounded Karim, shouting in English and Filipino. Fighting for breath, Karim scoured the roofline behind the men's heads. He couldn't spot Ayesha's red tracksuit. The jib of the crane was turning slowly through ninety degrees. A burly crew member, dressed like the others in a blue jumpsuit and white hard hat, prodded Karim with the barrel of his rifle while another man disarmed him.

'I'm with the Moroccan police!' Karim cried. 'Do you understand? I'm with the police!' He pointed. 'There are migrants in that container!'

The jib of the crane settled over the topmost container in the third row and the spreader descended. Karim was seized with despair. Ayesha had made it to the bay but it looked like she hadn't found Joseph's container in time. Without warning, a high-velocity rifle shot made everyone jump. It was followed by a crackle from the walkie-talkies. 'He's a terrorist! Shoot him!' Looking down the ship towards the bridge, Karim could see the stocky outline of Mohammed Mansouri on the bridge wing, pointing a rifle.

'There are people in that container!' Karim cried to his captors. 'That's what your job is – to drown migrants!'

There was a gabble from the crew members and the man with the rifle spoke into his walkie-talkie.

'Are there migrants inside the container?'

Karim could hear a *click* fifty feet in the air as the twist-locks engaged, then a judder as the container ascended on four steel cables.

'Of course not!' Mansouri's voice came over the walkie-talkie. 'There's nothing inside but sandbags! I've explained to you! It's an insurance scam! We jettison containers and claim the insurance!'

An argument broke out among the men.

'Kill him,' Mansouri barked over the walkie-talkie. 'Kill him!'

The long arm of the crane was now swinging out from the vessel, the container suspended high above the waves. The men had taken off their ear protectors and were watching to see what happened. Karim, too, was lying on the deck spellbound, gazing up in appalled anticipation. The jib came to a halt above the ocean and the container swayed gently, silently, a black rectangle against the starlit sky. There was a horrible silence. At that moment Marie-Louise's baby started crying. Whether the wind had changed, or the hum from the engines had dropped, the sound carried down to the deck of the ship.

Several things happened in quick succession. The gunman, who up to that point had his rifle trained on Karim, put his rifle aside. Instantly, a shot rang out and the man fell dead. The other crew members scattered in terror. Karim, hitherto shielded from Mansouri's eyeline, rolled against the platform as another shot rang out, which missed his foot by inches. Above him, the crane operator was crouching in the doorway of his cabin, mouth wide in shock. There was a *crack* of gunfire and a moment later he, too, slumped dead. From his hiding place Karim saw everything. But Mansouri had made an error. There was now no one to operate the crane; as long as the container was attached to the cables, the migrants had a chance.

Suddenly, there was another *crack*. Karim looked around in panic, wondering what Mansouri was firing at. A moment of dread: was Ayesha the target? He didn't dare raise his head above the parapet in case it was blown off. Karim stared help-lessly at the container. Then he realised that it was hanging by only three of its cables. *Ya rabee!* By God! Mansouri was shoot-ing at cables. How could Mansouri see the filaments, let alone find them with his rifle? A second shot rang out and another cable snapped. The container fell forward with a violent lurch. Karim gave a cry. Try as he might, he could hear no sounds of life, no shouts or screams. The people inside would be crushed to death!

The container swung back and forth, a giant coffin skimming the waves, a red *X* on the lid. *Zing!* The third cable snapped. One last strand remained. There was a loud *crack* and it, too, gave way. The near-vertical angle of entry meant that the ten-tonne container, full of men, women and children, disappeared instantly into the ocean.

Karim ran to the side and stared at the point of impact, already receding from view. Would the container resurface? There was no sign of it. Just ripples. *People are nothing but lines scribbled on the water.* He had failed to rescue his friends – Jean-François, Franco, the ever-smiling Louis, Amadou, Bouboucar, possibly Joseph, too – just as he had failed Abdou.

The sound of shearing metal brought him back to his senses. Freed of both the container and the heavy steel spreader, the counterweight was causing the crane to tilt. The jib swung one hundred and eighty degrees and crashed into the hazardous goods containers like a giant's arm swatting a pile of shoeboxes. Instantly flames erupted, spreading quickly to the other containers.

Grabbing the dead man's rifle Karim ran back along the walkway. His only thought now was to rescue Ayesha. The crew had forgotten him in their rush for firefighting equipment. He crossed the deck underneath the accommodation tower, pausing behind a bulkhead door to take off his yellow waistcoat and tie it around his face. The smoke coming from the shattered containers was thick and noxious. Heaven help Ayesha if she was trapped!

He went down each bay and row in turn, unable to see more than a few feet ahead. Soon he was in the thickest part of the fumes. He pressed the bandana to his face. One ravine was impassable: burning drums wedged between the stacks like sticks of dynamite. The fire was burning fiercely and it seemed that the crew was having little success in getting it under control. He called out. 'Ayesha?' A bullet ricocheted. He looked up into the pall of smoke, his eyes streaming, trying to see where the shot had come from. As the smoke cleared he spotted a figure standing high up on the corner of one of the stacks . . . a sniper, his outline veiled by smoke . . . Karim fired and the figure disappeared.

Running along the dark, choking canyons was like being trapped in some hellish maze, his face and hands burning from the fumes, his eyes straining to see. Two shots hit the ground between his feet. He turned, glimpsed a lofty silhouette, aimed and fired. Again, it was impossible to tell if he had found his target. Karim emerged on the starboard side, steadied himself against a container and took great gulps of air. A lifeboat was already in the water, sailing away from the ship. Karim scanned the passageway in both directions, turned and went back into the maze. All of a sudden, he saw it: a flash of red, darting from left to right. *Praise God the Merciful!* He raced down the canyon. There she was again – about a hundred feet ahead, running erratically, as if she couldn't see straight.

'Ayesha!' His voice was a barely audible croak.

When he reached the intersection he stopped and looked around. Suddenly she appeared again, this time on his left, running between the stacks.

'Ayesha!'

He ran after her, then stopped. There was no sign of her. The sniper, too, had disappeared – either because he had been hit by a bullet, been overpowered by fumes or joined the exodus off the boat. Peering down a canyon, Karim saw an open container, one door ajar. Tentatively he edged down the row past the familiar names, the Maersks and MSCs and Hapag-Lloyds, holding the rifle with both hands. He pushed open the door of the container with the barrel of the gun. It was hard to see in the gloomy interior but he could make out a huddled figure in the corner.

'Ayesha?'

It was silent inside, insulated from the smoke and hubbub, and he could hear his footsteps as he crossed the floor. He rubbed his eyes. Ayesha had her back to him but there was something about her that wasn't quite right. She was clad in the red tracksuit top of the Commissioner Corps but she also appeared to be wearing dark trousers and a gas mask around her face. Karim reached down and touched her shoulder.

'Ayesha?'

Karim lifted off the gas mask – it wasn't Ayesha, but a Filipino man, his mouth somewhere between a grin and a sneer. Before Karim could do anything he heard a voice from behind, inflected with a Riffian accent.

'It's like shooting a dog in an alleyway.'

Standing behind Karim was Mohammed Mansouri, his rifle levelled at Karim's head. An armed commando stood by his side with a torchlight.

'What have you done with her?' Karim cried.

'We knew you'd come looking for her, although I must admit I thought you'd provide a little more sport.'

Mansouri swung the butt of his rifle into Karim's chin, sending him flailing across the floor. The Filipino stripped Karim of his gun. Karim was spluttering on his hands and knees and Mansouri was cocking the trigger, and Karim knew that it was all over and he would die like Abdou had died, his body tossed into the sea to provide fodder for creatures of the deep.

As he raised his eyes in silent prayer he saw the barrel of a shotgun protruding from the ventilation grille. There were periods in Karim's life – entire years – when he had only a hazy recollection of what happened. But he remembered the next ten seconds with absolute clarity. They started with an explosion, a one-hundred-and-forty-decibel gunshot that rent the dark air in the container and briefly illuminated, through the ventilation grille, the face of Joseph – *Joseph!* – who half an hour ago was drowned beneath the waves; a second later, the commando was lying dead and Mansouri was unleashing a volley of explosions that shattered the ventilator until there was nothing left, just a sliver of plastic hanging from a square-shaped hole. Ten seconds had passed, and it was now the Filipino man's turn to take the stage. Frightened out of his wits – unlike Mansouri, he was directly beneath the vent and had seen Joseph's face – he scrambled to his feet and hurtled towards the door. Too late! His exit was barred by two silhouetted figures wearing puffa jackets, and now both Mansouri and the Filipino were frozen in shock, as if they had seen ghosts. More explosions reverberated and Mohammed Mansouri – the most dangerous man on the Maghreb coast, Scourge of the Rif, crack marksman, wife-killer and drug-trafficker – was now lying on the floor, clutching his wounded arm, quivering in fear, his Amazigh tattoos powerless against men who had come back from the dead. Another man's arm, dark and marked with a different tattoo, reached down and lifted Karim to his feet.

'How—?'

Without waiting for explanations Karim ran with Joseph onto the deck, into the melee of smoke and flames. They charged through a bulkhead door into the interior of the vessel, past offices and storerooms. Crew were running in every direction. In the ship's office it was pandemonium, crew fighting for gas masks while a panicked officer fired shots at the ceiling. Seeing two of the lucky ones rush towards them, Karim and Joseph blocked their path, seized the masks and raced up to the next deck. Peering around the corridor they spotted one of Mansouri's thugs, gas-masked and armed, standing outside a door. At a sign from Karim, Joseph gave a shout. The guard came running and Karim barrelled into him sideways, sending his gun skittering along the floor. Karim kicked open the door of the cupboard.

Ayesha was sitting on the floor in her t-shirt and track bottoms, gasping from the fumes. Karim kneeled down and placed a mask over her head.

'*Labas?* Are you all right?'

She gave a weak smile and nodded.

'She let us out!' exclaimed Joseph. 'She opened the door to the container!' In a tone of awe, he added: 'Who is she?'

As Karim helped Ayesha get up a can of red spray paint fell from her tracksuit pocket and rolled across the floor. Karim picked it up and smiled.

'She is . . . a very clever woman.'

'What do you mean?'

'If you were to look over the roofs of the containers – the ones at the bow – you would observe a field of red crosses. Am I right?' He gave Ayesha a questioning look and she nodded.

Joseph only half-understood. His thoughts were on getting to safety.

'*Allons-y!* The fire is spreading!'

He led the way up another flight of stairs to the lifeboat station. Mansouri was standing by a yellow submersible, being held at gunpoint by Franco and Jean-François. Mansouri had recovered his composure.

'It looks like there isn't room for us all, Marrakchi. Who are you going to leave behind?'

Karim stepped inside the lifeboat. Every seat was taken, a host of anxious faces. Oussuman was standing by the controls waiting for orders.

Karim turned to Mansouri. 'There's room for one more.'

Karim pulled the Riffian so hard that he toppled over the threshold and sprawled on the floor of the lifeboat between the feet of the migrants. Murmurs rippled among them.

'Listen, fellow Africans!' cried Karim. 'This is the man who killed your friends, your cousins, your brothers and your sisters. He would have killed you tonight, but for the grace of God.'

Mansouri lifted himself from the floor. For a man surrounded by a hostile crowd he seemed remarkably calm, even dignified. He addressed his onlookers.

'It was nothing personal. If you need a scapegoat, blame the Europeans. They're the ones who started this.'

Karim turned to Oussuman. 'Make sure he returns to Tangier.'

'*Tangier?*' Oussuman could hardly believe his ears. '*Mais . . .* we could get to Spain in this boat!'

'We will see each other in Tangier,' said Karim in a voice that brooked no disagreement. 'Close the door and turn the handle.'

At seven o'clock the next morning two boats limped into the small fishing harbour of Tangier. One was a launch carrying Karim, Ayesha, Louis, Amadou and twelve officers and crew of the *Mustafa*. The other was the yellow lifeboat. When the door of the lifeboat was opened, Mohammed Mansouri was no longer on board.

His body was never found.

Chapter 17

There had been a change in the weather. An area of high pressure had moved up the Atlantic coast, displacing the easterly wind. In Marshan, the cemetery was a riot of purple sage. Ayesha, Karim and Joseph were staring at a newly dug grave.

'Who left those bird-of-paradise flowers?' asked Ayesha.

'The Widow Khoury.'

'The woman you stayed with? Why did she leave flowers?'

'She used to be married to Mokhtar.'

Ayesha was astonished and delighted. 'The sly old fox!'

'He was lucky to get a space in the cemetery,' remarked Joseph. 'They're running out of room.'

'Mokhtar knew everyone in Tangier. He would have slipped someone a few dirhams a long time ago, before he became ill.'

A workman came up to Karim and spoke in his ear. Karim looked at Joseph.

'Do you want to see the plot?'

The three of them walked over to a spot near the wall where Joseph had slept a fortnight earlier. Workmen were leaning on their spades, next to a trench.

'The memorial will be ready in fifteen days. The men will return to put it up.'

'How high will it be?' asked Joseph.

'High enough to be visible from the sea. Although only with binoculars!'

'And the inscription?'

'To *Sidiki, Ismael* and *Askanda*. Along with a dedication in French to the thousands of unknowns who perished in the Strait.'

'In Hausa as well?'

'In Hausa, Yoruba, English, French and Swahili. The Tangier-Tetouan district council will pay for it as an act of atonement.'

After a few minutes Ayesha asked Joseph the question that had been uppermost in her mind.

'Are you going to keep trying to cross the Strait?'

'No.'

'Why not?'

Joseph regarded them shyly. 'I was at Chez Kebe last night. The men said that the Moroccan government is going to grant an amnesty to migrants. We'll be allowed to stay in the country and get official papers.'

'Oh, that would be wonderful!' Ayesha clapped her hands. 'The King is a good man. He will make it happen, *inshallah*!'

'Where are you going to live?' asked Karim.

'*Alors* . . . Jean-François, Louis, Franco, Amadou, Marie-Louise and her children want to rent an apartment in Boukhalef. Although I think Franco and Marie-Louise will look for a place on their own. The baby is due in October.'

'And you?'

'The custodian of St Andrew's Church has a spare room. I can stay with him in return for looking after the churchyard.'

'He sounds like a nice man,' commented Ayesha.

'Do you know what his name is?'

Karim and Ayesha looked blank.

'Mustafa.'

The container ship *Mustafa* had been towed back to Tanger-Med with what remained of its cargo. In the days that followed, forty-two public officials, including officers from the Sûreté, Gendarmerie and Marine Royale, as well as numerous security guards and port workers, were arrested on charges of murder, manslaughter, corruption, racketeering and theft. Driss El Hajjem, the EDS chief at Tanger-Med, was among those indicted. Only Police Chief Larbi, Lieutenant Hammoudi, Lieutenant Jibrane and the tall man with the harelip had escaped. Operation MEDIHA was already being hailed as one of the most successful operations in the history of the Tangier Sûreté, one that had cleared out corruption and left the city of Tangier and the port of Tanger-Med in good shape for the future.

Karim embraced Joseph. 'Will you live in Tangier if you're allowed to stay?'

Joseph nodded. '*J'espère* – I mean, *inshallah*.'

'You're speaking like a Moroccan already!' Karim said, clapping him on the back

Ayesha shook hands with Joseph and she and Karim strolled off. Before they had gone a hundred yards Karim stopped and went back to the cemetery, where Joseph was still contemplating the trench.

'I almost forgot.' Karim reached in his pocket and took out three ten-dirham coins. 'For the umbrella.'

Joseph laughed. 'Thank you.' The two men embraced.

Karim hurried after Ayesha. Seeing him running, Ayesha cried, 'Race you to the café!'

They sprinted past the King's audience palace with its smart-looking guards, across the green park, past the children playing on the swings. Ayesha flung herself down under the eucalyptus trees and grinned as Karim came running up a few seconds later.

'Come with me,' he panted, pulling her to her feet. 'I want to show you something.'

He led her over the grass and across the road to the area of scrubland with the Phoenician Tombs. Ayesha was enchanted. They sat for a while among the courting couples, gazing out to sea. She held up her phone and took a selfie, Karim in Abdou's grey hoodie and Ayesha in her taupe *jellaba*, with the blue Mediterranean behind them.

'You look better without your moustache.'

'*Besahh?* Is that so?' Karim had gone to the curved-backed barber that morning, after prayers. He offered to pay for the broken shelves but the barber was so remorseful for what had happened that he gave Karim a free shave.

'I've decided that I prefer being clean-shaven,' Karim mused. 'I don't want anyone coming near my nose with scissors again.'

'Even if you get nose hairs?'

'I'll clip them myself. Or I'll ask you.'

Ayesha didn't reply, or she didn't hear. She was gazing out to sea with a dreamy look on her face. 'This place has a strange atmosphere. Does it have a name?'

'The Phoenician Tombs.'

'So it's a cemetery?'

'I suppose so.'

'Strange – two cemeteries in Marshan, both looking over the Strait of Gibraltar.'

'This one is very old.'

'How old?'

'The man over there – the guy selling sunflower seeds – told me that it's a hundred thousand years old. Another woman said that it's a hundred years old. I think the real answer is somewhere in-between.'

They watched the Tarifa ferry emerge from the harbour down to their right. Further out to sea, container ships moved slowly back and forth.

'Clowns' shoes.'

'What?'

'I've been trying to think what container ships remind me of,' said Karim. 'Do you remember when Si Brahim took us to the circus in El Harti park? The clowns had long shoes. That's what the ships look like.'

'They don't look anything like clowns' shoes,' snorted Ayesha. 'They've got lumps on them. That one over there is so full of lumps it looks like an overloaded fruit bowl.'

'Very well. The empty ones are clowns' shoes. The full ones are fruit bowls.'

For a while neither of them spoke. Ayesha shaded her eyes.

'I don't know why everyone wants to go to Europe. I'm happy exactly where I am.'

There was something about her words that Karim found comforting. Ayesha's phone rang and Karim went off to buy sunflower seeds. When he came back Ayesha's cheeks were flushed and she was taking deep breaths.

'Colonel Lalami is gone.'

'Gone?'

'Arrested.'

'*Al-hamdulillah.*'

Karim hailed a taxi to take them to the station. The taxi drove down past the Mendoubia Gardens and through the Grand Socco. Couples were pushing strollers in the park or sitting at tables outside the cinema, enjoying the afternoon sun.

'I'm going to miss Tangier. I never thought I would say that about a city with so many hills and such strange weather, but it's true,' said Karim.

'I like this city, too,' said Ayesha, catching a glimpse of the Mediterranean. 'It has a strange quality, as if it's not quite part of this world.'

Karim pointed. 'I bought some perfume for you in that shop.'

Ayesha reacted with surprise. 'Really? Where is the perfume?'

'In a locker somewhere.'

'Will you pick it up when we return?'

'*Inshallah.*'

Ayesha and Karim had been asked to appear at the trial. The state prosecutors had a lengthy case to prepare and it could be months, even years, before they returned to Tangier.

At the station the two of them walked along the platform and Karim handed Ayesha her bag. She found a seat on the train and opened the window.

'*T'halla frasek.* Give Safee a pat on the head.'

'Ayesha . . .'

'Yes?'

'Do you think I'm a failure?'

'What? No!'

'I came to Tangier but I didn't really do anything.'

'Karim, you saved the lives of some of the most downtrodden people in the world. Fewer patients will die from illegal medicines because of you. You're the best police detective I know.'

'You only know *one* police detective,' Karim grinned.

'Take care.'

'You too.'

They didn't kiss. But Ayesha's hand lingered in Karim's as the train pulled out of the station. He watched until the train had disappeared then returned through the scaffolding, glad that that he had practical matters to attend to.

Outside the station, a white ambulance was waiting to take Abdou's body back to Marrakech. The toxicology report had revealed liquid ketamine in his bloodstream. The presence of water in his lungs indicated that Abdou had still been alive when he was thrown into the sea.

Seeing the ambulance parked by the roadside, Karim felt a wave of grief. He had never imagined that he would bring his colleague back in a white van marked *For the Moroccan dead*. He drew consolation from the knowledge that Abdou had solved the mystery – that he'd been so near to proving the connection between the migrants and the pharma cartel. As Karim approached the ambulance, Hicham – Abdou's driver – jumped out and opened the passenger door.

Karim laughed. 'You make me feel like the King of Morocco rather than an out-of-town policeman!'

He settled back and looked through the reams of paper-work that had to accompany the body. There were forms to be filled in and letters to be signed. Only in the most exceptional circumstances was a corpse allowed to be taken across provincial lines. Abdou's family, backed by a letter from Commissioner Badnaoui in Marrakech, had obtained a special dispensation from the Tangier authorities to return the body for burial.

Karim was glad that Hicham wasn't the talkative type. It was a six-hour drive to Marrakech and he needed time to process his thoughts. The journey would also give him an opportunity to prepare some words of condolence for Abdou's parents.

The ambulance headed out of town along the airport road. As he pored over the documents, half in French and half in Arabic, Karim felt his eyelids droop. He pushed his seat back for a nap. He must have slept for longer than he realised, for when he opened his eyes the ambulance was trundling down a country road.

'This isn't the motorway!'

Hicham stared fixedly ahead. 'I was told to take you this way.'

'No! You were meant to take the N1 to Casablanca then the A7 to Marrakech!'

They turned a bend and a police car came into view, parked by some oleander bushes. Karim's palms were sweating. Hicham came to a stop behind the vehicle. The doors of the police car opened and Police Chief Larbi got out. Panic flooded Karim's brain: his Glock was in the back of the ambulance. With Larbi was Ali Hammoudi from the Tanger-Med prefecture. Larbi came up and tapped on the window.

'Please step out of the vehicle, lieutenant.'

Karim rolled down his window and replied in a cold voice.

'A police officer is dead. We have a duty to return his body to his family.'

'And so you shall, lieutenant,' said Larbi. 'A finer man has not walked this earth.' Ali reached through the window and shook Karim's hand.

'I – I don't understand,' said Karim, getting out of the ambulance.

'We just wanted to offer our thanks,' said Larbi. His breath no longer stank of tobacco and he seemed better groomed than the last time Karim saw him.

'And our apologies,' added Ali.

'What are you talking about?'

Larbi explained. 'Mansouri controlled the port like a drug baron. The place was so riddled with EDS guards and corrupt officials that we – myself, Ali and Abdou – had to give the impression that we thought the scam was taking place in Terminal 1. We had to throw Mansouri off the scent.'

'But why lie to me? Surely you must have realised that I was honest!'

'We knew about your role in MEDIHA, but this conspiracy went way beyond that. We found listening devices in the prefecture and EDS had access to all our cameras. The case was so sensitive that we instructed Abdou not to tell anyone outside a tiny circle – Ben Jelloun, Ali and myself. Of course, once the container fell on you we knew you were on our side, but you never came back to the port.'

354 James von Leyden

'We also knew that your phone had a trace,' added Ali.

'But I saw the Raja scarf in your office! You were the last person to talk to Abdou. And you were in the Sûreté van after he went missing!'

'You're right. I did speak to Abdou, God rest his soul. I offered to do the surveillance of Terminal 2 with him but he refused. He said it was best not to arouse suspicions.'

'Ali and I were in the prefecture,' Larbi said. 'Watching the CCTV cameras.'

'So what happened?'

'The cartel found out that Abdou knew the secret of the *Mustafa*. It could have been as the result of a phone tap, or through Simo – we don't know. They set an ambush, at least two men, perhaps more, hidden in the gap between the containers. When Abdou hadn't returned to the prefecture by seven-thirty, Ali and I drove into the terminal to look for him.'

'But what did they do with Abdou's body? How did it end up in Tangier?'

'We think at first they hid his body in an empty container,' said Larbi. 'You were right about that. We checked all the empty containers at ten o'clock but by then an EDS van had been through the storage yard. When he was arrested El Hajjem said that they dropped the body at Cap Spartel. They probably thought that the current would carry Abdou's body far out into the Atlantic.'

'Instead of which,' continued Ali, 'it ended up back in Tangier because of the unusual currents we discussed. That part was true, by the way.'

Karim let this information sink in.

'Incidentally,' Ali added, 'I don't know why I support Raja Athletic. They've had a terrible season.'

A comment that Bouchaïb – the parking attendant in Marrakech – had made in early March popped into Karim's brain.

'That's a little harsh,' he smiled, 'considering that Raja beat Tunis a few weeks ago.'

'I'm impressed. Are you a fan?'

Before Karim could put him right Larbi looked at his watch. 'It's six o'clock. You have a long drive ahead.'

'Wait!' said Karim. 'What about Simo?'

'Simo was – how shall I put it? – *compromised*. He took bribes from the cartel. He didn't want to, but they threatened his family. After he met you at the Cap Spartel lighthouse he decided he'd had enough. Unfortunately, the cartel got to him first.'

'Why didn't you tell me this earlier?'

Larbi sighed. 'Lieutenant, men I would have trusted with my life ended up working for Mansouri. He had a trace on every mobile and a spy in every corner. I've had two heart attacks because of this case.'

'At least you've stopped smoking.'

Larbi grinned. He shook Karim's hand.

'We'll see you again for the trial, *inshallah*. Then we shall celebrate. My son is the head chef at the Hilton. He will lay on a proper celebration.'

Karim raised an eyebrow, remembering his assumption that Larbi was an unmarried man. When Karim was back in the ambulance the commissioner looked through the passenger window.

'Please give the heartfelt condolences of the entire Tangier Sûreté to Abdou's family. He was a brave officer and one of the finest men I have ever worked with.'

The driver did a three-point turn and headed back towards the A1 motorway.

'He's my boss now.'

'What do you mean?' asked Karim.

'Larbi has taken over as chief of police in Tangier. A new man is going to head up Tanger-Med.'

'Who will be Larbi's second-in-command?'

'Lieutenant Jibrane. He's a rough sort, but he wasn't part of the conspiracy.'

For a long while Karim said nothing.

'*Labas?* Are you all right, Lieutenant Belkacem?' asked Hicham.

Karim stared at the motorway toll booth, backlit by the evening sun.

'I was just thinking how wrong one can be,' he laughed.

'Don't look for dates in the olive tree,' said Hicham.

Karim laughed again. This time, Hicham joined in.

Author's Note

This book is set in March 2013, twelve years after the EU–Morocco cross-border cooperation pact came into effect. In September 2013, King Mohammed VI of Morocco announced a new, more liberal immigration policy that included settlement for 25,000 sub-Saharan Africans. Despite these measures, attempts to reach Spain from Morocco (including assaults on the walls at Ceuta and Melilla) have risen steadily, with 56,480 crossings and 769 deaths in 2018.

In 2008, a Moroccan drug baron called Mohamed Kharraz, long considered virtually immune from the law, was jailed along with the former head of Tangier's judicial police. Kharraz named more than thirty members of the security services in the trial.

According to estimates by the World Health Organization seven out of ten medicines sold in Africa are counterfeits and cause around 100,000 deaths a year.

Tanger-Med 2 opened in June 2019, increasing the port's capacity to 9 million containers a year. Chez Kebe is now closed. At the time of writing (February 2020), the Teatro Cervantes is still in ruins.

Acknowledgments

I am indebted to my agent Jane Gregory and to Mary Jones at David Higham Associates for suggesting changes to the final draft. I would also like to thank my publisher Krystyna Green at Constable. Josh Shoemake's *Tangier: A Literary Guide for Travellers* (I. B. Tauris, 2013) was an invaluable source of information. So, too, was *Moroccan Noir: Police, Crime, and Politics in Popular Culture* by Jonathan Smolin (Indiana University Press, 2013). The story about Mansouri shooting his wife comes from a reminiscence about Mohammed Mrabet's grandfather by Paul Bowles, quoted in an interview in *Rolling Stone* magazine (Michael Rogers, May 1974). *Chukran bezzaf* to Peter Solomon for checking the Moroccan Arabic and to Nasio Attanasio for checking the French. Thanks, also, to the captain and crew of the CMA-CGM *Africa 2* with whom I spent two weeks sailing between Antwerp and Tangier. Finally, my wife Czarina has been my sounding board and loyal supporter throughout.